William P. Fogg

Round the World

Letters from Japan, China, India and Egypt

William P. Fogg

Round the World
Letters from Japan, China, India and Egypt

ISBN/EAN: 9783337173135

Printed in Europe, USA, Canada, Australia, Japan

Cover: Foto ©Andreas Hilbeck / pixelio.de

More available books at **www.hansebooks.com**

"ROUND THE WORLD."

LETTERS

FROM

JAPAN, CHINA,

INDIA, AND EGYPT.

By WM. PERRY FOGG.

CLEVELAND, OHIO,

1872.

PREFACE.

This volume is not published in its present form for public sale, but design-ed as a *souvenir* to personal friends who have expressed a desire to have copies of these " Letters " for preservation; and I have endeavored to enhance its value by sketches and photographs of scenery and costumes in the countries through which I passed. The " letter press," I regret to say, is not what it should be, as it was printed before my return from the forms as originally published in the Daily *Leader*, and abounds in errors resulting from hasty proof-reading, unavoidable in a morning paper. The annexed *Errata* will rectify some of these most glaring mistakes, but the minor errors in orthogra-phy and punctuation are left to the intelligence of the reader to correct for him-self.

I was not ordered abroad "by the doctors," but started in perfect health, which I retained through all the vicissitudes of climate, and was so fortunate as not to meet with any serious mishap to mar the pleasure of the journey. Only once, during that eventful night of the typhoon on the Chinese coast, did I question my prudence in being there, without the excuse of ill-health or busi-ness. My motive was not merely the pursuit of pleasure, but the desire to gratify a long-cherished passion to see once in my lifetime the strange and curious nations of the Orient, books of travel among whom have always had for me a strange fascination.

In these sketches I have confined my descriptions, in a great measure, to what passed under my own observation; and have endeavored to paint the curious and novel scenes in Japan, China, and India, as they appeared to a fresh traveler, without any attempt at fine writing, or high-flown description. The unexpected courtesy and kindness everywhere met from both foreigners and natives, and the many chance acquaintances which have ripened into friendships that will endure for a lifetime, are among the pleasantest souvenirs of my journey.

This first volume does not complete the circuit "round the world." Perhaps another may follow giving the incidents of travel from Egypt through the Holy Land, over the Lebanon to Baalbec and Damascus, to Smyrna and the site of Ephesus, to Greece and Constantinople, up the Black Sea and the Danube, through Hungary and Austria, Germany and France to England, thence home across the Atlantic. A portion of the latter series of letters has been published over the signature of "Nebula" in the Daily *Herald*.

With this explanation of the anomalous form of the present volume, I so-licit the kindness and indulgence of the reader to overlook the many faults and imperfections of these hastily-written sketches,

W. P. F.

Cleveland, May, 1872.

CONTENTS.

—— ——

NUMBER THIRTY.

NUMBER THIRTY-ONE.

NUMBER THIRTY-THREE.

ERRATA.

11th Page, 32d Line, for *one* read *our.*
23d " 28th " add *expected.*
30th " 4th " from bottom, for *happy* read *matchless.*
37th " 20th " discard the word *of.*
37th " 33d " for *ong* read *long.*
40th " 16th " from bottom, after the word *higher* insert *rank.*
42d " 10th " for *Duel* read *Dual.*
45th " 2d " from bottom, for *raising* read *using.*
45th " 27th " " " " *have* read *has.*
48th " 30th " " top, after the word *sold* insert *to them.*
54th " 25th " " " " for *sacrificiously* read *sacrilegiously.*
54th " 24th " " bottom, for *peats* read *pates.*
54th " 2d " " " " for *Sea* read *Tea.*
55th " 6th " " " " for *notions* read *natives.*
55th " 2d " " " " for *eft* read *left.*
59th " 15th " " " top, after the word *and* insert *great was.*
61st " 21st " for *second* read *sacred.*
75th " 22d " " *when* read *where.*
78th " 11th " " *novel* read *naval.*
84th " 18th " " *party* read *family.*
89th " last line, " *iden* read *in olden.*
97th " 8th " " *hurried* read *honied.*
99th " 23d " from bottom, for *started* read *stared.*
102d " 2d " " top, for *shall* read *should.*
106th " 16th " " " for *of* read *on.*
108th " 1st " " " for *patrial* read *patriæ.*
108th " 2d " " bottom, for *firm* read *fine.*
109th " 17th " " " for *Domingo* read *Francisco.*
110th " 5th " " top, for *arrows* read *arms.*
110th " 31st " " " for *slide* read *glide.*
112th " 25th " " " for *five* read *fine.*
112th " 7th " " bottom, for *Albert* read *albeit.*
115th " 9th " " top, for *sight* read *site.*
116th " 3d " " " after the word *grounds* insert *attached.*
117th " 19th " " bottom, for *Kennshaw* read *cumshaw.*
123d " 9th " " top, for *out* read *but.*
124th " 27th " " bottom, for *sloped* read *shaped.*
126th " 11th " " " for *orchards* read *orchids.*
128th " 11th " " top, for *cunnshaw* read *cumshaw.*
130th " 9th " " bottom, for *shore* read *board.*
132d " 9th " " " for *cologne* read *Cologne.*
135th " 5th " " top, for *servants* read *steamers.*
135th " 12th " " bottom, for *north* read *earth.*
137th " 14th " " top, for *music* read *mimic.*
139th " 11th " " " for *drays* read *drags.*
139th " 16th " " bottom, for *nations* read *natives.*
142d " 22d " " " for *so* read *as.*
149th " 24th " " top, for *clan* read *clang.*

151st page, 15th line from bottom, for *contracted* read *committed*.
152d " 11th " " " for *river* read *view.*
153d " 12th " " top, for *hand* read *hands.*
155th " 5th " " bottom, for *miles* read *yards*
158th " 19th " " top, for *onclean* read *unclean.*
160th " 11th " " bottom, for *break* read *breach.*
164th " 21st " " " for *as* read *and.*
169th " top line, should read, "The cenotaphs are of marble."
171st " 6th line from top, for *vested* read *rested.*
171st " 15th " " bottom, for *clean* read *clear.*
172d " 22d " " top, for *remarkable* read *venerable.*
172d " 23d " " bottom, for *head* read *beard.*
172d " 8th " " " for *brick* read *breach.*
175th " 18th " " top, for *ear-rings* read *carvings.*
176th " 24th " " bottom, for *and culture* read *in colors.*
177th " 13th " " " for *covering* read *carving.*
180th " 8th " " " for *for* read *from.*
185th " 11th " " " for *shule* read *thule.*
193d " 7th " " " for *touper* read *toupee.*
199th " 24th " " " for *parts* read *yards.*
200th " 4th " " top for *leave* read *visit.*
200th " 12th " " bottom, for *small* read *much.*
202d " 29th " " " for *that* read *than.*
202d " 26th " " " for *Waitre* read *Maitre.*
204th " 17th " " top, for *when* read *where.*
204th " 6th " " bottom, for *when* read *where.*
207th " 8th " " " for *hold* read *held.*
209th " 14th " " top, for *thin* read *their.*
210th " 23d " " " before the word *all* insert *from.*
216th " bottom line, for *ornament* read *armament.*
217th " 5th line from top, for *flint-locks* read *flints.*
217th " 5th " " bottom, for *by* read *in the.*
219th " 18th line " top, for *August* read *March.*
219th " 15th " " bottom, for *unnecessary* read *incessant.*
220th " 23d " " " for *loose* read *lose.*
223d " 11th " " " erase the last *these.*
227th " 8th " " " add *in Paradise.*
229th " 15th " " top, for *September* read *April.*
229th " 10th " " bottom, for *when* read *where.*

ROUND THE WORLD.

NUMBER ONE.

Good-Bye' to Cleveland—The Kansas
Pacific Route—Buffalos, Antelopes
and Prairie Dogs—A Savory Stew—
Denver and the Rocky Mountains—
Greeley—Cheyenne to the Summit—
Down Grade to the Salt Lake Valley—The City of Deseret—Several
Landladies in One Hotel—Visit to
the Theater—The Prophets' Wives
and Daughters—A Mormon Audience.

[Special Correspondence of Cleveland LEADER.]
SALT LAKE CITY, October 26, 1870.

"Westward the Star of Empire takes its
way." This is my motto; and as the lights
of our Forest City grow dim in the distance, I try in vain to realize that, leaving
all that is so dear to me behind, I am really
started on my way "Round the World." A
day in Chicago, another in St. Louis, and I
take the Kansas Pacific route to California,
via Denver, in preference to the Omaha or
Northern road. This route takes the traveler across the young and growing State of
Kansas to Denver, the central city and capital of Colorado, about nine hundred miles
west of St. Louis; thence north along the
base of the Rocky Mountains, one hundred
and ten miles, to Cheyenne, where he connects with the Union Pacific road at a point
five hundred miles west of Omaha. The
through fare is the same by either route,
and although this may be half a day longer,
it is far more interesting, as it passes
through the towns of Leavenworth, Lawrence, Topeka and Lecompton, places his-
torical in "border ruffian" times, where
still lingers the memory of John Brown and
his friends, many of whom sacrificed their
lives in trying to save Kansas to freedom.
The events of the great rebellion that followed, and the names and places then made
famous forever, have almost driven from
recollection these famous men.

Of the six hundred miles from Kansas

City to Denver, the first two hundred m ay be briefly described as prairie, where thriving towns are rapidly springing up along the line of the railroad, and well cultivated farms will soon form a continuous line to the border of the plains, which stretch westward another two hundred miles, over which the buffalo still range, but are growing scarcer every year; then two hundred miles of desert, parched and arid, where the great drawback to settlement and culture will always be the lack of water. Here the stations on the road are few and far between, being rarely dignified by names, and distinguished only by numbers. But exactly where the plains end and the desert begins is difficult to tell. This is the famous "Smoky Hill route," the scene of nearly all the Indian outrages upon overland travelers before the railroad was completed. As it passes through the great buffalo range, the sweetest pastures and best hunting-grounds of the Indians, they resisted the encroachment of the "iron horse" for a considerable time after they had yielded the valley of the Platte. And now it is an attractive feature to the traveler by this route, that speeding along twenty five miles an hour in a Pullman car he can see occasional herds of buffalo, and be regaled on buffalo and antelope meat at every eating station. A few weeks ago a large herd of buffalo crossing the track compelled the engineer to stop his train. Antelopes are almost constantly in sight from the cars, and fall an easy pray to the hunter. He fastens a red flag to a stick, and, lying quietly on the ground within rifle distance, the graceful, gazelle-like animal, with ears erect, gradually approaches, and falls an easy victim to his curiosity.

As we approach Denver, the second morning from St. Louis, we catch our first view of the magnificent scenery enjoyed by the traveler "across the continent." We have been gradually and almost imperceptibly climbing until we reach the plain upon which Denver is built, over five thousand feet above the level of the sea, and stretching westward twenty miles further to the "Black Hills," behind which rise the lofty, snow-covered peaks of the Rocky Mountains. Silvered with the first rays of the morning sun, we see Pike's Peak, fourteen thousand feet high, on the extreme south of the range, and Long's peak, still higher, as far north as the eye can reach. Between these is a continuous line of snow-capped summits, some clear and distinct in lines, as if cut from marble, others partly obscured by clouds and mist. The mountain air at this elevation is remarkably clear, and objects can be discerned at a great distance. It is hard to believe that Pike's Peak is over seventy miles away, and the nearest summit of the Rocky Mountain range fully fifty miles distant.

Denver is a quiet, well-built city of seven thousand inhabitants. Brick blocks have taken the place of board and canvas shanties; a good city government, enforcing law and order, has replaced the vigilance committees that found it necessary a few years ago to hang the cut-throats and desperadoes who infested the place. The mineral wealth of Colorado is almost boundless, and all she needs now is the discovery of some simple and cheap process by which her ores can be desulphurized.

From Denver to Cheyenne the road runs due north over a smooth plain, with the "Rockys" in plain sight on our left. We watch with interest the herds of antelope almost within rifle range of the cars, while the fat little prairie dogs attracted by the bright warm sun can be seen in thousands as they sit barking at the passing train within a few yards of the track. Each one is squatted on the little mound of earth thrown up from his hole, and they seem to wink at us with a comical self-satisfied air, as much as to say, "We know you are in too much of a hurry to trouble us;" but if the train stops they dodge into their holes as quick as a flash. They are not, in fact, "dogs" at all, but a species of rabbit, light brown in color and but little larger than grey squirrels. They frequently share their holes with rattlesnakes and owls, and all fraternize like Barnum's happy family. Their great enemy is the prowling cayote, the cowardly wolf of the plains, whose teeth are against every animal smaller and weaker than himself. One of the most savory dishes yesterday morning at the eating station was called a "rabbit stew," of which we all partook freely. Before leaving the table it occurred to me to enquire of the colored waiter whether rabbits were plenty in that region. His reply was rather startling—"Oh yes, mas a, de prairie dogs is nice and fat just now."

Half way from Denver to Cheyenne we stop for a few minutes at the new town of Greeley, containing 1,500 people, and only five months old. This place has sprung up like magic. The father and projector of this colony is Mr. Meeker, for many years the agricultural editor of the New York *Tribune*. This town is a marvel of industry and enterprise, established and managed on eastern principles. No liquor saloons are allowed in the place, which so scandalizes the rough Coloradans in that region that as one of these outsiders expressed himself to me, they are "down on the d—d Republican puritanical fanatics." However, their heads are level, they mind their own business, ask no favors of their rough neighbors, and are going straight forward on the road to prosperity and wealth. If Greeley meets with no setback it bids fair in a few years to outstrip even Denver in population.

At Cheyenne we strike the Union Pacific line, and here commences the ascent of the great mountain range, the backbone of this continent. A steep up-grade for fifty miles brings us to Sherman—named after the tallest general in the service—the highest point on the whole route to the Pacific, and perhaps on any railway in the world. We are now 8,242 feet above the sea, nearly half a mile higher than the summit of Mount Wshington. The extreme lightness of the atmosphere tries our lungs as we draw in long breaths of the pure mountain air. Active exercise is here very difficult, and although our wind may be good, a short foot race makes us puff like so many porpoises. Then comes the descent of the grade, and we pass through some of the grandest mountain scenery in the world. Another night and a day brings us across Wyoming and into Utah territory, over the Laramie plains—a splendid grazing country—through the wonderful Echo canon, where 1,000 feet above our heads we see the fortifications built by the Mormons thirteen years ago to resist the passage of Uncle Sam's troops, under Johnston, afterward a famous general in the rebel service. Thence through the Weber canon, past the thousand mile tree, winding round the mountains on a narrow shelf, with a steep rock on one side and a dizzy precipice on the other—dashing through dark channels, rattling over high trestle-work bridges across deep gorges, and now through a narrow cleft in the rock called the "Devil's Gate," we emerge from the Wahsatch range of mountains to a scene of light and beauty. Before us in the dim

distance is the great Salt Lake, at our feet
are broad plains and green fields, dotted
with cosy houses and surrounded with gardens and orchards. This is Salt Lake Valley, the Canaan of the "Latter Day Saints."
Soon we reach Ogden, one thousand and
thirty-two miles from Omaha, the junction
of the Union Pacific with the Central Pacific railroad, from which point Brigham
Young has built a road thirty-six miles long
to Salt Lake City. A visit to Brigham and
the Mormons being on our programme, we
here branch off, and, soon after
dark, find ourselves in the midst of
Mormondom at a hotel which has *one* landlord and *three* landladies. Which one of the
latter attend to the culinary department I
cannot say, ut she deserves the credit of
giving us th best supper of tender steak
and fresh brook trout that we have tasted
for weeks. We notice that the landlord has
a sad, downcast look, which, under other circumstances, would excite our sympathy and
compassion.

It is Wednesday evening, and we are informed that the theater, one of the Mormon
institutions, is open on this and Saturday
evenings, so we hasten up the street two or
three squares to this temple of histrionic
art, regardless of mud, rain and darkness,
gaslight being here unknown. We are a
little late, but paying a dollar for one ticket
we quietly make our way to near the center
of the parquette, with a view to see
the audience rather than the play.

The theater is plainly finished, painted
white, without gilding or fresco. Four
tiers of boxes rise one above another from
the parquette to the ceiling, and it will seat
about two thousand five hundred people.
To-night it is but partly filled, owing to the
mud and rain, but the audience seems in a
very appreciative and enjoyable mood. After glancing quietly around for a few minutes I asked an intelligent looking man in
front of me whether President Young is
here. "No sir, he is not here to-night, as
usual, as he has just returned to-day from
Provo and is tired out." Encouraged by
his polite answer I ventured to inquire if
any of his wives are present. "Oh, yes,
those two ladies in the proscenium or stage
box are his wives, and that little boy with
them is his son, and there," pointing to a private box on the right, "are a dozen or more of
his daughters." For the next fifteen minutes
my opera glass was directed as often as could
be done without attracting attention to the

wives and daughters of the prophet. They
were all well and even fashionably dressed,
one of the wives decidedly good looking,
the daughters having healthy, ruddy complexions, none of them handsome, however,
and in the dim light of coal oil chandeliers
I could not detect any family likeness. Several of them had opera glasses, which they
handled as gracefully as any *habitue* of the
opera; all were neatly gloved, and they
formed an attractive group. Returning to
the charge I quietly asked my friend
in front whether any other distinguished
persons were in the house. "Oh, yes, those
two young ladies directly behind us with
light hair are Elder Smith's daughters, one
of the two associate presidents of the church
with Brigham, and yonder is Bishop So and
So, and there is Elder Brown and his family.
A little to the right of them is Elder Jones
and two of his wives," etc. My communi-
cative friend, who saw that I was a stranger
in pursuit of knowledge, kindly pointed out
a dozen or more family groups, all of whom
were paying such close attention to the p ay
as to scarcely notice that our eyes w te
directed towards them. Up to this tim I
had hardly glanced toward the stage, but
when I was told that one of the actresses
was the daughter of a high dignitary in the
church, I looked at my bill and found they
were playing the comedy of the "Wonderful Woman." All were amateurs, and the
actir.g was decidedly good. Noticing quite a
number of small children in the audience, I
asked my Mormon friend whether it was cus-
tomary for so many young people to attend
the theater. "Ye?," he replied, "we never
put on the stage those immoral plays
so common in other theaters"—a good
hit at the *Gentiles*, thought I. The
orchestra consisted of nine musicians, all amateurs. After the comedy
came the "Essence of Ole Virginny," in the
shape of a negro dance, which set the young
people half crazy. The performance then
closed with a laughable farce called the
"Young Widow."

A survey of the audience convinced me that
the female portion were decidedly superior
in intelligence and refinement of manners and
dress to the males. Many of the latter
were rough and coarse in looks and dress,
and they especially enjoyed the negro dance,
which they loudly encored. They did not
look *rowdyish*, nor were there any cat calls
or other such demonstrations not uncommon
in Eastern theaters, but they seemed to be-

long to a lower order of society than their
fair companions.   Brigham owns and runs
the theater. He believes in a "personal government," and caters for the amusement or
his people. The performance was over before
eleven o'clock, and I picked my way through
the mud back to the hotel without the
slightest feeling of danger, for the streets of
Salt Lake are safer in the darkest night
than are those of most cities of half its size.

To morrow I must see the institutions,
call on the Mormon prophet and the elders,
an account of which will be found in my
next letter.   W. P. F.

The Mormon City by Daylight--Its
Location and Surroundings -- The
Tabernacle--A Polygamist in The-
ory, But Not in Practice--The Mor-
mon Banker--Bishop and Colonel
Little--Lo, the Poor Indian--Not
for Joe--No Outsiders Admitted--The
Bishop's Benediction -- Interview
With Brigham Young--He Is Not
Posted in Politics--But too Shrewd
to be Caught Napping--Solution of
the Mormon Problem.

[Special Correspondence of the Cleveland LEADER.]

SALT LAKE CITY, October 27, 1870.

As I arrived here last night after dark I
could form but an imperfect idea of the location and appearance of the city. Taking
an early start this morning I am surprised
at the beauty and impressed with the grandeur of the surrounding scenery. The city
is located in the center of a broad basin,
the Wahsatch Mountains on the north
and east, a spur of the same range extending across the southern horizon—on the
west, perhaps ten miles distant, is the great
Salt Lake, a body of water eighty miles long
by forty to fifty in width, and so salty that
it is literally a "dead sea." No living
thing can be found in its waters. Lofty
promontories on the further side jut out
into the lake and bound our view in that direction. The city covers a space of three by
four miles, and is laid out in squares of ten
acres. The squares are subdivided into eight
lots of about one and a quarter acres each.
Water is brought from the mountains on the
north and flows through every street on
either side. It is pure and cold, and never
fails in the dryest season. Double rows of
shade trees line the streets and the water is
conducted into the gardens and orchards.
This is the secret of the wonderful fruitfulness of this land, which, without artificial
irrigation, would be an arid desert. When
the Mormons came down through the
canon of the Wahsatch into this
valley, twenty-three years ago, it was

literally a desert. They had fled a thousand miles from their enemies across the barren plains, and the one master mind and controlling spirit, Brigham Young, told them here to halt and lay the foundations of the "City of Deseret." The sufferings of this infatuated people for the first year or two were intense; but labor skillfully directed soon changed the face of nature, and they have "made the desert to bloom and blossom like the rose." However much we may condemn the practices and institutions, we cannot deny that their material prosperity is something wonderful. To-day there dwells in this once desert waste a population of 120,000 souls. Everywhere may be seen the fruits of enterprise and persistent energy.

This city contains about 25,000 inhabitants, and its appearance is very attractive. The houses are nearly all built of *adobe*, or sun-dried brick, and if more than two stories in height, the upper one is built of wood, as is the case with the Theater and some other public buildings.

The first place visited this morning was the Square, inclosed by a high adobe wall, which contains the Tabernacle and the foundations of the Temple. There is an entrance from the street on each of the four sides. Passing in by the east gate, I found the Superintendent, who very politely showed me everything of interest. The Tabernacle, which takes the place of the former "Bowery," is an immense building, oval in form, 250 feet long by 150 wide; the roof of wood, and self-supporting, being 80 feet in height. From the outside it has the appearance of an immense dish-cover. The audience room one of the largest in the world, will seat by measurement 13,000 people. It contains an organ built entirely by Mormon mechanics that is second in size only to that in Boston Music Hall. This immense room is a perfect whispering gallery, the arched form of the ceiling carrying the slightest sound from one extreme end to the other without echo. A gallery extends around the whole interior, and my conductor says that the ordinary congregation on Sunday is from 8,000 to 10,000 people, but he has seen 14,500 here on one occasion. There is no means of heating this immense building, and a smaller tabernacle is used in winter, which will seat 3,000. My informant is an intelligent man, English by birth, has been here eighteen years, and in answer to my inquiries talks with apparent frankne-s of their institutions, including, of course *polygamy*. He says he has but one wife, but believes that polygamy is right, and ordained of God. "Brother Brigham" has *seventeen regular* wives, besides a great many others who are *spiritually sealed* to him, and each one expects to be a queen in heaven. He says a plurality of wives is not obligatory, but every *true Mormon* must be a polygamist in theory if not in practice. When I tell him that this institution is a scandal and disgrace to the civilization of the nineteenth century—that it is degrading to woman and debasing to man—that on account of it the whole civilized world regards them as outcasts, disgracing humanity. etc., without taking offense, he says: "Nevertheless it is right—It is no more degrading to us than it was to the patriarchs of old. God has ordained it, and if God be with us we can not fail if the whole world be against us." He is an enthusiast and a fanatic, and I think is sincere. Whether the same can be said of the other brethren remains to be seen. While talking we are standing upon the granite foundations of the great Temple, which, when completed, will cost $5,000,-000. Upon the foundations alone they have spent a million. It will be, if ever built, the finest structure on this continent. I do not believe it will ever be completed. Brigham is the architect, as he is the all in all of Mormondom.

When at St. Lou's a friend gave me a letter to Hon. W. H. Hooper, delegate in Congress from Utah. He remarked at the time that it would "introduce me into the bosom of his family!" This was rather *startling;* but he relieved my apprehensions by telling me that Mr. Hooper had "but *one* wife." Mr. Hooper is the head of a large banking house—the only one in Utah. He is an affable and courteous gentleman, and received me very cordially. His office was full of bishops, elders, generals and colonels, to all of whom he introduced me, and, though full of business, he kindly offered me every service in his power. And here let me say that there was a frankness, cordiality and heartiness in the greeting of every Mormon whom I met in Salt Lake that surprised me. They court investigation, and say they have nothing to conceal. This is not entirely sincere, but is partly assumed for effect. Mr. Hooper put me in charge of Bishop Little, a colonel in the Mormon Legion as well as a dignitary in

the church. The Bishop, who is a native of
New Hampshire, came here with the first
settlers. A plain speaking, plainly-dressed
man, hearty and bluff in manner, with
only five or six wives. The functions of his
office are more civil than religious. A
Bishop is appointed over each ward, who
settles all quarrels and disputes among his
people, keeps them out of lawsuits and
sadly interferes with the business of lawyers. He took me first to the City Hall, a
fine brick building, and from the cupola
pointed out the interesting localities in the
city and surrounding country. " Now," he
says, "come down to my house, and let me
show you my carriage factory." Walking
along we were overtaken by a mounted Indian, whom he introduced to me as " Soldier," a Utah chief. Soldier was short and
fat, wore a red blanket, his face daubed with
red paint, hands not very clean, and he carried across the saddle in front a fine rifle.
He gave an Indian grunt as I shook his
hand, and turning to the Bishop said,
"Squaw run away; you catch him; gimme
paper." "Where has she gone?" Soldier
pointed to the South. The Bishop told him
where to apply for the proper document,
and was turning to leave when the chief
extended his dirty hand and jerked out, "two
bits." There was no mistaking the pantomime, and my Mormon friend handed him
a quarter. Soldier looked as if he would like
to make "two bits" of me, but relented
and without a word of thanks, rode off.
"That's the way with these red skins, always begging," said the Bishop, "but we
must keep on the right side of them." I
am told that every Indian within two hundred miles of Salt Lake will stand by the
Mormons in event of any collision with
the United States Government.

Approaching the Bishop's residence
I felt quite sure that I should now see
something of the *inside* of Mormon life.
But I was doomed to disappointment. He
showed me into his office, took me through
his large workshops, introduced me to
Brothers Smith, Jones and Brown, his part-
ners, blacksmiths and wagon-makers, and,
returning to his office, said he was sorry
that his family were "house cleaning," so
that he could not ask me into his house.
Although overrun with business, he devoted
half an hour to the history of the Church,
told me about Mormon, Maroni and Nephi,
quoted fluently from the Old and New Tes-
taments, defended polygamy and pitched

into the Gentiles, and as I rose to leave
gave me a dollar bill of Salt Lake currency
for a memento, and bestowed upon me with
great fervor his apostolic benediction.

At twelve o'clock I called, by appointment, on President Brigham Young. His
houses and grounds occupy two ten-acre
squares, enclosed on all sides by a wall ten
feet high. Two long buildings, one surmounted by a bee hive, the other having a
large stone lion over the porch, could be
seen within the enclosure. They are connected by a row of offices, into which the
gate opened from the street. Sending in
my card, I was soon ushered into "the presence." He received me quite cordially, and
I took a rapid mental photograph of one of
the most remarkable men of this generation. He is in his seventieth year, but
looks at least five years younger; about five
feet ten inches in height, portly in form,
florid in complexion, with small gray eyes
set far apart, sandy whiskers closely
trimmed, abundant hair, false teeth, which
makes his mouth seem prominent, somewhat carelessly dressed, wearing a
black over-coat, with a red handkerchief
tied loosely around his neck outside his
coat—a quiet, self-possessed air and manner,
as of a man conscious of his power,—such
was the inventory I took of the man who is
to-day a more absolute ruler of 120,000 people than any potentate, prince or president
in the civilized world.

I told him I was about to go abroad, and
as I expected frequently to be asked about
Utah and the Mormons, I wished to take with
me some more positive knowledge of the
community than I had been able to gather
from books or newspaper accounts. He
glanced at me rather sharply, surmising
perhaps that I was "interviewing" him as
a newspaper correspondent, and said that
he was glad that the Pacific railroad had
opened Utah to intelligent travelers. He
and his people had been cruelly misrepre-
sented, and he referred with some bitter-
ness to the speech of Senator Cragin of New
Hampshire, which I had mentioned as my
native State, said it was a tissue of lies;
"but," he said, with a malicious twinkle in
his eyes, "he is not re-elected to the Senate."
This remark surprised me, for I knew Mr.
Cragin *was* re-elected last June, but I did
not undeceive him. "All we ask is to be
let alone. Congress had been very unfair
in not admitting Utah as a State, and in
legislating against our institutions." There

is where the shoe pinches, thought I. In
answer to my enquiry whether Utah as a
State would be Republican or Democratic,
he said, "that depends upon which party
does us justice." He spoke of the wonderful prosperity of his people, driven into
the wilderness with nothing but their
strong arms, they had in little more
than twenty years converted a Sahara-
like desert into well cultivated farms,
producing larger crops to the acre
than any eastern state. Neither Utah nor
Salt Lake City owed any public debt. He
referred to the "Cullom bill," passed at the
last session, making polygamy a crime, and
providing for the appointment of jurors
who shall all be "Gentiles." I ventured to
inquire whether he thought that law could
be enforced. But he was too shrewd to be
caught, and was non-committal on that
point. I complimented him on being the
heart and brains of his community, and tha
to his good management they were indebted
for their wonderful prosperity, and asked
if, in the course of nature, he should be
taken away, could any other man carry his
people forward as he had done. He replied
with energy, "We are God's chosen people;
I am his servant; He will never permit me
to be removed until in His own good time
He has provided another to take my place."

After spending an hour I rose to leave and
apologized for having occupied so much of
his time while others were waiting to see
him. He walked with me to the door of
the outer office, shook my hand warmly at
parting and wished me a pleasant journey
and a safe return. He said, "Come and see
us again after you have been round the
world."

As I walked down the street, I glanced at
the buildings inside the wall which contained the prophet's harem, and thought,
this is all fair on the outside, but within is
rottenness and corruption. Is Brigham a
sincere and honest enthusiast, or a corrupt
and sensuous knave? His cold gray eyes
and calm, unimpassioned manner do not indicate the fanatic; nor do the lines about
his mouth, or his face generally seem that
of a gross sensualist. I can understand now
why he is so popular, or rather so worshipped among his followers, *He can read
human nature* and can adapt himself to and
make a favorable impression upon any one
with whom he comes in contact.

I stepped into a store to buy some stereo-
scopic views, and picking up one of Brig-

ham, I remarked that he is a good looking man. "Yes," said the artist with fervor, "and he is just as good as he looks."

The solution of this Mormon problem is puzzling wiser heads than mine, but the end is not far distant. In the course of human events Brigham cannot live much longer. The mantle of the prophet cannot fall upon any other living Mormon. I trust no event will occur to precipitate a collision between the government and this people while he lives. When he dies the bubble will burst. The Pacific railroads and the opening of new mines are drawing crowds to Utah. The Gentile population is increasing much faster than the Mormon, and in ten years Mormonism, or its accursed feature, polygamy, will be a thing of the past.

W. P. F.

From Ogden Over the Central Pacific—
Alkali and Sage Brush—The Sierra
Nevadas—Rounding Cape Horn—
Glimpse at the Golden State—San
Francisco Approached at Night—
Aladdin's Lamp—Hotels, Stores and
Public Buildings — Churches and
Schools—Starr King—The Cliff House
and the Lions—Lone Mountain Cem-
etery—Mission Dolores—The Chinese
—Adieu.

SAN FRANCISCO, Nov. 1, 1870.

The Central Pacific from Ogden to California is by no means a duplicate of the Union Pacific from Omaha to Ogden. The
sleeping cars and eating stations are inferior;
gold and silver take the place of scrip, and
a "good square meal" cannot always be had.
Chinese laborers and track-repairers replace
the Irish. California fruits, especially pears
and grapes, grow cheaper at every station,
and we begin to realize that we are on the
Western Slope of the Continent. But one
train a day each way is run between Omaha
and San Francisco, which leaves Ogden at
6 P M. We wake the next morning in the
valley of the Humboldt, and the day before
us is perhaps the dreariest and most un-
uncomfortable on the whole route.
Vast Alkali plains surround us,
where sage brush alone grows, and
ot a drop of water can be had which man
or beast can swallow. The ground is white
with alkali as if covered with snow, the fine
dust penetrates even through double windows and makes our hands and faces feel
sticky and uncomfortable. Our eyes are
slightly inflamed and reading becomes difficult. Water affords but a temporary relief,
and a "dry wash" with a soft towel is much
better. Such are a few of the annoyances of
the railway traveler, while dashing over
this worse than Sahara desert, twenty-five
miles an hour in a first class car. Imagine
what were the sufferings of the early emigrants, hundreds of whom perished miser-

ably on the way, overtaken by storms of
alkali sand, and the bones of thousands of
oxen and horses bleach on these barren
plains.

After three hundred miles of sage brush
and alkali, we commence to climb the Sierra
Nevadas, and for the next ten hours we
see results of engineering skill that seem
almost marvellous. Constantly ascending,
we wind around the mountains on narrow
shelves of rock, bri ge chasms at dizzy
heights on trestle-work, and where no
other course is practicable; boldly plunge
through the hills, and emerge from dark
tunnels to dash onward through the gloom
of miles of snow-sheds, by which alone this
route is kept open in winter, and the road
protected from the avalanches which sweep
down the mountain sides. There are over
fifty miles of these snow-sheds, built of
heavy timbers, and covered, roof and sides,
with four-inch planks. They are somewhat
aggravating to the traveler, as they cut off
all view of the scenery, and leave him in a
gloomy twilight which is neither night nor
day.

On we glide past the summit, and the
second morning after leaving Ogden commence the descent of the Western slope.
We round "Cape Horn," a bold promon-
tory, which juts out and overhangs a valley
2,000 feet below, and half way up the face
of the mountain on a narrow shelf of rock
the trains wind round like some huge
monster, where but a few years ago there
was not even a foot trail—a place well calculated to unsettle the nerves of timid
ladies. We pass it in safety, and turning to
the left cross the valley on the high trestle
work bridge, and we feel inclined to hold
our breath until the train reaches the solid
embankment on the opposite side of the
chasm.

Lower and lower we go, leaving the
Alpine scenery behind us, and now, as if
by magic, there opens before us the beautiful valley of the Sacramento. It is our first
glimpse of the "Golden State," and the picture is one long to be remembered. Pleasant farm houses, orchards loaded with fruit,
smiling fields and fertile meadows, as far as
the eye can reach, are in striking contrast
with the desolate scenes of the past thirty-
six hours. A short delay at Sacramento,
the second city and Capital of California,
and we continue on to Stockton, near which
gold was first discovered in 1848.

Thence through several western looking towns, over the coast range of mountains, the high volcanic peak of Monts Diabolo, looming up 3,800 feet on our right—a landmark far out in the Pacific—and just at dusk we reached Oakland, the terminus of the railroad, and the Brooklyn of San Francisco. Here we are transferred to a steam ferry boat, and crossing over the broad bay we watch with no little interest the myriad lights from the great city before us which reflected and doubled in number on the smooth water, stretch from the wharves high up to the summit of the hill upon which the city is built. Arriving at the pier the rush of passengers, shouting of hackmen and omnibus drivers, and the general confusion are worthy of New York City. The streets through which we are driven to the "Grand Hotel" are most brilliantly lighted. We pass block after block of splendid stores where the plate glass and rich display of wares remind us of Broadway. On the street corners the large, white California grapes are being sold, "eight pounds for a quarter." The pears, which we have frequently seen East, but rarely felt rich enough to buy, are here offered "three for a dime." No indication this of the high prices we had on the Pacific coast.

I have heard it predicted that in a few years this trip across the Continent will become as stale a subject for description as that over the Alleghenies from Pittsburgh to Philadelphia, and such was my own impressions before passing over it. And now, perhaps, I owe your readers an apology for occupying so much space in trying, though very imperfectly, to sketch the salient points of the route. The novelty, beauty, and grandeur of the scenery can hardly be exaggerated. One should return by the same route, at least as far as Cheyenne, to properly appreciate it, and then he will agree with me that no *word painting* can do it justice.

We reach San Francisco on Saturday night. The "China steamer" sails at noon on Tuesday, so what we see of this city which has grown up within a few years as if the genii of Alladin were the slaves of the builders, must be quickly accomplished. Here are hotels that compare favorably with the "St. Nicholas" or the "Fifth Avenue"—stores on Montgomery street that can only be matched on Broadway. But splendid blocks, expensive public buildings and fine hotels alone do not constitute a great and prosperous city. In churches and and schools and in the quiet observance of the Sabbath, San Francisco compares favorably with any city of its size on the eastern slope of the continent. The prosperity of this city is not all *material*. Boston has furnished the model of her public school system, and New England blood and training can be recognized in many of her institutions of charity and benevolence.

On Sunday we attended the church founded by Starr King, beside which he is buried. Kind hands still supply the flowers that decorate the grave of one whose loving heart so attached his friends, and whose genius and patriotic labors did so much to save California to the Union.

The vicinity of the city is full of places of interest. Every stranger is taken to the Cliff House to see "the lions"—here real "sea lions," or monster seals, which seem half human as they splash, gambol and climb over the conical rocks near the shore. Lone Mountain Cemetery is one of the most beautiful and romantic burial places in America—a splendid marble monument of the lamented Broderick is here a conspicuous object. In the outskirts of the city is the old Mission Dolores—where for more than a century the Jesuits held absolute sway over thousands of their dependant Indians and Mexicans—now occupied in part as a woolen factory. The "Celestials" are here an institution—every third person one meets in the streets wears the loose, dark blue blouse, baggy trousers, pointed shoes and long, braided "pig-tail" of a Chinaman. They are quiet and reserved in manner, go about their business, turning neither to the right nor the left. Housekeepers here are unanimous in their praise as servants—but I will leave the "Chinese question" for discussion hereafter when I have seen them at home.

At twelve o'clock the largest and newest of the China steamships, the America, will leave her dock. Our Cleveland friends, Messrs. Worthington, Beckwith and Pannel, will come down and see us off. My next letter must be dated beyond the "Golden Gate," far over the waters of the broad Pacific.   W. P. F.

Pacific Mail Steamers—Splendid Ships
—Creditable to America—Chinese
Passengers—How John Chinaman
Eats - Chop-Sticks Lively and Useful
Tools—Smoking Opium—An Invita-
tion Declined—The Opium Trade—
England's Shame—A Day Lost—
Thrown Overboard—Our Thanks-
giving and Christmas Ahead—Fusi-
yama Almost in Sight—The First
Glimpse of Asia.

STEAMSHIP AMERICA, ?
November 21, 1870,
N. L. 30 deg. 30 min., L. 158 deg. 24 min. E

The great disparity of surface on this
globe between land and water is forced upon
our minds by the thought that we have now
for twenty-one days been pushing steadily
westward over the vast desert of waters,
and have seen neither land nor sail. Day
after day is the same dreary expanse, and
during the twenty-five days from San Francisco to Japan it is rarely that a vessel of
any kind is seen. When about eight days
out, and 1,800 miles from land, we anxiously
watched for the smoke of the eastern bound
steamer, hoping to meet her and exchange
mails. For two days we had all been writing
letters full of last parting words to dear ones
at home, but to our great disappointment we
missed seeing her, having probably passed
during the night, which was cloudy, so that
the smoke or lights could not have been
seen more than eight or ten miles away. It
would seem surprising that we had any
chance to meet on this trackless Pacific.
Night and day there has been no cessation
of the steady clang of the machinery, the
quiver and crackling of the immense steamer,
as she pushes westward ten miles an hour,
never varying from her course, and regardless alike of wind or storm. We have seen
old Ocean in all his moods—for days smooth
and glassy, reflecting the bright sun and
cloudless sky with scarcely a ripple, remind-
ing me of Lake Erie in midsummer. Then
gathering clouds and the angry waves lashed
into fury, tossing our huge ship to and fro

like a cockle shell. "Pacific" seemed then a *misnomer* for this wild Ocean. But the steady clang of the engine never ceased as it pushed our leviathan onward—a triumph of skill and brains over the elements, of science over matter.

I had read of this Pacific mail line as unequaled in the world in size of ships, completeness of appointments, and comfort to passengers, but I was unprepared for such a floating palace as the "America" proves to be. If there can anywhere be comfort or even pleasure in a sea voyage, it is here. Our fifty cabin passengers have more space in state rooms and saloons than would be allowed to two hundred on a Cunarder. The table is supplied with every delicacy of a first class hotel. Vegetables and fruits, either fresh or canned—beef, mutton and poultry, were shipped, "on the hoof," before leaving port, and the steward is saving the fattest of turkeys for our Thanksgiving dinner. The crew, firemen and waiters, one hundred and fifty in number, are Chinese—the officers, of course, being American. The captain says they are as good sailors as the average of white men, and much more docile and obedient. They do not seem to me as strong limbed and broad chested as our Yankee sailors and fishermen, but few of these can be found in this section except in the position of officers. As table waiters the Chinese are remarkably quick and active, and very quiet. A glance of the eye toward any dish you may want is enough, they seem to know by intuition almost, what you require. They never hand you a cup of tea or coffee and leave you to get the sugar and milk as best you can.

This line of steamers consists of four ships, the China, Japan, America and Great Republic. The three first are in constant service, and the last named is held in reserve in case of accidents. They make one trip a month each way from San Francisco to Hong Kong, touching at Yokohama, in Japan, where they connect with a branch line to Shanghai. They are allowed a government subsidy of half a million dollars a year for carrying the mails between these ports. They are wooden, side-wheel steamers, with air-tight compartments, built in New York, and cost over a million dollars each. They are about 5,000 tons measurement, the "America," the largest and newest, being 5,600 tons, and the largest merchant ship afloat except the Great Eastern. It is gratifying to our national pride that this line of ocean steamers, the only one we have, is a success. They cannot carry all the freight (principally teas) that is offered in China and Japan, and the number will soon be increased so as to make semi-monthly trips. These ships are the continuation of our national Pacific railroad, and the pioneers of a commerce the extent of which we cannot now realize between Europe and Asia across our continent. When they first appeared in Hong Kong, their size and elegant accommodations for passengers surprised the English, who build only screw ocean steamers, and they predicted that the first ty·phoon they encountered would send them under. But for four years they have run without accident, riding out in safety the fiercest storms, typhoons and cyclones of the Chinese and Pacific seas. Their great size and breadth of beam give them steadiness in rough weather, and also enables them to carry a large number of passengers.

This ship will accommodate fourteen hundred persons in the steerage, and is always full going east. These are all Chinese, who pay $45 each for passage to California, there to be kicked and cuffed by the roughs, denied all the rights which "a white man is bound to respect," but economical and saving in his habits, patiently enduring insults, quiet and reserved in manners, in a few years he saves enough of his earnings to return to China a rich man.

We have now on board seven hundred returning Chinamen, each with his little fortune of two or three hundred dollars, the saving of two to five years hard labor and exile from the "flowery kingdom" among "western barbarians." What wonderful stories they will have to tell to their friends and neighbors! Stories as marvelous as the early voyagers four centuries ago, carried back from the far west to Spain and Portugal. The space on this ship is so large, and the discipline so perfect, that we see nothing of the Chinese unless we go forward among them. They occupy the whole main deck, 400 by 50 feet in size, and also a portion of the upper deck forward. Several are pointed out to me as wealthy merchants of San Francisco, who could well afford if they chose to pay $300 for cabin passage.

They are all neatly dressed and clean in personal appearance, and politely answer in "pigeon English" all my questions. The Chinese are inveterate gamblers, and many groups are scattered around the deck playing dominoes, the little piles of copper coin indicating the stakes. They are so intent on the game that they do not notice my standing by and watching them. Winning or losing, they take it very philosophically, without loud words or quarreling. Presently the gong sounds for dinner, and all start up "eager for the fray"—for eating, whether in cabin or steerage, is an important matter on board ship. The 700 Chinese are divided into fifty messes of fourteen each. Two from each mess, as its number is called, are detailed to bring the rations, consisting to-day of a large tin pan of boiled rice, another of beef and vegetables chopped up into pieces about an inch square, and a small dish of pickles by way of *relish*. Each mess has, also, a tin can holding about two gallons of tea. Placing the provisions on the deck, the mess forms a group around, and each man, squatted on his heels, pulls out his "chop-sticks" and "goes in" without ceremony or saying grace. The chop-sticks are of dark wood, about the size of a penholder or lead pencil, but longer, and are held between the thumb and two first fingers of the right hand. This is the "knife and fork" of nearly one half of the human race, and it is a curious sight to watch with what dexterity they are enabled by habit and practice to use them. Holding them like a pair of tongs they can pick up the smallest kernels of rice and transfer them to the mouth as rapidly as we could accomplish the same by the use of a table spoon. Besides chop-sticks, each one is provided with a small bowl, which he fills with rice, and, holding near his mouth with his left hand, its contents are speedily transferred down his throat. This exercise is varied by an occasional dive with the chop-sticks into the dish of meat and the transfer of a choice bit to accompany the rice in its downward course. Wo to the slow eater in this crowd, if any there be! The typical American who bolts his dinner in five minutes at a railway eating house, using knife and fork indiscriminately, is *slow* compared with John Chinaman, armed with his two bits of wood. The pan of rice is soon empty and is refilled as many times as desired, and the quantity of rice these people can eat when the supply is unstinted is wonderful. At last the "chop-stick exercise" flags, the last kernel of rice and scrap of meat has disappeared. With a sigh of regret at the transitory nature of all human happiness, John carefully wipes his "tools" and stores them away in his pocket for future use. In the meantime the can of tea has remained untasted, for the Chinese never drink while eating. And now he closes his repast with several bowls full of tea, of course, without milk or sugar, then he smokes his cigar or pipe with all the gusto inspired by a well filled s'omach. These ships are very liberal in the food provided for the steerage, the quantity being unstinted, and the quality much superior to the average fare of the Chinese at home or in California; and yet the cost of boarding them for the thirty days trip is less than five dollars each.

In the centre of the forward deck I notice a temporary room of thick canvas, about eight feet square, on the door of which is an inscription in Chinese. Upon inquiry I am told with a grin on the face of my informant that it is the "Opium smoking room." He opens the door and I glance inside. At first it seems dark, the only light being from a small lamp upon the floor, beside which is a box about half as large as a sardine can, which contains the drug prepared for use. There are three or four persons in the room, squatted on a floor or reclining on a bench in various stages of intoxication. One of them, with a silly smile on his cadaverous face, holds up a pipe and invites me to take a whiff. I decline and beat a hasty retreat, for the air of the place is so loaded with mephitic vapors that a few minutes stay would have overcome my senses. The pipe used for smoking opium is quite different from that ordinarily used for tobacco. It is of bamboo, as large in diameter as a flute, and two-thirds as long. About three inches from one end is a small bowl, in which the drug is placed, which is of the color and consistency of tar. A small quantity being put in the bowl, it is held in the lamp while from the other end of the pipe the fumes are drawn into the lungs and then slowly ejected through the nostrils. The intoxication, unlike that from alcohol, produces no howling maniacs, but lulls its victims to dreams of bliss from which he wakes to horrors worse than delirium tremens, which can only be assuaged by another indulgence and another descent into his infernal paradise. The habit once contracted, it is next to impossible to break off, and the miserable victim, possessed, as the Chinese say, by an "opium devil," becomes imbecile in mind and thoroughly demoralized body and soul, is speedily carried to a worse than prunkard's grave. The cost of opium is so great that but few of the very poor class can afford to use it. The Chinese authorities have used every effort to stop its sale, but the British government, to afford a market for the opium of India, has forced the accursed drug upon the Chinese at the cannon's mouth. The Emperor of China, when asked to license its sale, replied in words that should mantle the cheek of every Englishman with shame. "It is true," said he, "that I cannot prevent the introduction of the flowing poison. Gain-seeking and corrupt men will, for profit and sensuality, defeat my wishes, but nothing will induce me to derive a revenue for the vice and misery of my people." So Christian England deals with heathen China!

On Monday, 14th of November, we passed the 180th meridian from Greenwich, and were just half round the world from London. At this time my watch—set in Cleveland—was eight hours too fast, and when the dinner gong sounded at five o'clock, it was one o'clock at night in Cleveland and five A. M. in England. It makes one feel that he is indeed far away when his noon lunch or "tiffin" comes at the moment when his friends are seated round the evening lamp in that quiet room at home to which his mind so fondly turns. But to us the day following Monday, the 14th, was Wednesday, 16th of November. Tuesday, the 15th. was an unknown day—dropped in the bosom of the Pacific ocean. This will make our calendar agree with that of China and the East Indies, who have taken theirs from the Europeans coming eastward round the world. We are now eleven hours ahead of London and fifteen ahead of Cleveland. In a few days we shall eat our five o'clock Thanksgiving dinner long before daylight on the lake shore, and my Christmas at Shanghai will be thirteen and a half hours ahead of Cleveland. The day lost is past recovery to us who go on round the world, but it will be picked up by the steamer on her return, and if she should pass the 180th meridian on Sunday, the 25th of December, her passengers will have two Sundays in that week and a duplicate Christmas for 1870.

I can only wish them as pleasant weather and as agreeable a ship's company as we have been favored with. On Thursday we expect to sight Fusiyama, the "happy mountain" of Japan, whose volcanic peak, rising 14 000 feet above the sea will be the first object to meet our gaze in Asia.

W. P. F.

NUMBER FIVE.

A Pleasant Sunday—The Pacific Gulf
Stream and What Came of It—A
Typhoon—Frightful Scenes on Ship—
Cyclones Ahead of Hatteras—Peru-
vian Repentant—The Dangers Over—
All's Well That Ends Well—A Bright
Morning After the Gale—Good Resolu-
tions Forgotten—A Genuine Thanks-
giving.

STEAMSHIP AMERICA. ⎫
THANKSGIVING DAY, Nov. 24, 1870 ⎬
LAT. 32, 55., LON. 142, 57. ⎭

Our third and last Sunday on the America
was a very pleasant one. We had on board
three missionaries who were returning with
their families after a brief absence to the
scenes of their labors—one to Yokohama,
one to China, and the other to India. As
usual, we had religious services in the main
saloon in the morning, and in the evening
Rev. Dr. Scudder gave us a very interesting
lecture on India. The weather was de-
lightful, a bright sun and a cloudless sky,
the sea as smooth as an inland lake, and the
air as warm as a September day at home. In
four days more we expected to sight Japan.
But, as our Scotch friends say, "The best
laid plans of mice and men aft gang agloe."

On Monday night we were within eight
hundred miles of Yokohama, in the edge of
that current of warm water which corre-
sponds with the "Gulf Stream" of the Atlantic—here as there the fruitful source of
typhoons, cyclones and hurricanes. This
current, which is supposed by some savans
to have its origin in submarine volcanoes
south of the Island of Formosa, sweeps
thence along the coast of Japan, through
the North Pacific to the Aleutian Islands,
then over to the coast of California, down
which it follows until lost in the warm seas
about the equator. The day had been warm
and sultry, with occasional showers, but
the barometer had indicated no storm brew-
ing, until at ten o'clock it dropped in forty
minutes from 29-80 to 28-68. So sudden
a fall boded us no good, and our vigilant
captain at once prepared for one of those

terrific storms, called *typhoons* or *cyclones*,
peculiar to the east coast of Asia, and the
dread of all naviga'ors in these waters.

Within less than an hour from the first
premonition it struck the ship, the tremendous force of the wind throwing her instantly almost upon her beam ends. I had
retired early and was rudely awakened by
being pitched out of my berth, and with
trunk and other loose articles, shot over to
the lee side of my state room. Fortunately
the room was small so that I did not have
far to go. Hastily dressing I managed with
some difficulty to open the door leading to
the main saloon, and there the sight was
truly appalling. The skylights had all been
dashed in, chairs and everything moveable
were sweeping to and fro across the room,
the floor was covered with broken glass
from the racks over the tables, the lamps
were all extinguished, the howling of the
wind and dashing of the rain and spray
through the open sky lights, the lurid glare
of the lightning which seemed one incessant flash, made up the most frightful scene
I ever witnessed. But more startling than
all this were the shrieks of some of the
ladies who had rushed half-clad from their
rooms, and losing all presence of mind at
every lurch of the ship uttered most heart-
rending screams.

My experience of storms off Cape Hatteras, and in the Gulf of Mexico, was nothing
compared with a typhoon in the Chinese
sea. Every few minutes a heavy wave
would strike the ship, dash the water over
the top of the cabins, and as it thundered
against the guards our staunch vessel would
quiver and tremble as if going to pieces.

Being high up out of the water the wind
had a tremendous sweep against her cabins
and paddle boxes. But she was very strongly built, and having one thousand tons less
coal on board than when she left San Francisco was very buoyant; her machinery was
strong, and her officers all thorough seamen.
Every man was at his post, and when Captain Doane came down and spoke a few
cheerful words to the affrighted passengers
the panic subsided. By his direction the
ladies and children were removed for greater
safety to a small cabin on the lower deck,
in case the upper works should be carried
away. After the first fright was over the
passengers became quiet and self-possessed.
The course of this storm was from South-
west to Northeast, and it moved with great
rapidity, probably three hundred miles an

hour. These typhoons are circular and perhaps a mile or more in diameter. In half an hour we had passed through the outer rim into the center, and for about twenty minutes there was a lull of the wind, although the sea was running very high. Then as we again approached the edge of the cyclone it struck the ship with increased fury from the opposite direction. This was the crisis of the storm. For a few minutes we lay in a trough of the sea, and before steerage way could be got on the vessel she shipped several heavy seas, which tore up the guards around the paddle boxes, demolished the bath rooms and cattle pens, dashed one of the sailors from the upper deck, injuring him so severely that the poor fellow died the next day. Any accident at this moment to the machinery would have been fatal to the ship. She would have become a wreck and foundered in spite of the most skillful seamanship. No small boat could live for a moment or even be launched in such a gale.

We clung to the positions we had taken in the upper cabin and main deck, and for a while we held our breath, waiting for what was to come next. Such was the noise of the wind and banging against the ship of the waves, that we could not tell whether the engines had stopped or not. The Chinese passengers had been securely fastened below, lest they should rush on deck in a panic and do some mischief. To say that at such a time I was not alarmed, would be idle bravado; at all events I kept *quiet* and held on, and thought what a fool I had been to put myself, without any good excuse, in such a position. Even then I could not help laughing at a comical scene within a few feet of where I was standing. Among our passengers was a Peruvian, of very gentlemanly appearance and excessively polite manners, who was on his way to China to purchase a cargo of coolies. He was now the worst frightened man on the ship. He fell on his knees, and, crossing himself, muttered his long neglected prayers in Spanish to the Holy Virgin and all the saints in the Romish calendar.

But the engines moved steadily on, although at times one of the paddle-boxes would be completely under water, so that the strain upon the shafts was fearful. In the meantime, while the gale was at its height, one of the boats and all the settees upper deck had broken loose from their fastenings, and were dancing a lively jig over our heads before they finally *chassaed* into the ocean.

About three o'clock the Captain came down and assured us that the danger was over, although it was yet very rough, as we had passed through the outer rim of the cyclone, and most of the passengers returned to their rooms to find everything in confusion, and their bedding and clothes soaking wet. This, however, we cared very little for. I threw myself, in my wet clothing, upon the sofa, and in half an hour was fast asleep.

The next morning the sun shone bright and clear, and as we gathered in the saloon to a late breakfast we were a hard looking set. Everybody shook hands with everybody else, and each had his or her personal experience to relate. The events of the night before seemed like a horrible dream. But the bruises some of us had received, the heads of some of the waiters cut in falling against tables and over chairs, the smashed bulwarks and battered guards, and the stains of the salt spray to the very top of the smokestack, were evidence that our experience of a typhoon had been real. The captain said that in his twenty-three year's experience he had never seen a harder blow, although fortunately for us it was of short duration. Our Peruvian was especially demonstrative in his congratulations. If he made any good resolutions in the hour of peril to let the poor Coolies alone, I fear he has since forgotten them, for I overheard him yesterday discussing with another passenger the chances of getting a cargo.

To-day is Thanksgiving, and to us it is an occasion of genuine heartfelt thanksgiving and gratitude to Almighty God for the dangers we have escaped, and we need no fat turkeys nor sparkling champagne to give fervor to our thanks.   W. P. F.

NUMBER SIX.

Arrival in Japan—Bay of Yeddo—
Junk's and Fishing Boats—Harbor of
Yokohama—No Hacks, But Fat and
Jolly Porters — A Good European
Hotel—Situation of Yokohama — A
Former American Consul Disgraces
His Country—Bettos or Grooms—
Their Unique Dress — Out For a
Walk—Japanese Group—How They
Are Dressed—A Paradise of Bu-
bies—Married Women Sacrifice Their
Beauty—A Pair of Moos-mies—A Jac-
onin—Street Performers—Porters and
and Coolies—Ohaio and Saionara.

YOKOHAMA, JAPAN, Dec. 1, 1870.

On the morning of the 25th of November
I was awakened by a rapping at the door of
my room on the America, and recognized
the voice of my friend, the Consul at Swa-
tow, saying, "Come out and see Japan; it
is in plain sight, right before us." In a few
minutes I was on deck, and no one, unless
he has been for twenty-five days without
seeing land or even a sail, can appreciate
our delight as we gazed on the scene. We
were approaching the entrance of the Bay
of Yeddo, which very much resembles the
"Narrows" at New York. The high wooded
hills in front were dotted with small houses,
looking very cosy, surrounded with ever-
greens and fruit trees; on our left were several conical-shaped mountains rising out of
the water, some of which were extinct volcanoes; all around us were fleets of junks
and fishing boats, manned by a strange
race, dark-skinned, bare-headed, with no su-
perabundance of clothing, who watched our
steamer as she glided by with even greater
curiosity than we looked at their queer
craft, outlandish and clumsy as if modeled
from Noah's Ark. The sun was not yet
above the horizon; but, through an occasional rift in the clouds which obscured
Fusiyama, we could see the gilding of the
snow-covered cone of this "Matchless Mountain," which forms the background of every
Japanese landscape. Attracted by so many
strange sights we lingered on deck even

after the gong had called us to our last meal on the ship, for at eleven o'clock we expected to reach Yokohama, twenty miles up this beautiful bay.

Trunks are packed and baggage put in order for shore, stovepipe hats replace the wideawakes and Scotch caps, which have seen service on ship board, and after breakfast all are gathered on the upper deck as we pass the light ship and carefully thread our way through the fleet of foreign ships anchored in front of the city. Besides the eight war vessels, two, each, of French, American, British and German, there are now in this port over fifty sailing ships and fifteen steamers, representing every maritime nation in the world. The gun is fired, the anchor dropped, and the wheels stop for the first time since leaving San Francisco.

Trim looking boats come along side from the different men-of-war for letters and papers, for we bring ten days later news from the seat of war in Europe. We recognize the tricolored flag, and notice the disappointed looks of the French officer when told of the surrender of Metz. The steward and waiters are especially polite this morning and have an *expectant* air as they help us off with our baggage. We go ashore in a Japanese boat which lands us at the custom house pier, where we submit our trunks to the inspection of the officials, two-sworded men, in semi-European uniform, wearing no hats, but sometimes carrying one under the arm. They are very civil, and take our word that we have nothing subject to duty, which may be a rash statement, as we profess to know little about Japan "tariffs." A crowd of coolies surround us, each eager for the job of carrying our baggage to the International Hotel. These fellows are both dirty and ragged—if the latter term is possible, in view of the small amount of clothing they wear—but they are faithful and honest, fat and jolly, and satisfied with what seems to us very trifling compensation for their labor.

Yokohama is situated on the south shore of the bay of Yeddo, and contains about 35,-000 inhabitants. It is one of the four ports open to foreigners, and has nearly all the export trade of Japan. Along the *Bund* facing the harbor are the foreign commercial houses, mostly twe stories high, built of stone, and many of them enclosed in substantial stone walls. Each enclosure is

called a *Compound*, and contains an elegant
residence surrounded by shrubbery, warehouses or *go-downs*, offices, &c. Other
streets parallel with the *Bund*, extend back
for some distance, and are occupied by the
European retail dealers. Separated by a
large canal on the east are the heights, an
aristocratic quarter, where the foreign ministers reside, and also some of the wealth-
iest merchants. Back of the European town
and adjoining it on the west, is the native
quarter, full of *curio shops*, where Japanese life and manners can be seen, and a
place especially interesting to strangers.
There are only about twelve hundred foreign residents here, one half of whom are
English; perhaps two hundred Americans,
and the balance French and German. Kanagawa is a large native town two miles from
here, and was by the treaty of the port to
be opened to foreigners in 1860. But the
government, in accordance with its policy
to keep foreigners distinct from the Japanese, laid out the town of Yokohama on the
low, marshy shore of the bay, isolated it
from the main land by canals, filled up the
marsh from the adjoining hills, built extensive piers of granite, a large custom house,
and gave the land without charge for con-
sulates, warehouses and stores. Its location
is much better for harbor facilities than
Kanagawa, with which it is connected by a
long causeway, and it can be more easily
defended in case of disturbance. At that
time the exclusion policy of the Yeddo government was gradually giving way, but a
strong party in the country was bitterly opposed to the foreigners and had to be concil-
iated. By making the foreign settlement an
island the government could say that no
Aliens had been allowed a dwelling place
in Nippon, and the letter of the unrepealed
law against the admission of "barbarians"
was evaded.

After securing comfortable quarters at
the European hotel, let us go out for a walk.
Holding a horse in front of the hotel is a
betto, or groom. He wears neither coat
nor pants, but his clothing is elaborate, and
is easily washed, and certainly is a perfect
fit. It consists of a very narrow girdle
and suit of *tattooing*, the colors being red
and blue. On his back is a frightful dragon
with his tail curled around under the *betto's*
arm. Nondescript monsters, and curious
designs of tigers, lions and human figures
cover nearly his whole body, and he is evidently gratified at my admiration of his

unique dress. It may be said that he is "scantily dressed but decently painted." The custom is said to have originated with the fishermen, who being much employed in the water, imagined that in this way they could frighten away sharks. As, however, this beautifying struck the fancy of the bettos, it was next adopted by them from motives of vanity. These bettos always run alongside of horsemen and in front of carriages when out for a drive or on a journey. They have wonderful power of endurance, and will keep up with a fast trotting horse without apparent fatigue.

Walking down the nicely swept street, past the custom house, we come to a large *compound* where the British flag is flying. This is their Consulate, and a high stone wall encloses several acres. A red-coated soldier stands in the doorway of a large building containing the dwelling and offices of the Consul. A friend points out to me a large tree inside the wall, called "the treaty oak." Here the treaty with Commodore Perry was signed in 1854. As an American, I am ashamed to say that this piece of land, which is the most desirable in Yokohama, after being assigned for our Consulate, was sold for seven thousand dollars to the English and the money put in the Consul's pocket. The American Consulate was pushed back on to a small piece of land in the rear, and is not even the property of the United States.

A short distance further and we come to a broad street which separates the foreign from the native town. Here is a group of men and women of the laboring class. Their dress is very much alike in cut, as well as color, which is generally sombre. The broad sleeves of their outer garments, which are sewed up half way, serve as pockets. They all wear straw sandals on their feet, but no covering for their heads. Their hair is universally black, the heads of the men being partially shaved, and the hair drawn up and tied in a little cue on the top. The women wear their hair most elaborately dressed in waves and bands, with bright-colored *skewers* for hair pins. More than half the women in the street have babies in their arms, or slung at their backs, whose heads, shaved in fantastic patterns, look very comical peeping over their mother's shoulders. The race is undoubtedly prolific, and Japan must be a paradise of babies. Here we meet a woman of the better class —perhaps some shopkeeper's wife. That she is married is evident, for every hair is plucked from her eyebrows, and her teeth are varnished jet black. These are the distinguishing marks of married women, and are said to have been originally adopted by the wife of the Emperor many hundred years ago, as a sacrifice offered on the shrine of conjugal fidelity, she having thus destroyed her beauty to prove the absence of all wish or design to captivate admirers! It seems to me that it was making the husband pay rather dear, although it doubtless fully answered the purpose. But the fashion set by the wife of the Emperor of Japan five hundred years ago was universally adopted and remains to this day, in *permanancy* quite different from the fashions set by the late Empress of France.

In all countries the appearance of the female population is interesting to the stranger. This is especially true in the East; the *status* accorded to them, and their treatment by the "lords of creation," differing so widely from what is seen in western lands. In some eastern countries hardly any females are seen out of doors, and those who are visible are only of the poorer class. In few of them is the freedom allowed equal to that enjoyed by the sterner sex. But in Japan, although the wives and daughters of the aristocracy are seldom seen, all other classes of women enjoy perfect liberty. Women and girls are met with—shopping, walking, or visiting—in numbers hardly inferior to the men, and their nice, tidy, modest demeanor is remarkable. Their peculiar dress—perhaps it is the absence of crinoline—at first seems unbecoming, and the awkward, shuffling gait, produced by their high wooden pattens, is anything but graceful. But it is the "fashion of the country" and as the eye becomes accustomed to them the females convey a very pleasing impression, both in appearance and manner.

Here come two girls nicely dressed, of the respectable middle class. One is carrying an umbrella of bamboo, which are made here very light and cheap, and universally used as a sunshade, as well as for protection against rain. Their teeth are very white, their complexion light as Octoroons, their robes are of fine, dark-colored material, which is relieved by the large, bright-colored sashes worn around the waist. This, with the Japan lady, is *the* article of dress *par excellence.* It is called the *Obi,* and is always of the finest texture that her means will afford. It is tied in a very large knot

5

behind, and falls in a neat fold about half a
yard from the waist. These young ladies
are chatting together so lively about their
beaux, perhaps, that they do not even
glance at us, while behind them are following two little girls, or *moosmies*, about
eight years old, and evidently sisters.
I notice that their shoes, or pattens,
are highly polished with lacquer round
the sides, and the sandals by which they
are held by the toes to the foot are neatly
covered with red velvet. Their eyes are
black and sparkling with fun, and they are
really very attractive and pretty. In passing one of them looked at us who were
watching her so closely, and made some remark to her sister, which pleased them immensely. Perhaps they were laughing at
our funny looking European dress and hands
covered with gloves, which by them are
never worn.

But here comes a very important person
age, in his own estimation. He is *Yaconin*
and a government employe. He puts on
much the same airs as persons sometimes as-
sume in civilized lands when "dressed in a
little brief authority." His rank is shown
by the two swords, one very long and one
short, which are stuck through his girdle.
His wide trousers are made of silk, which
can only be worn by men of his rank; his
tunic is semi-European in cut, a sort of
Raglan. He wears no hat and has adopted
the innovation of letting his hair grow like
a foreigner. His countenance shows that
he is proud and overbearing. It is likely
that he can be genial in his manner toward
his equals, but the common people surrounding him in the street, honest, industrious and polite, as they are, he regards as
scum. The tradesman here bows very low
to an officer, and should he meet a Daimio,
or one of higher, the officer bows as low in
turn. Such is the custom of the country.
The Yaconin glances at us, but we look him
square in the eye without flinching, as an
"American sovereign" should, and he bows
politely, which we return with equal ci-
vility.

As we walk back a group of little urchins, street performers, wearing caps decorated with feathers, run in front of
us, turning somersaults, walking on their
hands with feet in the air, trundling along
like cart-wheels, and performing a variety
of gymnastic exercises creditable to a well
trained circus troupe. They keep alongside of us for several squares, and we can

only get rid of them by throwing them a dozen copper coins called *tempos*, about the value of one cent each. Before we reach the hotel we meet several coolies propelling heavy two-wheeled carts loaded with boxes of tea, or sugar and rice in sacks, marking time with a laud monotonous cry, *whang-hai! whang-hai!* Other porters are bearing merchandize to and from the quay, each pair with a burden between them on a pole, others singly, with baskets slung on each end of a pole about six feet long, which rests upon the shoulder. These porters are very mus ular and healthy-looking fellows, although their diet is entirely fish and rice, both of which are very cheap, and of excellent quality.

The first word which I have learned in the Japanese vocabulary is one easily remembered, and reminds me of home. The ordinary salutation is "*Ohaio*," signifying "good day." When uttered by a "Jap" it is always accompanied with a graceful inclination of the body, in strong contrast with the slight bob of the head with wh'ch Jones, Smith and Brown jerk out "How are you?" The parting word is "*Saionara*," which loses nothing in softness by contrast with the French *adieu*, or the Italian *addio*, and the elaborate courtesy of all classes in Japan makes a very favorable impression on the stranger.   W. P. F.

NUMBER SEVEN.

The Shops and How Customers are
Treated—Very Sharp at a Bargain—
The Currency—Mexican Silver Dol-
lars the Standard—Pasteboard Money
Drives Out Coin—A Financial Smash
not Improbable—Calculating Ma-
chines—Chinamen in Yokohama—
Statistics of Trade With this Coun-
try—Political Sketch of Japan—The
Mikado and the Tycoon—A Dual
Government—The Late Civil War—
North Against the South—A Great
Mistake—The Mikado Triumphs and
the Tycoon is Deposed—The British
Minister Omnipotent in Foreign
Affairs—Americans Can Take a Back
Seat.

YOKOHAMA, JAPAN, Dec. 6, 1870.

The islands forming the Japanese empire
stretch along the east coast of Asia, and are
the barriers which separate a great ocean
from a great continent. Except Formosa
all the islands of this chain belong to Japan.
The number is variously estimated from
1,000 to 3,800, large and small, having an
aggregate area of 170,000 square miles, and
a population of about 35,000,000. The
four largest islands are Nippon, 900 miles
long by about 100 miles wide, with about
95,000 square miles; Yesso, about 30,000;
Kinsieu, about 16,000; and Sikok about 10,-
000. Nippon signifies the "Land of the
Rising Sun," and the imperial banner is a
red sun on a white ground. Near the center, on the east side of Nippon, is Yokohama, in about the latitude of Philadelphia,
although the average temperature is con-
siderably warmer than the corresponding
points on the eastern coast of America. To-
day, the 6th of December, the sun is quite
warm, and I sit with my window open.
although the nights are chilly as October.
Snow sometimes falls to the depth of a few
inches, and ice an inch thick is not unusual
in January, which is the coldest month of
the year. Farther north, in Yesso, they
have weather as cold and snow as deep as in

New England. This chain of islands extend from northeast to southwest, through so many degrees of latitude as to give every variety of climate from that of Canada to Florida. The houses are never built with chimneys, the whole group being subject to earthquakes, and are rarely more than one story in height. "Air-tight" stoves and "base-burners" are unknown, the only means of heating rooms being brasiers of charcoal, around which on a damp and chilly day, in every shop one can see a group of natives squatted on their heels, warming their hands, smoking pipes with bowls half as large as a thimble, and sipping from tiny porcelain cups hot tea, or a rice wine called *saki*. The family of the shop-keeper lives in the rear, separated from the salesroom by light sliding screens covered with thin oiled paper. Window glass is never used except in the foreign houses, although the Japanese are quite skillful in the manufacture of glass into ornamental articles. These paper windows are very cheap, easily repaired, and said to be as effectual in keeping out the cold as thin sheets of glass. The Japanese depend in cold weather more upon thickly wadded clothing than artificial heat for comfort. The floors of the shops are raised about a foot above the ground, and are covered with nice straw matting. The customer always slips off his clogs or sandals, which he leaves outside and in front of the shop. There are sometimes a dozen pair, which to me all look alike, and suggest the very natural mistake of stepping into and walking off with another man's shoes. Of course foreigners are exceptions, and are permitted to tread with muddy boots on the clean mats of the shops; but if invited to visit the house of a Japanese gentleman, I would take a pair of slippers along in my pocket.

The places most visited by strangers in Japan are the curio shops. The outsides of these stores are by no means imposing. No high marble or granite structures, no plate glass windows, no army of elegantly dressed salesmen are to be seen, but a room perhaps fifteen feet square, open to the street, the shelves crowded with lacquer-ware, bronzes, fancy goods of every imaginable description, jewelry, straw-covered boxes, and hundreds of articles that are made nowhere else in the world. If you are a "Buckeye," the proprietor salutes you with the name of your state, which you return with equal politeness. You look about, and there being no counters, can handle all the goods in sight. If he thinks you want to purchase, and can appreciate a nice piece of bronze or a fine lacquered cabinet, he will perhaps invite you into the back room or up into the attic, where his choicest goods are kept. Although the front shop is so small you are surprised at the extent of the rear premises, and the large amount of stock on hand. He can furnish you with a hundred lacquered cabinets of which you have only seen one sample—or five hundred fans of any one of twenty different varieties. It is just at this time an expecially favorable opportunity to buy old and rare bronzes and lacquerd ware. The recent revolution having ruined many of the rich Daimios, who formerly kept up large establishments at Yeddo, where they were compelled by law to reside six months of every year, all the articles of *vertu* with which their palaces were filled, are now offered for sale. The best and most valuable pieces of bronze and lacquer the proprietor assures you are "very old," and "came from Yeddo."

If you believe all this literally you are in danger of being made to pay double price, although it would scarcely be polite to look incredulous. The "Japs" are good traders, and to one of their own people it is said that they never ask more than the actual value of their goods. But the curio dealers have become demoralized by contact with foreigners, and have as many prices for their goods as they have customers. Unless you have been round enough to know the actual market value of the goods, it will not be safe to offer more than a half or a third the price asked. He will never take offense at the smallness of the offer, but if he claps his hands, which means that "it is a bargain" too quick, you may be sure that your offer was too high. If after spending an hour in examining his finest goods, he does not accept your offers, and permits you to go away, you can return the next day, add a trifle to your bids, and conclude your purchase, tolerably certain that you have secured a *bargain*. But whether you purchase or not, you are treated with equal courtesy, offered a cup of tea, and, with a polite "*sionara,*" bowed into the street.

Shopping in this way takes a great deal of time, and is not altogether pleasant to one who counts his "time as money." But it would be a perfect delight to some ladies whom I know in Cleveland, and whose sharpness at a "bargain" would be more than a match for any one of the two million Japanese in Yeddo. I will say, to their credit, however, that two or three shops here have established a reputation for having *but one price*—a reform which all foreigners, not "shoppers" from taste and inclination, should encourage.

But before starting out on a shopping excursion, we must be provided with the right kind of money. No foreign gold, much less greenbacks or scrip, is current here. The standard of currency in Japan, China and India is the Mexican silver dollar, which is worth ten per cent. more than European or American gold. Your gold eagle can be exchanged at the banks here, or in China, for nine "Mexicans." The Japanese coins are, a gold *cobang*, formerly worth five dollars, but now depreciated; silver *itzaboos*—or *'boos*, for short—four for a dollar; half and quarter *'boos*; an oval copper coin, the *tempo*, one hundred to the dollar; and copper or bronze *cash*, about ten to the *tempo*, or one thousand to a dollar, which circulates only among the very poor classes. But the government has learned some lessons in finance from the Western nations, and within two or three years have issued a large quantity of paper money, representing every denomination from a *cobang* to a *quarter boo*. It is printed on thick paper like pasteboard, covered on both sides by Japanese characters, the smallest denomination being about three inches long by one inch wide, the size increasing with the value represented. This paper money has driven the gold and silver coin out of circulation, and is received by everybody, foreign and native, more readily than "Mexican dollars," which are inconvenient to carry and dangerous from the number counterfeited. It is hinted that the government has no record of the quantity of paper money issued, and in adopting the convenience of making paper represent coin, they must take the chance of an over-issue and a financial crash, of which we Americans have had several experiences in our history.

The "Japs" have no faculty for mental arithmetic. If you ask how much for a dozen or a hundred pieces of an article, instead of taking a pencil to figure it out, they have recourse to a calculating machine, made of wooden buttons strung on a wire frame, much like those used in primary schools at home. Every shop is provided with these machines, as are, also, the banking offices, where the receiving and paying tellers are generally Chinamen. There are hundreds of Chinese here holding the positions of higher servants and *compradores* for the hotels, banks and business houses. They are to be seen in the streets nicely dressed in silk and broadcloth, and as many of them occupy positions of trusts in the largest establishments, they consider themselves very much above the natives. The "Japs," in writing, use the Chinese characters, and like them, commence at the right hand upper corner, the lines running from top to bottom of the page.

Yokohama is the great shipping emporium of Japan. The present United States Consul at this port, Mr. Lyons, unlike some of his predecessors, is very popular with the American merchants here, and has the reputation of being a thoroughly upright, honest man. The importance of the trade will be seen from the fact that the export of merchandize to the United States in 1870 will exceed five and a half million of dollars. The greater part of this is tea, of which the export to the United States in 1870 will be over fourteen million pounds, paying a duty to the government of $3,500,000. Nearly all the Japan tea goes to America. The first cargo ever shipped was to England, but finding no sale there, was sent to New York. Unlike the Chinese teas, it is all uncolored, the natural leaf, and free from the copperas poison of the green teas of China.

The political situation of Japan has changed so materially within the last two years that no books or account of the method of government written five years ago are at all applicable to the present status of affairs. By Japanese chronology the history of the Mikados, or Emperors, goes back six hundred years before the Christian era. Honors were paid to him as the great high priest, son of heaven, and absolute spiritual as well as temporal ruler. His person was so sacred as to be veiled from all profane eyes. If he ever left his palace at Miako, every face was laid in the dust, as if in the presence of a god. In the twelfth century one of the most powerful of the Daimios, a man of great ability and ambition, during a period of civil commotion, assumed the real sovereignty of the empire, under the name of Tycoon. The Mikado then became a mere shadow, retaining the name of emperor, and all the honors and reverence due him in his spiritual capacity, but the Tycoon and his successors, who established their capital at Yeddo, were the actual rulers of the empire. Law, however, or custom and usage rather—for I believe there has been until lately no written law in Japan—required that all the acts of the Tycoon should be ratified by the Mikado. Many of the Mikados have devoted their lives to literary pursuits, and Miako has been the center of learning for the empire, while the spirit of war and military science has found its home in Yeddo.

In the early part of the seventeenth century the Jesuit missionaries under Xavier, the disciple and friend of Loyola, obtained a foothold in Japan, and made converts by thousands, including some of the princes of high rank. They soon incurred the enmity of the powerful priesthood by their wholesale destruction of the temples of Buddha and Sintoo, which led to an edict of banishment. The Portuguese, who then monopolized the foreign trade with Japan, took sides with the missionaries, and a decree ordered that the whole race of Portuguese should be banished forever. The foreign trade then passed into the hands of the Protestant Dutch, which they retained under the most humiliating restrictions and indignities, being imprisoned on a small island at Decima, and never allowed to penetrate beyond the limits of their own trading post, for over two hundred years, until in 1864 Commodore Perry inaugurated a new era in the history of the country. The Christians were bitterly persecuted, and after a bloody struggle were exterminated. The decree of the Emperor, issued two centuries and a half ago, prohibits any foreigner from setting foot on Japanese soil, and renders it lawful for any subject to kill any one of the hated race. This law is still unrepealed, although it has become a dead letter.

The treaties negotiated by Commodore Perry and his successors were made with the Tycoon, and it was not until several years later that the *dual* government of Japan was understood, and it was found that none of these treaties had been ratified by the Mikado. In the meantime, the foreigners had obtained a foothold in some places, and could not be dislodged. Many of the most powerful of the Southern

Daimios, who are almost absolute rulers in
their own districts, and number their
armed retainers by thousands and their in-
comes by millions of dollars, were bitterly
opposed to the foreign policy of the Tycoon's government, and the numerous murders and assassinations of Europeans were
attributed to them. The law requiring all
the Daimios to reside with their families
half the time at Yeddo gave frequent opportunities for foreign residents to meet these
bitterly hostile soldiers while travelling
back and forth on the Imperial road, or
Tocaido, which passes through Kanagara,
and was one reason why the Tycoon's government removed the foreign settlement to
Yokohama two miles away, and built upon
the causeway connecting the two places a
strong gateway for their protection. Al
though it was doubted at the time, it is now
well understood, that the Tycoon's government was sincere in their professions of in-
ability otherwise to protect foreigners from
assassination.

The hostility between the North and
South, the latter supporting the Mikado and
the former rallying around the Tycoon, at
last culminated in a civil war two years
ago. An immense quantity of military supplies had been sold by foreigners. Enfield
and Springfield rifles, breech loaders, revolvers, rifled cannon, shells and solid shot.
Both sides had a navy composed of
English and American built ships
of war commanded and manned entirely by Japanese. Just at this crisis
the ex-rebel ram Stonewall, sold by us to
the Tycoon, arrived at Yokohama. She
came into port with the Tycoon's flag flying, but Sir Harry Parks, the British Minister, who favored the Mikado and the
Southern side in the quarrel—not the first
time England has favored the South—per-
suaded our Minister, Geo. E. Van Volken-
burgh, not to deliver her up to the Tycoon.
This was a great mistake, and probably
turned the scale in favor of the rebels, for
the Stonewall with her powerful batteries
and formidable ram could have run down
and destroyed the whole Southern fleet.

The struggle was short and decisive. The
Tycoon's army was beaten in several bloody
battles, he gave up the game as lost, abdica-
ted his office which was then abolished,
and was allowed to retire to his estates
where he now lives a quasi-prisoner of war.
The Mikado is now the sole ruler, temporal
and spiritual of Japan. He is a young man

of about twenty-one, said to be of no great mental ability, but is in the hands of his ministers, the ruling spirit among whom is Satsuma, the most restless and ambitious of all the great Southern Daimaos. The Mikado now resides part of the time at Yeddo, and his government has shown great leniency toward the defeated and dethroned Tycoon and his adherents. Sir Harry and British influence is now all powerful in Japan, and controls the foreign policy of the government. The country appears to be tranquil. Foreigners can travel freely anywhere within the treaty limits, which extend from ten to fifteen miles around Yokohama, and by obtaining a pass from the government can visit Yeddo or any other place of interest. A large tract of land on the heights near the city has been granted to the British, where they have built a marine hospital and have a camp of one thousand men. A most beautiful site and spacious grounds have been assigned to the British Legation, and we Americans, who are entitled to the credit of having first opened Japan to the world, must take a back seat and suck our thumbs until another revolution brings us to the front.

W. P. F.

An Excursion to Daibutz—Japanese
Horses—County Roads and Shady
Lanes—Hedges Unrivalled in the
World—Everybody in Japan Knows
Ohaio—Large Crops With Rude Im-
plements — Two Triologies, One
Poetical and One True—Kamakura
and Its Temples—Collossal Statue of
Buddha—A Wonderful Work of
Art—A Sacrilegious Betto—A Japan-
ese Dinner—The Original Grecian
Bend—The Ride Back—A Funeral
Procession—A Pleasant Experience
Leaves a Painful Impression.

YOKOHAMA, JAPAN,
December 12, 1870.

Taking this place as the base of opera-
tions, I have made two excursions into the
interior—one to the great city of Yeddo,
eighteen miles distant to the west; the
other to Kamakura, the site of the ancient
capital of the Empire, about the same distance in the opposite direction. Near the
latter place is the famous bronze statue of
Buddha, called "Daibutz," to see which,
was the special object of the excursion. I
started before the sun was up, the sky clear
and bright, and the sharp morning air exhilarating for active exercise. A white
frost covered the ground, which disappeared
as the sun came up, and for the first mile or
two we gave our ponies loose rein to try
their quality. My companion was a young
Englishman, and we were accompanied by
a "Betto," who professed to know the way,
and who kept alongside the horses, with
less appearance of fatigue than the horses
showed, for the whole distance out and
back. After my forty miles' experience of
the tender mercies of a Japanese horse—or
pony, rather, for the breed is quite small—
untrained, hard-bitted, rough in gait and
vicious in disposition, I would recommend
the traveler to go on foot. It would, however, be unjust to the Japanese pony not to
give him credit for being remarkably tough
and sure-footed. Our route for a short dis-

Bronze Statue of Buddha

tance was along the main road, which was crowded with market people, some loaded with vegetables in baskets slung across their shoulders, others leading ponies almost buried under huge panniers of all kinds of country produce. No wheeled vehicle did we see of any description on the whole journey.

Turning to the left, we followed a bridle path, which skirted the shore of a beautiful bay, dotted with small islands and fishing boats, and named after the Mississippi, one of the first American men-of-war that visited Japan. The country was very broken, full of hills and ravines, up and down which our pathway led, in many places so narrow that two horsemen could not ride abreast. From the summits of the hills we had beautiful views of the bay on our left, the white sails glistening in the morning sun, and on our right was a most, picturesque, undulating country stretching many miles away, teeming with an industrious population. In the background, sixty miles distant, was the conical peak of "matchless Fusigama," from base to summit white with snow, the lines clear and distinct against the blue sky.

The highly cultivated valleys were unmarred by fences, but divided off by embankments into paddy or rice fields at different levels, which permits them to be overflowed at certain seasons of the year. The ravines are terraced to the hill tops, the upper part being devoted to wheat and vegitables, while the lower half, as well as the valleys to which the ravines open, are given up to rice culture.

Our course lay through shaded lanes past brown farm houses with strawthatched roofs. Some green with moss and climbing plants, and shaded with handsome live-oak and evergreen trees over innumerable little rivulets, across which our ponies stepped daintily on plank or stone bridges, scarcely two feet in width, without railings or parapets on the sides. Then the path would lead along the narrow partitions between the rice fields, where a misstep would leave both horse and rider floundering in the mud. We passed several water wheels turning the rude machinery of rice mills, through frequent villages where the people, especially the women and children, turned out to see us go by, the latter greeting us with the salutation, "Ohaio!" "Ohaio!" It seemed as if at least *one State* of America was well known to the people here, for it was called after us from nearly every cottage and hamlet which we passed.

We wind along through shady lanes where the sun's rays pierce only at intervals, while on the banks above, the pine, evergreen, oak and bamboo are mingled with the bright crimson foliage of the maples; all making a picture of autumnal tints, which in richness and variety, surpass anything I have ever seen. The dark glossy leaves of the camelia, a native of Japan, are frequently seen. It grows wild in the woods, covered with flowers of various colors, some red and single like hollyhocks. Japanese gardeners here attained great skill in cultivating the camelia, which, in America is more frequently called from its native country, the "Japonica." Very large, double asters and cryeonthenums of various colors are seen in the gardens which we pass, and very many other late autumn flowers, the name of which, with my limited knowledge of botany, I cannot give.

But the most beautiful feature of the road is the extent and great variety of the hedges, which, in some places line the path for miles. It is said that nowhere out of England can such hedges be seen, and not even there, in such variety. They are well kept and nicely trimmed in the Dutch style, (which was introduced, perhaps, from Japan to Europe,) Wild-orange, camelia, bamboo, and the tea-plant, all give variety to the hedgerows, which enclose fields of rich dark soil, without a pebble or weed. The implements of husbandry are very rude, and not constructed on the labor-saving plan. It is to the credit of Japan that women are seldom seen at work in the fields, their time being devoted to the lighter labors of the household. Large crops are raised, but the land is never allowed to rest, and without any proper succession of crops. It is richly dressed to keep up its fertility. Perhaps perpetuating the same seeds and plants without change may be the cause why many fruits and vegetables are either rank or tasteless. Some one disgusted with Japan has said that, although it is one of the most fertile and beautiful countries in the world, "There the flowers have no scent, the birds no song, the fruit and vegetables no flavor." To which another *triology* may be added, which is much more literally true, if not so practical. "Women wear no crinoline, houses harbor no bugs, and the country no lawyers." Since I have been in Japan I have heard the singing of birds, have scented the Cape-Jasmine, and have eaten many fine-flavored oranges, but I have seen neither "crinoline, bugs, nor attorneys," native to the country.

But as we must return before dark to Yokohama it will not answer to linger among these charming green lanes, however attractive they may be. At eleven o'clock we reached Kenesawa, a pretty fishing village on the bay, and a great resort among the natives for spending a holiday and for picnics. The road from here to Kamakura passes through a narrow cleft in the rock, sixty feet deep, with perpendicular sides; a pass that a handful of men could defend against thousands. The old city which, seven hundred years ago was the capitol of the empire, is said to contain, even now, over a hundred temples and shrines. The road to it is thronged with pilgrims to the sacred city. But its glory has departed, and many of its temples are in ruins. We visited a few which, like all the temples of Japan, were built very strongly of wood, with very heavy cornices and gateways, carved with figures of dragons, fish, birds and flowers. They are situated on high terraces, approached by wide stone steps, and command beautiful views over the surrounding country. The elaborate carvings were once covered with gold, but now the gilding has become dim with age and neglect, and nearly all have a dilapidated appearance.

About a mile South-west of what remains of the ancient city, surrounded by a grove of evergreen, and approached through a broad avenue, flagged with stones, is the famous colassal statue of the Great Buddha, which is one of the most wonderful works of art'in the world. It is of Bronze, 50 feet in height, 96 feet in circumference at the base, and rests upon a granite pedestal about six feet high. It represents the great prophet sitting in the oriental manner upon a lotus. The head is covered with small knobs representing the snails which, according to tradition, came to protect Buddha from the heat of the burning sun. It is no grotesque idol, but a work of high art, executed more than 600 years ago, and is said to have been originally covered by an immense temple, which was swept away by an earthquake wave from the sea. The face is of Hindoo type, the hands are folded in front, and the attitude easy, with an expression of placid repose. It is Buddha in Nirvana, a state of utter annihilation of external consciousness, attained after ages of purification. The bronze plates of which it is composed were cast in sections of a few feet square, and joined so skilfully that the seams can with difficulty be detected. The features are all in perfect harmony and proportion. The nose is three and a half feet long, the ears six and a half, the thumb nailes eight by ten inches. The thumbs are joined in front of the body, and upon them is room for six persons to sit abreast. The statue is hollow, and contains within many small gilt images of the Buddish pantheon. Upon the walls are inscribed the autographs of many visitors in red and black paint, which the old priest in charge offered to us, that we might attain a cheap immortality by leaving our names or initials upon the ceiling. While looking about the room inside for some relic to bring away, our *Betto*, who seemed to divine my wish, most wickedly and sacri~~legiously~~ *legiously* broke off the hand of one of the gilt images. As I noticed that the other hand was gone, and this one could easily be replaced, I quiet- ly slipped the "relic" into my pocket and handed the fellow a Boo as a salve for his conscience.

Returning to the town of Kamakura we took dinner at a native inn, where we were served with the best the place afforded. Hot tea and *saki*, then little ~~pasta~~ *of* sweet- meats and confectionary; next came fish and rice, which we ate with chopsticks. After that several courses of native dishes, the material of which were to us unknown, but as they were savory and our ride had given a sharp appetite, we asked no ques- tions. I am sure no "bill of fare" at Del- monico's, or any other restaurant in Eu- rope or America includes them. We were awaited upon by very pretty attendants, (according to Japanese style of beauty,) and here we noticed the original "Grecian bend," the graceful wave called by Hogarth the "line of beauty." The wide scarfs around their waists were tied in very large knots behind, and represented the fashion- able "panniers." As they stooped very low in handing us the various dishes, we could readily understand how her Parisian sisters copied this posture from the Japan- ese "Moosmies" who waited on the visiters at the Tea house erected at the "Exposi- tion Universelle" in 1867.

The Original "Grecian Bend"

The difference between the "Moosmie" and the Parisienne is, that what the latter attains by much study and practice, the former grows into naturally, from politeness inculcated from the earliest childhood.

Our ride back was by an entirely different route, and our "Betto" several times lost the way. The country people were very kind in directing us, and in several cases insisted upon going along quite a distance to show the road. Just before reaching town we met a funeral procession, headed by priests, and a band of musicians playing upon samisens, a sort of banjo, and small drums, or *tom toms*. White is the color of mourning in both Japan and China. The coffins are large earthen jars, the Japanese being buried as he lives, with his heels tucked under him, in a sitting posture. This has the advantage of saving space in cemeteries, which is increased by burning the bodies of the poorer classes, and burying the ashes in still smaller jars. Their funerals are always at sunset, and they have a strange superstition against sleeping or being buried with their heads to the north. In sleeping rooms the points of the compass are frequently marked on the ceiling, that the sleeping mats may be placed 'in the right direction.

Soon after sunset we reached the hotel, our day's experience having given me a better insight of the nótibūe, their manners and customs at home, away from the influence of foreigners, than I could ever have obtained in the city of Yokohama. It, also left, for several days, a *painful* impression, of my forty miles ride on a Japanese pony.

W. P. F.

The Leader's Correspondent in Luck—
Interviewing One of the Royal Family—No Show for a High Private, but
a Colonel Can Go In—His High
Mightiness Good Natured and Affable—Enquiry After Mr. Emperor President Grant's Health—A Short Lesson
in History and Geography—Invited
to Yeddo—The Officers Curious but
Very Courteous—Homage Paid to
Royalty in Europe as Well as Asia—
Americans Can't See It.

YOKOHAMA, JAPAN, Dec. 12, 1870.

Some philosopher has said that "one
"might as well be born lucky as rich."
When I came to Japan, a private traveler, I
had no expectation of being able to approach
within gun-shot of any of the "blood royal;"
but my lucky star is in the ascendant and
to-day I have had the satisfaction, in behalf
of the LEADER, of "interviewing" the uncle
of the Micado, one of the royal family, and
the Minister of Marine and War. It happened in this wise: When I returned at one
o'clock from my morning walk in Curio-
town, I found the hall of the hotel filled
with Japanese officers of high rank, in various uniforms, military and naval, but all
wearing the two swords, and the coat-of-
arms of the Makado.

Upon enquiry as to what was up, I was
told that his "High Mightiness, uncle of
Emperor," etc., etc., had arrived, and was
taking breakfast in the grand parlor on the
ground floor. The landlord was in a flurry,
the waiters were running to and fro, and
the house was the scene of as much excitement as if the Queen of England herself was
the guest.

Glancing at the door of the room which
was guarded by a crowd of officers, I determined some way or other to *interview* this
high personage. I quietly took my lunch
while I studied the plan of the campaign.
Then I went up to my room, put on my
best toggery, which was not very *dashing*—
neither sword, gilt buttons nor shoulder-
straps—and descending, card in had, I
"*Ohaio'd*" a young officer, and requested him

to take in my card to His Excellency, and request permission to pay my respects. He
could not understand my English and politely referred me to the interpreter, a pleasant looking "Jap," whose knowledge of
English was not very extensive. He looked
at me with surprise, as I repeated my request, glanced at the card and spelled out
the name which he pronounced with a decidedly foreign accent, and asked me who I
was. I told him I was an American gentleman traveling for information and pleasure,
an independent "citizen sovereign" in my
own country, who expected to see somewhat of the world before I returned home,
and named some of the countries which I
designed to visit—that it would afford me
great pleasure to pay my respects to one of
the Micado's family and a high officer of the
government of Japan. I did not mention
that I was "connected with the Press,"
which would have been an *open sesame* to
any great man's presence in America—for
I do not suppose that any Japanese
is civilized enough to appreciate the
importance and value of newspapers. With
some hesitation he took in my card, and returning in a few minutes he handed it back
and courteously informed me that His Excellency was to remain but a short time and
begged to be excused from receiving any
private traveler. Nothing daunted, I then
played my best trump, which I had held in
reserve. I took my card and wrote on it
the military title which I held by virtue of
a commission from the Governor of Ohio,
and explained to the officers the rank it
signified, which at once raised me many degrees in their estimation. I said that I
would detain His Excellency but a moment.
In the meantime I had formed a rapid acquaintance with a young fellow, the captain
of one of the Japanese men-of-war, and
pleased him by admiring his sword, which
he told me was presented to him by the
Micado. He went into the room with the
interpreter and immediately came back with
the request for me to enter. *Literally* my
last card had won. At the door I was met
by an officer next in rank to the Minister,
who shook hands and led me to the other
end of the large room and presented me to
the great man, who rose from his seat,
shook hands very cordially and offered me a
chair. He seemed about fifty years old,
short and fat, with a very intelligent face
and remarkably bright and sparkling eyes.
I noticed on the table some bottles, which
showed me that he had washed down his

breakfast with some good English ale, and
he seemed a little *mellow*, and in good
humor with himself and all the world.
His hair was not tied up in cue, but cut very
short, and his dress was in Japanese style
of very rich material. One sword was in
his belt, and the larger one was lying on
the table. They were by far the most elegant I have seen in Japan. The scabbards
and handles were inlaid with gold and pearl.
His hat lay before him on the table, shaped
like an inverted wash-bowl, and richly decorated with gold lace. His lieutenant's hat
was similar, only with silver decoration.
He did not seem in a *bit of a hurry*, but offered me a cigar, while one of his attendants,
on his knees and with his head bowed to the
floor, handed him an elegant Japanese pipe.
His knowledge of the English vocabulary
seemed about equal to mine of the Japanese.
He could say "yes," "no," "How do youdo,"
and "good bye." So our conversation was
through the interpreter. He touched me on
the coat and intimated that I wore no uniform, which I explained by saying that I was
in traveling dress. The next question as put
by the interpreter so amused me that I could
with difficulty keep a sober countenance.
It was, "How do Mr. Grant, Emperor,
America?" I assured him the "Emperor"
was quite well the last time I heard from
him, and then tried to explain that we call
our "Emperor" by the title of "President."
I don't think he appreciated the difference.
I answered to the best of my ability many
questions about our army and how our battles
were fought, whether at long or short range,
hand to hand, or with big guns, with troops
massed or as skirmishers, told him something about the great battles of our war, the
number of men engaged, and the part taken
in the war by "Emperor" President Grant.
He asked the number of men in my regiment, and whether they were brave. I can
assure, I gave the Sixth and Seventh Ward
Germans, who composed the Third Regiment O. V. M., the credit of being as gallant a set of fellows as ever shouldered a
musket. He seemed quite interested in
hearing about our war, of which he knew
scarcely anything. When I rose to take
leave, and apologized for detaining him so
long, he requested me again to be seated,
and asked me where I was going. I think
his knowledge of geography was too limited to understand the route I propose to
take. When I told him I had been to
Yeddo, he said: "You go again and come
see me." Perhaps I shall do so. While I

was talking with him his officers were standing around, but none presumed to be seated in his presence. He offered me another cigar, shook hands, and I bowed myself out, with a pleasant impression of the only one of the Mikado's near relatives whom I expect ever to see.

After my interview with His Excellency, his officers were very friendly and agreeable. Their uniform and arms were a hybrid between the foreign and Japanese. They were very curious in examining my watch, and my sword-cane was something entirely new to them. I showed them some photographs which I had in my pocket, and their admiration of the "moosmies," or young ladies. They enjoyed being complimented on the good fit and elegance of their European uniforms and equipments. The whole Japanese race is singularly imitative, and ready to copy and adopt foreign dress and customs. The late civil war has done much to hasten the alteration in uniform of all the military class, and it is more than probable that in a very few years the time-honored and by no means unbecoming national dress will no more be seen among the military officers. The non-combatant officials, the princes, and the imperial household will for some time longer resist any change, and considering that the Japanese have worn the same style of dress for many centuries, it seems almost a matter of regret that it should pass away.

Etiquette, through all grades, is more observed in Japan than in almost any other country. The highest nobles might pass from the cradle (if cradles were used in Japan, which they are not,) to the grave, and hardly have spoken to persons of low station. All service is done in a posture of humility, and no trouble is undertaken by any man that his servants can relieve him of. The utmost respect and reverence is paid to the Mikado and to the members of his family. It is said that even the dishes used in serving his food are destroyed immediately after, for fear that may be put to some profane use.

When His Excellency passed from the hotel to his carriage, through the ranks of his officers and attendants, every head was bowed, the lower grade of servants almost to the ground. His bearing was that of one accustomed all his lifetime to such homage. To us Americans such servility on the part of the lower ranks inspires no awe, although the persons to whom it is paid may have descended from a long line of sovereigns, and

as Mikado, be a representative of heaven,
himself a deity of high rank, in whom is
centered the glory and veneration of a nation of thirty-five millions of people. What
is it but an exaggeration of the homage
which the more civilized nations of Europe
pay to the nobility and royalty "crowned
by the grace of God?" W. P. F.

Excursion to Yeddo—A Cosmopolitan
Turnout—The Asiastic has no Rights
the African is Bound to Respect—An
Undress Uniform—Musicians Without
Melody—Blind Beggars—A State Car-
riage—-Norimons and Cangos—-A
Traveling Dentist—A Fashionable
Tea House—Suggestion to Young
Housekeepers—Grimalkin Minus the
Tail—Fancy Pigs—Cheap and Primi-
tive Clothing—The Unfortunate Mr.
Richardson—-A Family Moving—
Young Sprigs of Aristocracy—Sinag-
awa—Inside the Capital.

YEDDO, JAPAN, December, 1870.

This famous city which school boys class
with Pekin and London, among the largest
in the world, and for over four hundred
years the "capital of the Tycoons," is, according to Japanese chronology, a modern
city. Kamakura, the second city, with its
hundred temples, its collossal bronze statue
of Buddha, though now but an insignificant
village, dates one thousand years further
back than Yeddo, when it was the great
Eastern capital of the empire. The Tycoon
dynasty removed the capital to Yeddo, and
under their rule it has become the most
populous and wealthy city in Japan. Its
name signifies "the river gate," and its location, about eighteen miles above Yokohama,
on the shores of the bay of the same name,
is very beautiful. It is beyond the treaty
limits for foreigners, but passes can readily
be obtained from the government upon application through the foreign consuls.

Starting from Yokohama for the excursion our turnout was indeed cosmopolitan,
and represented the four great continents.
An English built "trap" was drawn by
Japanese ponies and driven by an African
Jehu, whose style of handling the ribbons
seemed to us quite reckless. I did not feel
much compassion for the ponies, for they
are perhaps the worst horses in the world;
ill-shaped and vicious, given to kicking, bit-
ing, shying, rearing and bolting. Curiously
enough, except on the breeding grounds,

the horses and mares are carefully kept
apart. For two hundred miles on the *tokaido*, or imperial road, from Osaka to
Yeddo, a mare is never seen, and on other
portions of the high road horses are equally
scarce. But our driver, while lashing his
ponies into a sharp canter along the narrow
road, in many places crowded with pedes-
trians, seemed to take delight in occasionally upsetting the baskets of the street peddlers and trying the cracker of his whip upon
the back of an unfortunate beggar, who was
not quick enough in getting out of the way.
A *betto* accompanied us, running along side
the horses and keeping up a warning cry of
"Ah! hay! Ah! hay!" to clear the track.
He started with a fair amount of clothing,
but gradually threw it off and tossed it to
the driver until nearly reduced to first principles, a blue handkerchief tied around his
head, and a very narrow girdle around his
loins. This undress uniform, however,
showed his tattooing to the best advantage,
his body being completely covered with
blue and red dragons, birds, fishes, and non-
descript animals.

Passing through the native town, over a
handsome stone bridge which spans the
canal, across the narrow causeway connecting Yokohama with the main land, we
reached Kanagawa, and turning into the
tokaido, we were fairly on the road to the
capital, which is a continuous street nearly
all the way to Yeddo, lined with shops, tea
houses and wayside inns, and swarming
with travellers on foot and horseback, peddlers, priests and beggars, in every variety
of strange costume. We insisted that Jehu
should lessen his speed that we might enjoy
the curious scenes, and also for fear of
accident to the little half-naked urchins
who insisted upon running across the road
in front of our horses, to their eminent peril
of life and limb. Many of these sights
would have been enigmas to me, but for the
explanation of a gentleman accompanying
us, who had been a resident of Japan for
several years.

Here comes a strolling band of musicians,
who make up in noise and discord what
they lack in music and melody, and we are
glad to get past the crowd at their heels and
beyond the hearing of their ear-splitting
tunes. Now we overtake a blind beggar
leaning on a staff. His head is shaved entirely smooth, and shines like a white ball.
It seems to me that in this country all the
beggars are blind, or else all the blind are
beggars. There are no good oculists in

Japan, and eye diseases are quite common. Next comes a sedan chair or palanquin, called here a *norimon*. It is suspended on the shoulders of four men, two before and two behind, very much as a wild beast might be slung in a cage for safe transport. This vehicle is elegantly decorated with lacquer work and gilt, and its bearers wear a sort of uniform. It is doubtless the state carriage of some high dignitary, as it is accompanied by half a dozen two-sworded *yaconins* on horseback. It passes us so quickly that we can barely catch a glance a the occupant. It may be "my lady" out for an airing. The *Cango* is a more simple vehicle, and is quite frequently met on the road. It is carried by two men, and looks like a wicker basket without sides, slung near the ground upon two poles ten feet long. It is used for long journeys by the middle class, and kept for hire at the inns on the main road. A quilt is laid on the bottom, and with legs curled up under him, in what seems a very cramped and uncomfortable position, the occupant will ride for hours or even whole days without apparent fatigue or discomfort. A Japanese when tired, drops on his heels and squats with no other support than his legs and heels can afford, just as naturally as a European drops into a chair. It is said that as soon as the baby leaves its mothers arms, the first thing it learns is not to walk or run, but to squat on its heels in this baboon fashion.

A travelling dentist next attracts our attention. He indulges in the rare luxury of a beard, and is quite a venerable looking old fellow. His instruments, which are of very primitive discription, doubtless inflict the full amount of torture which may be expected for a fee. They are carried in a basket, which also contains charms as well as medicines of various descriptions for sale. As a class the members of this profession in Japan are not above tricks of jugglery and necromancy, and will extract teeth, cut out corns, and even descend to amusing the children with tricks, like swallowing swords, &c., when not otherwise employed. It may be to their credit, however, that the teeth of the men and also of the women before marriage when they make "open sepulchers" of their mouths by varnishing them jet black, are remarkably white and regular.

Our road winds along towards the head of the bay, and occasionally we come to spaces on the roadside unoccupied by houses

and shops, where we catch glimpses of the
water beyond fields and gardens nicely laid
out and cultivated in vegetables and fruits.
When about half way we reach the river
Logo, the boundary of the treaty limits,
within which foreigners may travel without a passport. Here is a famous tea-
house, and while our horses are being
changed we accept the invitation to alight
and refresh ourselves with little cups
of tea, and minute dishes of sweetmeats and confectionery. The garden about
the inn is laid out with much taste in miniature cascades, fountains, rockeries, etc., a
style of ornamental gardening of which the
Japanese are very fond. The proprietor
has added to the attractions of the place,
by employing very pretty and modest-ap-
pearing girls as waitresses, who show us
into a room about twelve feet square, which
is divided off from adjoining rooms by sliding paper screens, so arranged that to accommodate large parties all these rooms can be
thrown into one. Across the side is a platform about a foot high, and the floor is covered with white straw mats, very soft and
perfectly clean. A *mat* and a *fan* in this
country are the *units* of measurement; the
latter being about a foot, while mats are always made of one exact size, three feet by
six. In building houses, rooms are arranged
in size with reference to the number of
mats that will exactly cover the floor. The
room seems empty, but according to their
ideas it is completely furnished. A young
couple can go to housekeeping in Japan without making large bills at furniture warehouses and upholsterers. Two or three
rooms covered with soft mats, a few
cotton-stuffed quilts for bed clothing,
a pan to cook the rice, half a dozen
lacquer caps and trays to eat from, a
large tub to bathe in, and a charcoal
brazier to warm the room in cold
weather—this completes the outfit of very
respectable young people; no chairs, tables,
and array of furniture, with which civilized
people crowd their rooms to the great detri-
ment of their finances, are required. Perhaps some of our young folks at home, who
cherish a wholesome horror of running into
debt, may long for a country of such Spar-
tan simplicity of manners, dress and housekeeping. While at the tea-house I made
friends with a large and very handsome cat,
but expressed pity that she had been mu-
tilated by cutting off her tail. My friend
laughingly informed me that such is the

nature of the breed of cats in Japan. I afterward saw hundreds of beautiful "tortoise-shell" felines, all minus the "flagstaff." European cats with long caudal appendages were looked upon as very curious when first brought to the country by foreigners, and much sought by the natives. Except the wild boar of the mountains, swine were unknown in Japan. But lately, with the fondness of the people for novelties, they have come to be in great demand. A wealthy Daimio, who is establishing a farm on the European plan, has been paying almost fabulous prices for pigs. His agent will go aboard every vessel arriving in port in search of *fancy styles*. He is very critical on this point, and only pure white, with sharp pointed ears and curly tails will answer. For a choice specimen of this description he lately paid in Yokohama $450, but would not take a lop-eared, long-tailed one at any price. A hundred "Chester county whites" would be a fortune to a speculator if they should arrive before the "pig fever" subsides.

But our driver is getting impatient. We pay our bill, only one *boo*, (twenty-five cents) and the smiling *moosmies* bow very low and gracefully as they *sionara* us away.

We walk down to the bank of the river, show our passes to the two-sworded officials, and are ferried across in a large flatboat, on which men, women and children, horses, carriages and dogs are promiscuously crowded together. On the boat we notice a peasant whose coat is made of long finely-split reeds, which besides the advantage of being cheap, is light, warm and nearly waterproof. A countryman equipped for a journey in winter looks as if he had taken the cover of a basket for his head gear, a wisp of straw for his sandals, and a bundle of reeds for his cloak.

Crossing the river, we are again on the *tokaido*, and we are joined by two mounted Yaconins, which are furnished by the government for the protection of strangers. They wear the usual complement of swords, and on their heads are black lacquered hats, sharp pointed at the crown and secured by straps under the chin. I do not believe that a foreigner, conducting himself properly, needs protection anywhere in Japan from the *unprivileged* classes, civilians, merchants, shop-keepers and peasants. They are as harmless and well-disposed people as can be found anywhere in the world. But the two-sworded gentry, soldiers and hangers-on of the feudal princes, idle, lazy and overbearing, when full of *saki*, are sometimes dangerous, and have given foreigners in times past much trouble. The spot on the road is here pointed out to us where Mr. Richardson, a young Englishman, was killed eight years ago. He was riding with two other gentlemen and a lady towards Yeddo, and met by a band of Prince Satsuma's retainers, who stopped and assaulted them, killing Mr. Richardson, and severely wounding the other gentlemen of the party. Few foreigners can pass this spot without a sympathising interest in the fate of this unfortunate young man, who was just on the eve of his departure for home, after a long sojourn in the East. For this outrage $100,-000 indemnity was demanded, and after much evasion on the part of the Japanese, exacted. The murderers not being given up for punishment, the town of Kagosima, the capital of Satsuma's dominions, was laid in ashes by a British fleet. Thus England takes care of her subjects in the East, and no wonder that to claim that nationality here is like the ægis of a "Roman citizen," 2,000 years ago.

A ride of about an hour brings us in sight of what may be regarded as the entrance to Yeddo, which encircles the head of a sickle-shaped bay, with small insular forts to the right, and many houses and temples, and gradually ascending heights covered with stately trees to the left. Slowly we make our way through the crowded street, and as we approach the capital the traffic on the road increases. Here is a family of the poorer class, apparently with all their worldly goods, leaving the city, the wife and her child doubled up in a *cango*, the husband, with two boys and a porter, carrying the heavier baggage. And here we pass two little boys, certainly not over eight years old. They belong to the upper class, for each one wears a sword stuck through his girdle, nearly as long as the boy himself. It would seem quite impossible for the little fellow to draw his weapon, but the young sprig of aristocracy struts along with an important air, other boys, as well as men of lower rank, carefully making way for him. This seems most absurd and laughable to us, but here, as in England only a century ago, to wear a sword is the distinguishing mark of a gentleman.

As we approach Sinagawa, the great suburb a mile long immediately before Yeddo, we notice that the tea houses and saki shops increase, until they almost line the way. Long rows of fancy colored lanterns hang in front, which are illuminated at night, giving the street a gay appearance. But this is a place of ill-repute and not entirely safe after dark. And now we pass through a heavily barred gate, and are within the city, although three miles of streets must yet be passed before we reach our stopping place for the night.   W. P. F.

NUMBER ELEVEN.

A Spanish Legend—Wonderful Progress in Three Years—Foreign Devils Now Treated as Equals—Curious, but Respectful—The Mikado's Castle—A Progressive Ruler and People—Residences of the Daimios—Mount Atango—A Beautiful View—A Doubtful Legend—Frequent Fires and No Insurance—Temples of Shiva—Cleanliness, Not Reverence Required — Catholic or Buddhist—Christian or Pagan—An Enormous Bell — Stone Lanterns—Spirits Over the Water — Pic-Nic Grounds.

YEDDO, JAPAN, December, 1870.

A fruitful soil, a fine climate and an industrious people seems to be all that can be desired for any country in the way of material elements of prosperity, unless they are in the case described in an old legend of Spain, which tells how St. Jago, the Patron Saint of Iberia, went to his master and begged some special favor for the country he had adopted. And, first, he asked for a fertile soil, for a fine climate, for brave sons to defend, and for fair daughters to grace it, all of which were successively granted. Emboldened by his success he asked that they should be blessed with a good government. When his master, according to the Spanish version, either wearied with so much importunity, or in a spirit of justice to other lands, by way of compensation for so many rich gifts, replied with emphasis, "That was a blessing they would never have." And how all other advantages have been neutralized by the want of this one crowning gift is shown on the page of history.

Japan under the servile abuses of the feudal system, which for centuries has drawn the life blood from her common people, may be classed with Spain, as a country blessed with every material element of prosperity, except a good government. But a change is taking place more rapidly than ever before in the history of this nation. But a few years ago, it was a common occurrence in the broad streets of Yeddo, for the retainers and men-at-arms, following some petty Daimio, as he passed along, to cry to the people "shi ta-ni-rio," down, down—and as if by magic, a wide path was opened, and every head was bowed, the body disappearing in some mavellous way behind the legs and knees of its owner. The attendants, bearing their masters' ensigns and badges, stood ready to punish with instant death any insolent fellow who dared cross their line of march, while they scowled fiercely at every foreigner, muttering "intruders," "barbarians," "sorcerers," "devils." But all this is changed. Japanese officials of the highest rank now receive the foreigner as an equal, and visit him as a friend. Socially the people have been great gainers by the revolution. Except in some remote country districts the cry of "shi ta-ni-rio" is no longer heard. The people have cast off the manners of slaves and are taking to themselves the hearts of men, and before many years they will claim a voice in the affairs of the country, which has heretofore been ruled exclusively by the military class.

In all our excursions about Yeddo we were accompanied by Yaconius, and the distances from one point of interest to another were so great that we were compelled to ride, either on horseback or in a carriage. Foreigners are here but rarely seen, and as we alight to look through the shops, the people gather about the door, almost blocking up the street, and follow in a long troop behind. They are very curious n examining our clothes and watching our motions, but are perfectly quiet and respectful. How a couple of Japanese, in their odd costume, would be chaffed and hooted at, if strolling through some streets in New York.

One of the first places visited by us was the Castle of the Tycoon, now occupied by the Mikado. It is inclosed by three separate walls and moats, and the space occupied by the official buildings, gardens and parks is over three square miles. Few foreigners have seen the inside of the castle, and we are only permitted to pass within the first wall, which is of stone, perhaps forty feet in height, and surrounded by a broad moat with beautiful sloping banks of green turf. The gates are very massive, and the portals of hewn stone, fitted, not cemented, and look strong enough to withstand anything but the fire of heavy artillery. Within this triple tier of walls and moats are extensive pleasure grounds, shrubberies, gardens and dainty little tea houses. In one place the Mikado has caused a road to be constructed between an avenue of trees in imitation of the great high road of the Empire, with exact models of the houses occupied by the peasants, surrounded by rice fields, that he may see how his people live and how rice is produced. Here he takes his daily rides and walks, and occasionally goes to the gardens of the palace by the seashore, and sometimes reviews his troops and ships of war. His life is as yet very secluded, but he is gradually breaking through the holy imprisonment in which his ancestors have lived and died. He is surrounded by men of advanced and liberal ideas, who encourage him in his desire to learn to become an intelligent ruler of an empire of forty millions of people.

Nothing is more striking to the eye of a stranger when passing from the commercial part of the city to the official quarter than the vast dimensions of all the residences of the feudal Daimios. Several hundred of these princes, each with five or ten thousand armed retainers within his houses and grounds, one would think, would be dangerous guests of the government, and under the new order of things the Mikado has wisely changed the law, and they now usually reside on their estates, except such as hold office under the government. But, perhaps, being less under espionage, they may plot a revolution and be even more mischievous to the powers that be.

From the castle we drive about a mile to Mount Atango, one of the highest points near the center of the city, so-called from the god Atango, whose temple once crowned the summit. A giddy flight of one hundred stone steps, called *Otoko Zaka*, or men's steps, leads directly to the top, to which, however, there is an easier flight winding around the side, called *Onna-Zaka*, or Women's Steps. There is a tradition of a young Japanese prince who, many years ago, was dared by his lady love, as the price of her hand, to ride on horseback up and down this steepest flight, and having safely performed the feat, he claimed and received his bride. It may be a very pretty story, but unless the breed of Japanese horses has very much degenerated since then, I must consider it a legend and a myth. General Putnam's feat at Rox-

bury, in Revolutionary times, was but
child's play compared with such an exploit
as this.

From the summit of Atango we have a
grand panoramic view of the city and bay.
From the foot of the hill, for perhaps two
miles down to the very water's edge, the
countless dwellings stretch away in monotonous straight lines of gray-tiled roofs, beyond which is the gradual curve of the
bay, studded with the now dismantled
forts upon which the Tycoon's government spent millions, in the vain hope
of preventing the Western barbarians from
approaching the capital, and with war ships
and steamers of foreign build, but bearing
the Japanese flag, side by side with heavy
native junks and fishing craft. On our left
the view is bounded by the castle, which
stands in the midst of the palaces of the
nobles, like a prince among his vassals, a
splendid monument of feudality. On the
north and east as far as the eye can reach
are streets and houses, with here and there
the heavy cornices of a temple surrounded
by groves of fine old trees. At intervals on
all sides are high, black, wooden watch
towers, which are used during the fires,
which occasionally consume a square mile
or so of the town. Owing to the inflamma-
ble material of which the houses are built,
fires are very frequent and destructive.
Fire insurance offices are unknown, and it
is said that every Japanese counts upon being burnt out once in seven or eight years,
and such is their elasticity of temperament
that almost before the embers are cool, they
quietly, rapidly and good-humoredly set
about rebuilding their homes. These fires
and the frequency of earthquakes account
for the fact that in the whole of Yeddo,
giant city as it is, there are very few large
or ancient buildings to be seen. The temples being located in large groves, and the
residences of the Daimios being detached,
escape these conflagrations. But the charm
of the scene lies not in the architecture of
the city, but in the gardens and trees; for
here and there in the heart of the town are
to be found spots which seem to be transported from some fair country scene, where
the dark pines and firs are relieved by the
bright green of the bamboo, and the came-
lias and laurels are mixed with the tree-
fern, the sagopalm and the fruitless plain-
tain.

Atango would not be in Japan if without
its tea houses, and while we are admiring

the view, the young ladies are serving us with hot tea, fruits and other light refreshments. When we ask "how much?" they shake their heads, leaving us to bestow such gratuity as we please, which is, of course, many times their ordinary charge.

Our next visit is to the famous temples of *Shiva*, the burial place of the Tycoons. There are twelve or fifteen separate temples within the spacious grounds, overshadowed by very large and beautiful trees. Each building is surrounded by a nicely paved courtyard, and there is a great similarity both of outside decoration and arrangement of the interiors. These temples and the grounds around them are kept in perfect order, and are richer in architectural ornament than any others we have seen in Japan. A flight of fifteen or twenty broad stone steps leads to the main entrance. These buildings are all of wood, heavily framed, with room left at the joints for the whole structure to oscillate. Some are very old, and have doubtless withstood many earthquake shocks without injury, which would have destroyed buildings of stone or brick. The cornices, doors, and outside walls are most elaborately carved in fantastic and allegorical designs, and are richly gilt or lacquered. An old priest, with head completely shaved, invites us to enter. In anticipation of a fee, perhaps, he is very polite; and from regard to the sacredness of the place I remove my hat, which was quite unnecessary; but he points t o my boots as the objectionable article of dress. Glancing in at the clean straw matting on the floor, I see the point. It is not from reverence, as in a Turkish Mosque, but from motives of cleanliness that he objects to my muddy boots. I am bound to see the interior of the temple, and I pull off my boots—and here let me suggest to any reader who may travel in Japan, that he should always carry about a pair of slippers in his pocket. There are large bronze images of Buddha upon the central altar, immense vases of the same material, and a great variety of curiously carved figures and other decorations, such as artificial flowers, elaborately wrought candlesticks, etc. At the sides are smaller shrines, where the gilt images and votive ornaments were suggestive of a Roman Catholic church, only that the symbol of the cross was wanting. There were the same "bell and book" priests in their robes, behind them rows of chanting choristers, the same burning of incense and repeating of prayers and rituals in an unknown tongue—unknown not only to us but to the crowd of worshippers around. The great similarity between the Catholic and Buddhist form of worship prompts the suggestion that one must have been borrowed from the other—I will not say which—but to the devout Catholic the one is of apostolic or heaven-inspired origin, while the other is the "devil's counterfeit."

Outside the temple, and near by, is a belfry, open on all four sides and ornamented in the same style as the larger buildings. In it hangs an enormous bell, covered with Japanese inscriptions, shaped like a minnie bullet. It is eight or nine inches in thickness, and as I touch it with my cane it gives forth a very sweet and melodious sound. It has no tongue, but is struck by a wooden beam suspended by iron chains. Some of these bells are very large, and one is mentioned by an old writer on Japan, at Miako, said to be five times larger than the great bell at Moscow.

In the court yards surrounding the temples are long rows of carved stone pillars, six to ten feet in height. These are lanterns and are the votive offerings of rich devotees. Every year in the month of August the spirits of the dead are supposed to visit these sacred shrines. They come from somewhere over the sea, and are welcomed with a grand illumination, music and curious ceremonies. After spending the night in the sacred precincts of the temples, they are escorted at early dawn by long processions of priests and people to the water's edge, and launched in miniature paper boats to float off to the great unknown regions beyond the sea.

Besides the temples of Shiva, which are, perhaps, the finest in Japan, we visited several others in the neighborhood, all located in large parks and surrounded by magnificent trees. Some of these grounds comprise hundreds of acres, and are great places of resort for pleasure-seekers and picnic parties, of which the Japanese are very fond; and it would certainly be difficult to find spots more lovely for a day's pleasure and recreation.

Other interesting features of our excursions about Yeddo—our visits to the theatres, shops and bazaars, bath-houses and market places, would occupy too much time and space to describe here.

W. P. F.

NUMBER TWELVE.

From Yokohama to Hiogo—The Moon Temple—Osaca—The Venice of Japan—Manufacture of Paper and Its Use—Paper Handkerchiefs and Pillow-Cases—The Inland Sea—Outlines of a Picture—Simonasaki—The Gateway of Rock—Entrance to Nagasaki—An Episode in History—Japanese Junk—Decima—Fine Porcelain—Arts and Manufactures—Departure for China—Sionara, Japan.

NAGASAKI, JAPAN, December, 1870.

The route from Yokohama to Shanghai, a distance of about 850 miles, is down the coast of Nippon to Hiogo, which lies at the entrance of the famous Inland Sea; thence 250 miles through this wonderful strait—which is rather a succession of inland lakes, connected by narrow channels, than a sea—to Nagasaki, where, leaving Japan, we strike across the Yellow Sea to the east coast of China.

A branch of the Pacific mail line makes three trips a month each way, and is composed of American-built steamers of the same style, but not so large, as the leviathans that cross the Pacific.

Hiogo, our first stopping place, is 350 miles from Yokohama by water, though but 200 by land, and is on the *tckaido*, or imperial road, which traverses the whole empire. It is one of the four treaty ports open to foreign trade, and is rapidly increasing in business and importance. Our steamer, the Costa Rica, came to anchor early in the morning in front of the town, and having the whole day to remain in port, we improve the time by visiting the places of interest in the vicinity. The town is built along the shore of a beautiful bay, with a background of mountains rising by a gradual slope nearly two thousand feet above the water. Several fresh water streams from this range flow down into the harbor, which the Japanese have availed themselves of for irrigating the rice lands, grain fields and garden patches in the rear of the town, and for some distance up the mountain side. Seven miles up the steep path, and almost at the summit, is the

"Moon Temple," a very curious and interesting specimen of a Budjhist sanctuary, which well repays the wearisome climb, for it can only be reached on foot, with a magnificent view, which stretches away for many miles, over land and water, islands, bays and harbors, dotted with junks and fishing craft. At our feet is the town, which seems so near that we can almost toss a stone into its streets. About half way up a little streamlet issues from the side of the mountain, and dances down from rock to rock, until in one fall of one hundred and fifty feet it is lost in spray, like a miniature Yo-semite cascade.

Hiogo is the port of the foreign trade of Osaca, twenty miles distant, on a river which empties into the bay. Osaca is one of the great cities of the empire, with a population of half a million. This city is the center of a very fertile and populous district, famous for its manufactures of silk, sugar, cotton goods and paper. It is traversed by a winding river and numerous canals, over which there are about four hundred bridges, all of stone, and some of great architectural beauty and elaborate workmanship. It is the Venice of Japan, and a favorite dwelling place of the great Princes or Daimios, whose estates are in this part of the empire. The paper made here is remarkably tough and in great variety. The material used is the inner bark of the mulberry tree. Chinese and India paper is made of bamboo, and is much inferior in strength and finish to that of Japan, when it supplies for many domestic uses the place of linen and cotton. From paper the Japanese make a very ingenious imitation of leather, and pocket handkerchiefs of the material are universally used. A roll of paper handkerchiefs is always seen in the girdle of a Japanese lady. The narrow wooden blocks upon which they rest their heads at night are covered with a padding of several thicknesses of paper. Removing the outside one every morning affords a clean pillow case without the trouble of washing.

Leaving the harbor of Hiogo we enter the inland sea, which has been described by every traveler in such glowing terms, that all I can say in the way of descriptions of its surpassing beauty of scenery seems but a repetition of what others have said before. The lamented Bishop Kingsley, whom none will accuse of exaggeration, says, "I have seen and admired the far-famed Loch Lo-mond in Scotland, but it was meagre compared with the gorgeous beauty of this inland sea. If we could put twenty Loch Lomonds together, and for every beautiful mountain on the margin, and every lovely island in the placid waters, plant a hundred mountains and a hundred islands, we should approximate the wealth and beauty seen in these heathen waters."

Carleton, in his charming "New Way Round the World," exhausts his vocabulary of glowing prose description, and can only express his admiration of what he calls "the indescribable glories of this inland sea," by a beautiful poetic quotation, the last line of which is,

"Hither, come hither and see!"

Now, I doubt whether I can conscientiously advise my friends to come eight thousand miles to witness anything, however grand, or picturesque, or beautiful in the way of natural scenery, but I may safely say that in going "round the world," I expect to find nowhere else such a combination of all the elements of beauty, such a feast of the senses and delight of the eyes, as here. Take the thousand isles of the St. Lawrence, the grand mountains of the Saguenay, multiplied without limit, and extending through two hundred and fifty miles of smooth and placid water—a bright sun and a pure atmosphere, wooded hills and shaded ravines, a pretty village nestling in every narrow valley, fishing boats and sails almost innumerable, and you have the outline of a picture so beautiful as to be an excuse for any rhapsody of description. I know that we sometimes weary of other people's raptures in describing scenery, even when we ourselves are not insensible to such emotions when the scenes themselves are before us; and so I leave the unrivalled beauties of this inland sea to be fully realized and appreciated by such of my readers as may come after me in what will, in a few years, be a beaten track round the world.

At sunset we pass through its western gateway—a narrow strait, called Simonasaki, between the islands of Nippon and Kiusin, past a town of the same name containing about fifteen thousand inhabitants. The Daimio who owns this place thought proper, a few years ago, to levy toll upon the foreign as well as the immense native fleet that passed through this narrow gate, but was quickly brought to his senses by a descent of the war ships of the foreign allied powers, who sunk his gunboats, dismounted his cannon, and threatened to burn the town if his piratical attempts were renewed.

All night we coasted along the western shore of Kiusin, and soon after daylight we passed close to a remarkable gateway, which lies directly in our track. It is formed of two tall masses of granite, fifty feet apart, and perhaps one hundred and fifty in height, and pointed at the top. Between these two pillars, by some convulsion of nature, is lodged an immense boulder of rock. The water is deep on all sides at the base and between these pillars, and through this natural gateway a fleet might sail in grand procession.

It was a beautiful morning when we steamed in towards the entrance of Nagasaki harbor, which to our eyes seemed completely hidden from view. After twisting and turning round one island after another the long bay became visible with the town at the further end, clustering at the foot of a range of hills, and in some places creeping up the terraced sides nearly to the summit. The bay is most spacious, and so completely land-locked as to be secure against the most violent gales or typhoons. Just at the entrance to the inner harbor we pass close to an island of perhaps one hundred acres, with a steep, rocky precipice toward the sea, and a gradual slope on the opposite side next to the main land. This little islet, which now looks so bright and pleasant in the early morning sun, is said to be the place where twenty thousand native Christians were slaughtered, being driven up the sloping bank and forced over the edge of the precipice to be dashed upon the rocks a hundred feet below. The same year when the last of the Roman Catholic converts were buried under the ruins of the captured city of Nagasaki, or hurled from this rocky islet, just two hundred and fifty years ago, a few exiles landed on Plymouth Rock, in a newly discovered continent, where they were destined to plant the seeds of a Protestant faith and found a great Protestant empire. And it was the descendants of these Pilgrim Fathers who, two centuries later, were the first among western nations to bring a lapsed Heathen race once more within the circle of Christian communion, and invite them anew to take their place in the family of civilized nations.

In the harbor of Nagasaki we find a large fleet of foreign vessels, besides almost innumerable native junks. To show how rapidly the Japanese government is adopting western ideas, especially in methods of war-fare, I count no less than six trim-looking, foreign-built gunboats, carrying the Imperial flag, which in appearance would not discredit any navy in the world.

As we drop anchor within a few yards of one of the trading junks, it may be interesting to describe the appearance of this curious specimen of naval architecture. For many centuries boat and ship building have stood still on account of laws prescribing the shape and size of all water craft. The largest native ships are rarely over one hundred tons burden, and quite unfit for long voyages. The policy of the government has been to prevent a bold, sea faring population from hazarding voyages beyond their own coasts, and to visit foreign countries was especially forbidden. The junk has but one mast, which is a little aft of the centre, and but one large square sail, attached to the yard, which is raised or lowered by a windlass in the cabin. From the foot of the mast to the stern, the deck rises at an angle of fifty degrees, and the long curved helm looks like the proboscis of a colossal elephant. It is a mystery how sailors can keep their feet in stormy weather on such an inclined plane as the quarter deck of this craft. They are built with open sterns, and strong bulwarks to keep out the water, and the rudder, which is very large and unwieldy, is almost out of sight. Being flat-bottomed, without centre-boards, they can sail before the wind with great rapidity, but on the wind they go sadly to leeward. They have certain marks on the sails which look like patches, designating the owners and the section where they belong. From the high deck of our steamer I can overlook the proceedings on board our neighbor. Sacks of rice are piled so high midships, that, being covered top and sides with matting, it looks like a small house. This craft is evidently the home of a large family, for the skipper, his wife and nearly a dozen children are squatted on deck, partaking of their morning meal of rice and fish. Forward I see four or five sailors smoking the pipe of idleness. Their long robes look inconvenient as the "toggery" of a sailor; but when occasion requires they have a way of slipping out of their clothes, and appearing in a costume well adapted to the agile feats of their profession, but rather shocking to the unaccustomed eyes of western barbarians.

We land at the stone jetty of Decima, a small island in front of the town, separated from the main land by a wide canal, where for centuries the Dutch consented to be penned up and submit to every indignity, while they monopolized the whole foreign trade of Japan. The street through which we passed is lined with their warehouses now going to decay, while a new era of progress and advancement is opening to the country. The canal is now spanned by a wide stone bridge, leading to broad, well-paved streets, through which we stroll, making our last purchases of "curios." This place has a population of over 100,000, and is famous for its manufacture of fine porcelain, a few specimens of which I had seen in Yeddo. We visit several large shops where the display of beautiful vases and china ware, elegant in design, and decorated in good taste, surpassed anything to be seen even in Paris. The teacups are all covered to retain the aroma of the fragrant leaf, and are as delicate and fragile as egg shells. If I were only a few thousand miles nearer home, I should be tempted to send a large consignment of this beautiful ware to my friends on Superior street.

It is surprising that, with the remarkable skill, ingenuity and taste the Japanese show in some branches of the mechanic arts and manufactures, in the higher departments of art they are so rude and unskilled. In their porcelain, bronze, lacquer-ware, temper of steel for sword blades, and fabrics of silk and paper, they rival any nation of the civilized world. But painting, sculpture and music have few votaries. In knowledge of perspective they excel the Chinese, but take low rank compared with Western nations. Printing in colors from blocks of wood, with graduated shading, like our lithographic color printing, has been known for ages; but their drawing is defective, and the execution rude. Their books of highly-colored prints are curious and interesting only as illustrative of their life, costumes and scenery. Their carving in ivory of figures and animals are skillful, but said to be inferior to the Chinese; and in all these there is a tendency towards the grotesque. It is easy to see that the pursuit of the arts and sciences requiring actual labor is not common among the higher classes, while to the lower ranks of society no inducements of rewards, honors and competition are held out for excellence in these accomplishments.

"Street life" in Nagasaki, as everywhere else in Japan, is full of interest, and we linger until the warning gun from the "Costa Rica" urges us to re-embark. We steam out of this beautiful bay, winding around the islands that so effectually hide its entrance, and now in the open sea we shape our course due west for China We look back upon the hills, not vine-clad, but terraced and cultivated in crops of more practical value, and watch the fertile valleys that shelter an industrious, contented and happy people, as they fade from sight in the distance. Japan is a country with a future. Nature has been lavish in her gifts of a fertile soil and a genial climate. We wonder whether the change now so rapidly spreading in the manners, customs and life of her people will result in making them more virtuous, happy and contented.

With many regrets at parting, and carrying with me pleasant memories of the few weeks spent in this interesting country. I can only say "Sionara, Japan."

W. P. F.

NUMBER THIRTEEN.

My first impressions of this great empire,
containing one third the whole population
of the globe, were not altogether favorable. The four hundred miles of "Yellow
Sea" that separate it from Japan has a reputation almost as bad as the English Channel. One may escape sea-sickness during a
month's voyage across the Pacific, but here
the rough weather and short, chopping
seas are pretty certain to bring him down.
When one hundred miles away our approach to the coast was indicated by the
color of the water from the sediment of the
great Yangtse River which, rising in the
Himalayas, three thousand miles away,
flows through the heart of China and empties into the sea to which its discolored
waters give the name. In size and extent
of territory which it drains, the Yangtse
should rank with the Amazon and Mississippi. But both these together cannot compare with this great artery of China in the
population which crowd its banks, and the
commerce it bears upon its bosom.

The mouth of the Yangtse strongly resembles the lower Mississippi. The shores
are a dead level for nearly a hundred miles
through the delta which its waters have
formed, and are dyked to prevent inunda-
tion. It is so wide that for thirty miles but
one shore is visible from the deck of our
steamer. As it gradually narrows I catch
glimpses of frequent dwellings, neatly
whitewashed and thatched with bamboo,
surrounded with groves of bananas and
plantains. A dense population is indicated
by the number of people working in the
fields, which are cultivated down to the
water's edge. This rich alluvial soil is devoted to rice and grain, not a foot of land is
wasted, and even the mounds under which
dead are buried are green with crops of
millet or wheat. Hundreds of junks are at
anchor, or sailing up and down the yellow
current, thousands of fishing boats are
closer in shore, and though the steam whis-
tle is constantly sounded as a warning, col-
lisions seem at times inevitable.

These Chinese navigators have the faculty of running across the bows of a steamer,

and calculating their distance so exactly, as usually to escape being run down. Sometimes. however, they are sunk and set up such exhorbitant claims for the loss of their craft that they are accused of purposely causing their destruction.

Fifty miles up the Yangtse we turn to the left into the Woosung, a clear stream three quarters of a mile wide, upon which about twelve miles above its confluence with the Yangtse is built the city of Shanghai, the great foreign commercial mart of Northern China. The name suggests to us all that great, coarse, overgrown chicken, which (the *word* not the *fowl*) was in everybody's mouth while the "hen fever" raged. It is unfortunate that so fine a city should be associated in our minds with so awkward a bird. As we approach it from the water the magnificent buildings occupied by the merchants, which face the bund or praya, a wide avenue along the river, give it a very imposing appearance. We come to anchor and are immediately surrounded by a fleet of sampans or passenger boats, and are quickly landed at the jetty, where a fierce onslaught on my baggage is made by a score of coolies. It is a war of words in which I can take no part, and I stand quietly by and let them fight it out. After fifteen minutes of fierce conflict, I follow the six victorious "Celestials," who have slung my trunk and satchels on bamboo poles, to the Astor House, not a six-storied granite hotel, but a modest building of two stories, with a garden in front, as unlike its great namesake as can well be imagined. Why called the "Astor House" I have been unable to ascertain, for it is kept in the English style by a full-blooded John Bull. After securing a comfortable room I stroll along the bund, over a handsome iron bridge that spans a creek crowded with boats, and begin to realize that I am indeed in the "flowery kingdom," and receiving my first impressions of John Chinaman at home. The streets are full of people, coolies carrying heavy burdens on poles across their shoulders, or slung between them in pairs, sedan-chairs of light bamboo, behind the silken curtains of which are stolid Chinamen or bright-eyed "Canton girls," Europeans dashing along in two-wheeled traps behind diminutive ponies, who make up in speed what they lack in size. But the conveyance *par excellence* of Shanghai seems to be the *wheelbarrow*, of which there are thousands here, though entirely unknown

in Canton or any part of southern China.
This machine must be the germ of the Irish
jaunting car. It carries two persons, who
sit back to back on a narrow board on either side of the wheel, with one foot thrust
into a rope stirrup. The "propeller"
pushes along his squeaking vehicle,
whose wooden axle is innocent of
any lubricator, assisted in bearing up the
weight by a leathern strap across his shoulders. With but one passenger he is obliged
to tilt it up very awkwardly on one side to
keep the equilibrium. Since the wheelbarrow has become a recognized institution in
the foreign quarter of the city various de-
vices have been suggested for improving its
construction. But John is slow in adopting
foreign innovations, and especially obstinate
in adhering to the dismal squeak of his machine. No amount of persuasion, short of
a municipal ordinance enforced by the
dreaded policeman, can induce him to apply
a little oil to the axle. It is enough for him
that his father and grandfather used no
grease, and the dismal wail of a score of
machines is music in his ears. As I stand
watching these novel velocipedes go by
loaded with Chinese of both sexes I am reminded of the nursery ballad, but here the
roads are smooth and the streets broad, and
I see no necessity for the happy Benedict to
"carry his wife home on a wheelbarrow."
The final catastrophe, too, is wanting, unless some luckless sailor, out on a bender, is
unable to maintain his balance.

In the river opposite the city is anchored
a large fleet of foreign ships and steamers,
and near the shore are moored several large
hulks in which is stored the opium from
India. These opium hulks are under the
strictest surveillance of the Chinese custom
house officials, as this article pays a very
high import duty and offers great tempta-
tions to smugglers. For some years past
the maritime customs department of China
has been under the control of foreigners,
mostly English and Americans, holding
office from the Chinese government. They
are paid large salaries, and if not absolutely
proof against fraud and speculation, they are
reported to be as honest public servants as
the custom house officials of any foreign
civilized government. They are certainly a
great improvement on the native Chinese,
who formerly held the positions, under
whose administration scarcely a tithe of the
duties collected ever found its way to the
Imperial treasury. It is the commonly ac-

cepted belief among foreigners that the
Mandarins and native officials of every
rank, from the Imperial Council down, are
corrupt. The stranger constantly hears one
word used, which is most insignificant, and
has a world of meaning; that word is
"squeeze."

The government of this country is patri-
archal. The Emperor is called the "Son of
Heaven," and exercises supreme control
over the whole Empire, because Heaven
has empowered and required him to do so.
But with this power is imposed the obliga-
tion to treat his people with leniency, sympathy and love. He lives in unapproachable
grandeur, and is never seen except by members of his own ~~party~~ and high state officers.
In governing such an immense realm the
people understand that he must delegate his
authority to a large number of officers,
whom they regard as his agents and representatives. When they consider themselves injured or oppressed by these officials,
they do not blame the Emperor, but some
times rise in rebellion against their immediate rulers, upon whom they wreak fearful
vengeance, and then appeal to their great
father to appoint more merciful officials in
their place.

The method of collecting the revenue is
peculiar, and unlike any civilized nation of
the West. The empire is divided into
eighteen provinces, and some of them larger
in extent and with four times the population of New York or Pennsylvania. Each
of these is ruled by a Viceroy. The provinces are sub-divided into departments,
governed by Tou-Tais. The departments
are again sub divided into districts, under
Mandarins of various grades. There is no
system of uniform taxation which bears
equally upon all parts of the empire. The
Supreme Council signifies to each Viceroy
how much money is required from his province, and the Viceroy in turn notifies each
Tou-Tai, and so on down to the Mandarins,
who must collect it from the people as best
they can. It is one grand system of
"squeeze," from the apex of the pyramid to
its base. Each official pays over to the
next higher in rank the sum absolutely demanded, which he must do at the peril of
his head, and putting the surplus, if any, in
his own pocket. Under such a system the
people who form the base of the pyramid
are often subjected to intolerable exactions,
and if the Chinese were not the most patient
and long-suffering race upon the face of the

globe, the country would be in a chronic state of rebellion.

The ruling dynasty is Manchu or Tartar. When this race, coming from the north, overrun and conquered the "Flowery Kingdom," they imposed upon the Chinese the wearing of the long queue or pigtail in token of subjection. In the course of many centuries it has become the most necessary and essential part of the Chinese dress, and to be deprived of it is the greatest indignity. To cut off a man's pigtail is a worse punishment even than to cut off his head, and would result in suicide. The military officers throughout the empire are all of the Tartar race, and in most of the large walled cities there is an inner wall, within which the Tartar families reside. Upon this colony or garrison the Emperor depends to hold possession of the city in case of a rebellion or insurrection. In every province and district there is a military officer, whose authority is co-ordinate with that of the civil governor. Although the government is an absolute despotism, it embodies some decidedly republican features, and the people have a good degree of personal liberty. The civil officials are all selected from the literary graduates, and persons of almost any condition in life may rise to the highest position of honor and influence through a most complex system of competitive literary examinations. Hundreds of thousands spend years in study, and yet fail to pass this ordeal; or if successful in taking the first degree, are unable to reach the second or third, which would make them eligible to the higher offices under the government. This class of literati scattered throughout the whole empire, are thoroughly imbued with the doctrines of Confucius, are earnest supporters of the government, (which they regard as the embodiment of the wisdom of their ancient sages), and exercise great influence over the common people. Some idea of the enormous scale on which these competitive examinations are carried out, may be had from the fact that at the last triennial examination at Nanking in September, 1870, over eighteen thousand candidates appeared, and they were from only three of the eighteen provinces. A novel feature on this occasion was that Kiang-si, the Governor, placed two steamers at the disposal of the candidates to convey them to and from their homes without charge. These examinations are frequently attended by demonstrations of dislike to foreigners, a feeling which generally pervades the whole literati, as a class.

Now we look upon the Chinese as barbarians, but is not this system of government appointments an improvement on that of our own enlightened land, where party service, personal favor and political considerations, and sometimes beer and whisky, are the *open sesame* to official positions, regardless of merit or qualification. When Mr. Jencke's civil service bill shall become a law, as in time it certainly must, we may hope for a reform that will place us in this respect almost on a par with the "Heathen Chinee."

No event connected with China during the present generation has created so much interest in foreign lands, or raised such great expectations which were doomed to disappointment, as the great Tai-ping rebellion. It commenced in 1850, and after a struggle of fourteen years duration, which nearly overthrew the Manchu dynasty and destroyed millions of lives, it was only put down at last by the help of foreign bayonets. It rendered desolate some of the richest and most fertile portions of the empire, leaving behind it tracts hundreds of miles in extent, marked with blackened walls and heaps of ruins, uncultivated fields and depopulated towns and cities. It originated with a man who had received from a native teacher near Canton some imperfect ideas of Christianity, and at first it seemed that he was to be the instrument of a great religious reform and the downfall of paganism. Having overcome a greater portion of Southern China the Tai-pings swept northward, and after a siege of two years captured Nanking, the second great city and ancient capital of the empire. In this contest the loss of life was frightful, as no prisoners were taken on either side. The professed object of the rebellion was the destruction of the Tartar dynasty and the restoration of the ancient Chinese race to the government of the empire. They allowed their hair to grow, repudiating the Manchu custom of shaving the front part of the head and cultivating the queue, and so were called "Long-hairs," this being a synonym for *rebels*. In the meantime the early promise that the success of the rebellion would result in a more beneficent government, with modern ideas and a Christian civilization, had faded away. The leader announced himself the brother of Jesus Christ, and his followers became more and more erratic and fanatical, until they degenerated into a superstition more absurd than the paganism it sought to replace. At this crisis, when the Peking government was tottering, and its downfall seemed inevitable, there appeared upon the stage a man whose career is one of the most remarkable in modern times, and seems like a romance of the middle ages. An American, who had first come to China as a common sailor, and had acquired some influence with the Mandarins, offered his services to the imperial government, and, as drowning men catch at straws, they were promptly accepted. Although entirely without military education or training, he showed such remarkable talent and energy in the reorganization and management of the Chinese army, everywhere defeated and demoralized, that he soon rose to supreme authority in the conduct of the war. He raised a foreign legion, established order and discipline in the imperial army, procured improved arms, checked and drove back the rebels marching on Peking, retook city after city, and in two years, having broken the back of the rebellion, met an untimely death at the storming of an insignificant town in one of the central provinces.

If General Ward's life had been spared ten years longer it is impossible to calculate what his unlimited influence with the government he had served might have enabled him to accomplish in reforming ancient abuses and corruptions, and introducing western ideas and civilization. Since his death the Chinese have placed his effigy in their pantheon of gods, and regard him as a special gift from heaven to save their nation. Here, on the *bund* at Shanghai, they have erected a marble monument to the memory of General Ward and the brave foreign officers of "that ever-victorious army" which he commanded, who fell in the struggle with the "long-haired" rebels.

And now, having returned at last to the *bund* whence we started, let us go back to the "Astor" for tiffin, leaving further record of experience among the Chinese for another day.   W. P. F.

NUMBER FOURTEEN.

SHANGHAI, CHINA, January, 1871.

First impressions are not always the best,
but in attempting to describe the strange
and curious sights of a foreign country,
where the traveler expects only to skim
over the surface, and has no time to dive beneath and comprehend the *rationale* and
philosophy of the people, his first impressions
are often of interest, if photographed at
once. An old traveller or long resident will
cease to notice and wonder that a stranger
is interested in scenes which are full of interest and novelty to the fresh comer. To
Bayard Taylor, there would be nothing
novel in seeing people eat with chop-sticks,
old men flying kites, or women toddling
through the streets with feet only three
inches long. I do not propose to wait until
familiarity with such sights has destroyed
their novelty and freshness, but shall try
and give the first impressions, which to me
are very curious and vivid, of the habits and
manners of this strange race.

China is said to be a country of paradoxes
and anomalies. Many familiar things are
strangely reversed. The people do not
walk upon their heads, to be sure; but the
old men fly their kites, while the children
look on; they write and print their books
from top to bottom, from right to left, in
perpendicular instead of horizontal lines
and their books end where ours begin; their
locks are made to fasten by turning the
keys from left to right; the carpenter uses
his plane and saw by drawing it towards
him, and the tailors stitch *from* them.
Their horses stand in the stables with their
heads where we place their tails; they
mount them from the *off*-side, and fasten the
bells upon the hind quarters instead of
round the neck; the anti-crinoline style
of their garments seriously impede locomo-
tion, and destroy all grace of movement; white is the color of mourning, and
their religion consists not in love of God,
but in fear of the devil. In this respect,
however, they do not differ so very much
from some so-called Christian nations.
Some other customs of the Chinese differ
materially from ours, but the comparison is
rather to their advantage. The children

pay the greatest deference and respect to
their parents. The most heinous offence
that a child can commit would be to strike
his father or mother; and by law and custom the parent would be justified in pun-
ishing the child with death. "Young China" never ignores or snubs "the governor."
So far is filial affection carried that grand-
parents are almost worshipped. "Sharper
than a serpent's tooth to have a thankless
child," has a significance ten-fold greater here than in America. The Scripture
injunction to "leave father and mother and
cleave unto the wife," is not according to
Confucius. The claim of one's parent upon
the affections and love of the married son
is considered to be paramount to that of his
wife. The reason given is that the
loss of a father or mother is irre-
parable, but that of the wife is
not. Women are treated with more respect and consideration as they advance
in years, and mothers are universally regarded with great affection and tenderness.
Although the husband and wife never see
each other before marriage, and have nothing to do with making choice of their part-
ner for life, a strong attachment often
springs up between them, and divorces are
rare and only justifiable if the wife is so
unfortunate as to be childless. While customs and theories vary, human nature and
woman's nature is the same the world over.
The Chinese have a *theory* of the infe-
riority of woman, which they often find it
difficult to carry into practice. They pay a
tribute to the "weaker" sex when they deny them education, for the professed reason
that they find it sufficiently difficult to keep
them in their proper place without it. In
many families here as well as in America,
the superiority of the wife's will and authority is sufficiently manifest and cheerful-
ly acknowledged, although "hen-pecked
husbands" are perhaps more rare than
among Western nations.

I attended, last evening, the Chinese theater by invitation of a friend, who took along
with him his *compradore* as guide and interpreter. It is situated in the Chinese quarter, and the streets in the vicinity were full
of restaurants and the walks crowded with
venders of fruits, sweetmeats and all kinds
of eatables. The outside of the building was
covered with immense pictures of the sensation order, representing dragons, lions and
nondescript animals, giants and dwarfs, and
reminded me of Barnum's Museum in olden

times. Inside we found a large and well-ventilated room, plainly finished, without gilding or decoration, with a gallery around three sides. The parquette was furnished with small tables, at which parties were regaling themselves with tea and refreshments. Most of the audience were men of the better class, some few of whom had their wives and children with them. A polite attendant showed us to our seats, which had been secured beforehand near the stage, and then placed before us very thin porcelain cups with covers. In each he put some tea leaves and poured hot water from small bronze kettles, which were carried around all the evening to replenish the cups. He then brought little dishes of dried fruit and sweetmeats, miniature oranges and roasted water-melon seeds, which are furnished to the audience gratuitously, and supply the place of peanuts in western theatres. Play-bills were furnished printed in Chinese on red paper. As we were the only foreigners present our entrance attracted some attention, but no rude staring annoyed us, and everybody around seemed studiously polite. Indeed, with the better class of Chinese, politeness is a science and gracefulness of manners, a study. I was much amused at watching a party of four gentlemen who came in and occupied a table near us. It was full ten minutes before they were seated, from the most excessive and persistent efforts on the part of each that every other one should occupy a better seat than himself. One seat being back to the stage each seemed determined to occupy it, with infinite bowings and compliments to his companions. The party were provided with the usual refreshments, and when the attendant brought a joss stick to light their pipes, which were ornamented with silver and very handsome, each insisted that the others should light first. The proverbial politeness of the Frenchman was not to be compared to this exhibition of Chinese manners.

Near us was seated a lady with nails on the third and fourth fingers of her left hand fully three inches in length. She frequently held this hand up to her face, as ladies sometimes do at home who wear elegant rings, and probably with the same motive. She was "got up" in great style, and often consulted a small mirror to make sure that her face and head dress were all right. She flirted her elegant ivory fan with all the grace of a Spanish Signorita, and ought to have had the mirror inserted in it—an idea that the Chinese ladies have not yet adopted from the French. Every person in the audience carried a fan, which when not in use was placed between the collar and the back of the neck.

I can only describe the play as a "comical, melo-dramatic farce." It seemed to me a most whimsical and ridiculous travesty; but the audience listened with the most serious earnestness, from the entree of the principal characters, which were harlequin-like, with a series of somersets over tables and chairs, to the finale, when the hero, after a painful and agonizing death, got up and quietly walked off the stage. I doubt whether the Chinese have any adequate conception of the ludicrous, either on the stage or in actual life. Making all allowance for the difference of national tastes and habits in dramatic performances, their more than Turkish gravity and impassiveness opened to me a new phase in the character of this strange race. The actors, who belonged to a famous troupe from Peking, and were all "stars," recited their parts in a high, drawling falsetto tone, frequently advancing and retiring, bowing, gesturing, twisting and turning in the most grotesque and ludicrous manner. There was an undue amount of action, loud altercations, the most violent gestures and frequent mock conflicts, with a great flourish of gongs, which seemed to inspire awe in the minds of the spectators. The play was in the Mandarin dialect, quite different from the colloquial language of Shanghai, and must have been unintelligible to the greater part of the audience, to whom, as well as to ourselves, it was a pantomime. The Emperor and other high officials were represented with a vast amount of tinsel, and long processions of "supes," with spears and tin helmets, marched in and out, looking as little like real soldiers as these characters do at home. Fire-crackers and blue lights, gongs and tom-toms, enlivened the battle scenes, and the whole wound up, like our evening campaign speeches on the Square, with "a grand exhibition of fireworks."

It is but just to Chinese theaters to say that vulgar and immoral plays are unknown, and the associations of the stage are quite different from those of western lands. The female characters are always performed by boys, and with remarkable accuracy in their imitation of voice and general appearance. The prompter sits on the stage, and beside him is a bowl of *saki*, or rice wine, of which the actor partakes after violent exercise. One of the most ludicrous things I saw was the two champions, who seemed to be rivals for the hand of the beautiful heroine of the play, after fighting most fiercely for ten minutes, agree to a truce, take a friendly drink together, and then resume their deadly conflict, which resulted fatally, of course, to the poor fellow who was not favored by the young lady.

In histrionic art the Chinese are far inferior to the Japanese. I saw a play acted at the Yeddo theater that showed an appreciation of the proprieties of "mimic life" that would be creditable in Europe or America. They had a revolving stage and very fair scenery. The acting in some parts was positively good, particularly the "old man" who in dress and manner, for of course it was all pantomime to me, reminded me of Ellsler at the Academy of Music. There were none of the absurdities which the Chinese auditors view with so much gravity, and frequent outbursts of laughter showed that the "Japs" appreciated the humorous passages of the play.

While walking yesterday along the Nankin road, in the Chinese quarters of Shanghai, I encountered a curious procession, and stepping into Chee-Kiang's shop I inquired in my best "pigeon English" what it all meant. Mr. "Chee" politely informed me that it was a wedding party, and explained to me in that particular dialect, which is the only medium of communication between natives and foreigners, some particulars which may be of interest to the reader. First came a dozen musicians beating gongs and blowing horns, each one apparently on his own account, and making the most ear-piercing and discordant article ever conceived of under the name of "music." They were dressed in fantastic costume of which yellow seemed the predominant color. Then a lot of boys carrying flags and lanterns, of which they seemed very proud. After them several coolies bearing between them the show presents, boxes and bales, including, I presume, the *trousseau* of the bride. Then a long procession of the bride's relations, all dressed in holiday attire, looking especially festive and jolly, as if bound to make a day of it, for behind them followed more coolies, loaded with baskets of fruit and every variety of eatables, among which I noticed a roast pig, brown and crisp, and done to a turn. These were to set off the

wedding feast. ᵍ Next came a gorgeous looking palanquin, decorated with paper flowers
silk and satin embroideries in the highest
style of the Chinese art, and carried by
eight coolies. This I suppose contained the
bride, but the curtains were drawn too
closely for any profane eyes to penetrate,
although I suspect that the "adorable crea-
ture" inside was peeping out. Then more
sedan chairs, but not quite so "stunning" in
appearance, containing the female relatives
of the family, and another lot of friends invited to the feast, and the long procession
wound up with more musicians, who seemed
trying   their   best   to   outdo   their
rival performers, who led the van. Behind
all were scores of beggars and street *gamins*,
the latter running from side to side of the
narrow road, as full of excitement and delight at the show as the same class would be
in following a military procession at home.
Having never had the pleasure of accepting
an invitation to a Chinese wedding, I can
only describe the *show part*, which is open
to the public, but I am told that they are
celebrated with a great deal of formality and
expense. Betrothals are contracted at a
very early age, and even among intimate
friends it is etiquette that all the negotiations
shall be conducted by a class of women called
"go-betweens," or match-makers. The boys
and girls are supposed to be entirely indifferent as to the whole matter. The idea of
courtship or love letters would be quite
shocking to all right minded persons. After
betrothal, which is consummated by an exchange of presents, and the making over of
a formal document to the parents of the
groom, the engagement is considered as legal
and binding as if the marriage had been performed. If the boy should die it is considered the proper and filial thing for the girl
to remain a widow for life, and devote herself to the care of her deceased husband's
parents—a custom which our girls at home
would consider particularly hard. Before
the wedding day the bride has her eyebrows
pulled out, which in China is the distinguishing mark of a married woman. On
the morning of the "lucky day" chosen for
the marriage, the bride is carried from her
own home to that of her future husband in
great state and ceremony. With her face
closely veiled, she kneels with her husband
before an altar, and they worship together
the spirit tablets of the ancestors of the
groom. The parties first see each other's
face when the bride's veil is removed and

they drink wine out of the same cup, after
the wedding day spent in feasting, congratulations, and general hilarity by their mu-
tual friends and relations. If not entirely
satisfied with the choice in which they have
had no part, it is certainly too late to repent,
and they have only to "make the best of it,'
—a conclusion which sensible in other lands
sometimes arrive at when they have entered
into the marriage relation with eyes wide
open, as they suppose, but in reality closely
bandaged by that blind little imp and match
maker, Cupid.   W. P. F.

Departure of Distinguished Guests—
Secretary Seward in Japan and Chi-
na—He Visits Pekin and the Great
Wall—Prince Kung is Grouty—The
Senator and Sailor Exchange Sa-
lutes—The Prince Relents—All Love-
ly and Serene over Sharks' Fins and
Birds' Nests—The Chinese Language—
Pigeon English—Coin and Currency
—Compradores Costumes and Queues
—Pawnbrokers Shops—Small Feet—
Fashion Makes Hideous Things Beau-
tiful—Visit to a Wealthy Chinaman
—Tea as is Tea—A Gentleman,
Though Wearing a Pigtail—Luxury
Next Door to Penury.

HONG KONG, CHINA, January, 1871.

The morning on which I left Shanghai, I
was awakened by a terrific din of firecrackers under my window. Fourth of July was
the first idea suggested, but then it occurred to me that it was nearer the fourth of
January than July. The fusilade was kept
up for several hours in the streets around
the landing place. The departure of distinguished guests is always celebrated in China
by burning firecrackers as a sacrifice to
"Joss" for good luck and a pleasant voyage.
Not that your humble correspondent was
the "distinguished personage" who drew
forth such a demonstration. The Hon. W.
H. Seward, who is "swinging round the circle," was to leave that day in the Hong
Kong steamer. The great sensation in
China this winter, especially among the
American residents, is the visit of the venerable ex-Secretary, who left San Francisco
in September, spent a month in Japan, and
after visiting North China, Peking and the
Great Wall, is now on the way to Hong
Kong, thence via. India to Europe. He is
accompanied in this tour through the East
by the two Misses Risley of Washington, the
elder of whom, Miss Risley Seward, his
adopted daughter, is his private Secretary.

A nephew of the distinguished Statesman,
Mr. George F. Seward, has for nine years
past held the position of Consul General in
China, and returned to Shanghai with the
party, bringing his young bride, one of the

most beautiful and accomplished daughters
of the Golden State. When appointed to
this important office, which is diplomatic as
well as consular, he was scarcely of age, and
it was looked upon by Americans in China
as a family affair, but during his long service he has won the respect and esteem of his
own countrymen as well as of the Chinese
officials.

In Japan Mr. Seward was received by the
Micado with all the honors accorded to the
Duke of Edinburgh, son of Queen Victoria,
last year. This was only accomplished
after long negotiations on the part of our
Minister to Japan, Mr. DeLong. Since the
arrival of the party in Shanghai, this city,
which is more American than any other
place in China, has been unusually gay with
balls and dinner parties. In their visit to
Peking, they were accompanied by Admiral
Rodgers and a large escort of marines from
the United States war ships on this statior.
A full band of music from the flag ship
Colorado enlivened the march, and the festive array of gold lace and blue jackets put
the visit on a semi-cfficial footing. Their
route was eight hundred miles by steam up
the Yellow Sea to Tientsin, thence eighty
miles by donkeys, mule litters, and Chinese
carts to the capital. The weather was very
cold, and the party suffered many discom-
forts, for this part of China is only accessible to travelers during the summer months;
in winter it is frozen up as solid as Canada.
The common people in the crowded cities
and villages through which they passed
doubtless thought it was a cortege bearing
tribute to their mighty Emperor, the "Son
of Heaven," from some tribe of western barbarians.

At the capital the party was most hospi-
tably entertained at the American and Russian legations, the English, of course, holding aloof, from that jealousy of American
influence in this country, which one sees
everywhere in China. Prince Kung, the
representative of royalty and Prime Minister of the Celestial Empire, declined to receive Mr. Seward at the Foreign Office,
on the ground of illness, and when it
was proposed to call at his private
residence, he replied that his house
was too small and mean to receive so great
a personage, but the proposal was so
flattering to him that he should "engrave
it on his heart and write it on his bones."
Such extravagant expressions are merely
the conventional forms cf Chinese etiquette

and mean nothing. If a consul proposes to call upon a *Tou-tai*, or Mandarien, they "will sweep their mean threshholds clean in honor of your presence, engrave your words upon their hearts, escort you back to their doorways and there wait weeping until your glorious return," &c. Notwithstanding these ~~hurried~~ words they both hate and despise you, although near the coast, where the power of outside barbarians is seen and realized, their dislike is tempered by a wholesome fear of foreign gunboats and bayonets.

Leaving the Prime Minister to recover from his "colic" the Seward party penetrated fifty miles further north to the great wall, that famous type of Chinese greatness and feebleness. The Shanghai *News Letter* gives a full report of the speeches made by the venerable statesman and the gallant Admiral while standing on this interesting spot, "surveying on one side the vast plains of China, teeming with population, on the other the desolate wilds of Tartary." The English newspapers in their account of the affair take occasion to speak of the American mania for speech-making on all and every occasion, and under the most adverse circumstances. They delicately hint at the slightly absurd aspect of these two old gentlemen standing upon a ruined wall, shivering in the keen blasts sweeping down from the plains of Tartary, and firing off a pair of formal speeches at each other. As the gallant old sailor was never before in his life known to make a speech, they intimate that these extended "remarks" were "cooked" by reporters for home consumption. But such ill natured feelings at one of our most cherished national characteristics is no more than we ought to expect from an Englishman.

After visiting the great wall and the *Ming Tombs*, where the Emperors of the *Ming*, or native Chinese dynasty were buried for thousands of years before the Tartars overrun and subjugated the Empire, the party returned to Peking, where in the meantime some pressure had been brought to bear on the government, and the Prince consented to invite the august visitors to an entertainment. There over a banquet of shark fins, birds' nests, and other Chinese delicacies, the best of feelings were mutually expressed, and compliments tossed back and forth between "China's best friend and treaty maker," and the head of a Ministry that rules one third of the whole human race.

Some one has said that the march of improvement in China has been a *dead march*, and one great impediment in the way of the introduction of foreign ideas is the difficulty of acquiring the language; which in part accounts for the extreme isolation ot the Chinese race from the other nations of the world. The written language has no alphabet, but is made up of forty thousand arbitrary characters, of which about five thousand are in common use. Each of these characters represent a word or syllable. While it is possible for the vocal organs to express only about five hundred distinct sounds, there are ten times that number of characters, so that the same sound may represent either one of ten different words. In English the number of words alike in sound but with different meanings are limited. In Chinese it is universal. One can readily see what an immense amount of study and how retentive a memory is required to learn this written language, which is understood by the learned class not only over the whole Chinese empire, but also in Japan, Loo-Choo, Corea, and the neighboring islands. Through it a far larger proportion of the human race can be reached than through any other language of the world.

The hundreds of thousands who are competitors for literary honors at the annual examinations perfect themselves by long and patient study in the written language, and become familiar with the writings of Confucius and the other Chinese classics. Of these but a small fraction are successful, and become the employees of the government, to whom every channel of wealth and power is open, from the Mandarin's button to the peacock feather of the prime minister. The great mass of unsuccessful candidates settle down into village schoolmasters and teachers, and form an influential literary class of society scattered throughout the whole empire.

The spoken language of China so differs in every separate province, that people living within a hundred miles can no more understand each other's dialect than an Englishman can understand a Spaniard. The Mandarin or court dialect is more common than any other, and is used at the capital and among officials throughout the empire.

The difficulty of acquiring a language so artificial and elaborate as the Chinese, and which only the missionaries attempt to learn, has given rise to a curious jargon

called "Pigeon English," which is the exclusive medium of communication between
natives and foreigners at the open ports. I
found merchants who had been for a score
of years residents of China, and could
neither read nor speak the first word of
Chinese. Ask a native to pronounce the
word "business," and he will produce a
sound that more resembles "pigeon" than
anything else, and hence the term "Pigeon
English." This dialect, which has to me a
most comical sound, consists of but a few
hundred words, and one can learn it so as
to be understood in a very short time. Many
natives think it pure English, and if one
seeks foreign employment he will sometimes take lessons from a native professor
for a few days, who advertises to teach
"Red-haired talk." It is a mixture of English, French and Portuguese, stirred up
with a plentiful sprinkling of Chinese, and
forms a *hodge-podge* which shocks people of very strict literary notions. It
dispenses with pronouns and surplus words,
is remarkably laconic and especially convenient for a traveler to learn who cannot
stay long enough in the country to acquire
a more elegant or polished language. I go
into a shop and ask "John" for some article,
he replies sententiously "got" or "no got,"
which he jerks out with a good natured
grin that always makes me laugh. Before
I became proficient in the language I one
day told a servant at the hotel to go up to
my room and bring the book I was reading
yesterday. He stared but stirred not, evidently not understanding my request. A
friend translated my message thus: *"Go
topside and catchee one piecee bookee, all
same read yesterday."* Off he started like a
shot. Built in the wall, just outside the
door of every shop is a little recess where
the proprietor, *Chin chin Joss,* or burns the
sacred Joss-sticks to ensure a good trade.
I go into Toe-Shing's shop, here in Hong
Kong, where I have made extensive purchases, and inquire how business is. He replies, *"No good pigeon, I, Chin-chin Joss,
he catchee melican man, all the same you
muchee buy."*
The Chinese currency in dealing with
foreigners is, like that of the Japanese, exclusively Mexican dollars. They have no
coin of their own, except copper cash, value
one-tenth of a cent, and you will sometimes
meet Coolies loaded down with this coin in
strings of 100 or 1,000. Tea is purchased
in the interior with cash, and steamers up

the Yangt se river frequently carry tons of it, bringing down about the same weight of tea. The Mexicans in common circulation are usually *chopped*, that is stamped with the name of well known Chinese merchants, which makes them more current among the people, and is a partial guaranty against their being counterfeit. So much bogus silver is in circulation that a Chinaman will hesitate to take a Mexican that has not the chop. Every shopkeeper is provided with curious little scales for weighing coin, and will take any foreign silver according to its weight. There are in circulation for larger transactions silver ingots, shaped like a Chinese woman's shoe, and hence called *sycees*. Their weight is stamped upon them and they pass for their value in silver, from ten to fifty dollars each. The native merchants and bankers have a system of bills of exchange, which are good all over the empire. They are capital accountants, and every foreign mercantile house has its *compradore*, a person of education and sometimes of considerable wealth, who could lend large sums to his employers if they require it. He dresses in broadcloth and silk, and occupies a position of high trust. He has charge of all the funds of the house, and checks are made on him as the treasurer of the establishment. His accounts are kept with great exactness, and instances of misplaced confidence are almost unknown. Every Chinaman received into the service of a foreigner is expected to give a bail bond for his honesty, which binds all his relatives. Father, mother, wife and children would all be ruined by his misconduct. Perhaps in western lands some such system will have to be adopted to insure honesty in positions of trust.

When a Chinaman has committed a crime which has made him amenable to the laws he is very apt to commit suicide and cheat the gallows. He is very sensitive to the disgrace which would be brought upon himself and his family; although I do not think the Chinese entertain any high moral sentiment which would lead them to do right because it *is* right. They are generous and hospitable to a fault, and for the sake of appearances will often involve themselves in expenditures, especially at weddings and funerals, that keep them under the harrow for years.

In the streets I have sometimes seen men quarreling in the fiercest manner, and the blustering tone indicated an immediate resort to blows; but it was sound and fury, signifying nothing. The sing-song tone of two Chinese talking together is very curious, and unlike anything I ever heard in any other language. Sometimes, in case of deep resentment, their method of obtaining revenge on an adversary is characteristic. He commits suicide by taking opium, having previously hired Coolies to take him to die at the door of his adversary. In this way he hopes for a double revenge, by the terrible fright he will give his enemy, and also the opportunity he expects to have, as a disembodied spirit, to do him harm.

Even in the cold climate of northern China there are scarcely any conveniences for heating the houses. Wood and fuel of all kinds are very scarce, and extra garments and furs are everywhere resorted to as protection against the cold. Furs of the most expensive kinds are worn by the wealthy classes, and seem to be looked upon as an indication of rank and wealth. In summer the pawnbrokers' shops are filled with expensive clothing, which is redeemed in the fall upon the payment of a rate of interest quite low compared with the extortions of these establishments among western nations. They are usually large, high, and nearly fire-proof buildings, under strict government surveillance, and the safest places for the storage of valuables to be found in the large cities where fires are frequent and very destructive.

The garments worn by both sexes are loose and flowing. the styles never changing and being the same for all classes. The fabric worn by the great mass of the people is blue home spun cotton, while the wealthy classes wear silks, satins, gauzes, furs and broadcloth. The front of the head is shaved, but the hair on the top and back part is braided into the queue. To this false hair is added and a braid of silk at the end, so that it reaches almost to the ground. For full mourning, white silk is braided into the queue, for half mourning blue is the appropriate color. A small silk cap is usually worn both in the house and street. While to work the Chinamen usually twists his "pigtail" round his head to be out of the way; but it is considered as disrespectful for a servant to come into your house with his queue round his head as to wear his hat into your drawing room. The women, of course, never shave the head or wear the queue, but they comb their hair back from the forehead and do it up in the most elab-

orate manner, with a profusion of gold and
silver ornaments. What I shall call the
"jug handle" style seems to be the most
popular.

The custom of binding the girls' feet is
not so universal as I first supposed. It is a
mark of gentility, and among the fashionable
and wealthy classes of women of whom the
stranger sees very few, it is said to be uni
versal. But the great mass of the poorer
women in the city and country appear to
have feet of the natural size. I have seen
in the shops elegant little shoes, which are
designed for the use of full grown women,
less than three inches long; and occasionally
in the streets ladies dressed in silks
and satins may be seen toddling
along, as proud of their little feet,
as a western belle would be of her
wasp like waist. Fond mothers commence
to bind their daughter's feet when very
young with narrow strips of cotton wound
tightly about them, until the foot assumes
the form of an acute triangle, the big toe
forming the apex, the others being bent
under the foot and almost absorbed. The effect of this deformity is to produce an un-
graceful, tottering gait, which, however, is
associated here with the idea of good breeding and gentility.

While at Shanghai I was glad to accept
the invitation of a very wealthy Chinese
merchant to visit his house, which was situated in the old Chinese city. Accompanied
by a friend, I entered through a half ruined
gateway, and threaded the narrow streets
reeking with filth, an abomination to any
one possessed of eyes to see or nose to smell
with. On one of these streets, where the
green and slimy water standing in the gutters on either side would breed a pestilence,
even in the temperate zone, was a high brick
wall and in the center a heavily barred gate.
At our summons the gate was opened by a
well dressed porter, and we entered a handsome courtyard, through which we passed
into the house of the merchant. He met us
at the threshhold and bade us welcome, then
led the way through several suites of rooms
elegantly furnished in the Chinese style.
Most elaborate carvings in stone and marble
over the doorways, and in one room the
wainscoating of dark wood was carved in
bas relief, so as to represent a legend or
story of Chinese history. Through four or
five rooms, each more elegant than the pre-
ceding, then across a miniature garden filled
with rare flowers, and bordered with dwarf

orange trees not more than two feet high, but covered with full-sized fruit, and we reached the inner sanctum.

Here our host showed us his most valuable "curios," rare gems and precious stones, a picture on silk which once belonged to the Emperor of China, and was five hundred years old. He took much pride in his elegant house, which we told him was "number one," to a Chinaman the highest praise you can express.

Inviting us to be seated he regaled us with tea served in the thinnest of porcelain cups —and such tea! I never was especially fond of the "cup that cheers but not inebriates," but this was delicious. A few dry leaves were put in, the hot water poured on them, and the cup covered to retain the aroma. Then partially removing the cover we sipped a beverage as much superior to ordinary tea as the delicate *Chablis* of the Rhine diff rs from last year's cider.

We were shown into the room especially fitted up for opium smoking, and invited to take a pipe, which we declined. Our hosts' wife is said to be very handsome, and we wanted to have a glimpse of her, but we were not gratified, and it is not etiquette to enquire after the wife and family. The higher class of Chinese never allow their wives or daughters to be seen by foreigners.

Wealth, luxury and good taste were everywhere to be seen about the mansion, and the owner in courtesy of manner is a polished gentleman. If he showed a pardonable vanity and pride in exhibiting his place to us, I think we have all seen the same feeling in showing one's beautiful house to visitors among western barbarians. After spending an hour very agreeably we took our leave, our polite host accompanying us to the outer gate, and urging us to come again. Outside the gate the squalor and the filth of the street seemed more disgusting than ever by contrast with the luxury we had just left, and we hastened away feeling that it is but a thin wall that divides great wealth and extreme penury here in China as well as in London, Paris and New York.

W. P. F.

NUMBER SIXTEEN.

Approach to Hong Kong—Safely Landed Under the Protection of a Young Amazon --Wonderful Prosperity of Hong Kong—The Greatest Smuggling Depot in the World—Manners and Customs of the People—The Most Snobbish Place in China—·Street Scenes—Sepoys from India—Parsees—Black Policemen—Justice Swift and Sure—A Chinese Jack Cade—Broad Brimmed Hats—Sedan Chairs--Climb·ing Victoria Peak—Reception to Mr. Seward—A Buckeye Abroad Who is Creditable to His Country.

HONG KONG, January, 1871.

It was a warm and bright Sunday morn·ing when the French steamer "Phase" dropped anchor in the beautiful harbor of Hong Kong, and my impression at the time has been confirmed by a ten days' residence, that this is the most picturesque as well as one of the most spacious harbors in the world. Rio Janeiro is said to resemble it, but neither it nor the Bay of Naples can rival the beauty of the scene before us. The mountain rises abruptly from the water's edge, and is crowned by "Victoria Peak," seventeen hundred feet above the sea. The houses are built tier above tier, and from the water it seems a city of palaces, stretch·ing far up the hill side, and for more than two miles along the shore. Beyond the town, on the left, I see the "Happy Valley," where I can catch a glimpse of the English cemetery embowered in tropical foliage; for with all its beauty of location Hong Kong is not healthy, and many an Ameri·can and European who has come to this Eastern land in search of a fortune, remains here in possession only of six feet of Chinese earth.

Landing here is but a repetition of the scene at Shanghai, but I have learned some·thing by experience. A hundred *sampans* surrounded the steamer, some *manned* by males, but the greater number by females, and the shrill pipes of the women drown the bass tones of their male competitors. I ean over the rail, and before leaving the deck close my contract with a young Ama·

zon to take me ashore, and have no further trouble. Sae fought her way to my pile of luggage, *manfully* shouldered trunk and valise, and I had only to follow in her wake to the boat, the crew of which, from a family likeness, I judged to be her mother and sister. In five minutes more I am landed at a fine granite pier, and follow six coolies carrying my luggage, which would be a light load for one Irish porter, to the Hong Kong Hotel, a spacious, airy building, with wide verandas extending round each of its five stories. This city, which is sometimes called the St. Helena of the Chinese seas, has grown very rapidly, and has a most motley population, made up of every European and Asiatic nation. It is not a part of the Chinese Empire, but the island on which it is situated, containing about thirty square miles, was ceded by the Chinese government to Great Britain thirty years ago, and forms the colony of Victoria, with an English Governor and a full set of officials appointed and sent out from home. The population is about 150,000, and it is growing more rapidly than any other place in the East. It is a free port, with no custom house or port charges of any description. The sum of five dollars, which a vessel pays on entering the harbor, is returned when she leaves. With a land-locked harbor, safe against any storm, and spacious enough to hold all the navies of Europe, so close to the ocean and easy of access that no pilots are required, Hong Kong has become the central depot for shipping and merchandise on the coast of China. The native population from the main land have made this barren rock their home, and built up a Chinese town of 80,000 people, which stretches along the western shore of the bay, and is creeping through the ravines and up the hillside, attesting the untiring industry, perseverance and enterprise of the native Chinese when in the pursuit of gain. Hong Kong is the postal and financial centre of the Chinese seas, and here are located the heads of mercantile firms, who determine the destination of ships and cargoes composing the foreign trade with China. Trade converges here as to a great centre of attraction. From my room in the hotel I can see ships of war, trading junks and mercantile craft from almost every country. Over twenty steamers are anchored in the harbor, and native vessels in great numbers from the adjoining coast, each differing in shape and color, according to the port they

are from, crowd the anchorage on the west
side of the harbor. Here are junks from
every port between Shantung, 1,200 miles
north, and Siam, Singapore, Java and the
Philipine Islands. A Chinese sailor will
distinguish where they come from by difference in shape and rigging, paint and decoration; and, if honest, may tell you where
stout-built junks are lying undisturbed, with
a pirate crew, and nearly fitted out with a
fresh supply of guns and powder. Only it
would not answer to trust him implicitly,
for he may belong to a piratical craft himself, and put you on a false scent.

It may be asked what is the secret of this
sudden and enormous growth of a barren
rock in population and commercial importance, when the main land close by has
many commodious harbors, nearer the producing markets and the native purchasers of
foreign goods. The answer to this question
shows another side of the picture, not creditable to British commercial ethics. When
poor China was forced, at the mouth of the
cannon, to cede this island, lying in the
highway of the immense commerce of Canton river, to Great Britain, she did not
dream that it would become the *greatest
smuggling depot* in the world. That the body
and soul destroying drug, which she was
trying to keep out of the reach of her teeming millions, would here be stored in immense quantities, and smuggled to the main-
land in spite of all her efforts to prevent
that cargoes of foreign goods on which she
had the right to levy an import duty, would
from this central point be run into every
creek and bay along the coast where they
could be landed by bribing the officials.
That tea, camphor, cassia, sugar and other
products of China, which pay an export duty
at the consular ports should go to Hong Kong
free. This illicit trade which an English
writer speaks of as the "encouragement of
commerce at the expense of revenue," is
neither more or less than smuggling, and
from it the fortunes of the Hong Kong merchants have been made. Verily the poor
"heathen Chinee" has very few rights which
John Bull is bound to respect.

Hong Kong has the reputation of being
the most *snobbish* place in the east, and in my
short experience I have seen much to con-
firm this idea. Being a miniature province
with a governor who represents royalty,
and a set of tide-writers and hangers-on
fresh from the old country, English habits
and manners are not only adopted as the

standard, but exaggerated, so as to become almost ludicrous. To be a "Royal Britain" here is to worship everything that bears the semblance of royalty—unicorns, lions griffins and crown. The effrontery and arrogance of John Bull is proverbial all over the world, but in the east the bovine animal roars and bellows in his loudest tone, paws the ground and tosses his head in the most defiant manner. This may be excusable in a nation on "whose dominions the sun never sets," but what shall I say of Americans residing here for a few years, who adopt the tone and air of the cockney, cultivate side whiskers, sneer at everything American, and especially affect to despise Republican institutions. At dinner parties you will hear sentiments expressed by Americans anything but complimentary to their native land, sneers at American consuls and officials abroad, and that, too, in the presence of foreigners. I am almost ashamed to record an instance of snobbery that occurred here not long since. An American merchant, born in Boston, but for some years a resident of Hong Kong, who aspires to social position among the English nobs, said to the Governor of the colony that "he would willingly give ten years of his life if he had only been born an Englishman." The bluff old Governor, disgusted at such flunkeyism, administered a stinging rebuke that brought the mantle of shame to the cheek of the renegade American. That line of Saxe, "Born in Boston needs no second birth," does not apply to him.

This loss of national pride among Americans which the air of China seems to produce, was illustrated last fourth of July by the captain of the Pacific Mail steamer China, on her way from Hong Kong to San Francisco. It was suggested by the Americans abroad that he ought to dress the ship with flags, and in some suitable manner celebrate our national holiday. But the captain declined to do so for fear that *the English passengers might take offence.* This, too, on an American built steamer, sailing under the American flag, and belonging to a line that was receiving a subsidy of half a million dollars a year from the American government.

I do not say that all Americans in China are like those I have noticed above—but the feeling which I condemn is so common as to give a tone to American society, especially in Hong Kong, and be noticeable to any one fresh from home, who cherishes

that *amor patriae* which, while not blind to
our national faults, would at least never pa-
rade our soiled linen before our neighbors
eyes.

One class of Americans wherever I have
met them seem to cherish a deep love and
affection for their native land, the Missionaries. There seems to be very little social
intimacy between them and the merchants.
They give no expensive dinner parties nor
entertainments, but devote themselves quietly to their blessed work. They are sometimes refered to sneeringly by their money-
making countrymen, whose conduct, as an
illustration of christian morality, is not always a bright example to the heathen.

These small communities of Europeans
are subject to rules of etiquette as inexorable as the laws of the Medes and Persians.
The gentlemen in society being far more
numerous than the ladies, it is considered
proper for a stranger to call on any or all
the ladies without special permission, or
even an introduction. If considered an eligible acquaintance, the husband of the lady
returns the call, the new-comer is invited to
dine, and considered as admitted to terms
of social intercourse. If not considered a
desirable acquaintance, his call is simply ig-
nored. The Hong Kong club excludes every
person who sells goods *by retail.* He is not
considered by the snobs here a *gentleman,* no
matter how extensive his business or how
great his wealth or culture. A. T. Stewart,
if residing here, could not become
a member of this woud-be aristocratic and very exclusive club, which
is the only one in the place. The thermom-
eter may stand at 120° in the shade, but a
black dress coat must always be worn at
dinner, whether ladies are present or not. I
was told that in some of the bachelor *hongs,*
as the dwellings attached to the large mercantile houses are called, it is not considered
the thing to appear at breakfast even except
in full dress. Such snobbishness carries its
own penalty and is a subject of ridicule to
strangers from every other country than
England, instead of impressing them with
the wonderful exclusiveness and high breeding of society here.

The streets of Hong Kong are more cosmopolitan than any others I have seen in
China. A regiment of red-coated Sepoys
from India is stationed here and I frequently
meet the soldiers in the street. They are
tall, firm looking men, dark complexion,
Asiatic profile, keen black eyes, and have

the bearing of men who can fight. Their commissioned officers are all Englishmen, but the *chevrous* on the sleeves show that there is a chance for promotion to a native up to a certain grade. I am told that they are *Sikhs* from the Paunjaub in Northern India, which did not join in the revolt against the British in 1857. They all wear white helmet-shaped pith hats, which are universal in India.

Here I see for the first time the *Parsees*, disciples of Zoroaster, and sun-worshippers. They are most numerous in Bombay, but a few can be seen scattered throughout the whole east. They are no darker in complexion than Cubans, but are a larger and finer-looking race, men of education, and first-class merchants. Their dress is European, except the tall *Mitre* or hat, which is peculiar to the sect. It reminds me of a brown, glazed ruff box, worn a little on the back of the head, without visor or any protection for the eyes.

The motly population of Hong Kong includes a large proportion of rascals from every clime, and makes a very large number of police necessary, over six hundred, of whom nearly one half are negroes. In answer to my enquiry to-day, one of them told me he "was a subject of the Queen from Jamaica." He had never been in the United States and thought there was too much prejudice against color there to suit him."

In the heart of the city is an immense jail with seven hundred inmates, mostly Chinese, who work on the street chained together and guarded by soldiers. Punishment to a Chinaman is swift and sure if caught transgressing the laws. A few days ago a friend of mine arrived on the Pacific Mail steamer "Great Republic," from San Domingo, and leaving his luggage locked in his stateroom, he took a walk up town. A waiter who was passing his room heard a slight rustling noise, and looking through the keyhole he espied a Coolie, who had crawled in through the window, rifling the baggage. He gave the alarm and the fellow was secured and taken ashore to the office of the Company. Here he broke away from his captors and dashed through the crowd, but was caught by his pigtail, which streamed out behind in his rapid movement. He was then led by the queue to the Magistrate's office, and within an hour from the time he was first caught, he found himself in the chain gang, with six months before him of hard work.

A Chinese "Jack Cade," before starting
out oils his body, wearing only such garments as will readily slip off, and fills his
queue with bits of glass. As they rarely
carry arrows they are not very dangerous,
but decidedly slippery customers and hard
to hold.

The hats worn by the natives are very
odd looking, and quite different from those
usually seen in Northern China. It is of
bamboo, very light, and often three feet in
diameter, curving up from the edge of the
brim to the centre like the lid of a tea-pot.
In Chinese towns, where the streets are
narrow, two such hats cannot pass each
other without colliding, and they have to be
carried under the arm.

The best institution I have seen in Horg
Kong is the Sedan chairs. The doors of the
hotel are besieged with them, and they are
everywhere to be hired for a very small
sum, which is regulated by the city government like the fare of hackney coaches. It
is cheaper to ride than go on foot, and they
are used by everybody, as the streets are
mostly too steep for carriages drawn by
horses. They are made of bamboo and cane,
very light, and comfortable, with a green
canopy to keep off the sun, and supported
by bamboo poles about ten feet long, resting
on the shoulders of two coolies, who slide
rapidly over the ground at a pace between
a walk and a trot. As I look from my window I see a sailor coming up the street in a
chair, with his feet elevated over the "dash-
board " and lying back with great dignity,
smoking a cigar. Late every night I hear
the "won't go home till morning," sung in
full chorus by bands of sailors, out on a
bender, who sweep through the center of
the street arm in arm. The police never
seem to interfere with such demonstrations
on the part of *white men.*

A few days ago, with some friends, I ascended to the summit of Victoria Peak,
from which there is a magnificent view of
the whole island of Horg Kong and many
miles out to sea. Four coolies to each chair
carried us up the winding path, and in some
places the ascent was so steep that I
pitied my perspiring "bearers" and got
out and walked—a piece of humar-
ity quite unexpected. On the summit
is a tall flag-staff, a powerful telescope, and
a cannon in charge of a guard, who signals to the town below the approach of
every ship long before she can reach the
anchorage. He explained to us his system

of signals by which the merchants are informed as to the character and nationality of the coming vessel while she is twenty miles away. The cannon is only fired at the approach of a mail steamer or a man-of-war.

While at Hong Kong I was present at a reception given at the American consulate to the Hon. Mr. Seward. It was a very pleasant affair, attended by all the American residents and several prominent English merchants. The venerable ex-Secretary was welcomed very gracefully in a little speech by our consul, D. H. Bailey. Esq., and replied in an address which showed that he has lost none of his ability as a diplomat. He gave the usual credit to commerce of carrying civilization and Christianity to heathen lands, but drew a picture of the future for China in too roseate hues for any one but an optimist, giving the Chinese credit for all the virtues, while he thought them entitled to all the consideration of the most favored nations. He defended the Burlingame policy, which is especially obnoxious to American merchants in China. It was evident that he does not agree with "Truthful James"—

Before leaving Hong Kong for the "up country," I must express my gratitude to Mr. Bailey and his estimable family for many acts of kindness and courtesy to a stranger. Mr. B is a Buckeye from Cincinnati, a lawyer of ability, and his eminent social qualities and liberal culture render him the most creditable representative of our country abroad that I have anywhere had the pleasure of meeting.   W. P. F.

American Steamers in China—Up the Canton River—My Fellow Passengers—The Bogue Forts—Pagodas—Commodore Foote and the Barrier Forts—Fleet of Boats—Charmine—Temple of Honam—Transmigration of Souls—Street Scenes in Canton—Cat and Dog Meat Shops—Pawnbrokers—Curiosity Shops—Soothing Syrup—Temple of 500 Genii—Temple of Confucius—Temple of Longevity—Flower Pagoda—Execution Ground—Examination Hall.

CANTON, CHINA, January 1871.

Although Americans are far behind the British in commercial importance on the Chinese coast, in the matter of river steamers, we have the monopoly. The swift, side-wheel, American built steamboats have driven the slower, black, English boats out of the market. The navigation of the great Yangtse river for 600 miles from Shanghai to Han-kow is in the hands of Americans. The five large steamers that ply on the Yangtse, some of them 1,500 tons burden, look precisely like those on the Sound or Hudson river. This great artery of the Chinese Empire, the Yangtse, is sometimes by our English cousins in derision, called the "Yankee," from the many American steamers on its waters.

From Hong Hong to Canton there is another line of American-built boats which control the immense passenger traffic between these two places. The distance is over one hundred miles, and boats leave daily at an early hour in the morning, reaching their destination in about seven hours. I stepped on board the "Fire King," was introduced to the Captain, an American, Albert, an ex-rebel officer from Georgia, but now tolerably well reconstructed, and could almost imagine I was in America and about to take a trip up the Hudson. One peculiarity of all these river boats is that the first-class cabins are forward, which makes them much pleasanter in a warm climate, as we are sure of a fine coast breeze, with a better view of the scenery, no smoke or bad odors from heated oil, and much less jar from the machinery.

After breakfast the captain very kindly showed me over the boat, which was crowded with Chinese passengers, although there were only ten or twelve Europeans in the forward saloon. The main cabin aft was filled with the better class of Chinese, mostly merchants, and quite a number of small footed ladies. Every party had their *chow-chow*, or lunch boxes. Most of the people were dressed in silk or broadcloth robes, and were squatted on fine mats on the floor, while the luggage was piled on chairs and seats. On the main deck were the second class natives, piled in so close that it was difficult to pass through. They were gathered in groups smoking, some tobacco, and a few opium, and nearly all were *gambling*. So inveterate is the habit of gambling that when a boy invests his *copper cash* in a handful of nuts he will bet with the seller whether the number is odd or even, or as to the number of seeds in an orange, agreeing if he loses to pay *two cash* instead of one. The officers of the Fire King are Americans, but of course the crew are coolies. The Chinese appreciate the value of time, for the common people pay a dollar fare for a seven hours ride in the steamer, rather than go in a junk for a quarter that sum and be two or three days on the way. To show how much behind the times are the English guide books, if you refer to "Bradshaw" you will find it recorded that "to go from Hong Kong to Canton you must take a native junk," although a daily line of steamers have been running for over ten years.

The first fifty miles of the route seems more like a broad bay than a river, and we thread our way swiftly, without a collision fortunately, through fleets of junks, some very large and gayly painted, and nearly all armed with rusty old cannon, that look more dangerous to the gunners than to the target they are aimed at.

At the narrow entrance to the Pearl River we pass quite close to the Bogue forts, once quite formidable but now in ruins. The British battered them down in 1856, and the shattered granite blocks remain as they were left at the close of the bombardment. Here I catch the first sight of a pagoda, perhaps 150 feet high with nine stories. It is curious that all the pagodas in

China are built with three, five, seven or nine stories—always an odd number. These towers or monuments, though sometimes connected with temples, are not considered especially sacred. Some of them are very o d and nearly all dilapidated. Frequently large shrubs and bushes are growing from crannies in the walls, where seeds have been lodged by the winds. They are substantially built of bricks or stone, with outside galleries round every story, and form a very characteristic and beautiful feature in Chinese landscapes. It is supposed that they were originally designed as depositories of revered relics or to commemorate some noted person. That they are now neglected and in ruins is quoted by Chinese *Old Fogies* as an illustration of the degeneracy of modern times.

As the river narrows we see on both sides people at work in the rice fields, and the country seems highly cultivated and very populous. We now approach Whampoa, quite a large city, where all the foreign ships are anchored, as there is not sufficient depth of water above for them to ascend the ten miles between here and Canton. Near by are the famous Barrier forts, dismantled and in ruins. These had an especial interest to me as the scene when the gallant Commodore Foote laid his ship alongside the Chinese forts and qu'ckly battered them down, the soldiers *skedaddling* through the gates in the rear and never returning. The boats from our squadron, carrying the American flag, had been frequently fired on from these forts, and to remonstrances and demands for explanation and apology, nothing but Chinese verbiage could be obtained; until at last the Commodore's patience being exhausted, he taught them to respect the "stars and stripes" by battering down their forts. This is, I believe, the only time the American eagle has set his claws in the Chinese dragon, and the lesson has had a very salutary effect. As an illustration of Chinese inconsistency and insolence, the Mandarin Governor of Canton, after an humble apology for the "mistake" of firing on the boats of a friendly nation carrying the national flag, proposes that an American flag be sent to him, so that in future his officers might know and be able to recognize it. This, after half a century of international intercourse!

As we approach the great city the "Fire King" slackens speed, for the boats and native craft seem to almost completely cover the water around us, and for miles ahead. Many of these boats are the homes of whole families who spend their lives upon the water. Here they are born, here they eat and sleep and here they die. It is said that more than one hundred thousand people thus spend their lives upon the river and know no other home. We land near the sight of the foreign "factories," or business houses, which were all destroyed by the Chinese in 1856. After the war the government conceded a tract of several hundred acres to the foreigners for their sole occupation, which is called "Charmine." It is certainly charmingly situated along the river bank, separated from the native city by a wide canal, and laid out in grass plots and avenues of trees. Here are the flagstaffs of the foreign consuls, a neat English church, and twelve or fifteen large and stately edifices of foreign merchants, that look like palaces in contrast with the vast collection of mean, one-story houses that spread out for miles in the rear. There are altogether but about fifty Europeans and Americans in this city of over a million inhabitants. The government is weak and feeble, and in case of a popular outbreak, nothing could save them from instant destruction.

Most of the city is built on the north side of the river, and the houses seem very low and mean. The pawnbroker's establishments, large, tall, square towers, rise high above the tiled roofs, and in the very heart of the town is an immense lattice work of bamboo poles, looking like a gigantic bird cage, which I am told is the staging around the new Catholic Cathedral, commenced three years ago and yet unfinished.

We reached Canton at two o'clock, and after reporting myself at Oliphant & Co's, whose guest I was during my three days visit, for there are no hotels here. I started out to see the sights, but I could not venture into such a maze of narrow streets, where not a soul understands a word even of "pigeon English," without a guide. I found Arr-Kum, a very intelligent Chinaman, who had been in California, and speaks quite good English. I can recommend him as one of the most civil and obliging of guides. He laid out a three days programme which we afterwards carried out to the letter. Our first visit was to the great Temple of Honam one of the oldest and richest in Canton, which is located on the south or Honam side of the river. Taking a

Sampean we were quickly set across, and landed at a stone pier near the gate of the temple. The grounds to this establishment, which is a Buddhist monastery, comprise perhaps fifty acres. Entering a long avenue shaded by fine old trees, we came to a flight of stone steps leading to a terrace, upon which is the principal temple, a very large building with projecting eaves and cornices richly carved with figures of dragons and other non-descript animals. The high curved roof and bright colors, as well as the general style of architecture, were similar to the Buddhist temple in Japan. On each side of the doorway was a huge, grotesque wooden image, armed with a club, to keep out bad spirits. Inside, upon a raised platform in the the center, were three idols, at least twenty feet high and sitting cross-legged upon a bed of lotus flowers. These, I was told, represented the Past, Present and Future. In front of the idols were burning many joss sticks, about the size of pipe-stems, made of sandal-wood and filling the building with fragrance. Worshippers were coming in and out, each one kneeling before the altar, bowing and muttering prayers, especially before the "Future," and lighting their votive joss-sticks, which they stuck in little jars filled with earth. There are about sixty priests attached to this temple, and we walked through the wide stone cloisters and large open courts to the gardens, where there is a pond well stocked with fish, and a great variety of tropical fruits and vegetables. We looked into the spacious kitchen and dining room, and met several of the priests, who looked as well fed and jolly as any lot of monks to be found in a Christian country.

The Buddhists believe in the transmigration of souls, and that in the future life we may have to do penance for our sins, by a descent in the scale of creation, and being condemned for a time to occupy the bodies of animals. This is a most suggestive idea, and will account for certain qualities which sometime crop out in the character and action of persons we know. Illustrations of this will occur to every reader. It also leads to humanity in the treatment of animals, for who knows but the ass, the horse, or the dog about him, may contain the imprisoned soul of some near relative. In the grounds attached to the temple, I was shown a dozen or more hogs, very fat and better fed than half the Chinese population. When I innocently poked them with my cane, they grunted entire satisfaction with their present condition. The priests care for them very tenderly, for they believe that they contain the imprisoned spirits of some defunct members of their own order. It is to be hoped that when they are once more elevated to the grade of humanity, they will leave behind all their *swinish* propensities and traits of character.

I arranged with Arr-Kum for an early start the next morning, and he was on hand at nine o'clock, with two sedan chairs, each provided with an extra set of coolies for a hard day's tramp, and we dove into the heart of the great city. I can give but the merest outline of the curious sights of these two days. To describe them all would occupy too much space. The streets are very narrow, scarcely admitting of two chairs passing each other, and all were paved with flat stones and tolerably clean. Each street is devoted to some especial trade, and the din of the venders of all sorts of eatables was sometimes terrific. The signs were all vertical, and in red or yellow letters. Every shop is open to the street, and all sorts of manufacturing can be seen without entering. My coolies slid along as rapidly as the crowded thoroughfare would permit, and in the two days they must have traveled twenty-five miles, winding, twisting and turning in every direction. I did not meet a European or American anywhere in the city, and was, of course, stared at by the natives wherever I went. A few years ago I should have been hooted at and called a *Fankwei*, or "foreign devil," but now the salutation was "Taipan" or "Lord," and many with outstretched palms solicited "Kennshaw," or a gratuity of copper cash. In some of the fashionable streets there are large shops filled with elegant silks, gold and silver embroideries, fine porcelain, most expensive furs and rich jewelry. In the silk-weaving quarter they were weaving with hand looms, the beautiful fabrics at the rate of half a yard a day In the paper *joss* shops are all sorts of curious decorations for their idols. One street was devoted to "wedding chairs," where these gay and festive vehicles are kept for hire. The cap business occupied a very long street, and the shoe trade another. The flour mills were most primitive, the work being all done by hand labor. In the cafes and eating houses were all sorts of tempting viands, among which the brown, crisp roast pig was the most conspicuous. One narrow lane was devoted to cat and dog meat, where pussy and Carlo were sizzling in the frying pans, and others with legs tied were lying on the floor, mewing and yelping most piteously. While in front of one of these shops a little girl came along with a pretty white kitten in her arms, destined for the spit. White is the favorite color with epicures in cats, but black is generally preferred in dogs. It is but fair to the ''Heathen Chinee'' to say, that this diet is not considered ''first-class.'' and is only eaten by the poorer classes.

I called at a pawnbroker's shop, and was introduced to the proprietor, a hard-faced, hook-nosed old fellow, with a corps of clerks behind him, busy making entries in large folios. He was seated on a high bench passing judgment as to the value of some article which a poor woman with downcast eyes was offering. Just the sight one may see in London, Paris or New York, for human nature is the same all the world over. One of the young Levis was detailed to show me up to the top of the building. Every story was crammed full of packages, each neatly tied up and labeled. As I stood on the roof, from which there was a fine view of the whole city, and of the White Cloud Hills far away to the south, I noticed that Levi was examining closely the quality of my coat, and with an eye to business, looking very sharply at the small diamond pin I wore. He was doubtless making an estimate of how much it would be prudent to advance on these articles in case I desired to put them "up the spout."

Fish in China are always sold alive, and are kept in large tanks of running water, from which the seller catches with a dip-net the one selected by the customer. The gold beaters' shops, lacquered and glassware factories, streets filled with carvers in ivory and sandal wood, fan-makers, jadestone shops, a blue stone like turquoise, of which most of the ornaments worn by Chinese women are made. These and many other similar places occupied the first day. I must not omit to mention the "curiosity shops," filled with odds and ends of every description, among which were a broken ivory-handled knife, and a pair of spectacles of European manufacture. Looking about I noticed a small bottle that had a familiar look, and upon examination I found it bore the label, "Mrs. Winslow's Soothing Syrup," with an uncancelled United States revenue stamp. How it found its way here to the interior of the Celestial Empire is to me a mystery.

The next day was devoted to temples, pagodas and public buildings, only a few of which I have space to mention. The "Temple of the 500 Genii," where that number of hideous wooden idols are ranged around the interior of a large building, looking like a lot of tobacconists signs, once gay with paint and gilding, but now dusty and dilapidated. The Temple of Confucius— where there is a colossal statue of that old sage. The roof and decorations of this temple are painted green—to him the sacred color. We entered the court-yard by a side door, and my guide pointed out the front gate, and just inside the inclosure a small bridge, over which, he said, no one had ever passed but the Emperor. Desiring what Margaret Fuller calls "a universal experience," I told Orr-Kum to engage the attention of the attending priest, while I quietly slipped round and passed over the bridge hitherto sacred to the foot of the Chinese "Son of Heaven."

In the "Temple of Longevity" was a fat and jolly looking old idol, with six hands. He was reclining on his side, with mouth wide open, apparently enjoying a hearty laugh. This is consistent with the idea that length of days is promoted by good humor. As I lit my cigar from a joss-stick burning in front of this "jolly old cove," the attendant stared at me with astonishment, but the usual *doceur* of a small piece of silver reconciled him to my seeming irreverence.

The "Flower Pagoda" was the most charming of all the sights in Canton. No hideous idols here, but beautiful flowers of every hue render it fit place of worship for Christian or heathen.

The execution ground is a small court surrounded by high walls. Here 75,000 rebels were executed in a single year during the Taeping rebellion.

We visited the Examination Halls at the southeast angle of the city wall. This is used once every three years at the competitive examinations. Here, ranged in long rows, are 14,000 cells, each 3½ by 6 feet, where the candidates are isolated during the examination, being allowed only writing material to compose their theses. Only five months ago all these cells were occupied.

It was quite dark before we finished our

last day's sight-seeing in Canton. The shops were all shut, and such a thing as a street lamp is unknown in China. Our coolies groped their way through the dark streets, compelling the porters to open some of the heavily barred wooden gates, which are closed at night to cut off communication between the different wards. When at last I reached my hospitable quarters at "Charmine," I felt that I had left behind the dark, hideous barbarism of the East, and, almost by enchantment, had reached the bright and cheerful civilization of the nineteenth century.   W. P. F.

Steamer Life in the Tropics - Arrival
at Singapore—A Boat Ride by Moon-
light—Chinese Festival—An English
Toddy Shop—Population and Climate
of Singapore—Character of the Ma-
lays—The Creese-Running a Muck—
Nature so Lavish that Mankind De-
generates—Picturesque Costumes—The
Gharry and its Driver—A Morning
Ride—The Asiatic Gardens—Fan
Palms — Victoria Regias — Tropical
Vegetation—A Chinese Millionaire—
A Courteous Gentleman—The Wham-
poa Garden.

SINGAPORE, February 5, 1871.

After six days of steamer life in the
tropic, with all its stifling annoyances
below deck, and a vertical sun tempered
only by an awning above, at noon to day
we enter the straits of Malacca, 1,400 miles
from Hong Kong. and steam past a light
house, a hundred feet in height, built upon
a dangerous rock in the center of this great
highway of commerce from Europe to
China. We hope to reach Singapore before
dark, and the engineer crowds on steam
and every stitch of canvass is spread to the
fair wind. We passengers are anxious to
spend the night on shore, for our supply of
ice has been exhausted for two days, and
we long for an iced-lemonade and a taste of
the delicious pine apples, bananas and other
fruit for which Singapore is famous.

It is eight o'clock before we drop anchor
within the crescent-shaped harbor, and see
the lights of the city spread out before us
three miles away. But it is too late and we
are too far off for the *sampans*, or shore
boats to reach us before morning. So we
resign ourselves to the inevitable, though
we dread the night before us, which will
be doubly hot now that the steamer is at
anchor. But the captain, pitying our disappointment, orders the gig to be cleared
away, and in a few minutes we are speeding
along over the moonlit water as fast as four
stout sailors can propel our light craft. The

phosphorescence in these Eastern seas is brighter than I have ever seen elsewhere. The water sparkles with gems at every dip of the oars, and our boat leaves a train of snow glistening with jewels in its wake. The soft air wafted from the shore is laden with incense, for we are now among the spice islands of the tropics, and almost under the equator.

We wind among the shipping at anchor, steamers and sail vessels from almost every part of Europe, junks from China and curious craft from India. Now we pass a leviathan steamer laden with the cable which is to connect Singapore with Hong Kong, and see upon her deck and over her stern the wheels and complicated machinery for paying out the wire thread which will soon put China in instant communication with London and New York. In a few minutes more we are landed at the stone jetty, from which a short walk brings us in front of the large inclosure of the Hotel D'Europe. It is bright with lights streaming through the open windows, across the broad piazza of several detached buildings in a large garden filled with tropical shrubbery. There is no glass in the windows, for in this hot climate the air must circulate freely everywhere, obstructed only by venetian blinds. We register our names, are assigned large airy rooms, and stroll out to see the place by gas and moonlight. But one of our party had ever been here before, and accepting his guidance we cross the river by an elegant iron bridge toward the commercial part of the city, where from the music and many flashing lights we think some celebration is going on. Passing through several quiet streets, we turn a corner and suddenly come upon a broad square crowded with people, all Chinese. Fire-crackers are popping all around, and the venders of fruits and eatables, with flaming lights, make the place bright as day. At the further end of the street, in a booth erected for the purpose, is a Chinese theatre in full operation. It is covered with gay flags and bright colored lanterns, and we quietly edge our way towards the stage and watch the curious pantomime and fantastic performances of the Chinese drama. If there is any dialogue it is drowned in the incessant rattling of bamboo sticks, beating on tom-toms, varied with an occasional boom of heavy gongs. It is evidently some Chinese festival and we have arrived just in time for the celebration.

Soon weary of the din and glare, we pass
on and cross another fine bridge in the direction of our hotel. Stopping at a native
shop to enquire the way and we learn that
the Hotel d'Europe is known to the Maylays
under the significant name of the "English
Toddy Shop." For more than three months
I had been beyond the range of telegraphs,
but here once more we seem to touch civilization, and the evening paper upon the
hotel table, gives us the war news from
Paris of yesterday.

Singapore, or the "town of lions," as the
word signifies, is situated on an island twenty-five miles long by about fifteen broad, at
the lower extremity of the peninsula of Malacca, which extends southward one thousand miles below the Continent of Asia. It
is a British colony and a free port, and was
ceded to the English by the Rajah of Ja-
hore, a native prince who lives in great barbaric splendor on the main land about
twenty miles from the city, and is the ruler
of a large portion of the Malayan peninsula.

He receives from the British government
a heavy annual payment in consideration of
the cession of this island and is *nominally*
at least, an independent prince. But if he
should quarrel with the Governor of Singapore a few gunboats and a regiment or two
of red-coats would squelch his sovereignty
as they have already done with the many
native princes of India. The Malays ar_ all
Mohammedans and as a race have no enviable reputation among Eastern nations. They
are of light copper color, with
high and very prominent cheek bones,
and a larger and better developed
physique than the Chinese. They
can be firm friends or malignant enemies, and in the latter case are most treacherous and cruel. There national weapon is
the *creese*, of which I secured a specimen in
a native shop. It is a wicked looking dag-
ger, about eighteen inches long, with a ser-
pentine blade, keen and glittering, in shape
like the deadly cobra, and, like it, the
point is charged with a fatal poison for
which there is no antidote. The sheath is
of hard wood, the handle carved and ornamented with gold and silver. In the interior every Malay carries this deadly
weapon in his belt, but in the territory controlled by the English no one is permitted
to wear it. Better meet the cobra
or the tiger in the thicknesses of the
jungle than an enraged Malay armed with
this savage weapon. In this country the

term "running a muck" had its origin, and
it is not an unusual occurrence. After a
native has gambled away his money, wife
and children, and his own life been staked
and lost, instead of blowing out his brains
like a sensible Christian, he draws his
creese and dashes through the village, cry-
ing "*A-mok! A-mok!*" striking at everyone he meets. The whole population turns
out in pursuit, and hunts him down like a
wild beast through thicket and jungle, a
large reward being given to whoever slays
the desperado.

The language of the Maylays is the Italian of the East, full of soft, liquid sounds,
vary musical and sweet and easy to be
learned by a foreigner.

Notwithstanding the cruel and blood-
thirsty character of the men, the women
are said to be kind and gentle. They have
soft, lustrous eyes, with drooping lashes,
and mild, pleasing countenances, indicative
of affectionate dispositions. They are neat
and tasty in dress, and in deportment are
modest and unassuming. Such a contrast
between the sexes seems an anomaly. In
riding outside the city I have frequently
met the native women wearing a curious
head gear made of bamboo, two feet or
more in diameter, and shaped like a cheese.
It is very light, and a perfect protection
from the sun.

The population of Singapore is about 120,-
800, of whom more than half are Chinese.
Their energy and enterprise is more than a
match for the native Malays and they control the business of the place. Every
steamer and junk brings a crowd of these
emigrants from the Chinese ports, and in
a few years by industry and economy they
accumulate what is to them a fortune, and
return to China, rich men. The climate
here is said to be the most agreeable in the
world, and is a perpetual summer. Though
but seventy miles north of the equator the
mercury rarely rises above ninety degrees,
with a variation of only about ten degrees
between summer and winter. No long
summer days nor long winter nights, for
the sun rises all the year round within a
few minutes of six o'clock. The abundance
and variety of fruits is unsurpassed in the
world, and nature seems to have bestowed
her choicest gifts with a lavish hand. The
typhoon of the Chinese seas and the cyclones of the Indian ocean are alike unknown.

But there is another side of the picture.
The woods swarm with venomous reptiles
and poisonous plants. In the jungles the
tiger lies in wait for his prey, and the native inhabitants, not unlike him in disposition, have not advanced a step in civilization, nor changed the face of nature by cultivating the soil. The waters around abound
in fish, the woods with fruit. The bamboo
and the palm furnish them with shelter and
the little clothing they care to wear. The
European degenerates, morally and phys'-
cally, by residence in this too favored'clime.
He comes here to make money, and this he
is bound to do, regardless of the rights of
the miserable and degraded native population. But he pays the penalty in the loss
of health and stamina, in a diseased liver,
and blood thinned by a tropical sun. Ten
years' residence here counts for fifteen or
twenty in the length of a man's life in the
Temperate Zone. Such is the inexorable
law of compensation.

In the streets and shops we see every
shade of color and every caste of race.
Scarcely five per cent of the inhabitants are
European. But Java and Ceylon, Hindostan and Burmah, and every island of the
East Indian Achipelago has here its repro-
sentatives. Turbans of every color, and
costumes as varied and bright as the flowers that everywhere blossom in the gardens
and woods, with red and scarlet intermin-
gled with white, and set off by the foil of
their dark skins give a picturesqueness to
the looks of the people quite in contrast
with the sombre hue of the costumes universally worn in Japan and China.

In this climate, to Europeans as well as
natives, a bath is the first duty of the morning, and every hotel and steamer has bath
rooms free to the guests. Before the sun is
up we take a *gharry* to ride out to the gardens of the Asiatic Society, about three
miles from the city. Our *gharry* is so peculiar a vehicle that it deserves a description.
It is a square, black van mounted on four
wheels, with two seats, and moveable slats
for windows—a rattling, jolting concern in
which every bolt and nut seems loose, and
ready, on the slightest provocation to col-
lapse into "everlasting smash." It is drawn
by a single horse, small as a Shetland pony,
with harness enough for a load in itself.
The driver is a dark skinned Malay, with
glittering black eyes, wearing a bright red
turban, which is his principal article of
attire, for besides that he wears only a nar-

row strip of cloth about his loins, and dangling around his neck a metal badge with the number of his vehicle, (310) Having secured his "fare" inside, he runs alongside the pony, plying his lash and screaming, until the animal is excited into a sharp trot. Then he jumps on to the shafts behind him.

We set off at a rattling pace through the European quarter, past two pretty churches and many foreign residences surrounded by fine gardens, thence through the outskirts of the city thickly populated by natives, and soon reach an avenue lined with palm trees, where we meet the market people loaded with vegetables and fruit. They are mostly Chinese, and baskets which they carry on their heads or swung on bamboo poles, are filled with curious fruits, many of which we have never tasted nor even heard the names. A half hour ride over this smooth road, past lanes shaded with cocoanut trees and lined with hedges of light green bamboo, leading to the bungalows of Europeans which we see on every elevation, and we reach the entrance to a park of several hundred acres, laid out with winding carriage roads and smooth graveled walks in the highest style of English landscape gardening. Clumps of tropical trees and shrubs, and parterres of gorgeous flowers are everywhere around us. The rare flowering plants which I had only seen in green-houses, are here growing to immense size in the open air. Over our heads are stately palms, wild almonds, and tall feathery bamboos.

But the most curious tree which I have never ceased to admire, is the fan-palm, each leaf six or eight feet long and radiating from the stem like the sticks of a fan. Imagine a fan for a giant, the handle ten feet long and six inches thick, the fan itself fifteen feet in diameter. In a small pond an immense *victoria regia*, with leaves two feet across which will bear the weight of a child. Mingled with the grass beside the path are large masses of the sensitive plant. Orchids in endless variety are hanging in rustic baskets under the trees. Wild heliotrope, masses of English roses and most beautiful ferns are arranged so as to give an artistic effect to the scene. Every plant and flower which I recognize seems magnified in size and intensified in color under this tropical sun. Rain rarely falls at this season, but the grass smoothly shorn, sparkles with dew drops in the early morning sun.

After an hour spent here which was crowded with views of the brilliant coloring and luxuriant vegetation only to be seen near the Equator, we return to breakfast, of which pine-apples, bananas, mangosteens and oranges formed the most agreeable part. This fruit was taken fresh from the trees surrounding the hotel, and I need not say that the flavor was delicious.

One of the *sights* of Singapore is Whampoah's Gardens. Mr. Whampoah (it seems strange to put this prefix to the name of a Chinaman) is a millionaire Chinese merchant, at whose office I called with a letter of introduction from our Consul. His counting-house is fitted up in first class European style, and he received me with the most flattering politeness. He is a man about fifty years old, in looks and dress as much a Chinaman as if in his native Canton. He told me that he had been a resident here for nearly forty years, and although he has several times returned to China on business, ho is contented to live and end his days in Singapore. He speaks English perfectly, and his table is covered with correspondence in that and other European languages. Among his clerks and bookeepers I notice a Bengalese and a Parsee, and several others whose dress and complexion indicate either Portuguese or mixed European and Asiatic blood. He is evidently gratified at my desire to see his famous gardens, and expresses a regret that he cannot be at home to do the honors. As he writes an order, or "chap," in Chinese, to his head servant to show me his place, I notice upon his fingers two most brilliant sapphire rings. He insisted upon sending his clerk to procure for me some Siamese coins of which I desired specimens, and I left his office with the impression that he is the most courteous and thorough bred gentleman I have thus far met in the east. It is an illustration of what a Chinaman is capable of, that Wampoa commenced his career as a ship's compardor, or steward, and by his energy and schrewduess has acquired great wealth and an enviable position for honor and probity among the highest merchants here.

We found his house and grounds most curious and interesting. Here everything is thoroughly Chinese in style, and in strong contrast with the Asiatic gardens visited yesterday. Miniature tea-houses, fanciful arbors, canals spanned by rustic bridges. Little ponds stocked with gold fish, gardens within gardens, curious imi-

tations of grotesque animals formed by
plants trained on wire frames, and such an
endless variety of shrubs, plants and vines,
all kept in the most perfect order, as woul l
fill with delight the heart of our esteemel
friend, the venerable Professor, whose
place we pass on our way to Rocky River.

Thanks to my "chop" the attendant
showed us the most assiduous attentions,
and, to my surprise respectfully declined
"cumsshan" which I offered them at parting—an instance of self-denial alike rare in
Christian or heathen lands.   W. P. F.

NUMBER NINETEEN.

Up the Straits of Malacca—Penang, and the Province of Wellesley—Malay Pirates—"Old John Brown"—The Penang Lawyer—Mount Pleasant—Pure Laziness—The "Marvel of Tropical Beauty"—A Granite Bath Tub and Natural Shower Bath—Loyal Britons Abroad—Royal Scapegraces—The Dorian—Difference of Opinion—A Wager—John Bull Against Jonathan—An Exciting National Contest—Yankee Comes Off Victorious—The Andaman Isles—"Life on the Ocean Wave"—Not All Pure Romance.

ON BOARD STEAMER "THALES,"
INDIAN OCEAN, Feb'y 10, 1871

After a sail of 360 miles up the Straits of Malacca, winding among islands covered from water's edge to summit with tropical foliage, where the air is fragrant with spicy odors, and the jungles swarm with venomous serpents and man eating tigers, with Sumatra on our left, and Java behind us, early this morning our steamer, the "Thales" dropped anchor in front of the town of Penang. This is another English possession like Singapore, and with the neighboring islands is known as the "Province of Wellesley." It has a population of 125,000, one third of whom are Chinese emigrants, the balance native Malays and Asiatics of various races, with only a few hundred Europeans, who by virtue of forts and gunboats, rule these vast hordes of natives in perfect security. The whole commerce by steam and sail vessels between western nations and China passes through the Straits of Malacca, of which Singapore guards the southern and Penang the northern entrance, so that the positions of these two dependencies of Great Britain are of great commercial importance. Penang is the limit of Chinese emigration in this direction, for to the westward stretches the broad expanse of the Bay of Bengal, 1,200 miles across which is India. Several very large Chinese junks are anchored near us which have

coasted down all the way from Tien-tsin,
2 500 miles from here, and within a single
day's journey of the capital of China.
They make but one round trip a
year, coming down with the favoring
monsoon during the winter months, and
returning the following summer, when the
winds blow steadily from the South. For
these huge, unwieldy craft to beat up
against a head wind would be quite impossible. On the one nearest I count twelve
large old-fashioned iron cannon, which I
suspect are more for show than service
against the piratical Malays, who despite all
the watchfulness of the English cruisers,
will occasionally scoop up a Junk, rob and
murder all on board, then sink the vessel
and dodge back into some inlet or sheltered
cove along the coast. These pirates now
rarely attack European craft, but lie in
wait for the more defenceless Chinese,
against whom they nourish a most bitter
hatred. On our steamers the sailors are
Malays, and the cabin servants and firemen
Chinese. The traditional ill-will between
the two races sometimes breaks out in a
fight in which knives are freely used. But
the control of the English officers, backed
by their revolvers, is supreme over all
these semi-savages.

Not two months ago there came floating
with the tide into the harbor of Penang
thirty Chinamen all *creesed* by Malay pirates. An English gunboat started at once
in pursuit, overtook the pirates before they
could reach the shelter of the coast, and sent
their craft with all on board to the bottom.

Among the flags of every nation I notice
over one large ship the "Stars and Stripes"—
the handsomest flag in the world. In going
ashore we pass close under her stern and I
read the name "Columbia of New York."
The sailors are hoisting in packages of nutmegs, pimento and other spices, and I catch
a few notes of an air that sounds like "Old
John Brown." My companions in the
boat are all Englishmen, and cannot
understand the memories suggested by
the inspiring refrain, " Glory, Glory,
Hallelujah." I want to go on ~~shore~~ and
shake hands with a genuine Yankee who
believes that " his soul is marching on."

We land at the government pier and are
beset by venders of fruit and rough sticks
to be made into canes. There are two kinds,
both a specialty here, the "Malacca joints,"
very light and tough from which all our
expensive canes and whip stalks are made,

and a heavy iron-like sprout, with a solid,
knobby head, called a "Penang Lawyer."
The origin of this name I could not ascertain, but when polished into a cane I can
imagine that it would furnish "knock-
down arguments" on a dry, knotty point of
law to any belligerent member of the legal
profession.

The streets are wide, and near the harbor
are large warehouses filled with pepper,
nutmegs and other spices, of which Penang is one of the greatest shipping ports in
the world. After a look at the fort and
public buildings, all of which are most substantially built and guarded by dark skinned
native soldiers in red coats, we take a
gharry and drive a few miles into ·the
country to a famous waterfall at the foot
of "Mount Pleasant," which rises abruptly
from the plain two thousand feet and commands a splendid view of the harbor and
the shipping. The roads are smooth and
shaded by cocoanut, nutmeg and bread-fruit
trees. Bananas and plantains stretch their
long leaves over hedges of bamboo, and the
bungalows of Europeans seem almost buried
in the luxuriant vegetation. The houses of
the Malayans are all built on posts, thus in-
suring dryness during the rainy season, al-
lowing a free circulation of air, and keeping out snakes and other vermin.
The entrance is by a ladder, and on
this the mistress of the house is usually
lounging, with half a dozen or more naked
urchins playing around, while the father
lies asleep in the shade of his domicile.
Nobody is at work, and nature, in the profuseness of her gifts, seems here to have relieved man from the injunction to earn his
bread by the sweat of his face.

At the end of our drive we came to the
Alexandra Hotel and Bathing Establish-
lishment, kept by an Englishman, whose
circular inviting us to visit his place which
is described as "a marvel of beauty, embowered in mosses and flowering plants,
where the murmuring flow of crystal
streams delight the ear and intoxicate the
senses," was put in our hands on landing
from the steamer. We find the waterfall
and baths, and the Bungalow or Hotel, surrounded by shade trees and covered by the
blossoms of bright tropical flowers, quite
up to the high-flown description. A pretty
mountain stream comes tumbling down
the ravine, dashing in spray from rock
to rock, and conducted through a series
of bath-rooms cut in the solid rock. The

water is very pure, and the luxury of a
swim in a bath-tub of granite, sixty by
thirty, shaded from the sun by a light bamboo roof, where a natural waterfall furnishes
the shower-bath, can only be appreciated
in this hot tropical climate. But the hotel
attached, where we ordered a tiffin after
our bath, is more pretentious than deserv-
ing. It claims, after the style of the loyal
Briton, to be "under the patronage of H.
R. H. the Princess of Wales, the Governor
of the Province," and a long list of other
local dignitaries. In the public room the
walls are decorated with engravings representing the "heir apparent" in the midst of
a happy domestic circle, a picture of home
felicity so notoriously belied by the facts
as to excite only pity for the poor
Princess. Here were also two engravings of the gay young Duke of Edinburgh,
whose escapades during his visit last year
to Australia and India so scandalized his
good mother as to lead to his being sent
home to England. Though but moderately
loyal at home, the Britain becomes intensely
so when abroad, and ruffles his feathers at
any allusion by a foreigner to the discredit-
able acts of these royal brothers. But I am
told that among themselves they do not
hesitate to condemn such conduct in terms
as severe as a republican would use in
speaking of rulers elected by his own vote.

Of all the fruits for which Penang is
famous, none has given rise to so much discussion on our way up the coast as the
dorian. One of our passengers, an old resident of India, is extravagant in its praise.
He says it is very wholesome and nutri-
tious, that he always eats at least one before
breakfast, and his wife and children prefer
it to pine apples, oranges or bananas. He
admits that to a stranger it has a slightly
unpleasant odor, but he describes the taste
as resembling custards flavored with pine
apple and strawberry. Another passenger
tells quite a different story. He says it is
the vilest and most horrid smelling fruit in
the world; that garlic, fried onions, assa-
fœtida, and the seventy distinct smells of
Cologne condensed in one cannot be compared with the nauseating stench of the
dorian.

Such a diversity of opinion results in a
wager between a full-blooded, rosy-cheeked
young Englishman, who has lately "come
out," and an American, as to which shall
partake most freely of this delectable fruit
when we reach Penang. In our rides about

the neighborhood we have seen *dorians*
growing upon large trees and piled up for
sale in the market. It is oval in shape,
a third larger than the pineapple, and
greenish-yellow in color. We selected three
fine specimens, and sent them on board
with our baskets of fruits. As they are
brought on deck the Captain sniffs the air
and calls out, "take them d—d dorians forward."

The next day at eleven o'clock is the time
fixed for the trial. A majority of our passengers are English, but the few Americans
on board are ready to back their national
champion. The Secretary of the Russian
Legation at Pekin is selected as umpire, and
the preliminary arrangements are very
simple. On the main deck, just forward of
the engines, is a small table, on which is
placed a dorian, a knife and two teaspoons.
Beside the table are two chairs for the principal actors. The conditions are that neither champion shall have the right of *holding his nose* during the contest. At the
given hour the table is surrounded by all the
passengers and most of the officers of the
ship. The question arises who shall cut the
dorian? Umpire declines and the steward
volunteers. The fruit is severed length-
wise, disclosing a white, custard-like pulp,
rather inviting to the eye—but, oh! the
smell is overpowering. The crowd fall
back to the rail, every man holding his
nose. At this stage the chances seem in favor of the Englishman, who is the younger
and more vigorous of the two; but Yankee
is tough, and not wanting in nerve, when it
comes to a question of national credit. Umpire gives the word "charge," and each
champion makes a dive with his spoon, and
swallows without blinking a mouthful of
the custard. It is done so quickly that
American can scarcely detect the flavor,
which is really not disagreeable. Russia
falls back one pace and again calls "charge."
Another mouthful is simultaneously swal-
lowed by the champions. At the third
charge, as American coolly raised a spoon-
ful to his mouth, he glanced across the table and saw the game was up. Britons'
cheek had lost its roses, his spoon dropped
before it reached his lips, and he bolted to
the side of the ship—he had thrown up the
spoon.

Umpire's decision in favor of "our American Cousin" was received with cheers, and
the waiters were summoned to throw overboard the remnant of the dorian, and wash

down the table and the deck. Yankee quietly withdrew to his stateroom, *removed a wad of cotton from his nostrils,* and returned on deck to receive the congratulations of all parties, who fumigated themselves with cheroots and washed down the flavor of the dorian with several bottles of champagne at the expense of Johnny Bull.

We left Penang late in the evening in the midst of a terrific squall of rain and wind. The water seemed to pour down in solid sheets. Half an hour later it was bright moonlight, and we steamed along the narrow channel, winding among islets for about thirty miles, when we reached the entrance to the Straits of Malacca. Here we dropped the native pilot into his boat without checking the speed of the steamer, and casting off the rope he was almost instantly lost to sight astern. Our course is now northwest across the Bay of Bengal to Calcutta. When about half way we sight the Andaman Isles, lofty, cone-shaped mountains, covered with verdure to their very summits, and a conspicuous land mark for sailors. On one of these islands the English government has established a penal colony which is visited only twice a year. The Andaman group comprises several large islands, some of which are said to be inhabited by cannibals. The suggestion of a possibility of a shipwreck in this neighborhood is not very pleasant. We pass the days on deck, where, protected from the blazing sun by a double awning, we can enjoy the breeze caused by the motion of the ship. But the monotony of a sea voyage in the Indian Ocean is very wearisome. Every day the same bright sun and clear sky. Books, conversation and cheroots lose their power to while away the listlessness, the absolute inanity of such a life. In the evening we lounge on deck with a full moon sailing over our heads, the water smooth as glass and sparkling in the phosphorescent light. What can be more charming than this "life on the ocean wave." I lingered late on deck enjoying this lovely picture, which all the elements have combined to render perfect, and at last reluctantly went below. The lamp is burning in the main cabin, which is deserted, and the air is close and stifling. I enter my state room and strike a match. Horror of horrors! at the gleam of the light a score of enormous cock-roaches scamper over the floor, trunks and bedclothes. I glance at the narrow berth and the thought of vermin worse than these, of which I had discovered "signs," makes me shudder. There is a most disagreeable odor prevading the whole ship below. Perhaps it is from the opium with which these servants are freighted on their return voyage from India to China. I call to the steward for a glass of water. It is lukewarm, for the ice is all gone. In disgust I go once more on deck, light a cheroot, pace back and forth, then lean over the rail and watch the glimmer of the moonbeams on the smooth sea, and calculate how many more such days and nights before we can reach Calcutta. The illusion of romance and beauty in a sea-life is fast fading away. R clining on a settee, I am soon asleep, but the officer of the deck taps me on the shoulder and very civilly says, "Excuse me, sir, but you ought not to sleep on deck; it is not prudent in this climate." I grope my way down to the main saloon, draw a chair to the table, rest my head on my arms, and fall into a fitful, uneasy, unrefreshing sleep. In my dreams I find "John Whopper's" hole through the earth. I am in the rink, listening to the music and watching the gay crowd of skaters. Then I hear the jingle of the sleigh bells and the crunching of the snow beneath the runners as they fly along the avenue. Anon and it is the splash of water clear as crystal and cool as melted icicles. I awake with a start, and I find it is daylight. The noise I hear is the sailors washing down the decks.

Sailing through tropical seas is not *pure delight*—by no manner of means.

W. P. F.

Approach to India—The Hooghly—
Garden Reach—Calcutta—The King
of Oude—The Landing—Native Mag-
pies and Blackbirds—The Great
Eastern—"New Varmint"—Morning
Races—A Gay Crowd—The Euras-
ians—Commerce of Calcutta—The
"Black Hole"—The East India Com-
pany—Government of India—The
Viceroy—A Perambulating Govern-
ment—Palanquins—A Catastrophe—
Good-bye to "New Varmint"—India
Railways—Iron Replaces Wood—De-
lights of Summer Travel—Native
Servants.

UP COUNTRY, INDIA, }
February, 1871. }

My first sight of India was from the deck
of our steamer as at early dawn we entered
the Hooghly River, whose strong current
and shifting sand-bars render the navigation
extremely difficult. The many mouths of
the Ganges, of which the Hooghly is one,
have formed an alluvial delta of several hundred square miles like that of the Mississippi,
which is a wilderness of timber and brush-
wood, the tall grass forming a jungle where
tigers and other beasts of prey have their
favorite haunts. Advancing up the river
the scenery gradually improves, the country seems more and more cultivated, the
shipping and bustle on the river increase,
and he many beautiful country seats on its
banks indicate that we are approaching the
capital. At length we enter "Garden
Reach" which for two miles is lined on both
sides with splendid Bungalows of the
wealthy European and native residents
which are shaded with palms and other
tropical vegetation, and surrounded with
highly cultivated grounds. As we approach
Calcutta, the metropolis of India, we are
struck with the magnificence of the buildings, public and private, the forest of masts,
and the many steamers anchored in the

stream, the numerous spires and vast extent
of the city which has a population of over
600,000. It is situated on a broad plain on the
left bank and but little raised above the Hoo'
ghly, 100 miles from its mouth, and extends
nearly five miles along the shore. Above
"Garden Reach," on our right is the residence of the ex King of Oude. The grounds
have a frontage of half a mile on the river,
and include several detached palaces vast
in size and gaudy in decorations. Among
them is a Mosque, whose gilt dome surmounted by a crescent glitters in the sun.
Here the King keeps up a court upon
an allowance of two lacs of rupees, $100,000,
a month from the government. He is said
to be a profligate old scamp, with a hundred
or more wives, and is surrounded by a set
of native princes and rajahs, who are altogether a bad lot. Always notorious for de-
bauchery, he has now become infamous for
his vices. Although his income is over a
million dollars a year he spends nearly
double that sum, and runs so recklessly into
debt that the government has lately appointed a guardian to check his extravagance.

We anchor opposite the "old fort *Ghaut*,"
an Indian word signifying *steps*, the public
landing, which rises in a broad flight of
stone steps from the water's edge to the top
of the bank. The deck is instantly swarming with the native Bengalese boatmen who
chatter like a lot of black-birds. A dozen
or more seize my baggage, hurry it into a
boat and in a few minutes I am on the soil
of India. As soon as the boat touches the
jetty a dozen more of these black fellows,
tall and slender, whose long, lank arms and
spindle legs make them look like a flock of
half starved crows, pounce upon my trunks,
carry them up the steps and pile them on a
gharry. It is useless to contend, so I quietly submit, and climb into the carriage for
protection. The magpies surround the
gharry, each clamorous after pay for a service which a single Irish porter could easily
have performed in two minutes. Not one
of these coolies has any other clothing than
a strip of dirty white cotton cloth around
the loins. I had procured from the pur-
ser of the ship a handful of copper coin
which I scatter at random among the
crowd and shout to the driver to go
on. In a quarter of an hour we reach
the "Great Eastern Hotel," where
I am saluted by another crowd
of Coolies seemingly identical with these I

escaped from at the landing. Four of them tug away at a moderate sized trunk, twice as many more cling to the other small parcels, and when I reach the office of the hotel they are after me once more for *bucksheesh*. My copper coin is exhausted and I hand them over to the tender mercies of the clerk who makes short work of them, for he talks Bangalese like a native. He makes one dash at them with hand, foot and tongue and they fly out of the door like a flock of black sheep.

The "Great Eastern" is an immense caravansary, occupying a whole square. The lower floor is used as a Bazaar for the sale of everything to eat, drink, or wear of European or eastern manufacture. The same stock company runs the hotel and the bazaars, and, of course, such a mammoth concern pays no dividend. This hotel, though said to be the largest and best in India, is not comfortable nor first class according to our American standard. The rooms are lofty and spacious, but ill-furnished and dingy. Having secured one of these barn-like apartments, my first movement is to engage a servant, for every guest is expected to have an especial lackey to take care of his room, bring his coffee, wait on him at the table, etc. For this position worth half a rupee (twenty-five cents) a day, there are twenty applicants, and each has his written "karacter" from a former employer. These are in English and some are curious and not entirely complimentary to the bearers. The candidates are dressed in white from head to foot, except the sash round the waist which is of fancy colors. I selected an honest looking fellow whose colors are red, white and blue stripes, only needing the stars to seem girded by an American flag. He repeats his name several times, and at last I catch the sound as "New Varmint." He is immediately installed, addresses me as "Sahib" makes a low salaam, touching his hands to his forehead and bowing almost to the floor. Nothing can exceed the obsequiousness of manners in these native servants, but most of them are great rascals. "New Varmint" never speaks to his master without a salaam so low that long practice alone prevents his losing his balance. But I am warned not to leave valuables lying around loose, and I soon find that in every purchase in any shop, native or European, the "*Varmint*" gets a commission.

Calcutta is just now in the height of the

season, and this is race week, a great attraction to the English at home or abroad. The races are advertised from 7 to 10 o'clock in the morning, before the heat of the sun drives everybody within doors. At this early hour the race ground is covered with stylish carriages containing the wealth and fashion of the metropolis. Europeans and Bengalese, Turks and Arabs, Hindoos and Mohometans, in clarences and broughams, gharries, dog-carts, traps, drags, and every conceivable style of vehicle, drawn by horses, mules and donkeys, crowd the road. The costumes are of every color of the rainbow, and the complexions of every shade, from the jet black with straight glossy hair, whose shiny skins are an excellent foil for their white cotton robes, up through half-caste and every shade of mixture to pure white blood. The gay turbans and rich flowing robes of silk and satin worn by the *Baboos*, or native merchants, give a picturesqueness to the scene peculiar to the East. The track is of solid, firm turf; the horses of Arabian stock, the jockeys dressed in fancy colors, the races run at full speed as at Epsom or Ascot in Old England. But I am more interested in looking at the spectators than in watching the race. I notice that no person on foot, horseback or in carriage, unless of pure European blood, is admitted to the inner circle, or near the grand stand. There is in India a large class of well educated, and often very wealthy people, called *Eurasians*, or English-speaking half castes, who inter-marry with the European, but who seem to be an intermediate race between the Hindoo and the Caucasian. The predjudice of color shuts them out from the best English society, while their own pride and superiority in culture keeps them distinct from the wealthy nations of full Indian blood.

Of the whole resident population of Calcutta, less than ten thousand are Europeans. Many of the English merchants are very wealthy and live in a style of luxury and splendor that impresses the stranger. Their houses are literally palaces, and their hospitality unbounded. The Armenians are a very numerous and influential body of merchants, and the native Hindoos, though formerely timorous, now as bankers, agents and money lenders, venture upon every kind of mercantile speculation, and goods belonging to native merchants, valued at several millions sterling are lying for sale in the warehouses. Calcutta is the great emporium of India. Its staple commodities of export, are indigo, opium, cotton, sugar, rice and silk, and by means of the Ganges, and its extensive connection with the interior, it commands an immense commerce.

Almost two centuries ago, the Emperor of Dalhi granted to the East India Company, a tract of land on the banks of the Hooghly, which is the site now occupied by Calcutta. On it was then a native village, called "Kallcuttah," from *Kali*, a goddess, *Cuttah*, a temple, hence the name of what is now one of the most splendid cities of Asia, and the seat of the supreme government of the British in India. Many years ago, in the time of Warren Hastings, when English power in India was almost extinguished, after a long siege, Calcutta was surrendered to Jrjad Dowlah, the Rajah of Bengal; and one hundred and fifty Englishmen were shut up for a night in an under ground cell. The next morning all were found suffocated in the "Black Hole" of Calcutta. The exact location of this spot, which is so often quoted, is between the Post Office and Court House, both large marble buildings on the strand.

Since the Sepoy rebellion in 1857 that great monopoly, the "East India Company," has ceased to exist. It was an anomaly in history, an *imperium in imperio*, with an army of over two hundred thousand men, levying war and making treaties, and ruling with despotic sway more than a hundred and fifty millions of human beings. The terrible exactions of this powerful corporation culminated in a bloody rebellion, which was trampled out with an iron heel at a cost to England of $200,000,000. During the mutiny the horrible atrocities of the half-civilized natives, goaded on by religious fanaticisms, were not more shocking to the world than the terrible punishment inflicted by Christian Englishmen in blowing Sepoy prisoners from the mouths of their cannon. After the mutiny was suppressed, the English government assumed the sovereignty of this immense territory, extending from the Himalayas two thousand miles to Cape Cormorin, and from the Indian ocean on the west fifteen hundred miles to the Bay of Bengal—as large as all the States east of the Mississippi. The change in the government has resulted in the reform of many abuses, which, in the old times of Lord Clive and Warren Hastings, were the text of burning denunciation in the British Parliament. But the country is still many years behind the age. Neither native nor European residents have any voice in making or administering the laws, or the appointment of their rulers. The members of the government, all being sent out from England, have an exaggerated sense of their importance and dignity. Laws for the government of this vast empire are enacted ten thousand miles away, taxes are imposed and tariffs arranged with little regard to the wants or wishes of the people of India. The salary of the Viceroy, or Governor General, is $125,000 a year, and every evening his carriage appears on the strand drawn by six horses, with postillions in scarlet livery, preceded and followed by red coated lancers. All this is but a part of the system of governing this country, to impress upon the ignorant natives the grandeur and power of their British rulers.

Calcutta boasts many large and imposing public buildings, among which is the Government House, which cost about $700,000, and affords ample accommodation for official business and grand levees for the representatives of royalty. The Mint is an elegant Doric edifice on the bank of the river, and is said to be the largest in the world, having a capacity of striking 300,000 pieces in a working day of seven hours. Besides these, there are numerous museums, libraries, churches and public halls, and scattered through the park and near the Government House are bronze statues of Lord Hardinge, the Earl of Auckland, Lord Bentinck, and several other rulers and benefactors of India.

Every year, as soon as the hot weather sets in, or by the middle of March, the Viceroyal court, with the whole machinery of the government, is packed off by railway to Simla, 1,500 miles north, at the foot of the Himalayas, and here it remains until the close of the rainy season in November. A more inconvenient arrangement, so far as the public business is concerned, can scarcely be imagined; but to the government officials their personal comfort is of more consequence than efficiency or regard for the public interest.

A week in Calcutta exhausted all the novelties, including a ride in a *palanquin*, which is a large sized black coffin borne by two dark skinned mournful-looking Coolies in white robes. It is tilted on one side to crawl in, and you must lie flat on your back and perfectly still. If you turn you are in danger of upsetting the machine and being spilt out. One trial of the Indian '*palky*," as it is called, was enough, and I voted the machine a humbug and not to be compared for comfort with the sedan chair of China.

One evening I found myself in a gharry, with my baggage and *New Varmint* on the top of the vehicle, bound to the station of the East India Railway, *en route* for the up country. On the way to the terminus I stepped into another hotel to say good bye to my Russian friend who had acted as umpire in the *dorian* contest, and while there I heard the boom of the nine o'clock evening gun in the Palace grounds near by, and then a loud shouting in the street followed by a crash. The driver had left his seat to gossip with another native, and the horse frightened at the report of the gun, had dashed away, the vehicle collided with a lamp post and upset, tossing poor N. V. amid a shower of boxes, satchels and bundles into the middle of the street, when he rolled over several times in the white dust. The poor fellow was not hurt, however, but so badly frightened that his complexion with the addition of a thick coat of dust was decidedly more European than Asiatic in color. After some delay I secured another carriage, but train time was so near at hand that I barely escaped being left by the ferry boat which conveys passengers across the Hooghly to the suburb of Howrah where the railway station is located. "New Varmint" stuck to me to the last, and so the train whirled away and I saw him from the window of my compartment bowing and salaaming lower than ever in consideration of the liberal *douceur* which he received in addition to his pay and perquisites.

I had not seen a railway since I left San Francisco four months previous, and the novelty was quite enjoyable. A few years ago the traveller who would penetrate-into the interior of India was obliged to travel in a Dâk Gharry at the rate of forty or fifty miles a day, and my proposed trip of nearly three thousand miles up the valley of the Ganges to Delhi, thence to the Himalayas, and back through Northwestern and Central India to Bombay, would have occupied many months, and involved too much risk and hardship to pay as a pleasure excursion. But to-day there are over six thousand miles of complete railway in India and several thousand more are building.

Since the Sepoy mutiny which came so near being successful, owing to the difficulty of transportation, the government has favored all railway projects for their military value in controlling provinces thousands of miles distant. But a much stronger impulse was given in this direction by our rebellion, in raising the price of cotton and stimulating its culture over a vast extent of territory.

These roads are all built and worked by companies, but the government guarantees a five per cent. dividend to the stockholders, and exercises a general control over the management. It was at first supposed that the natives would not ride in carriages where they would lose caste by touching an inferior; but happily this proved to be a mistake, and the principal income from passenger traffic is derived from the natives, who travel third and fourth class, at from a third to half a cent per mile. The great moral effect of railways upon India in weakening the ties of caste is perhaps of even more importance than the wonderful development of the country, in stimulating the production of the great staples by providing an easy and rapid transportation to the seaboard.

The Indian railways, like everything else English, are well and substantially built. Owing to the scarcity of wood and to the destructiveness of the white ants, iron takes its place almost everywhere. The station houses are all of stone or brick, with corrugated iron roofs; the ties and sleepers, all the bridges, and even the telegraph poles, are of iron. When it is considered that the engines and cars, as well as every p und of iron used in the construction and equipment of these 6,000 miles of road has been brought out from England, it will be understood how immensely expensive these railways have been. In the management everything is English, with only such modifications as are absolutely necessary in this climate. Here as in England the word "car" is unknown—we ride in "carriages" or "wagons," and the gentlemanly "conductor" is transformed into a "guard," who wears the uniform, buttons and badge of the railway. As in Europe the carriages are divided into compartments holding eight persons, with doors opening on both sides to the platform, which are locked by the guard before the train starts. Freight cars are here termed "goods vans"—every employee, from the General Superintendent down to the coolie, is spoken of as a "servant" of the company.

The first and second class are alike, except that one is *cushioned* and the other *caned*. The latter is just half the price, but quite as comfortable in hot weather. The carriages are stronger, larger and loftier than the English model, and are protected from the sun by a double roof, the upper one a few inches above the lower and projecting slightly on either side. Every window, in addition to glasses, has Venetian blinds, and frequently sun-shades beside, and ventilation is especially provided for. But what avail double roof, Venetian blind or sun-shade against the terrible heat of an Indian summer? Then the carriages became like furnaces seven times heated. The very seat is hot to the touch, and you are afraid to lean back lest your coat stick to the varnished panel. If no ladies are present you relapse into the free-and-easy, take off the boots from your swollen feet, denude yourself of coat and vest, hang your soaked collar up to dry, elevate your feet, if possible, to the level of your nose, light a cheroot, and dreamily subside into a patient endurance of the miseries of the situation.

Everywhere else but in the East a servant is considered a luxury to be indulged in only by those who can travel "regardless of expense;" but here it seems an indispensable requisite to comfort. A first-class ticket on railways, steamers and hotels includes the fare of a native servant, and one can enjoy the luxury of being called "Sahib" by his own "boy" at a very trifling draft on his purse.   W. P. F.

BENARES, ON THE GANGES,
FEBRUARY, 1871.

The unit of currency in India is the *rupee*, worth about two shillings or half a dollar. The other denominations of coin are *annas*, sixteen to a rupee, and *pice*, twelve to an anna. Besides these, *cowries*, white, glossy shells, are used for small payments among the natives in the bazaars. The great bulk of the currency is silver rupees with their fractions, all of which is coined in Calcutta. The Indian government also issues currency notes of ten rupees and upward, but these are redeemable only at the the presidency where issued, so that Calcutta notes are at a small discount in Bombay, and *vice versa*. A good supply of small coin is very desirable, and saves one from throwing away *annas* where *pice* would do just as well. The railway company furnishes no porters and the demand for small change soon depletes the deepest purse, for the Coolies flock round you at every station and tease you for *bucksheesh* if they barely touch the smallest piece of luggage, not to mention the poor beggars "whom ye have always with you" in the east. The European residents complain that travelers have spoiled the natives by paying them three or four times too much for trifling services, and it seems natural to an American to give a Coolie half a rupee for carrying his luggage a mile under a boiling sun, while a resident would pay him but a quarter that sum or two annas, and he would *salaam* quite as low and consider himself well paid.

Too much baggage in traveling is proverbially a nuisance—but no one can travel in India without a *rasai* (a stuffed cotton quilt), a pillow and a railway rug. The distances are long, and although even in winter the heat at midday is oppressive, at night it is quite cool. The differerce in temperature between midday and midnight is excessive. Every one here wears a *solar topee*, a hat made of pith half an inch thick, but very light, ventilated around the head, and shaped sometimes like an antique helmet, but more frequently resembling a wooden chopping-bowl. Around it is wound a *puggree* of white cambric, or thin lawn. Though very odd in appearance to a stranger, this is by far the most comfortable headgear for a tropical climate I have ever seen. One is allowed all the luggage free that will go under the seat or can be piled in the rack overhead, but trunks have to be registered and receipted for by a very complicated system and paid for at a high rate of transportation. Baggage checks, as well as Pullman sleeping cars, are unknown anywhere in the world except in America. My first night on the train was anything but comfortable, although the misery of sitting up all night was mitigated by an arrangement peculiar to these India carriages, of raising the cushion behind the seat and strapping it to the roof, thus affording *shelves* for four persons. The first-class carriages are never crowded, and I have frequently rode hundreds of miles with a whole compartment to myself. In this train there are nine fourth-class cars, each of which is crowded with at least forty natives, but not more than twenty Europeans all told.

As I described to an English fellow-trader this morning, the luxury of our drawing-room and sleeping cars he seemed much interested and surprised; but I was somewhat annoyed at a slight raising of the eyebrows, as if he thought I was drawing a long bow.

Our course was to the north-west, up the valley of the Ganges, five hundred and forty mile to Benares, a journey of about twenty-four hours, including stoppages. The country is very level, and thoroughly cultivated. This valley for fifteen hundred miles is the most populous and fertile in India, but every crop depends on irrigation by the numerous canal; and wells with the old fashioned sweeps, or where bullocks are drawing water to be poured by hand upon the fields are everywhere to be seen. Rice, tobacco, castor oil-beans, and poppies are the principal crops. The poppy is cultivated under the immediate supervision of the Government authorities, who take the crop at a fixed price and manufacture it into opium. This monopoly yields a yearly income to the Indian Government of *seven million pounds sterling*. The horizon is fringed with palms, and over there broad prairies the mango trees are scattered like the oaks in an English park. An occasional glimpse of the Ganges calls up no enthusiasm. It is now the dry season and the Sacred River is very low, with broad, sandy banks. The current is as rapid as the Missouri, and the water of the same dingy, yellow color. The railway is fenced with cactus hedges and its showy yellow blossoms form a bright feature in the landscape.

The natives have very little idea of time-tables and departure hours. They walk down to the stations and there sit on the platforms smoking their *hookahs*, waiting patiently for the train to arrive whether it is one hour or ten. But when they hear the train coming they loose all self-control and rush like a flock of sheep crowding and jamming, with an uproar that sounds like a Babel of tongues, towards the pens provided for them, as if for dear life, where they are stowed away like tightly-packed herrings. Here once seated the hubbub subsides, and they whiff at their hubble-bubbles in stolid indifference, and never complain to the guard at being behind time. For the convenience of this class of travelers, from whom the chief income of the company is derived, the stations are very close together, and as the trains stop at every station the rate of speed rarely exceeds twenty miles an hour. Nearly all the railway employees are natives, and the ticket clerks and book-keepers are usually half-castes, who speak English as well as Hindoostanic. They are addressed as *Baboos*, a title of honor, and feel infinitely above their native brethren. They are very civil to Europeans, but the way they kick and cuff the natives is an illustration of the effect of "a little brief authority"—the same all the world over.

During the night the innumerable stopping places with unpronouncable names disturbed many a comfortable "forty winks,"

and when morning came, and I tried to ascertain our whereabouts, it was quite impossible to understand the names of the stations as shouted by the attendant porter,
who yells out in a barbaric manner some
such euphonious name as *Chandaragore*, or
Dildaranuggur, meanwhile clanging his bell
to announce the approach of the train. As
the day grew hot a water-carrier with a
well-filled skin upon his back appeared at
every station and ran alongside the native
cars in answer to the universal shout of
'*ah! ah! Beestie!*" The dust and glare was
almost intolerable, but I had been warned
not to partake of this "cholera mixture," although an occasional ablution taken *al fresco*
at the carriage door, with a towel, soap and
sponge from my traveling bag, was quite a
luxury.

The scene when we stopped for dinner was
unique. The station-master and the sparrows alone were English—everything else
locked Eastern. Black Sepoy soldiers rushed
frantically among the screaming natives
who were crowding into the train, each
hugging a big bundle, sometimes containing
household stuff and sometimes babies—*pal-
kees* and *doolies*—palanquins and sedans, as
we should call them—waited at the back
door of the station—natives were crowded
around the "booking office" for tickets,
where the Baboo in attendance was coolly
smoking his water-pipe—an ibis was drink-
ing at the engine tank; a sacred cow looking
over the cactus hedge; a tame elephant
reaching up with his trunk at the telegraph
wire, on which was perched a bird with
bright plumage, while an Indian vulture
crowned the iron telegraph post. I was so
much amused at watching these strange
sights that I quite forgot my dinner, and
when the starting bell rung I made a rush
to the dining room and seized a couple of
sandwiches, for which I paid a rupee, and,
without stopping for the change, jumped on
board the train, which was already in motion.

In the broad cultivated plain through
which we pass there are no detached houses
to be seen, but we frequently rush past mud
villages which contain quite a colony of
people, and are the most wretched and
filthy imaginable. A moat full of black
looking water surrounds each, which an-
swers the double purpose of keeping off
snakes and wild animals, and of breeding
mosquitoes—especially the latter. The
thatched roofs and mud walls have a tumble

down look, and as there are no chimneys, the smoke escapes through the roof or low doorway, and keeps out the mosquitoes. The ditch is usually spanned by a narrow plank, which seems to be a favorite spot to perform the operation of tooth cleaning, for we rarely pass one of these narrow bridges upon which one or more natives is not perched, industriously scrubbing at his mouth, which I think must be a part of the religion of a Hindoo, for though his black skin may be filthy, and his hair frowsly, I notice that their teeth are universally white and clean.

Passing by one of these villages by midday one cannot appreciate the multitude of inhabitants it shelters. All is still and somnolent—even the trees. The men are away at work in the fields, their better-halves are asleep, and the children are at the schools supported by the government but for which the people have to pay in taxes. But in the early morning, or an hour before dark in the evening, all is clamor and bustle. The children are noisily playing and making mud-pies, the "lasses" are gathering cow-manure, which is stuck against the walls to dry for fuel, the father is washing himself and his linen in the ditch in front of the village, from which the women are filling water jars for culinary purposes. Here the village barber is removing the hair from the poll of a slightly clad gentleman sitting on his haunches in the street, while a Brahmin near by daubs a would-be dandy with a finishing touch of ochre on his forehead and nose. As the "fire carriage" whirls by, a crowd of swarthy, naked little imps line the moat to gaze at the sight, and the head of the family standing up to his waist in the filthy pond, ceases for a moment the cleansing process of daubing himself with mud to look at the train, which, though no longer a novelty, will always remain to him an unfathomable mystery.

Just before dark we reach Mogul-Serai, the junction of a branch road six miles long to Benares, the sacred city of the Hindoos. Here we cross the Ganges by a bridge of boats, and drive two miles through the narrow streets to the English Cantonment, where a one-story Bungalow, called the "Victoria Hotel," the only one here, though not very promising in appearance, affords us a good supper and a comfortable bed.

We took an early start the next morning to "do" the sights of this curious place. Our guide was a high-caste Brahmin, a fine-looking and very intelligent young man who was educated at the Queens' College in that city. He wrote his name in a Sanscrit book which he gave me as "Shiva Dotta, Pundit." He laughed at the superstition of his countrymen and professed to disbelieve in *Brahma* and in his namesake *Shiva*, but I could not make out that in objuring Paganism he had embraced Christianity. Like many Hindoos who have been educated above the religion of their ancestors he was skeptical, and had no religion or theology of any kind to speak of.

This city has been over a century under the rule of the English, but it has changed less than any other large place in India. The most intense bigotry and superstition rules everywhere supreme. The inhabitants are almost exclusively Hindoos who support hundred of temples, while the Mohamedans have but one great Mosque whose stately minarets mark the triumph of the crescent over the object and superstitous Hindoos. As we rode through the suburbs we passed hundreds of women stepping gracefully along, bearing water jugs on their heads, while many others were crowded around the well waiting their turn to dip the bright copper cans holding about a quart, which every Hindoo carries, into the water to fill their jugs. They kept up a continual clatter like so many magpies, shouting and gesticulating in the most excited manner. A true Hindoo when not asleep, is always talking or playing on the tom-tom.

The great sight in Benares is the river front, which is lined with palaces, temples, and ghants for two miles, and where the Hindoo pilgrims come from all over India to wash in the sacred river. A drive of half an hour brought us to the Ganges at the upper end of the city. On the way we stopped to see the famous "Monkey Temple," where swarms of huge, fat-paunched, yellow-headed holy monkeys fill the enclosure, hang from roofs, are strung along every beam, and grin at you from all sides. Before we reached their temple we met the outposts running along the walls keeping alongside our gharry, and jumping down to secure the handfulls of parched peas thrown to them by my guide. Inside the temple and around the large sacred tank adjoining, are many thousands of these fat, well-fed fellows from the venerable patriarch to the "babe in its mother's arms." They are cunning, mischievous and quite

THE GHAUTS, BENARES

i gnorant of the laws of *meum* and *teum,* for
they steal everything they can put their
paws on; but the Hindoo venerates the ape,
and their sacred character protects them
from all molestation. They believe that
these are descendants from the Monkey God
himself who came to India thousands of
years ago. At the call of the priests, to
whom I gave some money to buy food, they
came noisily flocking from every direction,
along roof and parapet, from turret and pinnacle, down pillars, from every corner and
crannie each eager to receive his share,
cramming their pouches with frightened
haste, keeping one eye on us, as if ready for
attack or retreat. Some were large, ugly-
looking customers as if disposed to show
fight. When I shook my cane at them they
scampered away, but stopped at a safe distance to grin and "make faces," mocking
every motion in that comical, semi-human
manner peculiar to the tribe. My "shaking
a stick at them" made the attendant priests
scowl at me, and to strike one would lead to
serious consequences.

Arriving at the river's edge, we embarked
on a boat and floated slowly down the
stream, which is about six hundred yards
wide, keeping just near enough to the shore
to witness one of the strangest sights in the
world. The *Ghants,* or stone steps rise
eighty feet from the water, and are crowned
with splendid palaces of cut stone, four and
five stories in height, with carved saracenic
arches over the door-ways and windows.
Facing the east the early morning sun
gave a splendid architectural effect to this
river front, which Bayard Taylor says,
"cannot be paralleled or surpassed by any
similar scene in India, or in the world."
Many of these buildings are the palaces of
wealthy Hindoo princes who make peri-
odical visits to Benares to purge themselves
from sins contracted in less holy habita-
tions. There is no sin so abominable, not
even the crime of murder, which a dip in
the fetid waters of the Ganges does not instantly efface. At the foot of the Ghants
were thousands of bathers, men, women
and children, ducking and splashing in the
sacred stream. Many were entirely nude,
others were "next to nothing" in the way
of drapery, and as they stood waist-deep in
in the water, going through their prostra-
tions and pouring the filthy stuff over their
heads, they seemed perfectly indifferent to
the gaze of the crowd around. Mingled together and seemingly quite unconscious of

each others' presence, could be seen the sober, sedate matron, the young maiden, the venerable priest with his young disciple, and the nude ascetic with weasened aspect and withered limbs, engaged in rites and ceremonies hallowed to them by the usage of centuries. Thick, black smoke rose to the clear blue sky from bonfires between the Ghants on the bank, where the bodies of the dead are being consumed, after which the ashes would be thrown into the river to float straight to paradise. But the most horrible sights were the dead bodies, some of them partially consumed, which we saw floating around in the river. Along the bank in other places, were lines of prostrate sick people, brought to the sacred Ganges to die, or perhaps to be murdered by suffocation with sacred mud by impatient heirs, which is said to be not an unusual occurrence. No where in the world unless in Central Africa, can be seen such besotted superstition and idolatry coupled with such intolerant fanaticism as in Benares.

We land near a large stone building of tasteful architecture, but somewhat decayed, called the observatory of *Jai-Singh*, founded in 1680. Upon the flat roof are several charts of the heavens on stone, and a mural quadrant for taking the sun's altitude. In old times a posse of astrologers was maintained here to observe and record the motion of the sun, moon and planets.

From here we drove to the *Great Mosque of Aurremzebe* of *Vishnu*, which he demolished, to signalize the triumph of Islam over Brahminism. The foundation is eighty feet above the river, upon which is built the mosque, with high arched dome and two slender minars, each one hundred and forty-seven feet in height. Their diameter at the base is only eight and one-fourth feet, decreasing to seven and one-half feet at the top. Though so tall and slender they have an interior staircase of one hundred and thirty steps. Our ascent was not devoid of risk, for each is said to lean fifteen inches from the perpendicular. But the river from the summit was superb, and well repaid the trouble and fatigue of the climb. At our feet, for miles around, was stretched the crowded city, with its gaudily-painted buildings heaped together in tangled confusion, while the streets were so narrow and crooked as hardly to be distinguished in the mass.

Looking down from this lofty pinnacle I caught sight of a bevy of gaily-dressed

ladies, who were sitting in a little garden
within a high enclosure—the family perhaps of some wealthy native. Although
women of the common class can be seen
anywhere in the street, all ladies of high
rank are kept in the strictest seclusion.
These were richly dressed and seemed quite
pretty; but perhaps it was the "distance
that lent enchantment to the view." While
I was watching them through my opera-
glass they caught sight of me, and looked
up through their hands in imitation of my
glass, with a curiosity greater perhaps than
my own—for I presume they had never before seen the face of a Frank. But suddenly
an old grey-headed fellow (he might be hus
band or father) appeared on the scene,
glanced up at me, and drove the ladies, with
threatening gestures, into the house. I
hope my innocent curiosity was not the
cause of trouble in the family. Descending
from our lofty view-point to the busy hive
below we slowly threaded our way out of
the labyrinth to the wider street, where
our gharry was waiting, stopping at a toy-
shop to buy some curiously painted and varnished toys which are a specialty of Benares manufacture, the peculiarity of which
is that the bright-colored pigment is not re-
movable by use.

Later in the day, under the guidance of
"Shiva Dotta," I went to visit the famous
"Golden Pagoda," dedicated to the god
Shiva. It is situated in the most crowded
part of the city and only accessible on foot.
From the roof rise three irregular spires
and domes, covered with sheet copper gilt,
presenting the appearance in the sun of
glittering masses of burnished gold. The
throng around the temple was so dense that
it was only after a fearful amount of pushing and crowding through an excited throng
of both sexes and all ages that we could
penetrate the vestibule. The "holy of
helies" none were permitted to enter but
the priests and privileged worshippers.
Around us in the doorway was a frantic
crowd shouting, screaming and howling in
their eagerness to gain a sight of the holy
chamber. Not being permitted to advance,
the pushing and crowding behind us of
hese, who seemed frantic with religious
frenzy, nearly took us off our feet. Within
the sacred inclosure before the *lingam,* or
emblem of worship, was a marble basin into
which the priests were throwing yellow
flowers, and those permitted to enter were
pouring from their brass utensils the

holy water they had brought from the Ganges. After dipping the flowers, which
seemed to me like yellow marigolds, into the
fountain the priests threw them through the
doorway to the people, who scrambled after
them most frantically, believing that they
possessed some marvelous charm. A fat,
oily-looking Brahmin waddled to the door
and threw round my neck a string of flowers, at the same time holding out his hand
for *bucksheesh.* The crowd behind scowled
at my good luck, and my guide drew me
away, for no one could tell what the zeal
these deluded fanatics would lead them t
do to an unbeliever. Ten years ago my life
would not have been worth a minute's purchase in such a place. I bestowed my string
of marigolds upon some one who could appreciate their value, and we elbowed our
way into the comparatively fresh air of the
street, having seen enough of Hindoo idol
atry.

On our way back to the "Victoria," we
passed hundreds of shops devoted to the
manufacture of brass and copper idols of
Vishnu, Shiva and Buddha. In other shops
where no manufacturing was going on I
saw large quantities of hideous little idols
made of iron and covered with gilt lacquer,
which my guide assured me were 'made in
Birmingham. Verily, not India alone, but
Christian England also, is somewhat given
up to I-dollar-try.   W. P. F.

Allahabad Junction—The City of Al-
lah—An Invisible River—Paradise for
the Faithful—The Fort—A Puzzle for
Savans—Club for a Giant—The Fu-
ture Capital-Krusra Garden—Tame
Sparrows—-Cawnpore—-The Sepoy
Rebellion—The Memorial Garden—
Lucknow, the City of Palaces—First
Impressions Illusive—The Heart's De-
light—Martiniere- "Secunder Bagh"
—The "Palace of Cæsar"—The Mu-
seum—The Residency—An Impressive
Ruin—"Diana Ye Hear the Slogan!"
—The Grave of Havelock—Barbarity
of the Conquerors—Treatment of the
Natives.

LUCKNOW, INDIA, February, 1871.
I remember seeing upon one of the coupons
of a fanciful ticket, "Round the World,"
issued by the Erie Railway, "Calcutta to
Bombay (1,500 miles) *via Allahabad Junction.*" The latter place sounded to me like
a *myth,* but here I am, and find
the "City of Allah," as the name
signifies, a very substantial reality.
It is situated about one hundred miles above
Banares, at the confluence of the Jumna
and the Ganges. The Hindoos, from time
immemorial, have considered Allahabad one
of the most sacred places in India. Here
they say *three* rivers join. Only *two* of these
are visible—the third, unseen by mortal
eyes, flows direct from Heaven. It is said
that over two hundred thousand pilgrims
visit this spot every year. When a pilgrim
arrives, he sits on the bank of the river,
and has his head and body shaved so that
his hair may fall into the water; for his
sacred writings promise him for every hair
thus deposited a thousand years of Paradise.

At the junction of the two rivers is a
very strong fort, built three hundred years
ago by Akbar, one of the Mogul Emperors,
when the Mohamedan power in India was
in its glory. The walls are of red sandstone, and 2,500 ~~miles~~ in circuit, and present
a very imposing appearance. It is thoroughly armed and garrisoned, and one of the
strongest places held by the British in this
country. An English officer very politely

showed me through the fortress, and pointed out the vaults where all the Europeans of the station took refuge during the mutiny of 1857, where many fell victims to cholera brought on by pestilence and suffering. Under the fort is a curious subterranean passage which the natives believe runs all the way to Benares. I penetrated about two hundred feet to a spot where a sacred tamarind tree is shown, which the Hindoos say grew in this very place. The water trickling from the roof and the bad air made it impossible for me to proceed further. The fort contains an immense quantity of cannon and munitions of war, and large repair shops where several hundred men were at work. Within the walls was once the favorite residence of Shah-Jehan, but all that remains of his beautiful palace is the "Hall of Akbar," a magnificent room, two hundred and seventy-two feet long, now used as an armory. Here are arranged with great taste along the walls, and through the center of the hall, over 50,000 stand of arms.

In the center of the fort stands an ancient monolith, forty-two feet in height by about three in diameter, and slightly tapering at the top. On it are two long Sanscrit inscriptions, obviously of remote antiquity, which have puzzled the most learned antiquarians. The popular belief is that it is the *Club of Bhim Sen*, a hero who figures in the romantic legends of Hindostan.

Allahabad has a population of about one hundred thousand natives, besides many civil and military officials, being the capital of the Northwestern Provinces, and the junction of the two great lines of railway connecting Bombay and Calcutta. It is increasing rapidly in business and importance, and from its central location, healthy climate and important strategic position it is predicted that it will some day become the capital of British India. The new town is laid out with wide, handsome roads, lined with well-built bungalows, and when the trees are fully grown, which are planted along the avenues and so essential in this hot climate, it will become a very attractive place of residence.

After the fort the most interesting sight is the Krusru Garden, which adjoins the railway station. This garden, or pleasure ground, is surrounded by a high embattled wall, and is five hundred feet square. Inside it is tastefully arranged and cultivated, and contains some very fine old Mango trees of immense size. In the centre are three large stone mausoleums, surmounted by marble domes, from the roof of which is a splendid view of the city and surrounding country.

The dining room at the Allahabad Hotel is very lofty and opens with large doors to the surrounding gardens. At breakfast this morning I heard the twittering of sparrows, and was surprised to see them flying all about the room, so tame as to pick crumbs from the hands of the guests at the table. Everywhere in India I have remarked the abundance and tameness of the birds. It is part of the religion of a Hindoo never to kill a living being when avoidable. This is carried almost too far, when applied to wild beasts and noxious vermin, but it softens their treatment of animals, and is one ennobling feature in their system of idolatry and superstition, which might well be imitated by Christians.

Another hundred miles to the north and we reach Cawnpore, ever memorable as the scene of the most barbarous act of the mutiny of 1857. It is situated on the right bank of the Ganges, and was once a place of considerable importance and busy traffic. It is now a large military station, with long ranges of barracks and store-houses, and usually several regiments of troops are stationed here. I presume the sad story of the massacre of nearly three hundred women and children, and the casting of their bodies into a well, by order of the infamous Nana Sahib, is familiar to most of my readers.

The sudden breaking out of the mutiny and revolt of the Sepoy soldiers in May, 1857, found the government quite unprepared for such an emergency. At that time there were no railways or telegraphs in India, and these distant stations were completely isolated. The rebellion broke out simultaneously at several points and spread like wild-fire; and in a few weeks the whole northwestern provinces were in the possession of the rebels. The East India Company had an army of about two hundred thousand men, of whom only thirty thousand were English, and these were scattered in small detachments over an immense territory. The native troops were officered by Europeans, most of whom were instantly dispatched by the mutineers, and their places supplied by natives, who displayed considerable military ability during the struggle that followed. They fought with ropes

round their necks, and little quarter was
given on either side. The Sepoys were
well drilled and disciplined soldiers, and
amply provided with cannon, arms and munitions of war.

Only a portion of the native troops revolted, and in several provinces the judicious management and prompt action of the
civil and military authorities kept them
faithful to the English, with whom
they united in putting down the
rebels. Had the disaffection been general,
and any unity of action existed among the
rebels, every vestige of British rule would
have been swept from India.

The immediate pretext of the mutiny
was the use of cartridges greased with lard,
which the Sepoys were compelled to bite
off. To touch "the unclean animal" was to
them a defilement against which their religion revolted. Fortunately, though both
Musselmen and Hindoos united in hating
their foreign rulers, they bore no affection
for each other. The former numbered but
one in twelve of the native population, and
are high-spirited and brave. Their ancestors had overrun India and ruled the country for five hundred years before the English acquired possession. The Kings of
Delhi and Oude, with many less powerful
Rajahs, still retained their titles, but were
only nominal or titular princes, keeping up
the semblance of royalty, but in fact stipen-
diaries, supported by the allowances made
to them by their English masters. Jealousy between Mohamedans and Hindoos
created a division in their counsels, and
made the suppression of the rebellion comparatively easy.

But it was a narrow escape, and the English learned a lesson, costing them dearly
in blood and treasure, which resulted in a
more humane and less oppressive system of
government, under which the country is
now more prosperous than ever before.

The rebellion broke out in the spring,
and during the awfully hot summer that followed it was very difficult for the English
soldiers, sent out to India from home, to relieve the few isolated forts that held out
against the insurgents, in which were
crowded all the English residents with
their wives and children. The whole country from Delhi to Calcutta, more than
twelve hundred miles in extent, was in the
hands of the rebels; and in Delhi, the ancient capital, a descendant of the Moguls
was proclaimed Emperor of India. Here in

Cawnpore a large army of Sepoys, commanded by Nana Sahib, besieged the handful of British troops and half caste residents, and forced them at last to surrender, with the promise of being permitted to embark on the river. But before they could leave the shore fire was opened upon them, and only two escaped alive. In another part of the town, where several hundred invalid soldiers and women and children were collected, all were slaughtered, and their bodies, yet warm, thrown into an old well.

My first visit in Cawnpore was to this spot, where now on a raised mound is a beautiful memorial, erected over the well. It consists of a high stone platform, on which stands a marble statue of a female with wings, designed by Baron Marochetti. This is surrounded by a stone gothic screen of beautiful design and workmanship. Near by are the tombs of those who fell at Cawnpore during the mutiny. There are many nameless, grass-grown mounds, among which are shrubs and flowers. The keeper of the place pointed out some patches of ground where the grass but feebly sprouted, and which resembled the "fairy rings" one sometimes sees in country places, and said, "These are the places where the little children are buried, the grass won't grow here if I water it ever so much. It seems to me as if the curse of God is on the spot, and on the men who committed the horrible deed." A large tract of ground neatly laid out and beautifully kept, called the *Memorial Garden*, surrounds the spot, and no native is allowed under any consideration to enter the enclosure.

From Cawnpore there is a branch road, forty-two miles to Lucknow, the capital of Oude, which contains a population of over 300,000 people. It is a purely oriental city of great extent and very picturesque appearance. More properly than any other place in India it is entitled to the name of the "City of Palaces.

Approaching the city from the railway station, a mile distant, the picture was like a dream of fairy land. Majestic buildings, apparently of white marble, crowned with domes of burnished gold, scores of pinnacles and minarets, many of them very high and graceful, spacious grounds filled with choice shrubbery and flowers, made the first impression very gratifying. But a nearer view destroyed much of the illusion. What at a distance seemed the purest marble turned to whitewashed brick and plaster, and burnished gold became very dingy gilt.

During the two days spent there I visited many very interesting places, of which I have space for only a slight sketch. With an intelligent native who spoke good English for a guide, I drove first to the Dilkooshah Palace, or "Heart's Delight," an imposing, square edifice, with flanking towers and a gilt dome. It was built by *Sadut-Ah-Khan,* and was a favorite country residence of the ladies of his harem. The entrance is a noble portico, as high as the building, to which leads a grand flight of steps. This place was the headquarters of Sir Colin Campbell's force at the final attack and capture of Lucknow, during the mutiny.

Not far from the Dilkooshah is a whimsical pile of buildings of every species of architecture, called the "Martiniere." or "Constantia." The front is adorned with extravagant figures of animals and gods, enormous lions with gaping mouths, and lamps in place of eyes, goddesses with shaking heads, and fantastic figures of heathen mythology. This building was erected about seventy years ago by an eccentric French adventurer named Claude Martine, who came out to India as private soldier, amassed immense wealth, and died a Major General in the service of one of the native princes. He left five hundred thousand pounds sterling to endow schools in Lucknow, Calcutta and Lyons. In this building one hundred and eighty boys are provided with a good education free of expense. The interior contains some handsome apartments, with richly ornamented ceilings, which when new must have been strikingly beautiful, but now they are dingy and defaced.

From "Constantia" we drove to "Secunder Bagh," a garden one hundred and twenty yards square, surrounded by a high brick wall with a gateway. It was laid out by one of the old kings of Oude for his favorite wife, and is now interesting as the place where 2,000 Sepoys took refuge during the siege. A break was made in the wall, and it was carried by storm, and the rebels slaughtered to a man.

Our next visit was to the "Kaiser Bagh," or "Palace of *Caesar,*" the title adopted by the Kings of Oude. This immense pile of buildings is of marble and decorated in the most extravagant manner. It was built by the last King and finished in 1850. The cost is said to have been eighty lacs of rupees, or forty million dollars. Its shape is that of a series of quadrangles, approached through massive gateways of marble, adorned with royal emblems. The courts and gardens, fountains and pavillions must have presented in the days of its founder, a truly brilliant spectacle, surrounded by all gaudy and striking appurtenances of an eastern court, which knew no bounds to its extravagance.

Two other splendid palaces stand upon the banks of the river, one of which is called the "Chutter Munzil," from the *gilt umbrellas* with which the domes are crowned. This sheltered the ladies of the harem, and is now used as a club-house and a public library. In the other is a very interesting museum of natural history with one of the most complete collections of Indian animals, birds and reptiles in the world. On one side of the room I noticed a series of the skeletons of monkeys, evidently arranged by a believer in the Darwinian theory. Commencing at the lowest grade, there was a gradual rise through the different species (the *tails* becoming less prominent) up to the ourang-outang and gorilla, and the series was crowned by the skeleton of a man.

Lucknow has the credit of being the original source from whence the rebellion of 1857 sprang, and has become memorable as the scene of one of the most remarkable sieges on record. Here in a building called the *Residency*, for five long months, during the heat of summer, a little band of noble hearts held out with unexampled courage and endurance against a horde of well-armed and ferocious enemies. Within the enclosure were several large buildings used as public offices, and surrounded by a low wall. Close outside the Residency were other buildings occupied by the rebels, and it was wholly unfit for defense against an enemy provided with an abundance of cannon and skilled in the use of arms. The ruins have been allowed to remain as far as possible in the same state in which they were left after "the relief." The buildings were terribly shattered with shot and shell, and every spot has a sad story connected with the siege. In this room a plate on the wall shows where the gallant Sir Henry Lawrence was mortally wounded by the bursting of a shell. We descend here into the cellars, where the women and children and the sick were driven for refuge from the hail of shot, and where so many died. The roofless buildings stand in solemn ruin, a monument alike of the bravery and devo-

tion of that handful of heroic men who held
it so long against overwhelming numbers,
and of the self-denying heroism of the
women and children, who perished uncomplainingly in its cellars. In the church
yard adjoining which is kept in perfect
order and beautifully decorated with flowers,
are buried those who perished during the
siege.

The armies under Generals Campbell and
Havelock were twice repulsed in trying to
penetrate to their relief, and the garrison
were ready to despair, when the fainting
girl raised her head and cried, "Dinna ye
hear the slogan?" Her quick ear had caught
the sound of the bag-pipes, and the familiar
air of her native Highlands, "The Camp-
bells are coming."

Upon the tomb of Sir Henry Lawrence is
the simple inscription, "*Here lies Sir Henry
Lawrence, who tried to do his duty.*" About
two miles from Lucknow on the Cawnpore
road is the *Alumbagh*, formerly a garden
palace of the King of Oude. In the center of
this garden rest the remains of Sir Henry
Havelock, "the Christian soldier." A plain
stone obelisk marks his grave.

The atrocities of the mutineers at Cawnpore and Lucknow aroused the worst pas-
sions of the British soldiers. These were
the deeds of a race of half-civilized pagans.
By what name can we call the horrible cru-
elties by which these deeds were avenged?
For every English victim a score of natives
suffered death. The horrors of blowing
prisoners from the mouth of cannon have
never been half told. When all civilized
nations were shocked at the barbarity of
these proceedings the perpetrators became
cautious about mentioning the subject to
strangers.

On the railway between Cawnpore and
Lucknow I met a "guard," who was an officer in the army during the mutiny, and
from whom, by judicious questioning, I
drew some particulars on this subject. He
related among other things the method of
execution. It was a string of helpless men
tied in front of a cannon, a few pounds of
powder, and that was all. "A very simple
method, you see," said he. "Did they submit quietly?" I asked. "Oh, yes, they are
all fatalists in their religion, and sometimes
didn't need to be tied; but I remember one
keen-eyed fellow, who cursed me as I was
tying him up, and said he would come back
as a crow and pick out my eyes." "How
many do you think were executed here and

KAISER BAGH OR KING'S PALACE, LUCKNOW

at Delhi?" "Oh, many thousands. We made short work of them. Sir, I caught a dozen or more Sikhs one night trying to escape from the camp with stolen cartridges in their knapsacks. We blew them to pieces the next morning." These stories of deliberate barbarity were related, as he supposed, to a sympathizing auditor, with perfect *sang froid*. These atrocities were not confined to rebels taken with arms in their hands, for very few prisoners were taken; but whole villages were arrested on suspicion of "aiding and abetting," and thousands executed with a mere form of trial.

I heard often in India of the splendid "loot" at the capture of Delhi; and in marching through the country the soldiers could hardly set eyes on a native prince or a Hindoo palace without exclaiming, "What a place to *break up!*" "What a fellow to *loot!*" It is plain that the Danish-Anglo-Saxon still has the taint of the old sea-king robbers in his blood.

It was a maxim of the Portuguese Jesuits that men who live long among Asiatics seldom fail to learn their vices, and this is often illustrated here; but the older residents treat the natives with much more kindness than new-comers, especially soldiers. The pompous young sprigs of officers who have just "come out" are the most harsh and cruel masters. In some hotels I noticed the significant notice, "Gentlemen are requested not to strike the servants." No comment is necessary.   W. P. F.

Approach to Agra—Cotton Boats—The
Sights of Agra—The Fort—Hall of
Judgment—The Sandal Wood Gates
— he Emperor's Palace—A Mam-
moth Pachisi-Board—The Pearl
Mosque—Secundra Bagh—A Fancy
Team—Akbar's Mausoleum—The Tej
—A Thing of Beauty, and a Wonder-
ful Echo—The Taj Seen by Blue-
Lights—A Persian Description—Delhi
—A Great Scoundrel—Visit to the
Citadel—The Hall of Audience—The
Peacock Throne—Chandnee Chowk—
The Great Mosque—A Field of Anima-
ted Poppies—Relics of Mahomet—"By
the Prophet's Beard"—The Cashmere
Gate—A Gallant Deed.

Returning to Cawnpore on the main line,
I took an early morning train, and in seven
hours reached Toendis Junction, from
whence a branch road runs twelve miles to
Agra, the once famed city of the Emperor
Akbar. What wondrous changes have occurred since the days when the Mussulman
dynasty held sway over these rich and fertile countries, where now speeds the all-
civilizing locomotive, then swept by the de-
vasting hordes of Timour the Tarter; and
the battalions of "Akbar the magnificent"
in all the pomp and splendor of unbounded
eastern wealth, delighted the eye, as struck
terror to the heart of the worshipping
thousands who flock to the city to greet the
mighty Emperor.

Agra, or Akbarabad as it was formerly
called, stands on the left bank of the Jumna, and in the days of its splendor the
whole space from the river's bank to the
Fort, is said to have been covered with palaces, of which nothing now remains but the
ruins. Engaging a gharry at the station
after much chaffering with the native driver, for I have found that in India as well
as elsewhere in the world, to save trouble one
must always make a bargain before-hand
with a Jehu, and never agree to pay above
half the price asked, and rescuing my traps
from a dozen coolies, all of whom demanded
bucksheesh. I took refuge in the vehicle
from a crowd of beggars, halt, blind and
maimed, and drove across the rickety float-

ing bridge to Beaumont's Hotel, within the "civil lines" where the English officials reside.

Alongside the bridge I noticed two elephants fording the river and spirting the water about with their trunks in great glee, to the infinite disgust, it seemed, of their black drivers, who, seated just back of their necks, prodded them on with their iron-tipped poles.

Along the banks of the rapid stream I counted over thirty flatboats laden with cotton, their bows fastened to the bank, as one sees them in Memphis or Nashville. Their freight, brought down from the up country, is here transferred to the railway for Calcutta or Bombay.

The three principal objects of interest in Agra are the Fort, Akbar's Tomb and the Taj, the last named built by Shah-Jehan, about two hundred years ago, as the Mausoleum of his favorite wife Noor Jehan, or the "light of the world," who is said to have been of surpassing beauty. (Here let me say that in Hindoostanee words the letter a always has the broad sound, as if followed by r.) Besides these, at Fettehpore, twenty-four miles distant, are the magnificent ruins of a favorite residence of the Emperor Akbar, which he deserted at the instigation of a Mussulman ascetic, who passed for a *saint*, and who complained that his devotions were interfered with by the bustle of a city and the gaieties of the court. Akbar therefore built the city of Agra upon what was then an unpeopled waste. The court and towns-people removed thither, and Fettehpore, with a massive palace, its noble residences and its deserted streets, remains to this day a monument of the splendor and wealth of its founder, and a testimony to the despotic power which a reputation for *sanctity* has in all ages conferred. As a journey to this place could only be made in a Dak Gharry, and would occupy two days time, I left it out of my programme.

My first visit was to the Fort, the walls of which built of huge blocks of red sandstone, are sixty feet in height, with macchiolated battlements, and a mile and a half in length. It was considered of enormous strength when it was built, three hundred years ago, and the arrangement of its traverses, covered passages and inner bastions, every approach being commanded by guns, shows that the engineers of those days were well skilled in the art of fortification. It contains the Arsenal, Akbar's palace, and the celebrated Motee Musjeed, or "Pearl Mosque." Passing through a noble court-yard, five hundred feet by three hundred and seventy, we entered a splendid hall, now used as an armory, which was once the *dewan*, or judgment hall of Emperor Akbar. In a recess near the center is the throne of white marble, inlaid with mosaics. The lofty roof is supported by three rows of pillars connected by saracenic arches of great beauty. At the upper end of the hall are the celebrated gates of Somnath, cap-tured by Lord Ellenborough in the Aff-ghan campaign. They are twelve feet high, very massive, and composed entirely of sandal-wood, elaborately carved and inlaid.

Beyond the Arsenal, overhanging the Jumna is the Emperor's palace, still in tol-erable preservation. In the galleries, the balconies and the corridors is a perfect forest of carving and ornamentation—all of the finest white marble, which in the hands of the artists of those days seemed as tract-able as wood. Perhaps the greatest curi-osity of the palace is the *Shish-Mehal*, or "Hall of Glass." It was intended for a bath, and the walls and ceilings are covered with thousands of small mirrors, arranged in the most intricate designs. In the center was a marble basin into which mimic cascades poured from the walls. When lighted with colored lamps behind these tiny waterfalls, the fairy-like chamber must have realized all the fable splendors of Arabian story

In a tesselated courtyard of white and black marble, the Emperor's favorite game of *Pachisi* used to be played. Each square of this titanic board is large enough for a person to stand upon, and sixteen little girls, each four of whom were dressed in distinctive colors, ran from square to square, in accordance with the throw of the *cow-ries* or dice.

I was shown the curious under ground passage, near what was once the *Zenana* or women's apartments, where the ladies of the harem played hide and seek before the Emperor, clad only in the garb of Eve. At the end of the passage is an old and very deep well, in which the unfaithful ones were put when sentenced to death.

The remaining object of interest in the Fort, is the *Pearl Mosque*, of small dimen-sions, but absolutely perfect in style and proportions. It is an exquisitly beautiful building, surmounted by three domes of white marble, which in distant views of the Fort are seen like silver bubbles, rest-

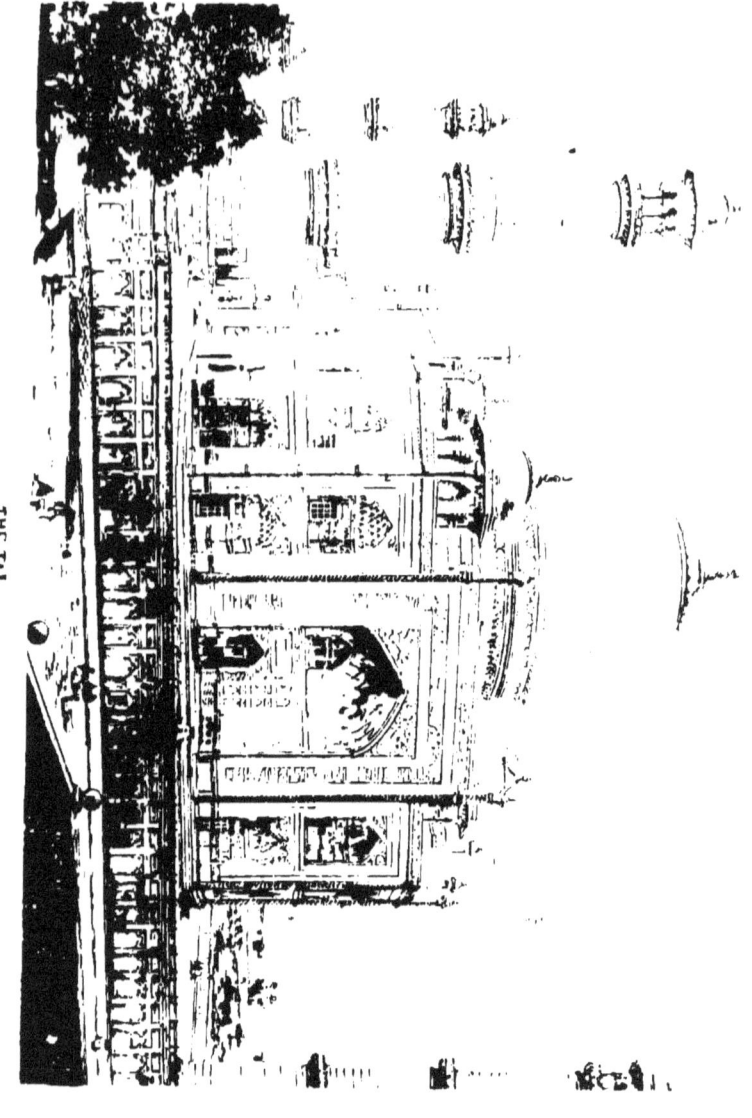

THE TAJ

ing for a moment on its walls, which the next breeze may sweep away.

Leaving the Taj for the last, I drove from the Fort eight miles down the river to *Secundra Bagh,* the Mausoleum of the great Emperor, over a road said to have once been lined with palaces, the ruins of which can be seen on either side. On the way we overtook an English built open barouche, drawn by a pair of milk-white oxen, whose harness was decorated with gold and silver ornaments. In the carriage were two wealthy nabobs, richly dressed and wearing large turbans of alternate white and red silk. My ambitious *Gharrwan,* who ought to have known better, essayed to pass this elegant establishment, but soon found his mistake, for the "cattle" when touched with the whip, were off at a pace that left our sorry steed far in the rear.

The tomb of Akbar stands in a spacious garden, entered by four gateways, seventy feet high, leading to a stone platform, four hundred feet square, on which is a splendid building of sandstone, with the two upper stories of marble. In a vaulted hall in the centre of this structure, which is five stories high and three hundred feet on each side, is a small plain sarcophagus, on which is sculptured a wreath of flowers. Beneath it is the dust of Akbar, the fourth descendant from *Tamanlane,* and one of the greatest men who ever wielded a scepter. On the top of the building under a gilded dome, and surrounded by screens of marble, wrought into patterns of marvellous richness and variety, stands another sarcophagus on which are sculptured in raised Arabic characters the ninety-nine attributes of Allah. This splendid tomb perpetuates no less the affection of the builder, *Jehangeen,* the son of the Emperor, than the greatness of him in honor of whose memory it was erected.

Returning rapidly to the city we drove to the Taj, which is esteemed the most beautiful building in the world. It is situated in a noble quadrangle, enclosed by lofty sandstone walls, and approached by a gateway, itself a splendid structure, with twenty-six white marble cupolas. The grounds are beautifully laid out with stately trees, shrubs and flower beds, and 'kept in perfect order at the expense of the government. The first view of the Taj is obtained as you pass the gateway at the end of a long avenue of tall cypress trees. Upon a platform of sandstone is raised a terrace of white marble three hundred and thirteen feet square, upon which is the beautiful pile itself. Its shape is an irregular octagon, the sides facing the four cardinal points, in which are the entrances, being about one hundred and thirty feet long. From the centre of the roof springs a marble dome, expanding grandly and rising to a height of eighty feet, tipped on its summit with a gilt crescent-pointed spire, two hundred and ninety-six feet from the basement. At each of the four corners of the platform is a minaret one hundred and thirty-three feet high, of exquisite proportions, and the smallest possible circumference in proportion to its height. On either side of the Taj is a red sandstone building, with lofty domes and handsome portals, erected, it is supposed, to enhance by contrast the beauty of the main building itself, and showing a more than regal disregard of cost in order to secure the greatest possible effect.

In the centre, immediately beneath the dome, are two sarcophagi, side by side, of Shah Jehan and his wife, the actual tomb being in the marble basement underneath. They are of the purest white marble, such as is said to be now unobtainable, and inlaid with flowers in a mosaic work of precious stones, each flower being a work of art in itself. The cornelian, agate, blood-stone and lapis-lazuli mostly prevail, wrought into a most perfect resemblance in color, shape and size of the lotus, the iris, and the tulip. An octagonal screen of trellis-work in marble, wrought in open tracery of most intricate design, surrounds the tombs. Upon the cornice, the arches of the doors and windows, and along the entrance passages, are inlaid in black marble, verses from the Koran; the whole book, it is said, being thus reproduced upon the walls of the building.

Under the dome is an echo so sweet, pure and prolonged, that it seems almost marvelous. A single musical note uttered by the voice, floats and soars overhead in a long, delicious undulation, fading away so slowly and imperceptibly that you seem to hear it after it is silent. I listened entranced and amazed at its wonderful effect, the strains sweetly prolonging themselves around the high-arched dome, like the harmonies of angels in paradise.

Descending a sloping marble passage from the outside near the main entrance, and surrounded by a crowd of chattering native guides with candles, we now inspected the actual tomb of Shah Jehan and his beautiful queen. The cenotaph are marble, profusely inlaid with precious stones, and inscribed with Persian characters. This chamber has no light but that reflected through the entrance, which falls directly on the marble tombs, greatly increasing the solemnity of the effect.

Not satisfied with having seen the Taj by the light of the sun, we resolved to view it again by night, illuminated by blue-lights; and it would have been a loss to have missed this aspect of the wonderful building. The many hangers-on who call themselves "guardians," will arrange the exhibition for a few rupees. Standing midway down the long garden walk we witnessed the brilliant illumination from minarets and terraces, the exquisite outline of the building thrown into striking relief on the dark sky, rendering the scene almost fairy-like, as in an instant, when the lights were extinguished the building vanished from sight.

Bishop Heber has said, "The Pathans designed like Titans and finished like jewelers." Great as are the dimensions of the Taj it is as laboriously finished as a Chinese casket carved in ivory. It cost fifteen million dollars and was twenty years in building. An old Persian manuscript gives a minute description of the Taj, in exaggerated Eastern phraseology, giving the quantity of the different marbles used, the names and cost of the various precious stones, many of which were received as tributes from different nations under the Emperor's rule; and in referring to its origin, says: "*Love was its author; Beauty its inspiration.*"

Next to their Mosques, the Mussulmen conquerors of India seem to have delighted in lavishing wealth upon their tombs. It is said that the Tombs of the Turks and Moguls form a complete and unbroken series of architectural monuments from the first year of the Moslem invasion to the present hour. In no country of the world do we find such wondrously beautiful sepulchers, in such a perfect state of preservation. They were built to last for all time, and the designs show us how much we have yet to learn before we can hope to rival the magnificence and exquisite beauty found in the Tombs and Palaces of the Mahometan era.

Leaving Agra with regret, and looking often back at the beautiful dome of the Taj, which can be seen for miles away, in five hours we reached Delhi, the famed capital of the Moslem Kings, which is situated on the left bank of the Jumna, one thousand

and nineteen miles from Calcutta. This place, made famous by the poets of Hindostan, whence in the days of its splendor issued the devastating armies of the Moguls. contains on its site the ruins of ten cities of the same name, having been captured, sacked, destroyed and rebuilt no less than eleven times, not always upon the same exact spot, but extending over an area of about forty square miles. This change of location was caused sometimes by the total destruction of the old towns, sometimes by a change in the bed of the river, and sometimes from the ambition of an Emperor who wished to build a more splendid residence. For wherever the King built his fortified palace, the nobles flocked around, and the people soon followed for the protection of the King's soldiers against the robber tribes.

Modern Delhi was built about two hundred years ago by the Emperor Shah-Jehan, and is enclosed by a turreted wall five and a half miles in circuit, and is approached through twelve strongly fortified entrances, the principal of which are known as the Cashmere, Delhi, Lahore and Calcutta gates.

We arrived in Delhi late in the evening, and had the choice of the only two places where strangers can be accommodated, the Dak Bungalow (or government caravanserai,) and the "United Service Hotel." We chose the latter, which was under the management of a native Bengalese, whose name approximated in sound, "Barrabbas." He proved to be a "thief and a robber," and his name was appropriate, for a more unmitigated scamp I did not meet in India. Smooth as oil in speech, cringing and fawning in manner, he watched over us as birds for his especial plucking, keeping everybody away except those who would pay the highest commission on our purchases, and coaxing silver rupees out of us which he pretended to pay as *bucksheesh* at the several places we visited, but coolly pocketed, giving only copper pice; and at last presenting a bill that was perfectly stunning. In fine, "we were strangers and he took us in."

Our first visit on the morning after our arrival was to the citadel, within which was the palace of the Emperor. It is enclosed on three sides by a high wall of red granite, the fourth side, which faces the river, being the wall of the city. The Palace and Hall of Audience, though now shorn of their grandeur and partly in ruins, attest the lav-

THE JUMNA MUSJID, FROM THE NORTH

ish decoration and beauty which once made
it the wonder and admiration of every beholder. The ceiling of this hall was once
composed entirely of gold and silver filagree
work, and the walls richly ornamented
with gold araberque. The roof vested of
massive square marble arches, around the
cornice of which is the inscription, quoted
by Moore in "Lalla Rookh:"
"If there be a Paradise on earth it is this, it is this "
In the center of this room stood the fa-
mous "Peacock Throne," so called from its
back being formed by jeweled representa-
tions of peacocks' tails. It was composed of
gold, studded with diamonds and precious
stones, and its value was estimated by Tave-
nier, a Frenchman, who saw it, at six millions of pounds sterling. A suite of apartments which formed the Seraglio and royal
baths, overlooking the river, were partially
restored and regilded last year on the occasion of the visit of the Duke of Edinburgh.
In each of these rooms is a fountain, and the
floor, walls and ceiling are of white marble, with inlaid borders of araberque designs. A large portion of the palace has
been cleared away since the mutiny to make
room for a splendid range of barracks which
have been built for the European troops.

Leaving the Fort, we drove through
Chaudnee Chowk, the principal street, one
hundred and twenty feet wide, a mile in
length, and adorned with an avenue of trees
Here are the best shops and several buildings handsomely decorated. In front of
their shops stand the richly-dressed, tur-
baned owners, who beseech you, in Parsee-
English, to come in and inspect their wares.
In the cool of the evening you will see the
native merchant in the narrow, projecting
balcony enjoying his *otium* with a *hubble-
bubble*, clad in a most invitingly cool disha-
bille of white muslin.

A canal of pure, clean water, brought
from the hills twenty miles distant, flows
through the centre of the city, adding much
to the health and comfort of the inhabitants·

We next visited the *Jumna Musjid*, the
largest and finest of all the Mahometan
temples in India. It is built on a small
rocky eminence, and is approached on three
sides by noble gateways, to which lead broad
flights of steps. In the center of the open
court is a large fountain, around which a
space, three hundred and twenty-five feet
square, is paved with blocks of white marble
three feet long and one and a half broad,
each being surrounded by a black border.

At the regular time of morning or evening devotion one can see four or five thousand worshippers in this vast open court, each kneeling upon one of these marble squares. Their flowing white robes and parti-colored turbans, as they bow with perfect uniformity towards the *Kibla*, or that part of the building which indicates the direction of Mecca, have a most picturesque effect, like a field of immense poppies swept over by the wind.

From the corners of the Mosque rise two graceful minarets one hundred and twenty feet high, inlaid throughout their whole height with flutings of white marble, and surmounted with the usual white marble cupolas. The view from the summit is magnificent. The vast city becomes an ant heap at your feet, and you instinctively peer out into space, and try to discern the sea in the direction of Calcutta or Bombay.

As we descended an aged and remarkable looking priest led us to one corner of the mosque, where he unlocked a strong door and took from a chest a manuscript volume carefully wrapped in folds of silk. It was an illuminated copy of the Koran, said to be seven hundred years old. It is in Arabic and the color of the ink, even now, a brilliant jet. He handled the sacred relic with all possible reverence, and was unwilling that our vile hands should touch it. He next displayed to our admiring gaze a lock of hair from the Prophet's *beard*, (being the *beard* sort, I suppose, by which the Mussulmen swear,) and a stone upon which was the print of his foot. This last relic capped the climax and we laughed outright, which so disgusted the old fellow, that he slammed down the lid of the chest, and seemed inclined to turn us scoffing unbelievers out of the room. But the sight of two silver rupees had a magical effect to smooth his scowling brow, and he *salammed* us to the door with great deference.

Near our hotel was the famous Cashmere Gate, where the British troops entered at the capture of Delhi in 1857. The *breach* then made yet remains, and is a memorial of the gallantry of the two soldiers, who carried the bags of powder along the ditch, piled them against the gate and lighted the fuse, with not one chance in a hundred of escaping the bullets of the besieged. One of the brave fellows was killed, but the other escaped unhurt.

W. P. F.

Indian Conjurors—Making a Mango
Tree Grow from the Seed—Hereditary
Occupations in India—Snake Charm-
ers—Bit by a Cobra—Shopping in
Delhi—Shawl Store of Manick Chund
—Indian Costumes —Observatory—
Mausoleums—The Koontub Minar—
Legend of the Iron Pillar—Huma-
yoon's Tomb—The Last of the Moguls
—A Sam Patch Leap—Memorial of a
Wicked Old King—One of the Results
of Polygamy—"Laying a Dak"—The
Horse Dak of India—Unique Style of
Traveling—Tame Squirrels and Birds
—The Mohun Pass—"Sudden Death"
for Chickens—Drawn by Coolies—
"Wiling the Hours by Cheerful Dis-
course" of Man-Eating Tigers—Arrive
at Deyra.

Delhi is famous for the skill of her conjurors and snake charmers; and Barrabbas
arranged for an exhibition to come off after
our late dinner. There were yet three hours
of daylight and we ranged ourselves in a
semi circle on the porch of the hotel—a
small and select audience of five persons—
with an indefinite number of natives in the
background. The chief performer, a thin,
wiry native, with keen and restless black
eyes, squatted on the stone pavement in
front, flanked on either side by his wife and
sister. Their entire apparatus consisted of
a few bowls, pipes, boxes and wicker
baskets, most rude in construction and not
suggestive of any marvelous mechanism.
And yet our conjurers went through with a
most astonishing series of tricks, some of
which would baffle even Hermann, the pres-
tidigitateur. A constant fire of words was
kept up in Hindoostanee between the performers, which seemed a sort of by-play,
connected with the various tricks, and was
translated by Barrabbas. Besides the ordinary performances, such as swallowing
swords, knives, and nails, and afterward
drawing a complete "old junk shop" from
his mouth, smashing our watches and burning up our handkerchiefs, which were afterward returned unhurt to our pockets, the
performer drank a mixture of three powders—red, white and blue—in a glass of

water, and immediately afterward produced the three powders in a dry state, separately, from his mouth. The formula often repeated was "ek-do-teen, choulon," (one, two, three, lock sharp, sister,) a rolling up of the eyes and pretended appeal to Vishnu, Shiva and Buddha, when a difficult transformation was about to take place. But the most wonderful thing was making a mango tree grow from the seed, which he planted in a pot of earth before our eyes. A trick which I think has never been performed out of India. These things and many others, showing wonderful skill in the conjuring art, were done in broad daylight, within a few feet of us, and in the absence of the usual mechanical contrivances of stage exhibitions.

All occupations in the East are hereditary—even "beggars" and "robbers." In the last census returns of the north-western Provinces, 2,000 are set down as "hereditary buffoons and corjurers," and 1,100 as "snake charmers"—and most curious of all, 6,372 are returned as "poets." I saw an exhibition of snake charming in Benares, which had almost a spice of tragedy in it. The performer opened out his stock in front of the Bungalow, where we were sitting, consisting of a *boa-constrictor*, ten or twelve feet long and as large round as my arm, two lively *cobras*, the most deadly of snakes, and a variety of *scorpions* He teased the cobras until they raised their hissing heads two feet from the ground, and with distended hoods, and quivering tongues, repeatedly struck at the man's hand. Not drawing it away quick enough he was bitten by the snake on the fore finger, and a drop of blood appeared on the wound. The man took from his pocket a small, black stone, looking like a bean, and pressed it for a moment on the wound to which it adhered, and went on with his exhibition. Then taking a small bit of light colored wood, he held it toward the cobras and they instantly slunk back, as if terrified and completely cowed; another piece of wood had the same effect upon the scorpions. A rupee paid the snake charmer and secured for me the two bits of wood and the little stone, which I brought away as mementos.

Our hotel was literally besieged by a host of itinerant venders of the specialties of Delhi. They tried to get across to us by bribing Barrabbas, who made a good thing out of the ten to twenty per cent. on all our purchases, which of course came out of our

pockets. Most of these venders are pro-
prietors of shops in the Chandnee-Chowd,
and bring quantities of Cashmere shawls,
Delhi embroidery, paintings and jewelry
for your inspection, some of which are very
tempting. Once admitted to your room,
before you have time to forbid them, these
men will have opened their bundles, and
displayed before your new longing eyes the
most exquisite fabrics of every color of the
rainbow, covered with the finest embroidery in gold, silver-thread and silk. If there
should be any ladies in your party you may
as well surrender at once, only stipulating
for enough to be left in your purse for the
expenses to Bombay; for the beautiful
opera cloaks, ravishing Cashmere shawls,
sandalwood carvings, and miniature paintings on ivory, gold and silver filagree ornaments, with which you find yourself sur·
rounded would tempt an anchorite, or any
other hater of the pomps and vanities of
life. The prices asked are of course very
different from what is gladly taken after a
half hour's bargaining; but it is a very un·
safe method of purchase, unless one knows
the actual value of the goods, for although
you may get the article at half the price
first demanded, you are by no means certain
that you have made a good bargain.

There are one or two shops, however,
where the prices asked are the fair market
value, and to these the traveler in search of
genuine articles should go direct. At the
shawl store of *Manick Chund* we were
shown up a narrow and steep flight of steps
to a small room, opening on one side to the
court, and on the other to a narrow balcony
overlooking the street. Chairs having been
provided for us by the proprietor and his as·
sistants, he unlocked a door leading into a
large closet, and brought out a bundle, like
a peddler's pack, tied up in white cloth.
When untied we found this contained about
twenty cashmere shawls, worth from five
hundred to one thousand rupees each.
These were held up for our inspection, one
after another, then pushed away, and another bundle brought out, exhibited to us
and thrown aside in the most careless manner. Bundles of bernouses and jackets of
cashmere cloth and velvet, most beautifully embroidered in silk and gold, *chogas*,
or loose dressing-gowns for gentlemen,
smoking caps, table covers, etc., until the
floor was two feet deep in a confused litter
of the richest dry goods I ever saw. To my
unsophisticated eyes these ravishing "cam·

els' hair" shawls are nothing near so handsome as the imitations made in England and France. They are neither smooth nor glossy, and suggested the idea of having been washed, but not ironed. But my judgment on dry goods had been laughed at so many times that I had lost all confidence in it, and under the instruction of the ladies of our party, who were familiar with Stewart's stock, I soon began to admire them. They are not made of "camels hair" at all, but of wool of the Cashmere goat; each shawl being composed of many pieces, woven by different families, perhaps, and the labor of months. They are sewed very nicely together, the skill of blending colors being something marvelous, and can be altered and changed, in borders and centres, and washed and mussed up without damage. In the East the wealthy natives do not wear them over the shoulders, but male and female alike, tie them around their waist. In India, dress serves the purpose of denoting rank. The peasant is clothed in cotton, and the prince in cloth of gold; and even religion, caste and occupation are distinguished by well-known and unchanging marks in costumes. The fixity of fashion is as singular in Hindoostan as its infinite changeableness in New York and Paris. The pattern we see in the bazaar to-day are those which were popular in the days of *Shah Jehan.* Hindoo workmen, though of the lowest class, possess such wonderful taste and culture, that their commonest productions are like poems in silk and velvet, which seems to prove the saying, that the finest taste is consistent with the deepest slavery of body and mind. Dress with the Oriental is an art, and a Hindoo will never wear a robe or a turban, the ornamentation of which is not consistent with his idea of symmetry and grace.

The expensive amusement of shopping in bazaar and hotel relieved the monotony of sight seeing for the first two days in Delhi. Early on the morning of the third day we started, under the guidance of Barrabbas, for an excursion to the many interesting places outside the city walls. Emerging by the Ajmere gate, a half hour's ride brought us to the observatory of *Jai-Singh,* the scientific Rajah of Jaypore, who erected a similar establishment, alluded to in a former letter, at Benares. The buildings are uninhabited, and in a very dilapidated condition. Three miles further we reach the Mausoleum of the Grand Vizier of the Em-

peror and Viceroy of Oude, erected about
one hundred years ago. It is a vast structure, occupying the center of a large enclosure. Under the marble dome is an
elegantly carved sarcophagus, but in accordance with the wish of the deceased the grave
is in a vaulted chamber, beneath, of plain
earth covered with a cloth, on which were
strewn fresh flowers.

Eleven miles from the city we reached the
famous *Koontub Minar*, which had been in
sight for an hour before we reached it, and
is said to be the loftiest column in the
world. It is built of red sandstone almost
as hard as granite, in five stories, narrow-
ing gradually from fifty feet in diameter at
the base to twelve feet at the top. A projecting balcony, supported by heavy stone
brackets, separates each story, and on horizontal bands extending around the tower,
are passages of the Koran carved in bold
relief. Its present height is two hundred
and forty-two feet, but it was originally
sixty feet higher; the top canopy having
been struck by lightning some few years
ago. The Koontub was built about seven
hundred years ago, and from the chaos of
legends and superstitious chronicles, it is
difficult to tell the real origin of this famous
structure. One legend is that it was erected
by the Rajah of Prithie for a favorite
daughter who desired to possess a tower
with its top nigh to heaven, from which she
might offer up her prayers.

From the summit, to which we ascended
by a spiral stone staircase, a most superb
view of the surrounding country is obtained.
Immediately below lie picturesque ivy-
covered ruins surrounding the tower, while
scattered in masses for miles around are
seen the ruins of the old cities of Delhi.

Adjoining the Koontub are extensive
Hindoo remains that date back to the ninth
century. The open colonnades which once
surrounded the Rajah's palace are so ornamented with covering that not an inch of
plain surface can be seen. In front of a tall,
wide-spanning arch, covered with creeping
plants, stands a curious pillar of wrought
iron, sixteen inches in diameter and twenty-
two feet in height above ground, and as
much more in depth below the surface
This pillar, as the Hindoos believe, was
erected by the Rajah who built the Koontub, by advice of the Brahmins, as he dreaded the fall of his dynasty, and was assured
that if he could pierce the head of the snake
god who supported the world his kingdom

would endure forever. He accordingly sunk the shaft, and his priestly advisers told him it was "all right." But he was skeptical, and against the advice of the priests, had the pillar raised, when they found the end covered with blood, to the great consternation of the sovereign, who was then told that the scepter would soon pass away from the Hindoos. He chucked the pillar back in the ground, but the serpent below had had enough of cold iron, and the charm was broken. The Rajah soon after lost his life and his kingdom, and from that day to this no Hindoo king has ever ruled in Delhi.

After a lunch at the government Bungalow, situated in a grove which seemed alive with birds of brilliant plumage, we started homeward, stopping at several interesting places on our way. One of the grandest buildings in the neighborhood is the Tomb of the Emperor Humayoon, who was the first of the Grand Moguls buried in India. The shape of the building is an octagon, of the usual red sandstone, most artistically picked out in relief with white marble. At a distance it has the appearance of delicate pencil inlaying. It stands in the center of an enclosure of about twelve acres, and is built upon a double platform, or terrace, the upper one two hundred and eighty feet square. You enter the building through a vast porch, with a pointed arch forty feet high, and in the center is an octagonal dome of marble forty-five feet in diameter and eighty feet high. Here are the sacrophagi of the Emperor, his wife and children; the actual graves being, as usual, below in the vaults. By a stone staircase in the thickness of the walls we ascended to a gallery, from which springs the huge dome, and looked down the giddy depth into the vast hall beneath. The wall of the dome is eleven feet thick, and covered with slabs of pure white marble. Though over three hundred years old this splendid mausoleum is in admirable preservation, and impressed me as a wonderful masterpiece of a by-gone age.

It was to Humayoon's tomb that *Baha-door-Shah*, the last of the Moguls, fled with his sons and hid themselves, after the capture of Delhi in September, 1857. They gave themselves up the next day, being promised that their lives should be spared; but on their way to Delhi, the two older princes were barbarously shot by Major Hodson. The spot where this tragedy oc-

THE KOOTUB MINAR

curred was afterwards pointed out by our guide. The King and his two younger sons were transported to Rangoon, where he died about two years ago.

In the neighborhood are several smaller tombs and mosques, one of which is built around a large tank, forty feet deep. While we were standing at the water's edge, a man suddenly appeared on top of the mosque, ran nimbly down the course of the dome, and sprang, feet foremost into the tank below. Several others followed in rapid succession, and swimming quickly to the bank, held out their hands for *buckshees;* then clambered up again to repeat the performance. It appeared to us a very dangerous feat, for the height could not have been less than one hundred feet, and the water, surrounded by tall buildings, was very cold; but they seemed to enjoy the plunge bath and kept it up as long as we threw them coppers.

Here is also the tomb of the poet *Chusero,* the reputed author of the "Arabian Nights," who died in the fourteenth century. Looking through the open-work marble screen, I saw upon the tomb a handful of rose leaves, some of which I secured as a memento.

About two miles from the Delhi gate we came to the massive ruins of a palace built by the Emperor *Ferose,* four hundred years ago, which was then the center of his capital city. Near it is a pillar three and a half feet in diameter, and forty feet high, of red sandstone, without a joint, called the *Lat,* or *staff* of *Ferose-Shah.* It was brought here by that Emperor, and is covered by an inscription so ancient that it puzzled for a long time the most skilled European savans. It has, however, been deciphered recently, and proves to be certain edicts in furtherance of religion and virtue, enacted by a king who reigned B. C. 320. This king obtained his throne by the murder of *ninety* of his relations, who had prior claims, and must have changed his character in his old age. The column is at least 2,200 years old, and is supposed to be the most ancient writing in India.

The records of these old Mussulman Kings are rarely free from the murders of relations, especially brothers. They were, however, but *half brothers,* and the jealousy and ambition of the mother often instigated the killing or putting out of the eyes of the sons of her rivals who were constantly plotting against the successful aspirant to the throne.

We left Delhi with a "left-handed blessing" for Barrabbas, and at midnight found
ourselves at *Saharunpore*, a station one hundred and ten miles farther north, where we
took a dak gharry the next morning for
Rajpore, fifty miles distant, near the foot
hills of the Himalayas, the highest range of
mountains in the world, which form the
"backbone" of the continent of Asia.

The arrangements for our vehicles and
relays of horses along the route to the Himalayas and back, which would occupy five
or six days, were made with the hotel
keeper, and is called "laying a dak." All
our heavy luggage was left here to await
our return, and we started on the expedition in "light marching order." The *horse
dak* of Northern India is so peculiar an
institution, that it merits a short description. Like the gharry it is a square, covered van, with sliding doors on each side.
It accommodates two persons and is fitted
up for continuous day and night travel. The
space between the seats is "floored over,"
and covered with a thin mattress, over
which we spread our *resais*, or thick cotton wadded quilts, and our pillows, shawls
and sundry "wraps," we recline at our ease
and make ourselves comfortable. The
springs of the vehicle are "packed" with
bamboo, which saves their breaking, but
does not increase our comfort when the
road is rough, and the hubs are wound
with straw-rope, frequently wet to protect
them from the heat of the sun. Two horses
are attached, one in the shafts the other
outside, drawing from a piece of bamboo
tied with a rope to the whippletree, and
projecting several feet on one side of the
dak. The horses are small and badly
broken, and can rarely be started without a
man pushing at each wheel, and two more
pulling at their bits. But when they do
go, it is with a rush, the bare-headed and
bare-legged native driver shouting and
cracking his whip, and all the hangers on
around the station cheering at the top of
their voices. This break-neck speed is kept
up until the next station is reached.

In this style, after several false starts, we
dashed away for the bungalow at Sahanpore,
with our luggage and "Chuddy-Lull," a native servant whom my friend had brought
from Calcutta, stowed on the top of the
vehicle to which he clung for dear life.

Before the days of railways this was the
universal method of travel for Europeans
in India; and all the daks seem to have

come down from a past generation, where they have figured in such trifling incidents as breakdowns and "spills," which even now are not of unfrequent occurrence and give a zest to the unique style of conveyance.

The stations are about six miles apart, and we make good time, for the horses are seldom allowed to hold up from the sharp canter into which they were started, except when we approached the river-channels, which at this season are nearly dry, but are frequently flooded by sudden storms, and by melted snow from the Himalayas, when all communication is stopped for days. Before passing one of these places the horses are always taken out, and bullocks harnessed to the dak, for the horses would be sure to "balk" in the middle of the stream, or in ascending the steep aclivity on the other side.

Our road was over a smooth plain, and the novelty and excitement of our conveyance, added to the cool, refreshing breeze sweeping down from the mountain peaks, which in the dim distance ahead seemed fleecy white clouds, produced an exhilaration like champaign. Along the road in front of the dak the ground squirrels trooped, and birds without number hopped fearlessly by our side, while paroquets, brilliant in blue and red plumage, were perched on the trees and gave us sidelong glances, as if amused and edified at our songs and laughter.

Before noon we reached the entrance of the *Mohun Pass*, and halted for three hours at the government bungalow, which is located on the summit of a high hill, commanding a beautiful view of the plain over which we had passed. The native *Khansamah*, the genius of the place, provided an excellent dinner, though his bill of fare was not very extensive. The omelet was delicious, and the "sudden death"—a fowl which we heard cackling in the yard as we drew up, and served up half an hour afterward in a *fricasee*, as appetizing as Delmonico's—together with our "small stores," were all that an epicure could desire.

Through the Pass, a distance of eight miles, our dak was drawn by nine coolies. The reason why horses are not used here was to us incomprehensible; for the road was smooth, and an American horse could easily have trotted up the steepest ascent. But in India the hire of nine men is less than that of two horses, and a *pas-seul* of

one of these unbroken beasts might have
sent our vehicle spinning over a precipice.

At the end of the Pass, which occupied
four hours, horses were once more attached,
after considerable delay; but it was now
dark and we had ten miles before us, part
of the way through thick woods and jungles. We closed the door of our carriage
and recounted all the frightful stories we
could remember of "man-eating" tigers,
which here are supposed to abound; concluding, however, that Chuddy Lall and
the driver would be the first victims in case
of attack, while we could defend our fortress with our revolvers. With such "pleasant discourse" we enlivened the hours, until at last the lights of the village of Deyra
appeared in the distance, where we roused
the keeper of the dak bungalow, who put
the whole establishment at our disposal,
and soon made us comfortable for the night.

W. P. F.

A Lively Start from Deyra--Scenes along
the Road—"Caravan-Serais"—War-
fare against Wild Beasts—Hindoos
take no part in it—Man-Eating Ti-
gers—A Paradise of Snakes—White
Skins are Patents of Nobility—Sa-
laam all—Approach to the Himalayas
—Up the Mountains—The Jampans
—Charming Scenery—Caught in a
Storm—Desperate Situation—Mussoo-
rie in Winter Quarters—Jolly as Mark
Tapley—Simla, the Hill Capital of In-
dia—The Snowy Range—Magnificent
Views of the Mountains—A Beautiful
Apparition—A Bengalese Handy An-
dy—"Grilled Boots"—Elephant and
Tiger Hunters—Right Royal Sport—
Return to Saharunpore.

We planned an early start from Deyra the
next morning to reach Rajpore in good season for our ascent of the Himalayas. But to
plan is one thing, to execute quite another·
Our late arrival the night before was unfa-
vorable to early rising, and when at last
breakfast was dispatched, the Daks were
not on hand. After much delay we were
packed bag and baggage, but then arose the
chronic trouble about starting the horses·
One horse was willing, the other refused to
budge an inch. Six grooms came running
from the stable, four placed themselves one
at each wheel, one held the horse by the bit,
another held up his fore leg, while several
boys pushed behind. The driver gave the
signal, the wheel men threw their whole
weight on the spokes, the obstinate brute
was fairly forced off the ground, and with a
wild yell of triumph we dashed off at full
speed, which the driver took care should
not to let up until we arrived at the end of
the stage.

Our road was again over the level plain,
and there was no lack of variety and charm
in watching the traffic on the road, and the
novel scenes in the villages through which
we passed. At frequent intervals are *serais*
or corrols, built by the Mogul Emperors or
the British Government, for the use of natives traveling, in caravans. Hence our

word "caravansary" or "caravan-serai."
The keepers of these places supply water,
provender and food, and at night the *serais*
along the road are aglow with the cooking
fires, and resound with the chattering and
laughter of thousands of natives. The villages, or *serais*, are about three miles apart,
and between them you never see a human
habitation. Although the north western
provinces are the most densely populated
country in the world, the jackals and wild
cattle roam over the space between these
villages, which are fortified with walls of
mud or brick, as freely as if it were an un-
trodden wilderness.

This is what makes India, despite its teeming population of two hundred millions, so
subject to the depredations of wild beasts.
The Hindoos are not a race of Nimrods.
They are naturally timid, and their religion
makes them averse to taking life, even of a
beast of prey. The government pays a reward of fifty rupees for every tiger killed,
and for leopards, hyenas and wolves, sums
that represent weeks of labor to a native;
yet these "varmints" are nearly all killed
by Europeans, and in the war between the
white man and the jungle owners, it is
doubtful which party are ahead. In some
interior districts a pair of man-eating tigers
have been known to eject the people of a
whole village and grimly hold it so long as
they liked the lodgings. In other places
the road is deserted because a tiger has possession.

The term man-eater is applied to a tiger
that has once tasted human blood. From
that time he becomes a cannibal, and doubly dangerous and savage. No longer satisfied with his former food, he prowls singly
or in pairs around the outskirts of a village,
watching his opportunity to gobble up some
unfortunate native.

The premium paid for a cobra's head is
three annas (ten cents), and the return of the
number annually killed is only about
20,000, while it is estimated that full that
number of men, women and children die
every year in India from the bites of cobras
and other venomous snakes. This country
is the paradise of snakes, for here they are
not only feared but worshipped. Sometimes a cobra will take up its abode in the
thatched roof or under the mud walls of a
native house, but the Hindoo will not kill
it; he sends for a snake-charmer to come and
play to it upon a reed or gourd, and respectfully ask it to go elsewhere. All this is

wonderfully in favor of the hideous reptile. Some witty essayist has written a paper "on the advantage of being a cantankerous old fool." If a cobra could reason he might congratulate himself "on the advantages of being an ugly, horrible 'sarpint,' with a fiend's eves, and a mouth full of certain death."

As we ride along the smooth road this beautiful morning we see neither wild beasts nor venomous reptiles, but meet long strings of camels, and great lumbering elephants loaded with packs larger than themselves, or carrying *howdahs* with gaily colored decorations, in which are stowed the family of some wealthy native traveler. At the villages the military police in dark-blue tunics, yellow trowsers, and bright red turbans, rise up from sleep or hookah, and give us the military salute—due in India to the white face from all native troops. Here your skin is your patent of nobility and passport, all in one. On the road the natives all *salaam* to us—except mere coolies, who do not think themselves worthy even to offer a salute—and as I make it a part of my religion never to be outdone in courtesy, I always return the low bow and humble "salaam, sahib," with a civil and polite "salaam."

At noon we reach Rajpore, a pretty village nestled at the foot of the hills that form the first range of the Himalayas. There can be no mistake now about our proximity to these grand old mountains. What all day yesterday seemed like white fleecy clouds, piled up along the northern horizon, and gradually rising as we approached, now stand sharply defined in lofty heights, uprising one above another, and extending as far as the eye can reach. Immediately before us are the mighty spurs of this mighty range, upon which is perched the town of Mussoorie, while a mile or two further on, at the summit of these hills, we discern the pretty white cottages of Landour, over 8,000 feet above the sea, and the *ultima-thule* of our journey.

From where we stand in the piazza of the hotel we can trace the narrow zig-zag path winding up the mountain side, in some places seeming like a shelf cut from the solid rock. By the path we are told that it is ten miles to Landour, although it can be scarcely one fourth that distance "as the bird flies." Here we exchange our Dak-gharry for ponies and Jampans; and all the luggage is packed on the backs of Coolies.

The *Jampa n* which is usually preferred by
ladies, for a skittish horse might back the
rider over a precipice, is a kind of sedan
chair, made very light, like those of China,
and closed on its four sides by curtains. It
is carried on the shoulders of four men by a
pole front and rear. Nine men are the complement of each Jampan, four to carry and
four as relays—the odd man assuming the
command of the squad, and becoming a
nominal security for their good behavior.

The *Jampan wallahs* have a most peculiar shuffling gait, caused apparently by
wearing slippers much too large for them.
Your comfort depends upon the sort of
bearers you get, as some keep step very
imperfectly, and the result is that you feel
the motion in every bone in your body. But
where they carry you with an easy sling
trot, you soon get accustomed and indifferent to the motion.

When our cavalcade started from Rajpore
the sun was shining brightly and it was
quite warm although a cool breeze was
sweeping down from the snow clad mountains; and I imprudently had my overcoat
strapped on the back of coolie, who started
half an hour ahead. The scenery, as we
ascended the winding path, was grand and
imposing. Huge rocky hills rise abruptly
to the height of five hundred to one thousand feet, or undulate along to a much
steeper ascent in the distance; down the
valleys through many a rocky ravine rush
bright, sparkling waterfalls, tumbling and
leaping in frothy beauty, as they are checked
in their course by massive boulders of stone.
Occasionally a troop of wild monkeys rush
chattering up the cliff, pelting you from the
top with pebbles—and loosening in their
ascent the shingly soil, which comes rattling
in a shower down the hillside. Masses of
wild honeysuckle, cactus and creeping
plants run over and clothe the rugged
points of rock, and the delicate foliage of
the feathery bamboo contrasts fancifully
with the lofty pine that towers by its side.

We came frequently to dangerous looking
curves, where it seems to require only a
strong puff of wind to tilt one over the
precipice. The path is usually about ten
feet wide and protected by a low stone parapet. But in some places it is too narrow
for two loaded horses to pass in safety, and
we here keep a sharp lookout that we may
meet no cavalcades bound down toward the
valley.

Having as we supposed plenty of time we

loitered on the way, frequently turning in
our saddles to gaze at the beautiful pictures
spread out on the plain below, for as we rise
higher and higher we can trace the road
over which we passed, all the way to Deyra.
But a sudden clouding in of the sun and
rumbling of thunder over our heads admon-
ished us that a storm was coming down the
mountain to meet us. A pattering of rain-
drops and a chilly blast of wind made the
Coolies drop the curtains of the Jampans;
but we on horseback had no such protection
from the rain that now came pouring down
in torrents. We were scarcely half way
up the mountain, and halting for a moment
under the protection of a cliff, we held a
"council of war," in which it was decided
that I should push ahead and secure quarters for the party, as the prospect of a severe
storm was now imminent. I gave my pony
the rattan freely and dashed ahead up the
winding path.

The higher I ascended the fiercer and
colder grew the blast, until the rain turned
to sleet and seemed to penetrate to the bone.
My poor nag could hardly be worried out
of a walk, and my wet clothes were fast being covered over with a coat of sleety mail.
Now I bitterly repented parting with my
over-coat, on which the Coolie was probably snoozing comfortably, having crowded
into some dry hole in the cliff. Through
the driving mist and sleet, the town of Mussoorie could be plainly seen, and I thought
every curve of the road would certainly
bring me to the summit. But *tantalus like*
it seemed to recede as I climbed upwards.
I fear my jaded poney thought I was a cruel
rider, as I plied my rattan and dug my heels
into his sides in the vain attempt to force
him into a trot.

Despite the desperate situation, wet to
the skin and chilled to the marrow, I halted
for a moment under a projecting cliff, impressed with the novelty and sublimity of
the scene. Looking back, I could see the
sun shining serenely on the plain below,
while half way up the mountain was a
pouring shower, which at my elevation
was turned to driving sleet. Over my head
and

> ———"Far along,
> From peak to peak, the rattling crags among,
> Leaped the live thunder—not in one lone cloud,
> But every mountain now had found a tongue."

But a short time could be given to the
poetry of the situation, unless I was willing
to realize the fate of that unfortunate
"youth who bore 'mid snow and ice a ban-

ner with a strange device." Another desperate push, and a few more curves of the road, which seemed interminable, and my pony pricked up his ears and struck into a lively gait, which soon brought us into the winding streets of the town. He instinctively trotted up hill and down through what might have passed for Goldsmith's "Deserted Village," straight to the hotel, without my seeing a single human being of whom I could have enquired the way.

Mussoorie is a summer watering place for Europeans residing on the hot and scorched plains, which extend for thousands of miles southward and is now in winter quarters. The hotel is dismantled with not a white man about the premises, and the furniture is piled promiscuously in parlors, drawing-rooms and bed-rooms. I am afraid I flourished my rattan threateningly over the heads of the native servants in charge of the establishment to expedite their movements. With poor Hindoostanee but good pantomime I made them understand that I wanted some rooms put in order and fires built for the "*memsahib*," or ladies, who were coming; and before they arrived there were bright fires blazing in two rooms, which, barring the smoke, made the place quite a cosy and comfortable retreat from the storm that raged out of doors. With hot water, *et cetera*, we soon made ourselves as jolly as a trio of Mark Tapleys, turning round and round like roasting jacks before the fire to dry our clothes. In the meantime the whole force of the establishment, with the addition of "Chuddy Lall," busied themselves in preparing something hot to eat and drink. Before dark the Coolies arrived with our luggage, and the evening was passed most pleasantly in "recounting the dangers we had passed," while the storm beat fiercely against the glass and rattled the casements as if enraged at our escape.

The next morning the sun rose bright and clear, and we found six inches of snow upon the ground, which to me was a novelty, as the only "winter landscape" I had seen for nearly two years. We started after breakfast, on foot, to ascend to Landour, the highest point, from which the best view can be had of the famous "Snowy Range." The buildings of Mussoorie, which in winter are uninhabited, are perched upon all sorts of funny places—here on the top of a hill, now on its slope, then deep in some cosy valley; and the streets leading to them twine, twist and turn in every direction.

The names over the gateways, "Rose Villa," "Waterloo Terrace," "Ivy Lodge," etc., have a thoroughly English look. But now the shutters are closed, the gates nailed up, and straw is twisted around the tender vines that in summer clamber over porch and doorways. It would be hard to realize, were it not for the signs over the closed and deserted shops, that within less than sixty days this place will be the home of five or six thousand Europeans, with bank and billiards, assembly room and theater, and possibly a daily newspaper, in full operation.

But the most fashionable resort for Europeans among the Himalayas is at Simla, where the government of India, seeking refuge from the host of Calcutta, is located for half the year. This place is called the "Hill Versailles," and is made up of cottages and bungalows, built like Musecorie along a narrow mountain ridge, and up and down the steep sides of an Alpine peak. It is connected by telegraph with the rest of the world, and during "the season" is gay with balls, picnics and private theatricals. The baggage of the Viceroy and suite fills a whole railway train, and is conveyed from the nearest station on elephants, camels, pack horses and coolies to this pleasant retreat among the mountains.

The snow is fast melting in the warm sun, as we climb up towards Landour. The air is exhilarating, but so rarified at this elevation of 8,000 feet, as to make active exercise rather fatiguing. At last we reach the highest point, on which is located a pretty cottage, now deserted, and taking possession of the porch we enjoy at our ease one of the grandest sights of mountain scenery in the world. In front, and extending to the right and left until lost in the dim distance are snow-covered peaks from 20,000 to 29,000 feet in height. Being draped in spotless white from base to summit the bright sun is reflected in dazzling brilliancy. The storm of yesterday has cleared the atmosphere, and the outlines are distinctly marked against the blue sky. The view of the Rocky Mountains from the plains of Denver is grand—perhaps the finest on the American continent. But here the mountains rise to double the height of either Pike's Peak or Mont Blanc. Covered with eternal ice and snow these lofty mountains seem radiantly brilliant, or frowningly gloomy, as the sun appears, or is hid by a passing cloud or by the uprising mists from the valleys. This beautiful view of the Himalayas impresses a picture on the memory of the beholder which can never be effaced; and amply repays the toil and fatigue of a journey thither.

In returning to the hotel at a point where the path for half a mile was nearly level, we were startled and almost run over by a horse that came dashing by at full speed along the road. We could catch but a rapid glance at the sudden apparition, but it showed us a pure white Arab, ridden by a beautiful girl, whose rosy cheeks belonged to some more northern clime than India. We all exclaimed, in one breath, "How beautiful!" "The horse or the rider?" "Both," was the unanimous verdict, as the apparition quickly vanished around a curve in the road. "Who can she be?" "Where does she belong?" were the questions asked, but they remain yet unanswered.

Melted snow is dampening to the feet, and our extra boots had all been left behind with the heavy baggage. So, ensconsed in slippers, we gave our wet boots to Chuddy Lall to be dried at the kitchen fire. This henchman of my friends was a Bengalese edition of "Handy-Andy"—simple, honest, and blundering as his Irish prototype—if as witty, it was hidden from us in his unknown tongue.

My friend wants his boots. Bells are rare in the East; when one wishes for a servant he steps into the hall and claps his hands. After some unaccountable delay Chuddy opens the door. His complexion, usually about "half-and-half," seems now almost white, and he looks frightened out of his wits. In his hands are the remains of a pair of boots, burned to a crisp. Leaving the door open to secure his retreat, he stammers out, "I go to sleep, fire blaze up and burn de boots—berry sorry, Sahib," and with both hands touching his forehead he *salaams* almost to the floor, then takes a step or two backwards towards the door.

His former experience with English masters led him to anticipate a volley of curses, emphasized by some missile like a boot-jack or a bottle. The provocation was certainly enough to start the ire of an even tempered man, thus condemned for three days in a wintry climate to wear his slippers, for no boots could be had short of Saharunpore.

But my friend is a gentleman, an Ameri-c\o, and a New Yorker.

Dismissing Handy Andy with a mild reprimand, he joined the rest of us in a hearty laugh at the irresistibly comical and frightened look of poor Chuddy, who kept shady the rest of the day as if afraid his master would change his mood. We had just finished dinner, and ever after, in speaking of our Himalayan experiences, "grilled boots" were referred to as a part of our "Bill of fare."

Another day was spent amid this splendid Alpine scenery, and then we descended to Rajpore, where our Daks were waiting to convey us back over the plains to Saharunpore.

At the Mohun Pass, where we exchanged *quadrupeds* for *bipeds*, we found a native Rajah encamped with several hundred attendants. They were on an elephant and tiger hunt; and with the party were three or four English officers, who very politely showed us through the camp and into the corrol, where there were about seventy wild elephants, all captured within the past week. Several splendid animals were chained by the leg to large trees, from which they had twisted in their fury every branch within reach of their trunks, and pawed great holes in the ground. They are allowed to give free vent to their rage, and after a few days they cool down and become docile and obedient. We were much interested in the description of the *modus operandi* of hunting elephants and tigers, and were strongly inclined to accept the invitation given us to join the party for a few day's sport. The possible chance of carrying home as a trophy the skin of a "Royal Bengal Tiger" was indeed a temptation—while the risk of leaving one's own skin in India as a trophy to the "Man-eater," would have been of no consideration whatever, if our other plans had not rendered this episode impossible.

When we reached Saharunpore after an absence of six days, and again took the cars southward, it seemed as if we had been on a grand pic-nic excursion, which to me had been made especially enjoyable by the society and companionship of most agreeable and pleasant friends.   W. P. F.

Return Southwards—Jubbalpore—Le-
gand of the Nerbudda—The Marble
Rocks—Prison of the Thugs—Traveling Companions—A Cigar Well In-
vested—The Russian Question—Will
The Russian Bear Drive the English
Bull out of India?

BOMBAY, INDIA, March 1871.

We now retrace our steps from Saharunpore to Allahabad, 500 miles, and here turn
to the southward in the direction of Bombay, 850 miles distant. We gradually
climb the Ghants, a long range of mountains
stretching across India from West to East;
and in ten hours had ascended 1000 feet
and reached Jubbalpore, one of the most
important cities of central India. It is situated on the Nerbudda, a large and rapid
stream, which has its source in a flat-topped
mountain, forming the eastern terminus of
this range of hills. The legend is that Her
Majesty, the Nerbudda, and another river,
rising in the same mountain, had intended
to be united in marriage, and to roll their
waters together toward the eastern seas;
but the course of true love failed to run
smooth; the little river Jobille, which has
its source hard by, cast in the apple of discord, and Her Majesty declared she would
not go a single pace in the same direction
with such wretches, and would flow *west*,
though all the other rivers in India might
flow *east*. So west she turned, and after a
thousand miles of wandering, pours her
waters into the Arabian Sea.

Ten miles from Jubbalpore are the celebrated "Marble Rocks," where the petulant
Nerbudda, becoming pent up between limestone rocks, flings herself tumultuously over
a ledge with a fall of thirty feet, called the
"Misty Shoot," then enters a deeply-cut
channel, carved through a mass of marble
and basalt for about two miles. The river
is here compressed into some twenty yards,
though more than five times that width
above the falls, and glides along in its narrow bed very smoothly and with great
depth, between a double wall of marble
from fifty to eighty feet in height. In some
places large masses of basalt, black as jet,
contrast strongly with the dazzling white

marble, and the reflection upon the water,
which has a bluish-green tint, is most curious and weird-like, especially when seen
by moonlight. Even at mid-day the utter
silence and solitude of the spot—as if the
spectator were left alone with the
Nerbudda in her marble dwelling—
strike the senses with a sort of awe.

The streets of Jubbalpore are wide and
well kept, and its many pretty bungalows,
surrounded by gardens and groves of mango
trees, make it an attractive place of residence during the hot season to the Europeans
from the plains. Here is located a prison
quite famous for the manufacture of tents,
carpets and other fabrics. The workers are
almost exclusively Thugs and their families,
many of them villainous looking fellows,
heavily ironed. They are the remnants of
that race of murderers and robbers that
once infested India, and were the dread
alike of natives and Europeans. The strong
hand of government has put an end to their
atrocities, and the few hundred here are
strictly guarded by soldiers, and made to
work to earn their own living.

From this place to Nagpore, one hundred
and sixty-two miles, is the connecting link
of the railway between Calcutta and Bombay, and has been opened but a short time.
The passengers and mails were formerly conveyed across this gap by Dak gharries, occupying thirty hours of most fatiguing
travel. The station house here is not finished, and while waiting for the train,
which was an hour late, I could but notice
how uncomplainingly the passengers, ladies
as well as gentlemen, sat upon their baggage on the stone platform, the midday sun pouring its tropical heat upon
their heads. A few only were protected by
white umbrellas held over them by coolies.
It occurred to me that in America there
would have been terrible growling over
such a matter; but to these Anglo-Indians,
who have been long in the country, the
railway is such an infinite improvement and
luxury in traveling, compared with the dak,
that this little annoyance was not considered
worth making a fuss about. But the sun
was too much for me, notwithstanding my
solar toupet, or pith hat, and leaving my
"traps" in charge of a native, I was glad to
take refuge in the shade of the unfinished
building. The train came up at last, and
with nearly a whole compartment to myself
where I could stretch out at full length on
a cane seat, I enjoyed the cool breeze that

swept through the car.

One advantage of traveling alone is the better opportunity it offers of making the acquaintance of your fellow passengers. I have met Americans aboard who boasted that they never spoke to their neighbors in railway cars, afraid, perhaps, of compromising their dignity. Such foolish people are to be pitied, for they miss many opportunities of gaining information about the country and people through which they are traveling. To my surprise I have found the English everywhere in the east extremely civil and polite to strangers, especially to Americans. I am told at home it is quite the reverse.

My companon du *Voyage* to-day was a very intelligent Englishman, to whom my cigar case was a letter of introduction. He had been for twelve years in the civil service, and was thoroughly posted on every point connected with the government of India. It was gratifying to see that he was as much interested in what I could tell him about America, as I was in the exceedingly valuable information so freely imparted by him, and which I could not have acquired from books.

Our route lay together for several days after, and I shall place to the credit of that *cheroot* one of the most intelligent and agreeable of the many pleasant travelling companions I have met abroad. But when my friend asked in a voice *almost plaintive*, whether we Americans would join Russia in a war against "our mother country,' I was at a loss what to reply. I have been asked the same question many times before, and it implies a *respect*, perhaps a *dread*, of our power which was not shown before the rebellion.

The fear of Russia and the dread that the Muscovite will work down and eventually drive them out of India, is the great nightmare that rests upon the English in the East. The Russians are steadily advancing southward in Asia, conquering their way step by step, until England and Russia are now almost face to face. That the English have got to fight for the possession of this magnificent empire in the East upon the plains of India is "manifest destiny;" but I am not the prophet to foretell the result. The intelligent natives watch with great interest the advance of Russia; not that they would be any better off under her than under the British, whom they fear, but do not love; but they would like to see the

English thrashed at all events, like the school boy who would be glad to see a new bully thrash his former master, even though he proves a severer tyrant. The country is infinitely better governed now than before the mutiny, and the wide-spread hatred of the English does not prove that they are bad rulers. It is merely the hatred that easterns always bear their masters; yet masters the Hindoos will always have. The English judges and civil officials are incorruptible, and the native, who is fond of law suits, is sure of exact and even justice, although his opponent may be a European. Under native rulers justice uninfluenced by bribes was unknown. For scores of centuries the Hindoos have bribed and taken bribes, and corruption has eaten into the national character so deeply that many people declare it can never be washed out. Bribes are constantly offered to English officials, and that they should be rejected is something incomprehensible to the ignorant native. The Russians are not thoroughly civilized: they are semi-barbarians, and their officials are notoriously the most corrupt and venal in Europe. "Scratch a Russian and you will find a bear beneath the skin." Were they a civilized European Power with "a mission" in the East, or even an enlightened Commercial Power, with benevolent instincts, but with no policy outside their pockets—such as the rule in India was under the East India Company—mankind might be benefited by their advance into Southern Asia. But as an organized Barbarism, of Asiatic origin, to replace the English would be a step backwards to the people of India. The great mass of the people are quite indifferent as to who their rulers are, if only their taxes are kept down. The Government is establishing schools and colleges in all the large cities, and thousands of young men are growing up with western ideas who will stand by the English in case of any future insurrection. They are identified with the government by minor official positions, and many thousands are employed on the railways. The danger is from the outside, not from any internal disaffection. There are 70,000 English soldiers in the country, and in reorganizing the native troops since the mutiny the government has wisely drawn most of their recruits from the Sikhs and other war-like tribes of the Punjaub in Northern India, who are all Mahometans and hate as well as despise the more effeminate Hindoos of the South.

My views of the "Eastern Question" are submitted in all modesty, and may not be correct. I can only say that they are the result of over 3,000 miles travel through the country, and the honest endeavor, without any partiality to the present rulers, against whom I was strongly prejudiced, to gain all possible information on the subject,

Lucky Crows—Summit of the Ghauts
—Perilous Descent—Bombay, the Cot-
ton Metropolis of India—Founded
by the Portuguese, Given to the
English—King Cotton Here Abso-
lute—The Parsees—Street Scenes—
Byculla Hotel—Yacht Race—The
" Live Yankee" Almost Wins—Wen-
ham Lake Ice—Caves of Elephanta
Hindoo Ideal of God—Farewell to
India.

BOMBAY, INDIA, March 1871.
All day we have been slowly climbing the
Ghauts; the Begra Hills on our
left are seen many miles away. Now
we turn sharply to the south,
pass through a deep rock cutting, then
dash through a half mile tunnel, and
cross the Begra river on a high iron bridge.
Again we pass over a hundred miles or
more of table land, highly cultivated, with
wheat fields of one thousand acres on either
side, almost ripe for the harvest. In the
middle of these fields upon high platforms
men are stationed to drive away the preda-
tory crows; but no one kills these marau-
ders, who ought to be thankful that their
lot is cast in a Hindoo not a Christian land.

During the few hours of darkness, for the
nights are here very short, we pass through
a wild section covered with wood and jungle, said to be infested by tigers and wild
beasts. Stopping at an early hour the next
morning for breakfast we find ourselves
upon the summit and enjoy a splendid sun -
rise five thousand feet above the sea. Now
commences the descent of the western slope
of the Ghauts. The grade is very steep and
our train is divided, each section being held
back by all the power of engine and brakes.
The curves are very sharp and the road rico-
chets like the tape on a card-rack. Around
the shorter curves there are three rails instead of two. One is laid so close to the off-
rail that there is barely space between them
for the flange of the wheel, and this is called
the guard rail. I do not remember ever to
have seen this in crossing the Alleghanies
by the Pennsylvania or Baltimore and Ohio
routes. The scenery is wild and grand, and
there are more bridges over chasms and

gorges, dark and deep, and more frequent
tunnels for the next ten miles than I ever
saw before in the same distance. At one
place the train comes to a full stop a hundred yards from the verge of a precipice of
one thousand feet; and here the track,
forming the letter Y, starts off again in the
opposite direction. A freight train coming
down this grade a few months ago during
the rainy season, when the track was slippery got beyond the control of the brakes
and went dashing over the precipice. We
run very slowly and are two hours in making the descent of fifteen miles. There is a
decided feeling of relief among the passengers when we "touch bottom."

For four hours more we glide smoothly
over a comparatively level country where
cotton seems to be the principal crop, and
most of the cars on the side tracks are
marked "cotton wagons." We are evidently approaching Bombay, the great cotton metropolis of India. This portion of
the road is old, and the track is lined with
hedges of cactus. The station houses are
pretty cottage-like buildings, surrounded
by flowers; and long rows of plants in pots,
gorgeous creepers and beds of roses and bal-
sams show the pains taken by these railway
gardeners, and the good taste of the superintendent of the line. Why cannot some of
our older roads in America follow the example of England and the continent in thus em-
belishing those most dreary looking places,
the country railway station?

At noon we reach Bombay, which claims
to be the second city in size in the British
empire, with a population of nearly a million, the rival of Calcutta as a seaport, and
the postal centre of India.

It is built on a number of small islands,
connected with each other and the main-
land by causeways, forming altogether a
peninsular so low and flat that during the
rainy season large tracts are under water.
Notwithstanding its location it is so open to
the invigorating sea breeze that Bombay is said to be one of the health-
ies places in India for Europeans. Many
of the rich merchants have beautiful villas
on Malabar Hill in the suburbs, which, surrounded by gardens and shrubbery, resemble the New Yorkers' cottages on Staten
Island. This city was founded three hundred years ago by the Portuguese under
that fearless old sea-dog, Vasco da Gama,
who won the title of "Admiral of the Indian, Persian and Arabian Seas," by first

doubling the stormy cape, and pointing out the new route to the Indies. For many years the Portuguese monopolized the rich trade of India, founding cities on both eastern and western coasts, which they enriched with most splendid churches, and like the Spaniards in the west, laid the foundation of an empire in injustice, and cemented it with innocent blood.

All that remains to them now is the little settlement of Goa, below Bombay on the western coast, once great and opulent, now a poor, faded place, with a harbor half choked with mud. There is said to be a caste in Western India called "Goaese," or "Portuguese,"—black as crows, and good for little except cooking—which represents the hybrid Lusitanian and native mixture. The city of Bombay was given away as a marriage *trosseau* along with the Infanta Catharine to Charles II.

But the Bombay of to-day is ruled by a potentate whom we once knew in America, "King Cotton," and his sway is here as absolute as it ever was in Charleston or New Orleans. Cotton has built the splendid stores and warehouses, which are unequaled in any city of the East. Cotton has collected the hundred steamers and the thousands of native boats that are anchored in the harbor. The export of cotton rose from twenty-five million dollars worth in 1859 to nearly two hundred millions in 1864; and the population from 400,000 to a million. Not even Chicago ever took a greater leap than did Bombay in these five years. But the sudden decline in cotton in 1865 brought on a commercial crisis that ruined nearly every merchant in the city. It has now in a measure recovered from the panic, and the rapid development of railways in India, of which Bombay is the western terminus, and the opening of the Suez canal, make this place the great entrepot for European goods as well as the most important export point for raw products, such as cotton, jute, spices, ivory and gums.

In numbers, intelligence and wealth the Parsees are the strongest of all the merchants of Bombay. This position they have gained by their superior capacity for business, enterprise and absence of caste prejudices, which have made the name of leading Parsee merchants widely known in Europe as well as their native land. Disciples of Zoroaster, and driven to India many hundred years ago, they have no nationality of their own, but are everywhere attached to the English rule.

In religion and education the Parsees are far in advance of Mahomitans and Hindoos. Their creed is a pure *deism*, in which God's works, such as fire, the sun and the sea, are worshiped as the manifestations or visible representatives of God on earth. Their temples are as plain as a Quaker meeting house, and disfigured by no idols or tawdry decoration. The men are well educated, and there is not a pauper in the whole race. The women of the higher class of Parsees are not secluded, but are frequently to be seen on the fashionable drives and promenades. They are quite good looking and but little darker in complexion than the southern races of Europe. The Parsee names on the street signs are as peculiar as Chinese. They are of many syllables, hard to pronounce, and all end in "*jee.*"

Bombay is farther south than Calcutta, and more Oriental and tropical than any other place I have seen in India. The street scenes are curious and novel, even to one who has been through Japan and China. The turbans, in size and gay colors, beat the world. They are from two to three feet in diameter, of bright colored fabrics, alternately twisted in the most elaborate and artistic style. Loose, flowing trowsers of pink or blue silk, and tunics to correspond, make the street costumes decidedly gay and lively. The turbans are sometimes composed of forty or fifty of different colored silks or cotton.

The "Byculla Hotel" is an immense building 200 feet long and perhaps eighty wide. The whole lower floor is in one room, twenty-five feet high, with doors and windows of Venetian blinds on every side, through which the air sweeps freely. The long dining table is down the center, and on one side are a few private rooms, luxuriously furnished and arranged with low moveable screens. The table is excellent and the variety of the fruits unsurpassed. Our landlord is a Parsee, who speaks English perfectly, but his dress is a strange mixture of the European and the Oriental—a tall Parsee miter-shaped hat, an English coat, vest and necktie, and loose trowsers of bright blue silk, tied round the ankle and flowing over Turkish slippers. The twittering of sparrows who fly in and out free as the wind and tame as canary birds, is a novel accompaniment to our meals. Besides the "voluntary" by the birds, during the dinner a band is playing behind a screen at one end of the room.

The spring races and regatta of the yacht club are now in full blast, so that we leave Bombay in its most attactive season. The yacht race in the spacious harbor was a beautiful sight. There were over forty boats of various classes called "Duboshee," "Lateens," "Sliding Gunters," &c., most of them very long, sharp and graceful in form, with immense lateen sails, and masts *raking forward*. One is named the "Live Yankee,' and her colors were "blue and red with a white star." She was entered for the fifth race, and came *within one* of beating. As she swept past the "flag ship" I thought I detected in her captain the face of a man born in Yankee land.

There are but few American ships or merchants in Bombay, but "Wenham Lake ice" is as well known here as in Boston. The company has five thousand tons in store—enough for a year's supply—and it is sold for an *anna* (three cents) a pound. Cheap enough after a voyage of fifteen thousand miles.

Among the sights in the neighborhood the most celebrated are the "Caves of Elephanta," situated on an island in the harbor, about two hours' sail from the pier. They are immense caverns cut in the solid rock, probably by the Buddhists, two thousand years ago. Though now partly in ruins, the gigantic statues and carvings upon the the rocky walls are very impressive. They embody the highest ideal of a pagan god. A three-faced colossal bust represents the Buddhist's idea of God in his three-fold character of Creator, Preserver and Destroyer, which is the Hindoo trinity. The grand reposa of the two first is not the meditation of a saint, but the calmness of unbounded power. The Destroyer's head portends not so small destruction as annihilation to the world.

The week spent in Bombay has been full of interest; and now with sincere regret I must say "farewell" to India. My travels here, so far from exhausting, have only increased my interest in this strange country, the home of one-sixth of the human race—a land where western ideas and a Christian civilization are now struggling for a foothold, but must eventually replace the effete idolatry and paganism of the past.

W. P. F.

ROUND THE WORLD.

NUMBER TWENTY-EIGHT.

From Bomay to Suez—The "Arabia"—
My Fellow Passengers—"Susianna"—
The Stage Yankee—Sea Voyaging in
the Tropics—Aden, the Gibralter of
the Red Sea—A most Desolate Situa-
ation—The Harbor Landing.—The
Padre and I Take a Run Ashore—
John Chinaman—An Abyssinian Ex-
quisite and his Bride—The Water
Tanks and Bazaars—The Padre's Gen-
erosity Gets Us into Trouble—Perim—
The British Play a Yankee Trick on
the French—Mocha, the Coffee City—
Navigation of the Red Sea—Why
"Red?"—Winds Always Ahead—Sinai
in Sight, but We Can't See the Chariot
Wheels—Welcome Suez.

[Special Correspondence Cleveland LEADER.

BOMBAY, July 1871.

From Bombay to Suez is a voyage of
about three thousand miles, and usually occupies fourteen days. One half the route
lies across the Arabian Sea to Aden, the
great coaling station where all steamers
touch, and the other half is up the Red Sea
to the mouth of the Suez canal. Our steamer,
the "Arabia," is one of the "Rubitine," or
Italian line, that make monthly trips from
Genoa to Bombay, passing across the Mediterranean to Port Said, through the Suez
canal, down the Red Sea to Aden, and
thence sixteen hundred miles across the Sea
of Arabia to Bombay. She is Clyde-built, of
iron, nearly new, with very civil and attentive
officers who speak no English, but understand a little French as well as Italian.
The first class cabins are forward—a good
improvement in a warm climate, for we
here get pure air and much less
jar from the machinery. The passengers are nearly all English officers with their families returning home
on a two years' furlough, which they are
allowed after seven years' service in India.
Of the eight officers' wives on board, six
went out to India as brides, and are now on
their way back for the first time. Several have
children sent home to "Grandpa" in England.

and the younger sheaves they are carrying home with them are generally healthy looking, and race about the ship, keeping their *Ayahs*, or native nurses, in constant tribulation, for fear they will fall overboard. In India every European child is expected to have a native attendant, from whom they learn Hindoostanee before they know a word of English. Upon their parents the tropical climate has left its mark. Their fresh complexions have turned sallow, their blood become thin, and their systems lost energy and elasticity. But now the thought of merry homes in Old England, to which they are bound, brings an unusual glow to the cheek and sparkle to the eyes.

Among our passengers and my next neighbor at the table, is a Greek priest, for twenty years the "padre" of the Greek church at Calcutta. His long white beard gives him a venerable, patriarchial appearance, but he is as full of fun and jollity as the youngest, and an especial favorite with the children. A Prussian of noble family sits on my left. To the disgust of his aristocratic relations he chose the life of a merchant in India in preference to the career of a younger son in the army; and has been so successful that he now returns home with an ample fortune. He believes in Bismarck and German unity, King William and a constitutional monarchy, but is more democratic, he says, than when he left Germany fifteen years ago. The head steward, or "Maitre d' hotel," who is known to us by the Royal title of Victor Emanuel, is continually making the most comical mistakes in misunderstanding our orders. But he is something of a *wag*, and the twinkle of his keen black eyes implies that he enjoys the fun as much as ourselves.

"Our American Cousin" can complain of no lack of courtesy on the part of the English fellow passengers; but their ignorance of America is amusing, and far exceeds that of well educated Americans about India. One of them told me he had it on good authority that the negroes had all refused to work, and the whole South was in a dreadful state of anarchy and desolation. That he expected to hear of their marching on Washington, getting possession of the government, and *making a negro president!* I was seriously asked if there was not a State in the South, somewhere near the mouth of the Mississippi, called "Susianna." The English in the East nearly all sympathized with the rebels, and I have been moved to give them pretty strong doses of the Northern side of the question of the

American war, and the Alabama claims. I laugh at their conventual idea of a *Yankee* as represented on the stage, who is supposed to talk through his nose, wear trowsers strapped half way up to his knees, and a hat and long-tailed coat of the last century. The new route from England westward to India is becoming better known and more popular every year, and opens to these Anglo-Indians new and more correct ideas of the American continent.

Our route is westward, inclining a little to the south, for Aden is three hundred miles nearer the equator than the last land we saw in India. This voyage has long been dreaded as hot, wearisome and full of discomfort. But the consolation is that it is the *last* long sea trip before reaching Europe. Sea voyaging in the tropics has its pleasures, but they are not unmixed. A month later and the Arabian Sea will be hot as a furnace, and even now the noonday sun pours down so fiercely that the awnings are an insufficient protection, while the air in the cabins below is stifling. We go down to meals and hurry up again on deck leaving our dinner half eaten, and gasping for a breath of fresh air. The sea is calm and the water smooth as a mirror. The engine has broken down and for half a day we float like a "painted ship upon a painted ocean." The captain and officers are annoyed at the accident and in bad humor so that we do not like to ask questions; and, besides, the sum total of *Italian* among the passengers is insufficient for much conversation. The nature of the accident we know not, but the relief is great, mentally as well as physically, when we once more feel the jar of the machinery and welcome the refreshing breeze caused by the motion of the ship.

After eight days steaming over the smooth and trackless Indian Ocean, without once seeing a sail or a speck of land, we sight far away the high peaks and desolate crags of Aden, which at first seemed like hazy clouds, but for five hours have been gradually becoming more and more distinct, until at sunset we anchor in a spacious sheltered harbor, so easy of access and with water so deep that no pilot is required. Unless the reader is well posted in geography, or fond of books of travel, he may know very little about this possession of England in the northwest corner of the Arabian Sea, which she has fortified like another Gibraltar.

Aden, the great half-way coaling station

between the Mediterranean and India, is situated on a peninsular that juts out from the Arabian coast, and in appearance is the most desolate, barren and forbidding place that it is possible to conceive of. Naked cliffs and volcanic ridges, without a tree, shrub, or scarcely a blade of grass, surround us on every side—some rising to the height of 1,800 feet—while forts mounting heavy guns, crown every peak, and water batteries command every part of the harbor and its entrance. Two years ago, during the Abyssinian war, Aden was the base of supplies for the English troops operating against King Theodore. Then the harbor was full of ships of war and transports. Annesley bay, where the British disembarked to march against Abyssinia, is about three hundred miles up the coast, full of small, rocky islands, and very difficult and dangerous of access. At Aden there are daily arrivals and departures of steamers, plying through the Suez canal between Europe and India and China. It is ninety-six miles from here to the entrance of the Red Sea, and this lonely, barren rock, this treeless, grassless, black ruin, which can most expressively be described as "Hell with the fires put out," where not a drop of fresh water can be had except that which is caught from the clouds or condensed from the sea, is growing into a busy town with a population of 30,000 people. A score of small native craft are in the inner harbor, and anchored around us are five or six large steamers and as many sailing ships.

Besides its importance as a coaling station Aden has secured to itself the export trade in Mocha coffee, amounting to 20,000 tons a year.

Our anchor is scarcely down when we are boarded by the port-officer, and five minutes afterwards I am on my way ashore in his boat. We land at the government pier, and on the *Bund* are a dozen two-storied buildings, including a hotel, post-office, custom-house, and a few mercantile establishments with Parsee names over the doors. These people are the *Greeks* of the east, and can be found among the most enterprising merchants of every city where the English hold sway (and where do they not?) between Ceylon and Astrakan. Here are the warehouses and water distilling machines of the P. and O. steamship company, and immense quantities of coals from New Castle are piled on the adjacent docks. This is the "Harbor

Landing," the town and cantonments of the troops is situated in a hollow among the volcanic hills five miles away.

The "Padre" and I had an early start the next morning, before the sun was visible over the hills that bound the horizon on the east. Our steamer was already surrounded by the natives in curious boats, some of them small canoes, scarcely larger than chopping bowls, and propelled by one man with a paddle shaped like a mustard spoon. These fellows were coal black, unincumbered by any surplus clothing, and ready to dive and quarrel under the water for the possession of the smallest silver coin thrown over by the passengers. Other larger boats were filled with men, who held up to us bunches of ostrich feathers, eggs as big as babies' heads, and corals of the brightest tints, which they offered for sale with great clamor. They were not allowed to come on board, for they have the reputation of being arrant thieves, and even the ports below were closed, lest the insinuating and slippery little scamps should crawl up from the boats into our state rooms. We selected a boat from the score soliciting our patronage, and six naked Ethiopians set us ashore in a jiffy. At the pier we engaged a dilapidated, one-horse, springless vehicle to convey us to the town. We had the choice between this and donkeys, which I would have chosen, but the Padre objected on the ground that his long black serge gown was not a convenient costume for riding *a la* Turk.

The road was hard and smooth, and for half the distance wound along the shore, then turned inland, and wound with many sharp curves through ravines and round the base of cliffs hundreds of feet high, on which not a particle of vegetable life could be seen. The scenery was unique and grand, but the very picture of desolation. We were in high spirits, like a couple of sailors taking a run ashore after a long confinement on ship. The Padre laughed jovially at the comical sights on the road, sung snatches of songs (perhaps they were *hymns*) in his native tongue, and seemed as full of fun and frolic as a boy. We met long trains of camels and dromedaries, some ladened with bags of "Mocha," others carrying each a dozen goatskins of water from a small stream fifteen miles away on the main land. These ungainly beasts, with crane-like necks and awkward gait, plodding along in single file, each one surmounted by a black urchin, perched high in the air, were in strong con-

trast with the little donkeys, scarcely bigger
than a Newfoundland dog, and carrying
burdens larger than themselves, or mounted
by natives whose feet dangled to the ground.
The people here are of every race known in
the east, and we met one unmistakable
" Johnny " with pig-tail and slanting, al-
mond eyes, who told me in "pigeon English"
that he was cook on a steamer in the harbor.
But most of the natives we met were Abys-
sinians, very black, with Asiatic, not negro
features, and hair cultivated in long cork-
screw curls, sticking out in all directions,
and by the application of lime faded out from
black to a dingy brown. These shock heads
in which both sexes seem to take great
pride, were not unlike the prevailing style
of young girls' hair at home. The appearance
of the women was by no means attractive.
All wore enormous silver ear ornaments and
nose rings, strings of glass beads, anklets and
armlets more massive than ornamental. One
couple especially attracted our attention.
They were got up in the most exquisite
style of Abyssinian art, especially the young
woman, and seemed to create quite a sensation
on the road. She was profusely decorated and
wore in her nose a large ring with the *three
pearls*, indicating that she was a bride.
Her " fellar's " wool, originally black, had
been colored to a dingy blonde, and
was elaborately curled until it would
fill a half bushel measure. The
lady rode a donkey and the groom
walked by her side (barefooted, of
course), and so absorbed were they in each
other that we drove slowly by and stared at
them without attracting their notice.

The entrance to the town was through a
deep gorge, where for a space of 100 yards
the walls rose from eighty to one hundred
feet in height on each side. A massive
gateway and cannon guarded the entrance.
and a squad of native soldiers in red coats
(sikhs from India), presented arms as we
passed. Emerging from the narrow ravine
the town was before us, occupying a basin
about a mile in diameter, evidently the
crater of an extinct volcano. A circle of
jagged peaks surrounded it, some of them
covered with forts and batteries. Several
regiments of troops are quartered here in
airy stone cantonments, forming a large fort
in the centre of the town. Notwithstanding its desolate and oven-like situation,
Aden is said to be quite healthy from October to April. If the " fires are put out "
during these months, the terrific, schorching
heat of summer must give the inhabitants a

foretaste of the lower regions with the fires in full blast.

The most curious thing about Aden is the series of immense water tanks, eleven in number, arranged *en chelon*, in a ravine opening to the north, where the rain falling upon a wide stretch of bare rocks is caught and carried through a succession of irregular-shaped tanks, cut in the solid rocks, or lined with masonry. These communicate through gates and sluiceways, and from the lowest one the water is conducted by an underground aqueduct to a large reservoir, which is always kept full, in the center of the town. Stone steps guarded by iron railings lead up to and around the tanks, each of which is numbered and marked with its capacity; the aggregate I made to be over *ten million gallons.* There is sometimes an interval of four or five years between the showers, but when it does rain it literally pours, and then the sight of these artificial cascades down the gorge and from one tank to another is said to be very beautiful. When the English took possession of Aden they found these tanks, which are very ancient, filled up with rubbish. They have spent immense sums in cleaning out, repairing and enlarging them; and they are now not only very curious and interesting, but absolutely essential to the occupation of the place.

From the tanks we drove through the bazaars which are very filthy and mean, with more gew-gaws of European manufacture than native goods. The specialities of Aden are ostrich and marabout feathers, ostrich eggs, leopard and lion skins, which we found very cheap. The Padre's profuseness in expenditure for ostrich eggs and feathers was only surpassed by his generosity in scattering small change among the crowd of beggars, that beset us on every side. This was pleasant enough at first, but the rumor spread that the venerable looking old patriarch was a *real Crœsus;* and we were soon surrounded by such numbers as to block up our way, and were glad to take refuge in our crazy vehicle and whip up our boney Rosinante. But escape was not so easy, for a crowd followed us at full run, and, despite our efforts, kept along side, hold out their hands and screaming for *backsheesh,* like a pack of half-famished wolves. While I belabored the poor horse the Padre threw the coin as far as he could on either side, which, as they stopped to scramble for, we at last escaped being devoured. Before we reached the wharf we heard the warning gun from our steamer, and hurried on board just as she was getting under weigh.

Ten hours from Aden we come to the little British island of Perim at the entrance of the Red Sea. Here is a lighthouse and flagstaff, but as yet no fortifications. This key which commands the gates is a rocky island some acres in extent, situated in mid channel, and we pass so near that a biscuit might be tossed from the high rock on board our steamer. The Suez canal being a French work and Egypt under French influence, the seizure of Perim by the English was especially annoying to their neighbors. It happened in this wise: The French Emperor had determined to take possession of the little island, and despatched a fleet for that purpose which put into Aden for coal. The Governor, of course, invited the French Admiral and his officers to dinner, and regaled them with unexceptionable champagne. In the course of the evening some of the junior officers "let on" that they were bound to Perim. The shrewd old governor, penciled a note to the harbor master to delay the coaling of the French ships; and the same night two British men-of-war left Aden and started up the coast. The next day after a ceremonious leave-taking, and courteous farewell to their British hosts, the French fleet sailed for Perim. But when they arrived to their great mortification and chagrin, they found the British flag flying and a great show of guns in position. Whether they put into Aden on their return history does not say.

Fifty miles above Perim, on the east coast, we pass within sight of the half-deserted coffee city of Mocha. Its minarets glitter in the morning sun, and a few small native craft can be seen in the harbor," but it is no longer a place of any commercial importance, the trade in its principal staple having been transferred to Aden.

That the navigation of the Red Sea is both difficult and dangerous is testified by the many wrecks scattered along its coasts. For thirteen hundred miles there is but one light house, which is located on a rock nearly in the center of the sea. The channel is not wide, and near the shores are many dangerous rocks and treacherous currents. They say the wind on the Red Sea is *always ahead*, whether a vessel is bound up or down. The shores which are either barren, sandy deserts, or sparsely inhabited by hostile tribes of Arabs, offer no hospitable reception to the shipwrecked sailor. Why it is called "Red" is a mystery. I could not see any *roseate hue* either in its stormy waves. bleak, sandy shores, or volcanic rocks.

Our first three days were genial and pleasant. Then the sea began to give us a taste of its quality. A fierce gale sprang up from the north and sweeping down right in our teeth caused us to lose half our speed. A defect in the machinery now, and we should have been driven back before the gale, or been dashed upon some island or rock. The temperature has suddenly fallen under this fierce north wind, and linen has given place to woolen. Our Indian friends feel the change keenly, and the native servants look very disconsolate as they shiver in white cotton robes, and repent that they ever consented to leave their sunny India. But our steamer pushes steadily ahead—though at times making but four or five miles an hour—and reaching the "Gulf of Suez," the last one hundred miles is in smoother water. Mount Sinai is now seen far away on our right, its summit wreathed in fleecy clouds; but between us and its base is a long stretch of sand hills and barren desert. I have read somewhere that when this sea is smooth and clear—(*which it never is*—the chariot wheels of the Egyptian hosts may be seen beneath the waves. We "Arabians" unanimously agree with old Pharaoh that the Red Sea is a disagreeable and treacherous piece of water; and we most heartily welcome the harbor of Suez.   W. P. F.

The Suez Canal—An Accomplished Fact —Reasons Alleged for Its Failure— Bugbears Exploded—Ferdinand de Lesseps—Is it a Pecuniary Success?— Rates of Toll—New Lines of Steamers —The Tides—Width, Depth and Rate of Speed Allowed—Mammoth Dredging Machines—Lac Amer—Lake Timsah —Ismailia—Lake Menzaleh—Port Said, the Silver Gate—The Sweet Water Canal—"Water is Gold"— "Have a Shine, Sir"—A Showy Old Turk—Across the Desert—Egyptian Soldiers—An Amusing Sight—Mud Hovels for Peasants and Palaces for Princes—Arrive at Grand Cairo.

CAIRO, EGYPT, March, 1871.

The Suez canal, one of the greatest achievements of the century, was opened at the grand fete in November, 1869, at which the Empress Eugenie assisted. It was then fully described by special correspondents all over the world.

What I propose to say now is that which I have myself seen, and such items as I have been able to gather in regard to its practical working, a matter which, eighteen months ago, was all conjecture, and about which the letter writers differed so widely. That it is now an accomplished fact, and a success, no one with his eyes open can deny. As Lardner scouted the idea of ships propelled by steam ever crossing the Atlantic, so Stephenson, the great engineer, and the English generally for years insisted that the Suez canal would be a failure. Perhaps "the wish was father to the thought." The English government, too, must now feel heartily ashamed of its intrigues with the Sultan to throw obstacles in the way of this great work, from that national jealousy of the French which seems inbred in every Englishman—on the ground of philanthropy in behalf of the forced and unpaid labor of the Egyptians—for no nation is now reaping so much benefit from this new route of steamers to India as the English people themselves.

The first great bugbear was the fancied difference in level between the Red Sea and the Mediterranean, by which locks would be

required, in accordance with the report of a commission sent out by Napoleon I. in 1798. This idea was exploded by more accurate surveys made fifty years afterwards. The next objection was that the channel would have to be made through hopeless quicksands at the southern or Suez end, and through centuries of Nile ooze at the northern part near the Mediterranean, where no channel could be made permanent, but the more you dug and dredged the worse it would be. This obstacle disappeared when it was proved that for most of the route the banks of the canal would not be of fluid sand, but of mud, clay and shelly earth—that below the Nile ooze and slippery mud of Lake Menzaleh there was a "hard pan" of clay, which, thrown up, gave solidity to the banks—and that so small a portion of the route passed through loose sand that no real trouble threatened the canal from the instability of its banks. These objections being disposed of, it was then urged that the sand drift from the siroccos of the desert would refill the canal as fast as it could be removed, thereby causing such immense expense in keeping the channel open, as to ruin the great enterprise financially. But it has been demonstrated by experience that not more than *five miles* of its entire length is liable to this drifting in of the sand; and at these places the encroachments of sand never exceed two yards in depth a month, which the company has contracted to be removed, at no great expense, as fast as it accumulates.

To Ferdinand de Lesseps, the "*Fondateur*" of the canal, as he is called, the world is indebted for having pushed through this magnificent work in the face of every obstacle, real and imaginary. With perfect faith in the eventual success of the enterprise, like Cyrus W. Field of Atlantic cable memory, he persevered when less sanguine men would have given up in despair; and to him belongs the credit of having opened this second Gibraltar inlet and outlet to the commerce of the world. I had the pleasure of meeting M. de Lesseps in Suez—a fine-looking man of sixty, with more brains than half the potentates of Europe, whose name should rank with Bismarck as one of the great men of the nineteenth century.

It is true that the Suez canal is a French work, but it is not owned, nor in any way controlled by the French government. Of the 400,000 shares representing the stock, 176,000 belong to the Viceroy of Egypt, Ismail Pacha, without whose active and energetic assistance it never could have been completed. The balance of the stock belongs to individuals, mostly Frenchmen. The first "Act of Concession" from the Egyptian government for a canal across the Isthmus of Suez was granted in 1854. Then followed five years of preliminary surveys and preparations, and the first ground was broken at Port Said in 1859. The Red Sea entered and mingled with the waters of the Mediterranean on the 15th of August, 1809. But it was not until about the 1st of January, 1870, that this thoroughfare, which all ages have wished for, but till now in vain, was opened as a highway to the commerce of the world.

And now after fifteen months trial it will be asked whether this costly work is a *pecuniary success.* Probably not as yet. The preferred stock last issued was guaranteed 5 per cent.—but to realize this dividend on its whole cost requires an income of four millions dollars a year, and two millions more for running expenses, repairs and management. The rate of toll is two dollars a ton register on every steamer, and two dollars for every passenger: sailing ships half that rate, beside pilotage, etc. It costs the steamer I am on $1,600 for passing through the canal, which seems a large sum for one day's toll, but it is a trifle compared with the expense of sending her around Cape Horn. To make the canal pay from tolls alone would require at least five such steamers to pass each way every day; and at present I am told that the average is about half that number. But the Suez Canal Company has other sources of income. The Viceroy made liberal grants of land to the company, a part of which have since reverted to him in consideration of a large sum of ready money; but 50 per cent. of all land sales in the towns of Port Said, Ismailia and Suez, where the company owns large tracts of valuable property, comes into its treasury! and since the opening of the canal new lines of passenger and freight steamers have been established, by which Russia, Austria, Italy and France are coming into competition with England for the trade of the East. When all the steamers now building for this purpose are afloat, it is estimated that the daily arrivals and departures at Port Said will be doubled.

During our half day's detention at Suez we had an opportunity of seeing this old town, which within a few years has taken a new lease of life. The harbor is mostly artificial, and contains a splendid stone dry-dock built for the *Khedive*, or Viceroy.

Anchored in the roads outside I counted not less than twelve war steamers flying the Turkish or Egyptian colors, the "Crescent and Star."

At noon the "Arabia," under the charge of a pilot, steamed slowly toward the entrance to the canal, and was soon enclosed between two walls of sand. There is here neither "tow-path" nor "heel-path," and little to remind an American of his former experience who has in old times traveled on the "raging canawl" in New York or Ohio. All measurements and distances being in French meters, kilometers and hectares, I will, for the convenience of the reader, reduce them to English. Our steamer draws sixteen feet, but under her keel is six feet to spare, which is increased three feet more at high tide. And here I may as well explain the matter of tides. The ordinary rise and fall of the tide at Port Said, on the Mediterranean, is one and a half feet, and at Suez three and a half feet. At the Equinox the maximum rise and fall is about double.

There being no gates or locks to interfere with the free inflow and egress of the ocean at either end, the tides slightly effect the depth of water in the canal, and produce a current which never exceeds two miles an hour, and is lost in the lakes which form *over one-half* the whole course. At the water line the width of the canal when finished according to its enlarged scale will be three hunred feet, the depth thirty feet, and the breadth at the bottom seventy feet. This will give space enough for the keels of two large ships to pass each other without inconvenience. At present the average width is about two hundred feet, with not less than twenty-four feet of water in the shallowest spots. At frequent intervals there are wider basins where ships can meet and pass each other. The management is by telegraph, and every few miles we see upon the banks a neatly fitted up telegraph station, from which the position of every ship in the canal is reported at head-quarters. The maximum speed allowed is eight miles an hour, which would take a ship through the ninety-six miles between Suez and Port Said in twelve hours, but no steaming is allowed after dark, so that we can only reach Ismailia, the half way station to-night.

From the deck of our steamer the view is unique. We are high out of the water and I can see over the top of the banks a desert of sand stretching away as far as the eye can reach. Near the entrance at Suez and moor-

ed to the banks we notice mammoth dredging machines, built entirely of iron. These
were not only constructed but invented by
the contractors to meet the special difficul-
ties and requirements of this service. Ten
of these gigantic machines, the use of which
I never should imagine if I had seen them
anywhere else, cost eighty thousand dollars
each, and twenty-five steam barges to carry
off the dirt brought up by the excavators,
cost fifty thousand dollars each. That these
were built by the contractors will give an
idea of the magnitude of the work.

Four hours slowly steaming through the
desert brought us to the Lac Amer or "Bitter Lake." This was an oval depression in
the land, directly in the track of the proposed canal, and is supposed to have been
originally the head of the Gulf of Suez. The
receding of the water of the Red Sea left it
an inland basin, from which the water
has long ago evaporated. Upon the bed of
this hollow was a layer of salt, in many places
several feet in thickness. When the water
of the Red Sea was again let into this bed it
formed a ready-made canal, twenty-one
miles long, in the widest part ten miles
across, and deep enough for the largest
ship. The water dissolving, the salt accu-
mulated in the bed of the lake is very bitter,
and hence the name given to it. Steaming
more rapidly through this we came to another section of the canal proper, eight
miles long, which connects the Bitter Lake
with Lake Timsah, six miles across, upon
the western shore of which is the new des-
ert-founded city of Ismailia. From here to
Port Said is forty-five miles, of which three
is through Lake Timsah, nineteen across the
desert, and then twenty-six miles to the
Mediterranean, through the shallow water
and deep mud of Lake Menzaleh. This
formed a part of the Nile delta, and was
originally one of its outlets. To excavate a
ship canal through the soft slippery mud of
this marsh, with banks that would stand the
rush of the Mediterranean within, and the
occasional storms on the lake outside, for a
long time baffled the utmost ingenuity and
skill of the engineers. But when it was discovered that by going deep enough they
would come to a strong, tenacious clay, un-
derlying the centuries of Nile ooze, which
being thrown out and mixed with the mud
would form a solid bank, this difficulty was
overcome. This double dyke is three or
four feet high, and within it is buried the
iron pipe through which the great "*Pompe-
a-feu*" (steam pump works) at Ismailia,

forces all the water-supply for the 15,000 inhabitants of Port Said, which is brought to Ismailia by the "Sweet-water canal" from the Nile.

Port Said is a lively town. The population is made up in great part of adventurers from every nation bordering the Mediterranean. The abounding hotels, restaurants, casinos, and the wide, sandy streets, remind one of a new town in America. French, Italian, Greek, Arabic and Turkish are heard in the streets quite as often as English. Speculation is rife, and the business of the place increasing rapidly. Every line of coasting steamers between Alexandria and Constantinople touch here, as it has the most desirable harbor on the whole southern coast of the Mediterranean. The sanguine talk of Port Said as the "Silver Gate between the Orient and the Occident," in fifty years to be another Venice, the rival of Alexandria. Its harbor is entirely artificial; formed by two parallel piers running out from the shore into the open sea a mile and a half—the longest piers in the world. They are built of artificial blocks of stone weighing twenty tons each, composed of desert sand and hydraulic cement. Some of these have been exposed for over six years to all the fury of the fiercest gales without in the least effecting their stability. This harbor is said to be better than that of Alexandria (one hundred and fifty miles west), and can be safely entered day or night at all seasons of the year.

Having thus made a rapid survey of the whole length of the canal from Suez to Port Said, we will return to Ismailia, which is connected with Cairo by a railway across the desert, where six years ago, was a trackless desert on the shore of the salt lake Timsah, without a tree or shrub within sight; there is now a pretty town of 5,000 people, with an excellent hotel and several handsome residences surrounded by gardens. The old bed of the canal, built perhaps by the Pharaohs, connecting a branch of the Nile with the Red Sea at Suez, and passing near this spot, has been widened and deepened so as to supply with fresh water this town and Port Said, forty-five miles away. That "Water is Gold" is as true in Egypt as in India. Its magic effect in converting a desert into a garden I have already seen in Salt Lake City. The public square and the wide streets are planted with shade trees, near which, along the gutters trickles a stream of pure, fresh water. Behind the town, and between it and the desert, is a wide sweeping double crescent of trees growing newly out of the sand, but fresh and green from a channel of water running near their roots. When fully grown these trees will protect the town from the encroachment of sand swept in before the fierce sirroccos from the desert. This sand, which looks so hopeless and useless as an element of fertility, is not pure silicious sand, but a mixture of calcarious loam and sand, needing only the addition of fresh water to form a rich and fertile soil. The desert of Suez, which stretches for ninety miles from the Nile to the Red Sea, was doubtless once well-watered and fertile, and cultivated like a garden. That it has now become a howling wilderness is accounted for by some depression of the Nile bed, or change in its course, by which its eastern outlets have become closed. As it never rains in this country, cut off the supply of water and it would all turn to a desert. Take away the Nile from Egypt and the whole land would become a mere continuation of the desert of Suez.

One of the first signs of western civilization I saw in Ismailia were the *boot blacks*, a dozen or more little black imps, who looked as if they might have slept the night before in the dry-goods boxes of Ann street, or the Bowery, surrounded the door of the "Hotel Pagnon," with "black your boots," "have a shine, Sir," in pantomime just as plain as if spoken in English. Of course I went in for a "shine." The whole double-handed performance, concluding with a sharp rap on the box, was so completely *a la New York*, that I am sure it never originated in this out of the way corner of Asia and Africa, but was introduced by some enterprising New York *gamin*, probably at the great celebration when the canal was opened. Perhaps, like the wandering Jew, he is still on his travels, and future explorers may trace this "march of civilization" among the little "pigtails" of Canton and Pekin.

While waiting for the train at the railway station I saw on the platform an old grey-bearded Turkish officer, with bright turban, loose blue trousers, and cashmere shawl tied round his waist, in which was stuck a pair of handsome silver mounted pistols. He wore an elegant sword, scimiter shaped, in a silver scabbard, and was what my English friend called a "great swell" among the humble *fellahs*, or Egyptian peasants, around him. Nothing daunted by his formidable appearance, I saluted him courteously, and by pantomime expressed my admiration of his ornaments which so gratified him that he unbuckled his scimiter for me to examine. Though silver mounted and very handsome I found it exceedingly dull and even rusty. The pistols were old fashioned flint-locks, *without any flint-locks*; and upon a close examination I could see that his whole "get up" was more for show than use. With my little "Smith & Wesson" and a good stout club I should have been more than a match for him at close quarters.

This railway, like all in Egypt, is owned by the Viceroy. It is smooth and well equipped, the cars and locomotives of French manufacture. Our course for three hours was over a sandy desert, that resembled the white alkali plains of the Humbolt Valley. The line of the "Sweet Water Canal" could be traced far away on our left, its green trees and narrow strip of fertile soil, the only relief to the eye in all that barren waste. The train halts for a moment at the edge of the desert, and as if by magic, the howling wilderness is transformed into a beautifully cultivated land, where every acre seems like a garden. No better evidence is wanted of the abject poverty and degredation of the laboring class than their miserable hovels, that look far less fit for human beings to dwell in than the worst mud huts I have seen in India.

At a station a few miles further on an amusing scene occurred. Near by is an encampment of perhaps a thousand Egyptian soldiers. They wear a neat, white undress uniform, are of fair size, and look well fed and serviceable. Their arms are breech-loading rifles of modern pattern. The officers are dressed in dark blue frock coats and red trowsers—and all, officers and men, wear the red fez cap. As soon as the train stops the soldiers make a rush for the cars, and clamber over them in every direction. The officers, armed with rattans, beat them back with solid whacks, laid on with a will. No one seems to take offense, and they run like a flock of sheep. To submit thus to blows shows a want of manliness and spirit characteristic of the modern Egyptian. It would never be submitted to by the soldiers of any civilized nation. Even in India a blow from an officer would fire the blood of the lowest Sepoy, and result either in immediate vengeance, or by suicide of the poor fellow, whose self-respect would be forever lost by such an outrage. Leaving the "scrimmage" in full blast we speed on, past more collections of mud huts, through long stretches of meadows

made amazingly fruitful by the sun-quick-
ened slime which the river leaves behind
after its annual rise, richer far than bone-
dust or guano; past fat cattle browsing in
rich pastures, like Pharoah's fat kine, in
striking contrast to the lean, ragged peasants or *fellaheen* at work in the fields; past
rows of graceful palms shooting up like so
many obelisks, behind which we catch a
glimpse of one of the Viceroy's many palaces;
and now the tall minarets of "Grand Cairo"
are before us.   W. P. F.

ROUND THE WORLD.

NUMBER THIRTY-ONE.

Cairo—Church Bells do not make a Sabbath—Dragomen—Scenes in Front of the Hotel—Peddlers and Mountebanks—Donkeys and Donkey Boys—A "Donk" with an Illustrious Name—The Fez—The Bazaars—Sprinkling Machines—The "Light of the Harem"—Old Abraham Comes to Grief—The Citadel—The Mamelukes' Leap—The Great Mosque—Island of Rhoda—Moses in the Bulrushes—The Nilometer—Joseph's Granaries—The Shoobra Gardens—A Mohamedan's Paradise—Mohamet Ali—Heliopolis—The Virgins' Sycamore Tree—Dancing Dervishes.

[From our Special Correspondent.]

CAIRO, August 24.

The sound of a sweet toned bell woke me early this morning, and for a moment it seemed that I must be once more in a Christian land; but a glance from my window across the little garden by the side of the hotel showed the sun rising over the domes and minarets of the capital of Egypt, and in the streets below were long lines of camels, crowds of swarthy Egyptians all wearing the universal red fez cap, and innumerable donkeys half buried under enormous burdens of fresh cut grass. A sonorous bray from one of these would for the moment drown all other sounds, even the chatter and clamor of their masters, which is unnecessary except during the hours of darkness. I now fully realized that I was not in America, nor in any other civilized land, and that the sound of the bell did not bring with it the Christian Sabbath. Opening the door I clap my hands, and a native servant appears with a tray on which are cafe-au-lait, eggs and bread. The regular breakfast is not served until twelve o'clock. Around the porch of the hotel, which faces a large and handsome square, is a scene full of amusement and novelty to the stranger. But before I can reach the door I am assailed by a crowd of gaily-dressed dragomen and guides, all most anxious to serve me, each provided with a handful of testimonials in various European languages. But I have learned by experience that this class are almost universally a set of thieves and swindlers preying upon strangers, and their exactions are only limited by the ignorance or weakness of those who may fall into their hands. It is a Levantine proverb that the three nuisances of the East are plague, fire and dragomen. So for the present I decline their urgent offers of service, and stand at the door watching the curious scene. Here are a dozen pedlers of antique relics from the pyramids, (probably *bogus*) canes, bright silk scarfs and turbans; another enterprising dealer has a basket full of young alligators or crocodiles, about a foot long, and holding up one of these charming productions of the Nile urges me to buy it—"*only one franc, sar.*" On the opposite side of the street a mountebank is swallowing swords and snakes, surrounded by an admiring crowd of donkey boys, cab-drivers and "hangers-on." Dogs without number fill every vacant space, their snarling and barking now and then varied, when a vigorous kick sends them yelping away. A private carriage drawn by a pair of handsome Arabs drives rapidly by, and in front of the horses run two Nubians with long white rods screaming to the people to get out of the way.

But a new face is descried by the donkey boys and they go for me at once. These boys and donkeys together form an institution without which Cairo would lose half its attractions. The latter are generally fat and tough, and endowed with all the laziness and obstinacy of their race. The large soft saddles are covered with red morrocco, and the trappings are flashy and ornamented with *cowrie shells*. The stirrup straps are not fastened to the saddle, but merely pass over it, and unless the boy holds the opposite one, in mounting or dismounting, you come down with a run. The fall, however, can never be much, although somewhat awkward to the stranger with so large a crowd of lookers on. The donkey boys, generally about half-grown, are the keenest little *gamins* I ever saw, and for antic drollery have no equals. One steps up to me, pulls his forelock with one hand and gives a corresponding kick behind, which *accidentally* hits another boy in the region of the stomach, and with a grin of humor on his dirty face says: "Take ride, sah? Mine splendid donkey. Name Prince"—then catching an English word I uttered,he quickly adds, " of Wales. Prince of Wales, sah"— if I had uttered a French word the name would have been "Prince Napoleon." Others behind him taking the cue call out, "Mine Billy Button," " Tom Jones," "Waterloo," "Duke Wellington," etc. But one bright-eyed little urchin (was he so much brighter than the rest?) calls out "Mine Berry good Jackass Yankee Doodle" "General Grant." That last shot told, and I followedthe boy to take my first ride on the " donk " with so illustrious a name.

Before I had been long in Cairo I discovered that it would be a matter of economy as well as comfort to invest in a fez. My friends at home will understand that to wear a *fez* in the East does not necessarily make one a *Turk*; but it will save by about one-half what you have to pay in the bazaars, as it implies that you are not a stranger to be taken in. English travelers are everywhere the least inclined to adopt the costume or language of a foreign country, and are made to pay accordingly. The French and Italians have that happy facility of identifying themselves with the people wherever they may be, which in the east has very much increased their popularity and influence. Here the nationality of a stovepipe hat is recognized on sight. In order to see and understand the peculiar customs and life of a strange people one should drop that haughty air of disdain and superiority, and so far as is consistent with propriety and comfort, mix with the people in a dress that will not attract the special attention of everyone he meets.

The bazaars of Cairo are only surpassed by those of Damascus and Constantinople in the extent, richness and variety of the thousand-and-one articles of oriental manufacture; and can best be seen on foot and donkey. The streets are so narrow and crooked that the older part of the city resembles a huge honey-comb. The upper stories project over the one next below, and the front is usually of lattice work, which enables the bright-eyed damsels to watch all that passes in the street without being seen themselves. There are no sidewalks or pavement, but the streets are cool and moist, the high projecting buildings shutting out the heat of the sun, and in many places canvas or boards completely roof in the narrow space at the top and form an arcade. Troops of hungry dogs do duty as scavengers and keep the streets in tolerable sanitary condition. The only sprinkling machine known here is the same generally used in India—a water-carrier with a goat-skin slung across his shoulders.

My donkey boy followed up the "General," making his presence known by frequent whacks over the flanks of the poor beast, and emphasising them with epithets rather rough and emphatic, than complimentary to his pedigree. The "donk" from instinct or long experience seemed to know when the blow was coming, and would make a sudden spurt to avoid it, which threatened the rider with being dropped off behind. The bazaars swarm with people. Men and women, donkeys, camels and oxen bearing heavy loads, are inextricably mingled, every one in the way of others, with no rule of turning out to the right or the left, all shouting, screaming, pulling and whacking the beasts, with most ludicrous appeals to the Prophet. It now requires a sharp lookout, not so much for fear of running over some one—for the foot passengers have a miraculous way of escaping danger—as to escape coming to grief by being wedged in between a camel laden with stone or wood, and the projecting panniers of a mule filled with vegetables or boxes of merchandise. Regardless of the hubbub and confusion of the street, you can see the turbanned merchant sitting cross-legged on a mat in front of his little seven by nine shop, smoking his chibouk and sipping his coffee with true Musselman coolness and gravity. Turning into a by-street I slipped off the "General," and leaving him in charge of the boy, I found a standing place on the corner to watch the passers by. As I wore the fez I attracted no special notice and a grim old Turk made room for me on the board in front of his shop. Here comes a woman out shopping, an occupation of which the fair sex are as fond of in Cairo as in New York, followed by a eunuch, black as Erebus, with an armful of parcels. She may be "the light of the harem," or her *grand-mother*, for all I can tell, for she is wrapped in the universal white cotton winding sheet, and her face is hidden behind a brown figured gauze veil. As she does not vouchsafe to shoot "an eyelash arrow from an eyebrow bow" in this direction, I presume she is old and ugly. Next comes the very personification of the "Father of the Faithful," with long white beard, a massive wrinkled face, and oriental dress, identical with that worn by the old

STREET SCENE IN CAIRO

patriarch. He rides an easy going mule and seems absorbed in holy meditation. But at the intersection of a narrow side street, he comes in contact with a mettled Arab, ridden by a young fellow at a sharp canter, and over goes old Abraham sprawling in the dust. This occurrence s not so unusual as to cause any excitement, and it is only the stranger who laughs at the catastrophe. He picks himself up, remounts his mule more astonished, perhaps, than his rider, and jogs on again, as if nothing had happened. Near by is a barber shop where, if I understood Arabic, I could hear the latest Caireen scandal, and in the cafe over the way a story-teller is surrounded by a crowd of eager listeners, as in the times of the Caliphs and the Arabian nights. For half an hour I watched the passing throng, and long for the pencil of a Hogarth or a Nast to fix on paper the comical scenes.

Then with "Billy Boy" and the "General," I take a quieter route toward the Citadel, which is located on a high bluff overlooking the whole city and its environs. The glistening domes and minarets of the four hundred mosques of which Cairo boasts are at our feet; to the east are seen the obelisk of Heliopolis and the tombs of the Mamelukes; on the west and south are the ruins of old Cairo, the grand acqueduct, the island and groves of Rhoda; while further on across the Nile are the pyramids of Ghizah and Sakharra, and beyond these the great Lybian desert. Close by is the famous "Mamelukes' leap," where fifty years ago that bloody old tyrant, Mahomet Ali having enticed these unruly chiefs into the citadel, shut the gates and slaughtered them all but one, Emil Bey, who dashed his horse over the low parapet, and down the face of the wall, forty feet, escaping with his life. although his horse was killed. As I looked over the wall down the steep precipice, the feat seemed a most daring one, and the escape almost miraculous. The tombs of the Mamelukes are magnificent monuments of these descendants of ~~these~~ Circassian girls, torn from their mountain homes by ruthless slave-dealers. But their sons lived to rule with iron hand the offspring of those who wrought their mothers' shame, and as bold warriors twice to hurl back the Tartars from Europe under the fierce Tamerlane.

In the center of the citadel is the mosque of Mohamet Ali, the finest in Egypt, and second only to that of St. Sophia at Constantinople. At the entrance an old priest takes

me in charge and points to my boots, which
I understand to mean, "Put off thy shoes
from off thy feet for the place whereon thou
standest is holy ground." I give him a franc,
and he brings a pair of large, loose slippers
which he ties on over my boots. Shade of
the prophet! how degenerate have we become in these latter days! An unbelieving
dog of a Frank enters the holy precincts
with his boots on. A circular marble col-
lonade encloses the large courtyard into
which we first came. In the center is a
fountain of marble, elegently carved, where
the faithful, having left their slippers outside, wash their feet before entering the
sacred mosque to perform their devotions.

Standing beneath the grand dome, which
is of beautifully-stained glass, the walls and
pillars of variegated marble, with hundreds
of lamps and chandeliers of fine crystal overhead, the effect was most impressive. A
"dim religious light," in strong contrast
with the noonday glare without, pervaded
the interior. The marble floor was covered
with Persian carpets, on which a crowd of
worshippers were kneeling, all facing toward
Mecca, and muttering prayers, while at regular intervals they reverently bumped their
foreheads on the ground. Some of them
glanced scowlingly at me, but I knew the
old priest, in view of the expected bak-
sheesh, would not let me come to grief.
In one corner, protected by a screen of
gilt lattice work, was the tomb of the
builder of the mosque, Mohamet Ali. In the
midst of all this magnificence, where marble and gold, crystal and precious stones had
been lavished without stint, I was surprised
at hearing the twittering of hundreds of
sparrows that seemed quite at home in the
cool and quiet interior of the mosque. They
were flying all around under the dome, and
their chirping could be heard above the
murmuring of the faithful kneeling on the
floor below. How much more acceptable to
the Almighty were their voices of praise
than the mummery of the ignorant and
superstitious crowd beneath.

This mosque, upon which immense sums
of money have been spent, with its stained
glass and somewhat gaudy decorations, bears
little resemblance to those beautiful temples erected by the Moslem conquerors
of India. There the lightness and elegance of Saracenic architecture have united
with most wonderful skill in carving the
pure white marble; and the "Pearl
Mosques" of Agra and Delhi seem infinitely superior in beauty and simplicity to

this tawdry specimen of the Mahomedan architecture of the present age.

During our ten days' stay in Cairo we visited many places and objects of interest. One fine cool morning we crossed in a boat to the island of Rhoda, where the Pasha has a palace in the midst of a beautiful garden, fragrant with orange blossoms. Here, according to tradition the infant Moses was launched among the bulrushes and found by Pharaoh's daughter. While musing on the strange scenes which this old river had witnessed, the lines of Dr. Holmes occurred to me, in which he comically inquires the whereabouts of the good, far-gone days of childhood, with their brightness and freshness:

" Where, oh, where are life's lilies and roses,
Bathed in the golden dawn's smile?
Dead as the bulrushes 'round little Moses,
On the old banks of the Nile."

Here on the Island of Rhoda is the famed Nilometer, a slender stone pillar in the center of a well, graduated with cubits—one of the most ancient relics of a remote age. Herodotus mentions that the measurement of the river's rise and fall, thereby to calculate the probable extent of the harvest, was a part of the priestcraft of the Pharaohs.

Returning to the main shore we visited Boulac, a portion of the city which contains an immense government foundry and a museum of Egyptian antiquities. In this neighborhood we had been told were the granaries of Joseph—the first great speculator in wheat of whom we have any record —but we were unable to find them, and I am inclined to think them a mith.

We also visited the Shoobra gardens and palace, having first obtained a government order through our Consul. The drive to this famous place is through a splendid avenue four miles long, shaded by very large and old sycamore trees. Here in the center of a beautiful garden was the favorite palace of old Mohamet Ali. Sparkling fountains, marble kiosks, elegant furniture, divans embroidered with gold and covered with the richest brocade, decorations of finest alabaster, nothing had been spared to make this an earthly paradise. The present Viceroy rarely comes here, but keeps up the place in honor of his grandfather, whose memory is held in great respect. Mohamet Ali, whose portraits hang on the walls and appear in several places among the frescoes, is represented as a grizzly old Turk, with an immense white beard, in Oriental turban and costume, surrounded by the ladies of his harem, as beautiful as the houris of a Mohametan's paradise. He was a crafty and ambitious, but a daring and energetic ruler. He massacred the Mamelukes in cold blood because they stood in the way of his ambitious schemes. Having made himself master of Egypt and Syria, he would have won Constantinople and perhaps have established there a strong government had not the English interfered to save the present effete dynasty.

It is a pleasant drive of six miles from Cairo to *Heliopolis*, the "City of the Sun." In old times, when Joseph ruled in Egypt, this was a place of much importance. It was called "On," and here Joseph lived and took the priest's daughter for a wife. All that now remains of the ancient city is a single red granite obelisk seventy feet high, covered with hieroglyphics. It was erected four thousand years ago, and successive inundations of the Nile have raised the surface of the ground twenty-five feet above its base—perhaps even much more, as it was usual to place these structures on a high mound. Near the site of this ancient city is the old Sycamore tree under whose branches, many centuries afterward, Joseph and Mary, as they journeyed to Egypt with their little boy, sat down and drank from a cool spring, the water of which instantly changed from salt and bitter to the pure sweet fountain which it remains to this day. Of course this is perfectly *authentic*. To doubt or question the genuineness of the old world's traditions and relics, would not only deprive these places of half their interest, but dispel those pleasant illusions so attractive to the visitor.

In the centre of Old Cairo, is a mosque and college of *dancing dervishes* or *fakeers*, and every Friday, they hold a *seance*. We reached the place after threading a labyrinth of crooked streets, and were ushered into a room in a building adjoining the mosque, where several other parties of foreigners were assembled. We were offered seats on the divan extending round the room, and a servant brought tiny cups of coffee of fine flavor but thick and sweet as syrup. Then came chibouks and and cigarettes for the ladies. After a half hour's delay we were shown into the mosque, where the performance came off. A circular space about forty feet in diameter and smoothly floored was enclosed in a low railing, outside which were the spectators and in a small gallery seats were provided for us as specially invited guests. In the gallery opposite was the *orchestra*, consisting of eight instruments like clarionets, and four small drums. Twelve dervishes then marched into the arena and ranged themselves around the inner space, after bowing to each other and to their superior or head priest, who wore a green robe and turban, indicating that he had made the pilgrimage to Mecca. All but the head *fakeer* wore tall, steeple-shaped felt hats, without any brim, short jackets and long white robes tied about the waist. Their faces looked pale and emaciated with fasting. One of them went into the musicians' gallery and read from the Koran for about twenty minutes in a drawling, sing-song tone, while his brethren knelt on the floor below, frequently bowing their heads to the ground. The music then struck up and the performers rose from their knees and marched several times round the arena. The head dervish, who seemed to be held in special reverence, stood on a mat by himself, and each one in passing him stopped to make a low salaam, and then turned round and salaamed the one next behind. Then the music became gradually more lively, and one after another threw up their hands and began to whirl. Faster and faster they whirled, their arms now extended at right angles, and with eyes closed in a sort of dreamy ecstacy, they spun round like tops, their gowns spreading out with the rotary motion to the size of most extravagant crinoline. I timed them with my watch and found that seventy times a minute was the maximum speed. They kept up this performanse for about an hour with occasional intervals of rest, when they would suddenly stop, fold their arms over their breasts, and march slowly around the arena, apparently made no more dizzy by their gyrations than the ball-room belle who has been "taking a turn" to the music of Strauss. At last the orchestra ceased playing and the *seance* was ended. As the performers, having put on their outside robes, quietly left the building, the true believers bowed very low as they made room for them to pass. They evidently considered them very holy men who would whirl themselves into very high seats *in paradise.*

This perfomance comes off every week and crowds of Mohamedens, as well as nearly all the foreign visitors in Cairo, go to see it. It is a free exhibition—no tickets being taken at the door—nor is any contribution box passed round. The dervishes are all Turks, and their complexion, pale from fasting and abstinence, is so much lighter than that of the native Egyptians, that they seem to us as white as Europeans. This curious sect is of modern origin, and Mohamet Ali brought them from Constantinople to Cairo, about fifty years ago. Nothing in civilized lands resembles their performances as much as the whirling of the Shakers.

Our visit to Memphis and the pyramids of Ghizah and Sakara will be described in my next letter.   W. P. F.

El Kaherah—The Nile—Ancient Knowl-
edge of the Egyptians—Lost Arts—
Visit to Memphis and Sakharra—An
Early Start—Sand Storm in the Des-
ert—The City of the Pharaohs—Tem-
ple of Apis—Cemetery of the Sacred
Bulls—Lunch Among the "Old Mas-
ters"—An "Antique" Factory—Ty-
phoons at Sea and Sirroccos on Land—
Pyramids of Ghizah—Egyptian Sol-
diers — Fertility of the Soil — Old
Cheops—Up We Go—View From the
Summit—The King's Chamber—The
Sphynx.

CAIRO, September 4.

It is written that "*El Kaherah*" which
the Europeans have metamorphosed into
Cairo, was founded by a general appointed by
Ali, the husband of Mahomet's fair daughter
Fatima; but the present city was not built
until some centuries later, and for Egypt is
quite a mushroom of a town only some nine
hundred years old. But it was built on the
ruins of much older cities, near the site of
the earliest temple-palaces of the Pharaohs;
and, after Constantinople, is the oldest Mahometan city in the world.

The Nile, the most mysterious of all
rivers, flows on the same from age to
age, its greasy, muddy, turbid waters the
source of fruitfulness in a land that without
them would speedily become a desert. Un-
changed they have rolled on since the touching story of Joseph and his brethren was enacted on their banks, since Pharaoh's daughter bathed in the turbid stream, since the
Israelites slaved along the shores, and many
centuries later they bore the gorgeous gal-
leys of the voluptuous Cleopatra.

Egypt was for ages the storehouse of
knowledge, and the art of magic is still
studied in the land, where of old the potentates, who united the Kingship and Priesthood in one person, called in its aid in hum-
bugging the masses of the people. We are
taught that the early race of men originally
was endowed with miraculous powers, the
knowledge of which lingered for centuries among the Chaldeans. They
were skilled, perhaps, in those wondrous sciences, such as mesmerism and clairvoyance,

of which the world is just now beginning to regain the knowledge. If these are among the "lost arts," it is not surprising that they represented *magic* to the people in that early age, for even now, with all the science and skill of modern civilization, they are almost a sealed book. We read in the Bible that Moses was skilled in all the knowledge of the Egyptians. What was his knowledge, known only to the wily priesthood to which all the Pharaohs belonged, and into which the adopted son of Pharaoh's daughter was doubtless initiated? The story of Moses leading God's chosen people through the desert toward the promised land discloses some of his skill in controlling the masses, who were probably quite as ignorant as the Egyptians among whom they had delved as slaves.

Having exhausted the sights of Cairo, except the bazaars, which one never tires of visiting, we arranged for a trip to Memphis and the pyramids of Sakharra. To accomplish this in one day required an early start, and soon after the sun was up we found ourselves on the banks of the Nile looking for transportation across its rapid, muddy current. The floating bridge had been rendered impassible by some accident, and we could only cross by boat. The struggle among the rival boatmen as to who should take us over was exciting. Being only passengers, my friend and I stepped back out of the crowd of shouting, screaming, scolding Arabs and let them settle the matter, in their own way. Any attempt to touch us or our effects was instantly resented with a rap from our rattans, for although we did not understand Arabic, the logic of a stick is well understood everywhere in the East. The shaking of fists and gesticulations were numerous, but we knew they were "mere sound and fury signifying nothing." At last the din and hubbub ceased, and we stepped quietly into the boat of the victorious party, and were quickly set across the river. At the railway station on the west side we took the train to Budershain, twelve miles up the river. There were crowds of filthy Arabs swarming over the third-class cars, and so much delay in starting on account of the broken bridge that we did not arrive there until ten o'clock. We hired donkeys at the station to go to the site of Memphis, five miles distant. Before starting we noticed that the sun was clouded in, and to me it seemed that a rain storm was coming up,

But it very rarely rains in Egypt, and to one familiar with the climate the signs indicated something infinitely worse—a *sand storm*. We had not reached a mile from the station when it came down upon us with great fury. The force of the wind was terrific, and the flying sand seemed to cut the skin like a knife. In a minute we were blinded in spite of the green goggles we wore, and the sand penetrated eyes, nose, ears and mouth We were in a desert of sand, and the air was so full of the fine cloud that we could not see ten feet before us. We turned our backs to the gale, and the howling of the wind and the braying of the donkeys made such music as I never heard before and hope never to hear again. I had read of caravans being overwhelmed and buried in the sands, but could never before realize the horrors of such a catastrophe. I took the *puggree* off my hat and tied it over my face for a veil, and holding on to our "donks" for dear life we took refuge under the lee of a sand hill until the gust had passed over. It lasted about twenty minutes, and left the sand drifted in places like snow. As soon as the storm lulled we pushed forward to a collection of mud huts where once stood the great city of Memphis, the proud capital of ancient Egypt—the city from which Pharaoh is supposed to have led forth the chivalry of the land in pursuit of the hosts of Israel on their march for freedom. A beautiful forest of palms covers a portion of the site, a noble burial place even for such a city. Its circumference, according to ancient writers, was over seventeen miles, and the ruins of its famous temples are now covered by the sand of the desert, and the alluvial deposits of the river. Excavations have been made in various places, and the ground was littered with broken statues of granite and marble. One colossal figure lies prone upon the ground. supposed to be the statue of Sesostris. The expression upon the upturned face is of quiet, benignant repose; or of pensive sorrow, in harmony with the desolate aspect of the whole place. It represents a once powerful king and ruler prostrate amid the ruins of his capital. A crowd of filthy Arabs surrounded us, screaming for *bakshecsh*, and they scrambled and quarreled for the few copper coins we threw them like a pack of half-starved dogs.

After a short rest we again started over the plain for the pyramids of Sakharra, four miles distant, but before reaching them we were overtaken by another sand-storm fiercer, if possible, than the first. Luckily it came from behind, and we fled before the blast which nearly took our poor donkeys off their feet. These pyramids are older and much more dilapidated than those of Ghizah, near Cairo. Near these crumbling mounds are the Sarapeum, or "Temple of Apis," and the tombs in which the sacred bulls are buried. These have lately been discovered and are among the most interesting monuments of Egypt. An enterprising Frenchman, M. Mariette, has spent two years and a large sum of money in bringing to light these wonderful relics of antiquity. We took refuge from the storm in a small building erected for his residence while superintending these excavations, where we found an old Sheik who claimed authority over this part of the desert—which simply means the privilege of levying blackmail on any visitor. We paid the fee, and with a young Arab for a guide commenced our explorations. The surface of the country for miles in every direction is a desert, and the sand-drift has covered many feet deep these ancient remains. It is probable that once this barren waste was as fertile as any part of the Nile valley, but a change in the bed of the river, and the gradual encroachment of the desert has made it what it now is.

We descend by a sloping path to the entrance, and lighting our candles find ourselves in a long rock-hewn gallery, which formed the cemetery for the bulls that were worshipped in the adjoining temple of Apis. Opening from this gallery like side chapels are twenty-four recesses cut out of the limestone rock, and in each of these an immense Sarcophagus, formed from a single piece of black porphyry. They are of uniform shape and size, about sixteen feet long, eight feet wide, and about nine feet in height. The outside is covered with hieroglyphics, with edges as clean-cut and fresh as if just finished. On two or three the figures are only traced, as if the work had been abruptly stopped. They are polished outside and in smooth as glass, and the heavy lids of most of them have been pushed off a few feet so that we can see the interior. They are now all empty, the sacred bulls they once contained having long ago crumbled to dust. With the assistance of my companions I let myself down into one and examined the interior. The space inside was large enough to contain a mammoth ox, the surface was beautifully polished, and the side, when struck by the hand, gave out a clear, bell-like sound. It seemed strange and almost ludicrous thus to stand, candle in hand, within the stone coffin of a sacred bull! "These be thy gods, O Egypt!" Strange that a people so advanced in the arts and sciences, so distinguished for wisdom, who have left behind ruins that are still the admiration of the world, should have religious ideas so low as to worship four-footed beasts, birds and creeping reptiles, What an immense amount of money, time and labor have been expended to excavate these long galleries, to bring these huge blocks of porphyry many hundred miles, to carve and polish them with almost miraculous skill, and then to fit each one in a niche to become the coffin of a—*bull*. And this was done, too, by a people without labor-saving machinery, who knew nothing of the use of iron tools—for I believe no iron instrument of any kind has been found in Egypt. The tools they used were of copper, but hard and pliant as steel. How to make it so is one of the "lost arts," which all the machinery and boasted knowledge of Birmingham or Sheffield cannot now accomplish.

We afterwards visited the temple near by and wandered through several rooms which have but lately been recovered from the sand. They are lined with white marble or cement, and upon the walls and ceilings are paintings as bright in colors and fresh-looking as if executed only yesterday.

In one of these rooms, seated on the sand, and surrounded by the works of the "old masters" (probably 4,000 years old), we took our frugal lunch, and drank in English ale to the memory of the quaint old fellows whose pictures stared at us from the walls—then tossed the bones to their descendants, a crowd of hungry Bedouins, who eagerly picked up every scrap.

Outside we found a lot of Arabs employed in unrolling mummies, thousands of which are buried in a pit near the temple. Great piles of skulls, crumbling bones and scraps of mummy cloth were scattered around. We secured here some genuine relics and antiques, old as the Pharaohs. Most of the so-called antiques sold in Cairo, especially the *scarabei*, or *sacred beetles*, are made, as I am told, at the factory of an enterprising Yankee or Englishman named Smith, in Assouan, at the foot of the first cataract of the Nile.

Having spent three hours at Sakharra we started on our return. Our intention had been to cross the desert from here to Ghizah, but the weather made such an expedition

dangerous, if not impossible. At intervals
all day the fierce sirrocco would break on
us, and we caught two more before we could
reach the station at Budershain. I have had
a little experience of typhoons at sea, and I
would much rather face the cyclone of the
Pacific with a good ship under me than the
sirocco of the Sahara desert when sand instead of water is the moving element,
mounted on a miserable little half-starved
donkey.

The great pyramids of Ghizah are situated
at the edge of the desert on the opposite side
of the river, and about six miles distant
from Cairo. To see the sun rise from the
summit of Cheops is well worth the effort
required to ensure an early start. There is
a fine, smooth carriage road all the way.
Having crossed the Nile by the bridge of
boats, we drive for three miles through a
beautiful avenue of acasia trees, past a large
palace of the Viceroy, and long barracks
around which soldiers are lounging—fat,
saucy-looking fellows, who look better fed
and clothed, and more happy than the miserable laborers from whom they are con-
scripted. In former times, to save a son
from being forced into the Pasha's army, it
was not an unusual thing for a parent to put
out the right eye of his child, or cut off the
first joint of the forefinger of his right hand.
But this mutilation was stopped when
the Pasha formed a regiment of *left-
handed men*, which proved quite as
efficient as the rest of the army—which
is not saying much. The last three miles of
the road is on a dyke or embankment which
saves it from overflow by the river. The
date-palms which we see scattered over the
plain are now in blossom, and produce the
finest dates in the world. We meet hundreds of donkeys and camels plodding slowly
along towards the city, bearing immense
loads of vegetables and fresh cut grass. On
either side of the road are fields of grain,
maize, clover and lentils, growing most
luxuriantly from a soil so rich that it actually
looks greasy, It is entirely an alluvial de-
posit from the Nile, and on it the crops
spring up very swiftly, having a peculiarly
bright green appearance, and are very tender to the touch from their rapid growth.
Two crops of grain, sometimes three, and of
grass and vegetables usually four crops are
taken from the same soil every year.

For a long time the pyramids were right
before us, and so deceptive is their appearance
under the cloudless sky, with no other object
upon the vast plain with which to compare

SCENE ON THE QUAY AT ALEXANDRIA ON THE ARRIVAL OF A STEAMER

them, that they seemed actually to grow smaller as we approached. We drove to the very foot of the great pyramid of Cheops, and our carriage was at once surrounded by a crowd of Arabs. We drove them all away and demanded to see the Sheik, who lives here and professes to control these wild children of the desert. We told him to select for each of us two good men from the expectant crowd, and commenced at once the ascent. Figures can convey but an inadequate idea of the immensity of this vast pile. It is 480 feet high; higher than the tallest spire in Europe; 200 feet taller than Trinity Church steeple. The base is 764 feet on each side, and it covers an area of *twelve* acres. The Public Square in Cleveland, including the streets that surround it, is, I believe, but *ten* acres. To build the causeway to carry the stone from the Nile, would require 100,000 men for ten years, and to build the monument, 360,000 men for twenty years. The difficulty of climbing the pyramid is not so much from the steepness of the ascent, as the great size of the blocks of stone composing each layer. An Arab taking hold of each hand lifts us up from one layer to the next, and it is a succession of steps about three feet high, with a space of one or two feet to stand upon. When about a third of the way up we stopped to rest, and another Arab popped out from behind a stone and urged us to engage his services. He explained by pantomime how useful he could be in pushing us up behind. Boys carrying small earthern bottles of water followed us up, knowing that we should be thirsty enough to give them a few piaster for a drink before we reached the top. Our Arabs wore no clothing, but a white cotton shirt, and kept up a constant chattering like so many black birds. To spring from block to block and pull us up after them did not seem to tire them in the least. On the summit is a space about 25 feet square, the apex as well as the casing of the pyramids having been removed by the Caliphs for constructing mosques and palaces at Cairo. We reached the top just in time to see the sun rise above the horizon of the great ocean desert, and spread out before us was one of the finest panoramas in the world. The dryness and purity of the air in Egypt enables one to see objects at a great distance.

We could see the Nile winding its way through a carpet of verdure, on which are many scattered villages—the city of Cairo with its domes, minarets and palaces glittering in the morning sun—and beyond all, the white shining sands of the desert.

The Arabs pointed out the autograph on stone of the Prince of Wales (*very badly cut*,) and offered us hammer and chisel, but we declined the cheap immortality of enrolling our names so high up on tablets of stone, along with those of Jones, Smith and Robinson which cover nearly every inch of the space. To descend was more difficult and dangerous than to climb up, for it requires steady nerves to look off from such a dizzy height, standing upon a shelf scarcely a foot in width. But our faithful Arabs never let go of our hands for a moment until we reached *terra firma*, where a liberal backsheesh made them dance round us like so many wild Indians. "Yankee Doodle, good, good," was the style of their returning thanks. This title seems to denote high rank in Egypt, and is used as an especial compliment to all Americans.

Resting on the huge blocks of stone on the shady side we took our lunch and indulged in a fragrant *chibouk*, before entering the long, narrow, dark passages that lead to the heart of the great pyramid. After climbing several inclines and sliding down others, with barely room to stand upright, we stood in the king's chamber, where our tapers made little impression on darkness so intense that it could almost be felt. This apartment is lined with polished granite, and is thirty-four feet long, eighteen broad, and about twenty in length. In the centre stands a red granite Sarcophagus, in which King Cheops was buried, ages before the time of Moses. The air here was so stifling that we did not tarry long, and were glad to escape into the open air once more. The second and third pyramids are somewhat less in size than that of Cheops; and the six others comparatively small. In front of the great pyramid and facing the river is the Sphinx. This most fantastic animal has ever been looked upon as one of the greatest wonders of Egypt. A colossal female head rises above the sand, attached to the body of a lioness, about which excavations have been made so as to show its form hewn from the solid rock. The features have the thick lips and high cheek bones of the Nubian which was the type of beauty to the ancient Egyptians. The circumference of the head measures over one hundred feet. Time and ill-usage have made sad havoc with the monstrous face, but there is a placid beauty about its features, an abstracted expression, resembling the large Budhist

idols of Japan and India. The conception
is a grand one, and well calculated to inspire
with terror the weak minds of its worship-
ers.

As we ride back to Cairo we turn back to
gaze upon these marvelous structures, and
are lost in amazement at the immense
amount of labor expended for no practical
utility. If their sole object was to perpet-
uate the names of the builders—Pharaohs,
Kings and Priests—whatever their titles
may have been, how futile the attempt at
immortality, for the names of the builders
have in most cases passed away.

Proud monuments of kings, whose very
    names
Have perished from the records of the past.

W. P. F.

www.ingramcontent.com/pod-product-compliance
Lightning Source LLC
Chambersburg PA
CBHW021052030726
47496CB00006B/1809